J. Margot Critch currently lives in St John's, Newfoundland, with her husband Brian and their two little buddies Simon and Chibs. She spends equal amounts of time writing, listening to Jimmy Buffett's music and looking out at the ocean—all the while trying to decide if she wants coffee or a margarita.

Rebecca Hunter is an award-winning author of sensual, emotional adventures of the heart. She writes sexy stories about alpha men and spirited women for Mills & Boon's Dare line, and her books reflect her love of travel. To find out more, or to join her newsletter, please visit rebeccahunterwriter.com.

If you liked
Turning Up the Heat and *Pure Satisfaction*
why not try

No Strings Christmas by Clare Connelly
Unwrapping the Best Man by Rachael Stewart

Also by J. Margot Critch

Miami Heat

Taming Reid
As You Crave It

Sin City Brotherhood

Boardroom Sins
Sins of the Flesh
Sweet as Sin
Forbidden Sins
A Sinful Little Christmas

Also by Rebecca Hunter

Fantasy Island

Pure Temptation
Pure Attraction

Blackmore, Inc.

Best Laid Plans
Playing with Fire
Baring it All
Hotter on Ice

Discover more at millsandboon.co.uk

TURNING UP THE HEAT

J. MARGOT CRITCH

PURE SATISFACTION

REBECCA HUNTER

MILLS & BOON

First Published in Great Britain 2020
by Mills & Boon, an imprint of HarperCollins*Publishers*
1 London Bridge Street, London, SE1 9GF

Turning Up the Heat © 2020 Juanita Margot Critch

Pure Satisfaction © 2020 Rebecca Hunter

ISBN: 978-0-263-27770-8

MIX
Paper from
responsible sources
FSC® C007454

This book is produced from independently certified FSC™ paper
to ensure responsible forest management.
For more information visit www.harpercollins.co.uk/green.

Printed and bound in Spain
by CPI, Barcelona

TURNING UP THE HEAT

J. MARGOT CRITCH

MILLS & BOON

For Johanna.

Five years ago, I submitted my very first manuscript
to Harlequin Blaze and it ended up on your desk.
Ten books later, because of your guidance and
support, you've helped me become the writer
I am today. It hasn't always been easy,
but it's always been fun.

It's been a privilege working with you. Thank you.

CHAPTER ONE

GEMMA REXFORD COULD feel the attention of everyone on her when she entered the hotel's banquet hall. She smoothed her hands down the front of her black dress and looked around for her brothers and their girlfriends. They were nowhere to be found in the crowd. As she walked deeper into the mass of people, she could feel them assessing her with open curiosity, jealousy and, as evidenced by the eyes that traveled up and down her figure as she passed, desire. Were they looking at her dress, her hair or the fact that they were all there to celebrate her, despite the fact that she was one of very few women in attendance at the International Rum Sellers and Distillers Convention?

Well, maybe *celebrate* wasn't quite the right word to use for the curious, envious glances that were thrown her way by the predominantly older male crowd. As a woman in the rum industry, she was part of a small but growing demographic, but none had been awarded a blending and distilling award from the association. It was a high honor, but even though Reid and Lila, and Quin and Celia were in attendance, Gemma was still the fifth wheel, and she felt incredibly out of place.

Gemma made her way into the room and took a quick look at the stage and saw the large trophy that she would somehow be taking home to the Rexford Rum Distillery in Miami. *Like it will even fit in the overhead bin.*

Smiling at those who politely waved and nodded in her direction, Gemma realized that she would need liquid fortification to get through the rest of the evening and made her way to the bar. If there was ever a place where one could get a drink, it should be this awards banquet. But when she arrived at the large bar, she found herself next to several men—all sniffing their glasses, swirling, sipping, smacking their lips. They were turning what should have been a casual drink into a spectacle. Owners and CEOs of some of the world's biggest rum brands drank their own brands, comparing the depth of caramel color and strength of spicy notes, boasting to their contemporaries about their own successes, but they all quieted when she approached, sliding their eyes over to her. Normally, Gemma didn't mind attention, but at the conference, she saw it as scrutiny. Everyone was trying to figure out the young female distiller who had been called one of the best in the world. She knew she made good rum. But the accolades made her feel uncomfortable.

"Ms. Rexford," the bartender greeted her, no

doubt recognizing her from her photo in the conference's itinerary. "What can I get you tonight?"

She eyed the rows of bottles behind the bar, where some of the best rums in the world were represented, and she almost asked for a drink from her own bottle—her usual short glass holding a finger or two of the spiced honey blend that had landed her such a prestigious award, but she changed her mind. She wanted something different. "I'll have a rumrunner."

The bartender blinked in what she imagined must be surprise. She was pretty sure that she was the only person in the room full of rum connoisseurs who'd dared to order a mixed drink. "With Rexford Rum, I assume?"

"No," she told him, still scanning the various bottles on display behind the bar. "I'll have Cain."

"Well, if that isn't music to my ears." The deep, smooth baritone voice spoke from behind her, causing her spine to straighten and making her nerve endings tingle. Gemma took a deep breath and turned around to see Tom Cain, of Cain Rum, standing there, a devilish smirk on his lips. "I always wanted to hear you say those words."

Gemma wasn't normally one to be flustered by a man, but with the heir of Cain Rum in front of her, she had to work her hardest at being cool, pretending he didn't affect her, even though he was easily one of the sexiest men Gemma had ever seen. "Don't flatter yourself," she told him, trying not to look directly into those icy blue eyes of his. "I figured if there was a rum that one had to load down with sugar and juice, it might as well be yours."

Tom clasped his chest dramatically. "Oh! You hurt me," he said while she laughed and shook her head at his dramatics.

Both of them were figures in the rum industry. While she worked out of the Rexford Rum Distillery, a small family business with her brothers, which had risen to international glory, Tom Cain operated Cain Rum in New York City, but they sold a mass-produced rum. Cain had a large facility and machines that she couldn't even fit inside the small building where most of their small-batch rum was made. Despite the differences in their companies and families, the Rexfords and the Cains shared quite an intense rivalry—but it was a personal one. Every time she thought of the Cains, Gemma was bitterly reminded of her brother Reid's ex-wife, Carolina, who'd stolen many of the Rexford family's rum recipes and then married Tom's father, John.

The air between them turned serious, and they stared at each other in silence. His wavy black hair was pushed back, and he'd put on an extremely well-tailored dark suit for the event. Despite the bad blood that existed between their families, she couldn't deny that she was attracted to him. Gemma could feel her heart rate speeding up as she looked up at him. He made his interest in her known. His eyes were on her body, and he absently drew the corner of his bottom lip between his teeth. His attention emboldened her, and she took a step closer, teasing him.

"Ma'am, your drink," the bartender interrupted, disturbing her thoughts as he passed over her glass.

Giving herself a moment to recover from the potency of Tom's gaze, Gemma turned to fully face the bartender, grateful for the distraction. "I'm too young to be a *ma'am*, aren't I?" she lightly scolded him with a smile. "But thank you," she said, winking as she accepted the drink. When she turned back to Tom, she could tell his eyes were on her mouth. It seemed he was still transfixed by her, and it was thrilling. She stepped a little closer to him as she brought the straw to her lips and drank.

The cocktail was much sweeter than she liked, but it was cool on her parched throat, and she sipped again.

She heard Tom clear his throat. "How's your drink?"

She took another taste and raised her eyes to meet his. Again, she had to fight to not screw up her face at the drink. There was a reason she never ordered cocktails. When she was done, she shrugged. "It's quite sweet. But the rum is fine."

"Especially when you load it down with sugar?" he asked before turning to the bartender. "A double of the Rexford Honey Blend, please. Neat."

"Exactly. You guys make a pretty good rum. But you already know that, don't you?"

"I know it's a good rum. We have great blenders and distillers."

"But they're not the best," she pointed out.

He looked her up and down again. "Apparently not," he said. "That title belongs to you this year."

Gemma looked over her shoulder at the dais on the opposite end of the conference room, where she would be accepting her award later that night. "So they tell me. You know, I didn't realize that you had actual employees. When I think Cain, I just picture a big factory full of automated equipment." She thought she saw the faintest flinch on his face, so she kept going. "But I guess you have to have *someone* on the floor, right? Maybe your guys could be the best in the world, too—if you weren't using my stolen recipes, that is."

She caught the twitch in his jaw, and she knew she'd hit a nerve alluding to what Carolina had done. He shook his head. "That had nothing to do with me."

"Your last name is Cain, isn't it?" she asked, pointing to the bottle behind the bar. "Your name is on that bottle."

"Trust me, if you taste the rum—*not covered up with juice*—you'll see it's not your recipe. We've never used the recipes that Carolina brought to us. I wouldn't allow it."

"Well, don't you suddenly have a whole heaping pile of integrity." He said nothing, and she smiled. "It's about time."

A beat of silence passed between them, and she tried to read his expression. He was impassable, but a grin turned up the corner of his lips. He turned his attention back to the bartender, gesturing to the bottle of Cain Rum behind the bar, and the server handed it over to him, along with a short glass.

"Try it," he said, pouring the amber liquid into the glass. "I mean, if you think your palate is sophisticated enough to tell the difference," he challenged, goading her.

"Oh, go fuck yourself," she told him haughtily. "My palate is plenty sophisticated."

He blinked, probably surprised at her profanity. "Clearly. Judging by that language."

She wasn't sorry. "I was raised with two brothers," she explained. "You don't like a woman with a foul mouth? That sounds like a *you* problem."

His eyes dipped to her lips again, and he leaned forward so his own lips grazed against her ear. "I don't have one problem with your mouth," he whispered, sending a bold shiver down her spine.

For a moment, the rest of the room fell away—the noise, lights and people disappeared as Gemma was caught in the moment. She imagined pulling him closer, inviting him up to her room and ripping off his clothing. Gemma might be attracted to Tom Cain—a bit of a crush she might have been harboring for a few years now—but there was no way she could act on it. Not with everything the Cains had done to her family. Whether Tom was telling the truth that they didn't use her recipes—she didn't know for sure—that act alone could have completely ruined her family and everything they'd worked for.

Tom nudged the glass closer to her, the sound of it scraping along the top of the wooden bar filled her ears. "You going to try that or not? It'll prove to you that we don't use your recipes."

"Why should I drink your rum? Just to appease you?"

"I want to clear my name," he told her. "I want you to get a taste of what Cain is doing right now. I never approved of what went down with Carolina and how we acquired those recipes."

"You *acquired* them through theft," she reminded him, keeping her voice low. She didn't want anyone to overhear their drama. While there'd been questions and rumors within the insular spirits community about Reid's ex-wife marrying John Cain, the full extent of what had happened, the theft, had never been revealed.

Tom flinched. Maybe he did have some remorse after all. "Listen, Gemma, I didn't even know about the theft until months after it happened." She didn't respond, not really caring what had happened to the recipes once they left her distillery. She'd moved on, creating new recipes for award-winning batches.

"If you say so. It doesn't matter what you did. Any blender can follow a recipe. But it takes a master to make the rum I do."

"Don't I know it," he admitted.

"Is that supposed to make me feel better?"

"Probably not. But if it means anything, soon I'll be in control of Cain Rum, and I'm making changes."

"How nice for you."

"And we're coming for you, Rexford. Once I make the necessary changes, you won't be on top for long."

Gemma's mind briefly flittered to an image of her naked, on top of Tom, riding him. She needed to get away from the guy. Even when she was supposed to be locked in battle with the man, she couldn't stop her hormones from taking over. When she blinked back to reality, she realized that he'd said something and was waiting for her response. Right, he'd challenged her. But it didn't bother her. Sure, Cain Rum was the biggest competitor on the East Coast; they mass-produced their rum and had vast distribution networks, but there was no doubt in anyone's mind that she and her brothers made a vastly superior product. "Well, I'm not going to make it easy for you."

He grinned again, and the smile creased his eyes. "I wouldn't expect you to. Especially with where you guys are at the moment. You have had one hell of a year."

She nodded. It had been Rexford Rum's biggest year yet. Business had never been better, and professionally, she'd reached many of her goals. Over the course of the last year, Rexford had seen an unprecedented increase in demand, and they hadn't had anywhere near enough stock to meet it. As a solution, she'd devised a way to quick-distill rum without sacrificing quality. The quick-distilled rum, while it only took a short time to create, still tasted like the handcrafted, barrel-aged rum that made them a highly sought-after commodity and had kept them in enough supply to meet the demand. And now she had almost every distillery in the world clamoring for her to design systems for them.

Tom pushed the glass a little closer to her, and Gemma realized that she'd forgotten all about the finger of rum he'd poured for her. "Drink it," he insisted. "On its own, without all of that mix. Actually taste it, and tell me that you believe it's your recipe."

"Why is it so important to you?"

"I don't know. Maybe I just want to impress you."

"Unlikely," she said, but still Gemma's fingers encircled the short glass, smoothing over the bumps and edges of the fine crystal. She didn't even need to taste it. That moment between her and Tom, the way his eyes bored directly into hers, was far more potent than anything that was in the glass. It could have been the scent of his cologne, his deep voice, his sure, almost-fluid movements that oozed sex appeal, that mischievous glint in his blue eyes or a mixture of all of the above... Whatever it was, there was something completely intoxicating about him. She looked at the glass in her hand and thought about how she would much rather taste Tom Cain than anything that came out of a bottle.

She raised the glass, but before she could lift it to her lips to taste, a voice stopped her. "Well, if it isn't the woman of the hour."

Gemma was pulled from Tom's influence and looked up at the familiar voice to see her brothers, Reid and Quin, approaching with their girlfriends, Lila and Celia.

"Uh-oh, you're busted now, Rexford," Tom murmured with a chuckle. "You're caught fraternizing with the enemy."

She frowned at her brothers' intrusion. "You haven't seen *fraternizing* yet," she told him, looking him square in the eyes.

"Hopefully I will sometime soon," he said before her brothers got to them.

She knew what her brothers thought of the Cains, and she knew she'd have some explaining to do when they saw her cavorting with the competition. Well, she wasn't exactly cavorting. She was conversing, maybe undressing him with her eyes, *definitely* imagining all of the things she might do to him if they were alone, and different people, pushed together in different circumstances. But not cavorting. She would never *cavort* with an enemy of her family.

Quin and Reid both pulled her in for hugs, as did Celia and Lila, before they even noticed whom she was with.

Reid saw Tom first. Gemma could tell when her oldest brother's mood shifted. His smile quickly turned down into a frown, and she noted the way his spine and shoulders straightened formally as he regarded the man she'd been speaking to. "Tom."

"Reid," Tom returned.

Gemma watched the battle of wills between the two men, wondering who would budge first. She didn't have to wonder, because Quin stood next to Reid.

"Cain," Quin held out his hand for Tom to shake. When Tom met his hand, Quin smiled cordially.

"How's your mother? I never imagined Carolina to be the maternal type."

Gemma couldn't help but snicker at Quin's crack.

Tom, however, didn't smile. But still he shook Quin's hand. "She's not my mother," he said.

"Carolina left my brother and married your father," Quin pointed out. "Sounds like she's your mother to me."

Tom smirked and looked at Reid. "Trust me, what my father and your ex-wife do is certainly none of my business, nor do I want it to be." He then nodded at Gemma. "I should be moving on." He picked up the glass of Rexford Honey that he'd ordered and clinked it against the one that was still in her hand—the one that held the Cain rum he'd poured for her. "Congratulations on the award. I'll be seeing you, Rexford."

Gemma said nothing as she watched him walk away. Both regret and relief filled her, but at least she was finally able to breathe.

Reid turned to her. He looked pissed. "What did he want?"

Gemma's eyes narrowed as she tried to recall what they'd even talked about that hadn't been innuendo-laced flirting and fighting. She shrugged. "I don't know. Nothing, I guess. We barely spoke about anything important. He just wanted to provoke me."

She saw that Lila, Reid's girlfriend, was watching her. "Based on the way you're blushing, mission accomplished, I guess."

"What's that supposed to mean?"

Instead of answering, Lila grinned and looked away and innocently sipped from her champagne glass.

"The guy's an asshole," Quin added, moving past her to the bar. He ordered two glasses of rum—the spiced honey, as well—and passed one to Reid. "Anything for you, Gem?"

She held up the glass in her hand—the rum that Tom had poured for her—and shook her head. "I'm good. Thanks."

Reid drank his own rum and nodded at the one that Gemma held with a white-knuckle grip. "What's that?"

She looked down at the glass. "Uh, just some rum." She still hadn't managed to drink even a sip of the Cain rum she'd been poured. She held the glass up to the lights and regarded it with a critical eye. The rum was clear—no impurities. She brought the glass to her lips and inhaled before taking a sip. It smelled clean, natural. When she tasted the rum, however, she was impressed. Instead of swallowing right away, she held the liquid in her mouth. The flavor was light but still had weight and substance, there was no trace of burn, and she swished it around in her mouth, over her tongue. It was sweet but smoky, smooth as silk. It wasn't as good as her own rum, but it was good enough to surprise her.

She raised her eyes to the crowd and found Tom Cain immediately. He was watching her, his eyes intense and a lazy grin on his face, as she drank his rum. He raised his glass and turned away from her and she missed the silent connection as she watched Tom cross the floor on the far end of the large banquet hall. Gemma finally swallowed the mouthful of rum. It flowed down her throat, warming her along the way as she watched him disappear into the crowd.

CHAPTER TWO

As Tom walked away from Gemma and the rest of the Rexford clan, he drank the rum in his glass. Gemma's spiced honey rum was some of the best he'd ever had. From across the room, he watched Gemma Rexford speak with her brothers. He knew that he should forget about her, but no matter where he was in the room, his eyes found her every time, picking her out of the crowd. Her long, wavy hair was dark and shiny, and looked so soft he wanted to run his fingers through it. She was like a beacon. He'd always been attracted to her, but in the past, their interactions had been limited to quick conversations about the industry at trade shows and conferences. Tonight, though, he hadn't been able to stay away from her. And as she stared up at him with those sharp, brown eyes, as she challenged him… God damn if she wasn't the most impressive woman he'd ever met.

She was smart, sexy as fuck, had a quick wit and—he drank from the glass of Rexford Rum in his hand—she made one hell of a bottle of rum. She really was the best distiller he'd ever encountered. Part of him wondered what she thought of the Cain rum he'd poured for her. He'd wanted her thoughts as a professional. But that was stupid. It shouldn't matter to him. His company made a fine product. Carolina may have tried to screw over her former family, but there was no way he would have let that happen.

From his spot across the room, he watched her speaking to her brothers. She looked guarded, however—on edge—as if they'd said something to upset her. Her posture was rigid, and she frowned. Briefly, he considered going back over there and pulling her away. But that was stupid. She was a strong, grown woman, and she didn't need rescuing from her brothers. Especially by him. And that would probably earn him a punch in the throat. From her.

She was still drinking from the glass—at least she hadn't thrown it down in disgust. He watched her hold it up to the light again. Looking for impurities, no doubt. She wouldn't find any. He hoped. God, he wished he could read her mind. Or at least her expression. The woman was a puzzle. She looked up and saw him—caught him looking. He grinned, and after a moment, he turned away. He sighed. If he had to stay away from Gemma Rexford, it was going to be a long conference.

With his mind on Gemma, he did several laps around the ballroom. Every time he looked in her direction, he saw her eyes on him, as if she was following him through the banquet hall. He stopped every now and then to talk with people he knew. But no one could hold his interest like the female distiller from Miami. Gemma outmatched everyone in the room with her intellect, her biting sense of humor—he subtly adjusted himself by shifting his pants—her raw sex appeal.

A server walked past him carrying a tray of questionable-looking shrimp pieces in puffed pastry. Tom might have passed them up, but he hadn't had anything to eat since that morning, and he was already feeling a bit of a buzz from the rum he'd had. He picked up an hors d'oeuvre from the tray and bit into it, immediately regretting his decision. The conference might be held at the nicest five-star resort in Jamaica, but it seemed that the catering was the same as any event at a three-star hotel. He bundled the remainder of the food into the small napkin and tossed it into a nearby trash can. When he looked up again, he was pleased to see Gemma standing in front of him.

"The food kind of sucks, right?"

"I would have expected better seafood from the Caribbean, but you can't win them all, I guess."

He noticed for the first time that she was holding two short glasses. She handed one to him. "I thought maybe since you enjoyed your first glass so much, you might want a second."

He laughed. "Thanks. At least it'll get the taste of that shrimp out of my mouth."

"You know, if you're looking for palatable shellfish, maybe you should head to Miami sometime. Nothing but incredible seafood restaurants there."

He sipped from his glass, hiding his surprise at their now pleasant conversation. "Is that an invitation?"

She shrugged and drank, too. "It's a free country. You can do what you want."

"So, if I were to visit Miami, where would you recommend I go?"

"Hmm," she started playfully. "Well, there's Arlo's. A great Cuban restaurant. But they're so busy now that it's almost impossible to get a table if you don't know someone."

"Well, I know you." She didn't respond, but he saw the blush that colored her cheeks. He liked that. He wanted to prod a little more, but he didn't want to drive her away. He took a look around. "Where are your bodyguards?"

"My bodyguards?"

"Your brothers. They obviously didn't like that you were talking to me back there."

She shrugged. "I'm a grown woman. I can talk to whoever the hell I want."

"Well, I'm flattered that you want to talk to me."

"Don't be too flattered," she told him, her smile playful. "I'm only here because everyone else is so mind-numbingly boring."

"Well, that's the trouble with being the most impressive person in the room," he noted. "No one's your match."

"You think I'm the most impressive person in the

room?" she asked with a small smile that let a little vulnerability come through.

"You are," he assured her truthfully. "No one else even comes close."

Gemma smiled, trying not to let Tom Cain's compliment go to her head. Well, it wasn't her head that she was worried about. Just being in the man's presence sent a drumline of desire straight between her thighs. What was she *thinking* going after him again? She hadn't been thinking—that was her problem. There was no way she could be attracted to a Cain. It was stupid. And given every other interaction they'd had with that family, she had no idea if she could even trust him. But if her brothers found out? She didn't even want to think about what they would do. Reid and Quin just might disown her. But tell all of that to the throbbing, needy desire that tapped out a message to her brain, telling her what to do. The message should have been SOS, because she was in serious trouble.

But Gemma just couldn't help herself. She took in their surroundings; there was a supply closet to her left, and no one in the room was paying them any mind. So, acting quickly, she opened the door and pulled Tom inside before shutting the door, leaving them in the dim light of the small room. She looked around and in the dark, she saw stacks of chairs and folded tables. There wasn't much room in there, but it would do.

"What are you doing?" he asked as she pushed him back against the closed door.

"Something totally irresponsible," she told him before she wrapped her arms around his neck and pulled him down to meet her.

Tom's lips captured hers in a blistering kiss that promised to devour her whole. That was exactly what she wanted. His taste, his scent, the way he pressed his hard body against hers, was enough to draw a needy moan from deep within her chest as she pulled him even closer, grasping at his shoulders, greedy for more, holding on for dear life. His kiss was unlike any she'd had before. She may be leaving the banquet dinner with an award for her rum making, but Tom should be given one for kissing.

Her hands were on his cheeks, and as his short, tidy beard tickled her palms, she imagined how the hair might feel between her thighs. She felt the thrum of desire in her core, and her panties grow moist, and she whimpered into his mouth.

With a desperate growling sound, he pulled away from her. Both she and Tom fought to catch their breath, and the sound of their mingled breaths filled the quiet room. She didn't know why he'd ended their kiss and wondered if he would leave her wanting in the dimly lit room. But he didn't make a move to leave. Surprising her, Tom put his large hands on her hips—digging his fingers in—and roughly turned her around before pulling her close again, pressing her back against his chest. She could feel the length of his dick against her ass, and he grunted against her neck when she rubbed against it.

Gemma knew Tom Cain was a smooth operator when it came to business—cool, collected—but there was nothing calm or gentle about the way his hands slid up and down her body. He pulled her hair away from her shoulder, exposing her neck, shoulders and chest. At the start of the night, she'd feared that the plunging neckline of her dress might be a little daring for the professional event. But when Tom put his lips on the sensitive spot at the hollow of her shoulder, she had no regrets about showing some skin.

Tom's lips worked their way across her shoulder, and he palmed her breasts through her dress. His touch was rough, insistent, but it wasn't enough. Gemma took his right hand in hers and pushed it down to her thighs. He needed no further instruction; his right hand immediately went under the hem of her dress and traveled upward. His touch tickled her thigh, and she stifled a giggle. The laughter died, however, when his right hand reached into her panties. There was nothing preliminary, delicate or timid about his touch. He knew what he wanted, what she needed. His breath warm and heavy in her ear, his fingers slid underneath the lace of her panties, skimming along her desire-slicked skin.

Anticipation kicked her heartbeat into overtime, and she thought it might burst out of her chest. When one of his fingers delved between her folds and brushed against her clit, she cried out as pleasure surged upward throughout her body, making her light-headed, completely forgetting about the reception happening on the other side of the door.

"Quiet, now," he ordered, murmuring in her ear. With one hand in her underwear, rubbing against her most sensitive flesh, he covered her mouth with his other hand, muffling her moans and cries. She was trapped between his chest and the door, but there was nowhere she would rather be than in this storage room with him—well, maybe she'd take a bed or something, but she couldn't wait for that. He slid two fingers inside her and her knees buckled, the heel of his hand bumping against her clit with every movement.

She threw her head back against his shoulder, exposing her throat to him even more. He took full advantage, kissing her, somehow finding that perfect spot at the base of her neck that made her feel like she was floating. She came without any warning. There was no notice, no buildup, as a furious bomb of pleasure exploded within her—starting deep inside and spreading to each of her extremities. She screamed against his palm and squeezed her eyes shut as he continued to touch her, drawing out every last drop of pleasure from her core.

When he finally released her, her legs felt weak, and she wasn't sure she could stand on her own without Tom holding her up. He stepped back, and she gripped the top of a tower of banquet chairs that were stacked to her right.

He reached out and put a hand on her shoulder to steady her. "Are you okay?"

Embarrassed at the way she'd lost control and become unhinged, Gemma's laugh was more of a breathless noise that she'd forced from her lungs. "Yeah, I'm great," she told him. "That was all just a…surprise."

He raised an eyebrow. "That wasn't what you wanted when you pulled me in here?"

She shrugged, trying to look cool and unaffected, but having already fallen apart intimately in his arms, there was no chance of that. "I didn't really have a game plan when I did that. I don't know what I was thinking." All she knew was that she wanted just one stolen moment with him.

"Really? I think you're lying," he challenged her, crossing his arms, watching her. "I think you knew exactly what you were doing."

"Why do you think that?"

"Because we can both feel the heat between us. We both feel that pull. I think that both of us knew that if we were ever alone, it would end exactly like this."

She couldn't disagree. "Don't get used to hearing this," she told him, "but I think you're right." His chuckle was deep, lustful, and she wanted him again. "But I don't think that's how you wanted it to end." She nodded at his midsection, where a very visible erection was still straining against his slim-fit pants.

"Honestly, I'd stay in here with you all night if I knew we could," he said, shaking his head. "But we don't have time or the space for everything I want to do to you. That can wait until later. But for now,

I'm pretty sure we have dinner, and you have an award to claim."

Even though his promise of *later* sent a shiver through her body, he was right. She could hear the crowd moving past the door, no doubt taking their seats for dinner. She had already been determined to be the big winner, and she couldn't go up on stage looking like a thoroughly sexed vixen. "We'd better get out there," she said, catching her breath. She straightened her dress and finger-combed her hair.

"You look great," he told her with a wince as he adjusted himself.

"You're just saying that because you want to get into my pants."

He cupped her cheek with his left hand. "I've already been in your pants, Gemma, and I'm going to be there again. But it wasn't a lie. You're beautiful. Although," he said, pulling her hair to cover her shoulder, "you might want to cover those little red marks."

"Did you give me a hickey?" she asked. "I can't go up there with a hickey."

He took a closer look. "It's not a hickey. It'll fade in a couple of minutes."

Their eyes met. "Thanks."

He kissed her again, and this time the touch of his lips was gentle. He unfortunately pulled away before she had a chance to settle into his kiss. "You let me know the next time you're feeling irresponsible."

She laughed. "Will do."

"You'd better get out there, Rexford," he told her, guiding her to the door with a small smack on her ass.

She put her hand on the doorknob. "See you around, Cain."

"Oh, you definitely will."

With that promise in her ears, she opened the door and joined the group of people headed for the round tables at the front of the room near the stage. She took a seat with her brothers and their dates.

"Where have you been?" Reid asked her.

"We thought we'd have to send out a search party," Quin added.

"I was in the ladies' room," she told them. "I just wanted a few minutes alone." Quin seemed to buy it, but Reid was still watching her, eyes narrowed. He was suspicious. But she smiled and drank her water. Her eyes drifted over Reid's shoulder to a few tables away, where Tom sat with some executives and representatives from Cain Rum. He laughed at something, the deep rumble traveling across the room and hitting her low in her stomach. Part of her wished she was sitting at his table—next to him. What would that be like? Would he would drape his arm protectively over her chair? Would she rest her hand on his thigh…?

She blinked quickly. *Whoa!* What was she doing? He'd made her come in a storage closet and now she was hearing wedding bells? *Come on*, she chided herself. They weren't in a relationship, and they never would be. It'd just been a while since she'd been with a guy who could make her fall apart in under a minute. That was all. She thought of his promise of later, and she drifted off briefly into a fantasyland where they spent the entire night in her bed. Tom caught her staring and smiled, as if he could read her thoughts. Gemma looked away quickly, suddenly embarrassed and unsure of how she could let the guy get under her skin so soon. *Nope*, she told herself. *It's never going to happen again.*

She let herself take one more look at him, though. He was still staring, and she felt heat crawl over her skin, starting at her chest, and she knew it colored her cheeks with the telltale sign of desire.

Right?

CHAPTER THREE

WHEN SHE DELIVERED the final words of her presentation and the audience politely applauded, Gemma exhaled with relief. A few months ago, she'd been asked by the conference organizers to prepare a workshop to discuss the new distilling processes she'd developed. She didn't like public speaking, and she wasn't sure what she would do to entertain her audience for forty-five minutes. But that she'd gotten through most of it without fumbling her words or boring anyone to sleep was a bit of a miracle.

For three months, she'd worked on the presentation day and night, memorizing it, but when the door opened and a latecomer had entered into the room, she completely lost her train of thought and almost swallowed her tongue when she saw it was Tom. Panic had set in and she froze up for about ten seconds before she realized that she hadn't needed to memorize anything. Of course, she could spend forty-five minutes talking about rum. Rum was her life, and she'd managed to revolutionize the distilling process. The impostor syndrome had drifted away, and every time she'd looked in Tom's direction, she could see his eyes were locked on her. But she'd been pleasantly surprised when her allotted time had flown by like it was only a few minutes.

As she closed her laptop, fellow distillers and others involved in the production of rum all came up to congratulate her and discuss the finer points of the presentation. But the one person who didn't come to her was the one she wanted to the most. Her attention was captivated by Tom hanging out in the back of the room, leaning against the wall with his hands in his pockets. He was so effortlessly sexy.

The crowd cleared after several minutes, and she was happy to see that that Tom had stuck around. She put her laptop in her shoulder bag and walked toward him.

"Great job," he told her. "Your presentation was very informative."

"Did you like it?"

"I did. You managed to present just enough information but not give away any of your secrets. Much to the chagrin of the people who came here to learn what you do."

Gemma laughed. "Like you? Is that why you came to my presentation? To figure out how I did it?" She began walking and they left the room, heading for the lobby bar, where conference goers mingled between events.

"I was curious. I'm still kind of amazed you were able to pull it off."

She stopped walking. "That was a crappy thing to say."

"I didn't mean it like that. What I meant is that for so long distilleries have been trying to find a way to quick-distill, and make it taste aged and hand-crafted. But you did it, and you did it well. If anyone could do it—and no one else could—it would be you. My guys wouldn't have figured it out."

"That's because they're talentless hacks who only know how to push a button. They don't live and breathe rum the way I do," she pointed out. "And that's too bad for you. You aren't getting anywhere near my secrets ever again."

"I've gotten close to at least one of them," he said, reminding her of what they'd done in the supply closet the night before. "How much would it take for you to come work for me?"

Gemma was stunned silent. Was that what he wanted? For her to work for Cain Rum? It was never going to happen. "It would take a lot more than whatever you're willing to pay me."

"Come on. You haven't even heard my offer," he teased.

She stopped walking again. This time she faced him. "Fine. Humor me." There was nothing that would make her leave her brothers and their family distillery, but she looked him up and down. She might play along that she could be convinced. Maybe he'd throw a little something extra into the deal. Maybe if he'd pay her with orgasms, she reasoned, it might be worth it. Her eyes roamed over his body, and she wondered what he looked like underneath the suit.

"My eyes are up here, Rexford," he said, drawing her attention to his face and into his deep, cool blue eyes. "Why don't you let me buy you a drink? We'll talk terms."

"We don't have anything to talk about," she said. "I'm not going to work for you."

"Gemma, you know we have lots to talk about."

He was right, but at the moment, she wasn't interested in talking. "I know."

"Uh-oh, it looks like we've been spotted."

Gemma looked over her shoulder and saw Reid and Quin at the other end of the hallway, watching her, both of them wearing matching frowns as they spied her with the enemy. She rolled her eyes and turned back to Tom. "I could really use that drink," she told him. "Let's go."

In the hotel lobby bar, Tom handed Gemma the glass of rosé she'd ordered. "I'm surprised by this, I would have figured you to be strictly a rum drinker."

She shrugged. "You how it is. I spend my whole day around rum. When I go home, I smell like rum. I'm sure it's coming out of my pores. I like the stuff, and I appreciate it. But it's not the thing I want to drink all the time. Some nights, after spending the entire day in the distillery, the last thing I want to do is sit down with a glass of rum when I get home."

"I get that," he told her. "When I spend all of my time freaking out over rum at the office, it's not always the most relaxing way to unwind, now is it?" He was already finding things they had in common. "So, what sorts of things do you like to do when you aren't making award-winning rum or revolutionizing the industry?"

"Why? Are you trying to get to know me or something?"

"I thought I might."

"Why?"

He shrugged, but the intimate way he looked at her was anything but casual. "I already know what you look like when you come. I might as well find out your favorite movie."

Gemma snorted over her glass. "You're such a jerk."

He laughed but then sobered. "For real, though, you really are impressive," he told her. "I'm intrigued by you. I like you."

"Do you really?"

"Yeah. You're smart, talented, beautiful."

"I'm also a Rexford."

"You are. And I'm a Cain. I feel like you'll make me regret ever talking to you in the first place."

Her laugh was sultry, and the sound went right to his dick. "You might be right about that one."

"I mean, if your brothers don't make me regret it first."

"Why are you so worried about my brothers?"

"Because they hate me, and I saw the way they stared daggers at me just for talking to you."

She casually waved off his concern. "I'm not worried about them. I don't really care what they think about who I talk to or what I do."

"What is it that you want to do with me?" he asked, enjoying how easy she was to talk to.

"I don't know yet. Maybe we'll see where the day takes us."

"What if the day took us up to my room?" he asked. "We can finish what we started last night in that storage closet."

She sipped her drink but didn't respond. He knew how to read women, and he knew from the way Gemma faced him openly, her eyelashes batting at him from over the rim of her glass, that she wanted him, too.

"You know, I was kind of disappointed that you didn't come find me last night."

She put down her glass and leaned an arm on the bar. "I considered it," she told him. "Briefly."

"So, why didn't you?" He trailed one finger slowly down her bare arm. His touch raised small bumps on her smooth skin.

She shivered. "I realized what a terrible idea it would have been."

"Why terrible? I know it would have been a great night, and so do you." If touching her in a storage room had been any indication, getting her in bed would blow his mind.

"You don't have to convince me," she said. "It would have been amazing. I didn't because I know how complicated it would have been. You're one of our biggest rivals. And you know as well as I do that there's some seriously bad blood between our families."

He knew that would be her answer. And he couldn't blame her. His father and Carolina had done some major unforgivable damage to the Rexfords, and he should consider himself lucky that she was even talking to him now. "Is that all you're worried about? Carolina and my father?"

"Isn't that enough?"

"What happened there was terrible, not to mention embarrassing." He'd worked hard to keep the drama to a minimum, keep the rumors out of the rum community. "But I'm not my family. No more than you are yours."

Gemma watched him for a bit. Her eyes were sharp, and he could tell she was trying to work something out in her head. "It can't be that simple. We can't just get a room and forget everything that happened, can we?"

"Why not? I want you." He dropped his hand to her thigh and walked his fingers up slowly. "And you want me too, don't you?"

She was quiet for a moment, as she watched his fingers. "Yes," she said quietly. "I do."

Gemma pushed up from the table and took a few steps away. She looked at Tom over her shoulder. He was still sitting, a curious, surprised look on his face. "Are you coming or not? Or were you just bluffing?"

In an instant, he stood. She noticed the way he

covertly pulled the front of his sport coat over his groin, and she kept walking, preceding him to the elevator, knowing he wasn't far behind.

She looked straight ahead, pushing the up button as he came to stand next to her. Conscious of anyone who might have seen them leave together, they both stared straight ahead, neither acknowledging the other's presence. The doors parted, and they both quickly walked inside. He pushed the button for the fourteenth floor—the same one that her room was located on. When the doors closed, she was surprised that he didn't make his move. They stood half a foot apart, and if he didn't touch her soon, she might explode in a ball of need. The elevator stopped on the next floor, and people entered to fill the car, forcing Gemma and Tom to the back, pushing them together.

At the back of the full elevator car, Tom placed his hand very low on her back. But it didn't stay there long. Her breath caught when his hand smoothed down over the curve of her ass. She stepped closer, and he gripped her, his fingers digging into her flesh, as the rest of the people in the elevator remained oblivious. It made her breath stop in her chest. She didn't dare move, afraid that if she did, he might pull away.

The elevator stopped again, and everyone else disembarked. Thankfully Gemma and Tom were left alone again. His hand went lower, feeling her through the thin, flowy skirt of her dress. Through the material of her dress, he slid his finger along the crack of her ass and touched her pussy from behind. She gasped, the light, but potent, touch sending a shock wave through her body.

Finally, they came to their floor, and the doors opened in front of them. Tom removed his hand from her and stepped out of the elevator. But Gemma hesitated. What was she doing? This was Tom Cain—her rival. The Cains had almost ruined her family, and even though she was attracted to him and wanted nothing more than to go to his hotel room and do all sorts of terrible things with him, this all felt like a betrayal to her brothers.

He must have noticed that she wasn't following, and he stopped, turned his head and cocked an eyebrow. "You coming or not?" He repeated her words from moments before in the bar, challenging her.

Gemma completely forgot her trepidation, and the betrayal, and followed him into the hallway. "Where's your room?"

"Just down here," he told her, taking her hand. They walked past the door of her own room, and that of her brothers', and she knew that if either Reid or Quin opened their doors as they were walking past—hand in hand—there would be hell to pay. But the same thought that terrified her also emboldened her. It made what was about to happen sexier, more illicit, and she smiled to herself, looking at Reid's closed door, daring him to come out at that moment.

Instead of walking further down the hallway,

however, they stopped outside the room next to the one Reid and Lila were sharing, Tom's room. *Well, this is interesting.* Tom unlocked the door and pulled her inside. When the door was shut, he pushed her against it. He took her hands in his and raised them above her head. She thought he might kiss her, but instead he just looked down at her while inhaling heavily through flared nostrils.

"You know, this is something I've been thinking about for a while."

"Really?"

"Yeah, this has been a long time coming for me. Seeing you at other conferences, at industry events, was always a highlight. I've always wanted you."

"Me too," she revealed. He'd always been strictly off-limits. But those boundaries didn't exist at the moment.

Especially when his mouth crashed down on hers. There was nothing preliminary or tentative about the touch of his lips. Their tongues stroked together, wrapping around one another, battering each other, plundering. The kiss was almost combative. Just like their relationship.

He still held her hands over her head, and she wanted them free, to feel him all over. But he held her in place. When he pulled away suddenly, she gulped for breath. "Worth the wait?" she asked.

"Definitely." He released her hands and smoothed his own down her body. She tried not to giggle as his touch tickled her ribs, before he gripped her hips roughly with his large fingers. He pulled her closer against him, and she moaned when she felt the rigid, hard length of his cock through his pants.

Tom lifted her easily and walked them to the bed. He stood her at the foot and kissed her again. His hands went to her back, and he lowered the zipper of her dress. Gemma quickly shucked the material and let it fall to the floor in a pool around her feet. She stepped out of it, kicking off her shoes, and she crawled onto the bed and leaned against the plush pillows at the headboard. She was still in her bra and panties, and with her knees bent and parted slightly, she watched him as he unbuttoned his shirt.

This was it; she was about to actually see him naked. The night before, she'd felt all of the lean muscles underneath his clothing, but that wasn't enough. She bit her lip, unable to take her eyes from him as he revealed his broad chest—well-formed muscles and neat, short hair that covered his chest and spread down his abdominal muscles and disappeared beneath the waistband of his pants. She moaned in satisfaction, and he paused unbuckling his belt.

"Like what you see?" he teased.

"I do. But there will be time to admire you later. Just hurry up and get over here."

He snapped his belt from the loops on his pants and tossed it to the side, and he pushed down his pants and boxer briefs at the same time. He stood before her naked, and she was stunned into silence. He was all lean muscle and tanned skin. He strode purposefully to the head of the bed, but instead of joining her on the mattress, he grasped her thighs and pulled her to meet him.

He lifted her ankles and held them to his shoulders. His hungry gaze roamed over her body, and he made her feel more desired than she'd ever felt. He reached down and pulled her panties from her body and threw them over his shoulder. "Lose the bra," he rumbled, dropping to his knees.

He spread her legs and leaned into the crevice formed by her spread legs. She pushed herself so that she was sitting. She removed her bra, just as he'd told her to do, and she watched as he extended his tongue and drew it up her seam. She gasped sharply at the contact and he looked up at her. He pulled her hips, and she fell back to the mattress as he tasted her again. His tongue teased her clit, drawing circles around the small bud, but then he used his fingers, dipping in and out of her. Gemma arched her back and pushed herself against him. His mouth was incredible, but she wanted more.

She grasped his hair in her fingers and pulled. "Ow," he protested. "That hurt."

"Well, get up here," she told him. "I need you."

"Glad to oblige," he whispered. He left her only long enough to reach for his pants and pull out a condom from one of the pockets.

"Prepared."

"I knew I'd have you today. I wanted to be ready in case you pulled me into another closet."

"Thank god for that."

She watched as he knelt over her and ripped open

the packet and rolled the latex over himself. Using his forearms, Tom lifted her thighs, raising her hips to him, lining her up, and he slid easily into her.

Their combined moans filled the air. Using controlled movement, he pulled back and then pushed into her again. He did it again and again, each long, slow thrust filling her, scorching each of her nerve endings. He began to lose control, and his thrusts became more frantic as she started to feel the burgeoning orgasm low in her core. She cried out his name, and he responded by pressing his body down against hers, still holding her thighs, and spreading her legs at an angle she hadn't known was possible. Her hips stung with the pressure, but with the change in angle, his cock hit her in a new, different place. It was enough to make her break apart and explode into a million different fragments. She cried out as she rode out the wave, feeling every last drop of the pleasure before he stiffened, gave a guttural sound and collapsed on top of her, releasing her thighs and supporting his weight on his arms.

With the exception of their heavy breaths, the room was now silent. She smoothed her hands up and down his back and heard conversation coming from the neighboring room—Reid's room. Then she heard Reid laughing through the wall. Her brothers were both in the next room together, and gone was the daring feeling she'd had when she'd entered Tom's room. It was replaced with the reminder that she was with Tom Cain, and what they'd just done—while incredible—was a complete betrayal of her brothers.

Gemma shifted underneath Tom. She didn't want him to move—she could have stayed there all day. But she remembered that it was still the middle of the busy day she'd scheduled. Tom stood and tossed the condom in the trash can, while Gemma stood. Naked, and without his warmth, the room was cool, and she shivered.

As she slid back into her dress, Gemma watched Tom, who had his back to her, as he reached for his shirt. The way the muscles in his broad back flexed and rippled pleased her, and she smiled, savoring the ache in her thigh muscles that she'd strained with him.

He pulled the shirt over his shoulders and turned to face her as he buttoned it up. He looked up at her and shot a devilish grin. "That was fun."

Understatement. Gemma laughed, forcing herself to look away from him, because she was afraid of the things that little smile would make her do. She turned to the mirror and tousled her hair to restore order to the thick tresses. When she caught her reflection in the mirror, however, she knew that there wasn't much she could do about her appearance— no amount of finger-combing would make her look any less thoroughly sexed, nor would concealer hide her flush. "It was a lot of fun." Her cell phone rang somewhere in the room, and she looked around trying to locate her purse.

"Over here," he told her, reaching down to pick it up from the floor. When she handed it over, their fingers touched before he pulled his hand back, sliding his fingers against hers—rekindling the spark between them.

Gemma snapped her eyes to his. "Thanks," she said as her phone continued to ring. But she could barely hear it.

"You going to answer that?" he asked, amusement in his voice.

"I guess so." She took out her phone and saw her brother's number on the caller ID. She sighed. "Do I have to?"

"Let me guess—your brother?"

She nodded. "Yeah, it's Reid. Obviously. If I answer this, can I trust you not to make any noise that he'll hear on his end?"

"Are you so embarrassed that you're with me?"

She didn't answer Tom and instead accepted the call. "Hey, Reid."

"Gemma, where are you? We have an interview with *Spirits Monthly* in twenty minutes."

Right. "I haven't forgotten, Reid. I'll be there," she lied. The truth was, Gemma had *totally* forgotten about the interview, but no way was she telling her brother that.

"The last I saw, you were ducking out of the lobby with Tom Cain."

She knew it had been a risk, going off with Tom when her brothers could have seen her. She'd been busted. "Nah, you must have confused me with someone else."

Reid was silent for a moment, telling her that he

wasn't buying it. "Twenty minutes, okay, Gem? Don't be late."

"You got it." She disconnected the call and put the phone back in her purse. She heard Reid cough in the next room. Her eyes widened. Would she be able to get out of Tom's room and into Reid's without being noticed? Her eyes slid to the rumpled sheets on the king-size bed.

"Are you wondering how loud we were?" Tom asked, wearing that same grin on his lips.

"No, I know we were pretty loud, and I know that the walls are plenty thin." She blew out a breath. "I've got to get out of here."

Tom moved in front of her and led her to the door. He opened it and ducked his head out, looking up and down the hallway. "All clear," he told her.

"Thanks." She brushed past him, trying to ignore the way her knees buckled at the scent of his cologne.

"Gemma, wait," he said, stopping her in her tracks.

"Yeah?"

"I want to see you again."

"I—"

"You're not sure?"

She shook her head. "I'm not," she whispered.

"Why don't you let me change your mind?" he asked, grasping her by the waist and pulling her to him. His mouth crashed onto hers. All it took was one taste of Tom's lips for her to melt against him. She snaked her arms around his neck and considered pushing him back into his room and shutting the door for another round.

"Have a good interview, guys." Reid's door opened, and before Gemma could dive back into Tom's room, Lila stepped into the hallway. Gemma stepped back from Tom and looked at her brother's girlfriend.

Lila pulled the door to her own room closed, thankfully barring Reid from seeing what had been unfolding in the hallway. "Hi," she whispered. "You're here for that interview already? The guys are both in there."

"I, um—"

Lila looked from Gemma to Tom and back to Gemma. "Or you're sneaking out of this guy's room and heading back to your own to freshen up before you face your brothers?"

"Uh—"

She smiled conspiratorially. "Well, either way, I'm sure it's none of my business. I'm going to get out of here. I'm meeting Celia at the spa for a massage," she explained. Gemma still couldn't find any words to respond. Lila leaned in and lowered her voice. "Let's talk later, okay?"

Gemma watched Lila walk down the hall, and when she disappeared around the corner, they were left alone again. Gemma turned back to Tom. "I've got to go. I have to get back to my room and get ready for the interview."

"You didn't answer my question."

"What question?"

"Can I see you again?"

"I don't know."

Tom's smile was crooked and boyish. "That wasn't a no."

Gemma shook her head. She knew in her heart that she wasn't done with Tom Cain. "No. It wasn't."

He leaned in for a kiss. "I'll be seeing you, Rexford."

CHAPTER FOUR

GEMMA ZIPPED HER coveralls and pulled her hair into a ponytail and walked out onto the distillery floor. It was her first day back in Miami, and she took a deep breath—not many people would count it as their favorite smell, but for Gemma, as she took in the pungent smell of distillation, she was home. The distillery was where she belonged, and she was glad to be away from Jamaica, back on familiar ground.

The sunlight was coming in through the small, high windows. It was still early, before everyone else came in. This was her favorite part of the day. It gave her a chance to go through the room, stirring, checking levels, testing flavors. But for the sound of the equipment working, the room was silent, and she reveled in it. She had to catch up on everything she'd missed the past week. She picked up several clipboards and read the notes that had been left by her crew while she was in Jamaica. Despite her fears that everything might fall apart without her, it turned out her perfectly capable team were able to keep things running.

"There's our distiller of the year," she heard Quin call from the door. She looked up and saw both of her brothers walking into the distillery.

So much for her quiet morning. "You guys are here early."

"We both have a lot to catch up on," Reid explained. He reached for the clipboards, and she snapped them back.

"The old Reid would have never taken a full week off," she teased.

"You got that right. But I'm glad I did." He paused. "Lila and I had a pretty interesting conversation after we got home last night."

Gemma's eyes widened. Had Lila told Reid about seeing her with Tom Cain? She hadn't had time to chat with her before they left the island. But no, Reid's girlfriend wouldn't have sold her out like that. "What is it?"

"I proposed."

"Oh, my God!" Gemma shrieked and threw her arms around her oldest brother. "That's amazing!"

Quin joined their group hug. "She said yes, right?" he asked, joking.

"Of course, she said yes," he told them. "I'm actually here early because I knew that she would call you as soon as she woke up. Hell, I had to physically stop her from calling you after midnight last night."

"And how did you manage to physically stop her?" Quin nudged him in the ribs.

"I think you know," Reid responded with a wink, not letting the innuendo escape them.

"Well, we have an engagement party to plan."

"That'll come." Reid put up his hands. "We're in no hurry." He nodded at the clipboards and turned to Gemma. "How does everything look?"

Back to work. The celebration didn't last long. But Gemma looked up at her oldest brother, and she could tell he was happy—happier than he'd ever looked. Before Lila had entered his life, she didn't think she'd ever see a smile on his face again. Not since what had happened with his ex-wife. Her thoughts of Carolina led to thoughts of Cain Rum, which led to Tom. A knife of guilt stabbed into her chest, and she felt it difficult to breathe as she remembered what she'd done with him in Jamaica. It might sound ridiculous, but Gemma knew that with one blissful act, she'd betrayed her family and the distillery.

When it seemed like it had taken her too long to respond, she cleared her throat. "Everything looks great. The crew did a great job of keeping the place running." If she could just keep the conversation about rum, she'd be fine. "We should be able to bottle more of the quick-distilled by the end of the week. Then they're on the truck and on shelves."

"Fabulous."

She thought they might walk away, but instead Quin smiled at her. "You know, Gem, I don't think we really had a conversation about it in Jamaica, but we're really proud of you."

Gemma shook her head. "We all made this happen."

"No, Gemma, listen. We would just be two guys

without a clue if you weren't running the distillery. You are the best in the world. There's no question."

Her brothers' praise felt good, but she needed them to leave, lest they be able to see the sin of Tom Cain written across her forehead. "Oh, my god, when did you guys turn so mushy?" She pushed both of their shoulders. "Get out of my distillery. I've got work to do."

"Fine."

"And tell Lila I'm calling her later."

Tom sat in his office, drumming his fingers on the desk. He stopped to flip through the week's worth of messages his assistant, Alison, had given him. Part of him had hoped to see a message from Gemma. But her name hadn't been among the list of people he had to call back. He tossed the little pink slips back onto his desktop. With the exception of Gemma Rexford, there was no one he wanted to speak to. He couldn't get her out of his mind, and it was driving him crazy.

Spinning around in his chair, he took in the skyline of New York City. The skyscrapers, the concrete jungle. The sky was gray and held the promise of snow, a far departure from Jamaica. He longed to be back there. Not just under the heat of the sun, but with Gemma. After she'd left him at his hotel room, he hadn't seen her again. He'd hoped she would come to him, but he guessed she must have come to her senses and stayed away. If only he could come to his senses, too.

"I heard you were back."

Tom turned in his chair and saw his father had come in without knocking. "John," he said. He never called him Dad, or referred to him as his father at the office. Not like the man acted anything like a father—especially in the last few years. "Come in, why don't you?" he asked ironically. His father never knocked, unable to fathom that someone might not want him in the room.

"How was Jamaica?" he asked, going to the wet bar and pouring himself a glass of rum, even though it was before noon.

"Good," Tom said. "Informative. I made some good connections."

"Did you run into the Rexfords?"

Tom nodded. If his father had any idea just *how* he'd run into the Rexfords… "Yes, of course."

"I heard the girl was the toast of the conference."

Tom bristled at his father's use of the word *girl*. Gemma was a grown woman, and he couldn't help but defend her. "Gemma Rexford is one of the best distillers in the world. And she has the product and awards to prove it. She gave a presentation on an overview of the process. But she obviously didn't share any secrets or the ins and outs of it."

John shook his head. "She must be more clever than she looks. Although, she looks pretty good, eh? There's a lot going on in that pretty little head of hers." Tom opened his mouth to defend Gemma, but his father finished his rum and left the glass on top of Tom's desk. He stood to leave.

"I've been looking at the profit and loss report from last month. I was hoping we could talk about it."

His father waved him off. "Ignore that for now. We're taking care of it."

Tom wanted to discuss it. Cain Rum was losing money every month. If they didn't make changes, Tom knew that when it came time to take over the company, there might not be a business left.

Before he could counter, his father was gone, and Tom was again alone in his office. He looked at the glass that his father had left on the corner of his desk. Condensation had pooled on the dark oak wood. Tom picked up the glass and wiped away the water. Polishing the shiny surface with the cuff of his sleeve, he saw that there was no damage. Much longer, and the wood would have tarnished. That was John Cain, all right—no consideration for anyone else. His father was selfish, dismissive, stubborn.

Tom hated that he hadn't stopped the things his father had said about Gemma. She was smart, capable, beautiful, sexy… His thoughts trailed off, and his tailored suit felt tight, restrictive. He was too hot, too confined. He needed to get away from the office.

Tom looked again at the stack of phone messages on his desk and the meetings and appointments that filled his schedule. He dialed his assistant in the next room.

"Yes, Tom?"

"Alison, I need a flight. Can you see if the jet is available?"

"Really? There's nothing in your schedule out of town."

"Something just came up. I need to leave as soon as possible."

"Sure thing. Where are you going?"

"Miami."

CHAPTER FIVE

LATER THAT AFTERNOON, Gemma was running late, and Lila and Celia were already seated when she walked into the restaurant. She'd made plans to meet her brothers' partners for lunch to celebrate Reid and Lila's engagement. She should have been there earlier, but there'd been a small hiccup with an order that she had to smooth over.

When she saw the girls, she almost ran over to the table in her excitement, and she squealed when she saw the smile on her future sister-in-law's face. And then again when she saw the large diamond on the fourth finger of her left hand.

"I can't believe you two are getting married. I never thought I would see the day that Reid settled down again."

"Yeah, especially after what his ex did to him and your family," Lila said, with one perfect raised eyebrow. "With how she left Reid and stole your recipes. Not that I'm upset that she left Reid—it certainly worked out for me—but I just can't get past that betrayal."

Gemma exhaled, blowing out a breath. Lila was the only one who knew that she had hooked up with Tom. "Yeah," she added, quietly, feeling terrible about her dalliance with Tom in Jamaica. His family could have destroyed hers, and she hadn't been able to look past her own hormones.

"And yet, I saw you coming out of his room…"

Celia perked up. "What's going on? What did I miss?"

"Why don't we talk about you?" Gemma suggested, as she poured herself a glass of champagne from the bottle they girls had ordered. "Tell us all about the proposal."

But Lila ignored the request. "Should I tell Celia?" Lila asked. "Or do you want to?"

"If someone doesn't start talking soon, I'm going to scream," Celia warned. "What's going on?"

"On our last night in Jamaica, I happened to see Gemma kissing someone outside of my and Reid's room."

"Who were you kissing?"

Gemma opened her mouth to respond, but Lila beat her to it. "Tom Cain," she revealed with a smile.

"Cain? As in Cain Rum?" Celia asked, her eyes wide. "That really sexy guy that Quin and Reid were grousing about the whole conference?"

"Oh, yeah."

Gemma sipped her wine and hoped they would continue talking among themselves and not turn their attention back to her. But no chance of that happening.

"So, come on, dish, Gem," Lila said. "I've been holding on to this for two days now, and I'm about to explode. What is going on?"

"You haven't told Reid, have you?"

"Of course not. He'd freak, and I wanted to get the story from you. So, what happened? How did you end up making out with Tom Cain?"

"Well," Gemma started, unsure where to begin. Should she start with the hotel room? The small storage room in the banquet hall? The heated looks they'd exchanged for several years…?

She shrugged. "We hooked up," she said simply. "That's it." *Keep it vague.*

"You're going to have to do better than that," Celia told her. "*Hooked up* can mean any number of things."

"Fine. We had sex," she told them. "It was dumb, it shouldn't have happened, but it did. It didn't mean anything."

"Was it good?" Celia asked.

Gemma felt her temperature rise—whether it was the wine or the memories of being with Tom. "It was—" she searched for the words, but couldn't come up with anything better than "—really god-damn good."

"So, are you going to see him again?" Lila asked.

"I'm sure we'll cross paths at some point. You know how the business is. But no, I'm not going to do that again."

"If it was so good, why not?"

"You both know what went down with the Cains.

You said it yourself. Do you think for a second that Reid and Quin would condone that happening?"

Lila laughed. "And since when do you listen to anything they say?"

Gemma considered it. She'd never been one to follow instructions. "Hmm, good point." As Lila and Celia laughed, Gemma thought about that. Maybe she would see Tom again. She didn't have to listen to everything her brothers said.

"Thanks, guys. Good work today," Gemma said to her crew as they finished bottling a large batch of dark rum and others were loading it onto the delivery trucks. She unzipped her coveralls to her waist and freed her arms from their sleeves and the bottom half caught on the more-than-ample curve of her hips. Her tank top was sticking to her clammy skin. She fanned herself with her hand. The interior of the distillery was stifling.

Her crew was about to leave for the day, but Gemma still had a few things to do. Back in her office, she heard someone step into the building. It was probably one of the workers coming back in. But Gemma just about fell over when she saw who was standing in the middle of her distillery.

"You know, none of my guys look as good in coveralls as you," Tom told her.

"I'm assuming you have no women on the floor, right? Maybe that's where you're going wrong."

"Perhaps you're right."

"What are you doing here?" she asked, crossing her arms.

"Honestly, I don't know. I just wanted to see you."

"You can't just show up in my distillery—" She stopped. "How did you even get in here?" They normally kept the facility locked up tight.

"One of the guys out front let me in."

"Our truck drivers aren't exactly the doormen."

"Oh, well. Listen, don't get mad at them, it wasn't their fault. I talk a pretty good game."

Oh, she knew. "Do you know what my brothers will do if they see you here?" Tom didn't have to know that they, and everyone else in the building, had gone home for the evening.

"I have some idea. So I guess you'll have to make it worth the risk for me then."

She could see the devilish glint in his eye, and she wondered why he was there. "What do you want?"

"Dinner. That's it. I just want to talk to you."

Gemma knew she shouldn't. Going anywhere with him would be a bad idea. But with all the talk of dinner, her stomach growled. She couldn't deny that she was hungry, and she had to eat anyway. "If I say yes, will you get the hell out of here?"

"Yes."

She sighed dramatically, looking like she was putting up a fight, indifferent to his charms. "Okay, fine. I'll meet you for dinner. I'm almost done here anyway, so I'll just go home and change."

"The coveralls and white tank top are a great look, though," he told her. His gaze started at her feet and traveled upward, and it felt like the temperature in the distillery rose another ten degrees.

"I'm all sweaty, though."

"Not the first time I've seen you get sweaty."

She couldn't help but laugh. "Get out, will you?"

"Fine, I'll go. Where should I pick you up?"

She almost told him that she would take her car and meet him somewhere, but she knew that if she did that, she might talk herself out of the dinner date. She gave him her address. "Where are we going?"

"You promised me some of the best seafood I'd ever had."

"It might be a little late to make a reservation."

"I've heard you know the right people. You can get us in. Unless you aren't the real mover and shaker down here that I've been led to believe."

He was goading her—challenging her again. She had no doubt of his ability to get a table at any place in New York City, and she wanted to show him that she held a little sway, too. "Oh, I know a place."

"Okay, great. I'll pick you up at eight."

CHAPTER SIX

TOM'S HAND SETTLED low on Gemma's back as they followed the hostess to their table. As much as she wanted his touch, as much as she wanted to squirm under his fingers, she stepped away from him and looked around. A couple of the faces in the busy restaurant were familiar, but none of them paid her any mind. But that didn't mean she didn't feel as if everyone was watching them acutely, already digging out cell phones to report back to her brothers.

You're being paranoid, she told herself. No one in the restaurant cared that she was on a dinner date with Tom Cain, heir to Cain Rum and son of the man the Rexfords had battled with for years.

They stopped at the table, and it surprised her when Tom held out her chair, waiting for her to sit. She dated quite often, but she couldn't remember the last time a man did something like that for her. "You're not only good-looking but a gentleman, too." She looked up at him as he helped slide in her chair.

He chuckled and walked around to his own side of the table. "You sound surprised."

"I am a little. You weren't very gentlemanly in Jamaica."

A self-satisfied smile adorned his face. "I guess I wasn't."

He picked up his menu and as he studied it, she studied him. His thick, black hair was brushed back, but the waves were a little messy. The humidity no doubt played with his usual style. She appreciated his high cheekbones; his nose had a slight bump, but it did nothing to take away from his good looks. His blue eyes were cast down at the wine list. He must have felt her watching him, and he looked up and smiled.

"So, what looks good to you?" he asked, no doubt about choice of food.

"The guy holding the wine list," she said with a grin. She couldn't help but flirt with him, and she felt herself relax a little. His company did something to disarm her. It surprised her how comfortable she was with him.

He laughed. "I'd believe you if I didn't feel like I just ran five miles outside. It's December, but it feels like New York in the summer. The humidity kills me."

"This is as cool as it gets," she told him.

"Well, it sounds terrible."

"You get used to it," she told him. "I'll take the humidity over the snow in New York any day. I would freeze to death up there."

"I'd keep you warm," he said. She believed it, too,

as his gaze lit a fire within her, searing her insides. "Unless you want to visit sometime in the summer."

She said nothing and sipped her water. Was he already making plans for them? "Let's pump the brakes there a little, why don't we?" She might be attracted to the guy, but she didn't think there would be anything for them beyond this night. "Before you set a wedding date or anything, this really isn't anything but dinner."

"Well, let's see what happens *after* dinner," he said with a wink. "But I guess I should count myself lucky that I got you here."

"Yeah, you should."

"But everyone's got to eat, right?"

"That's true." She would have probably gone home and ordered some Thai food and binged some of the episodes of *Real Housewives* that cluttered her DVR. Going to one of her favorite restaurants with an attractive man and an evening that might end in incredible sex was a far better option. She could always watch reality TV after he went back to New York.

The waiter returned to take their order, and Tom deferred to her. "You go ahead," he told her. "Whatever you recommend is fine with me."

"Well, you won't be disappointed." She turned back to the server. "We'll start with the shucked oysters," Gemma told the server. "Then I'll have the shrimp linguini."

Tom nodded in agreement. "That sounds good.

I'll have the same. And a bottle of sauvignon blanc with that?" he finished, asking Gemma.

"Yeah, that sounds great."

As the server walked away, Gemma wished he'd hurry back with the wine. "Tell me, Tom. What are you really doing down here?"

"I was honest with you before. I don't really know what I'm doing. It was probably a dumb thing to do. I didn't know if you would even want to see me. But I was in New York, and I was restless. And all I could think about was you. All I wanted was to see you again."

His admission stole her breath, and she leaned forward. "Really?"

He shrugged. "You did something to me. Something that I've never felt before."

She rolled her eyes. "Oh, what? You're in love with me now, or something?"

He chuckled. "No, I didn't say that. But you stuck with me, grabbed hold of me and I just couldn't shake you. You're an itch I couldn't scratch."

"Very cool. You make me sound like I'm a disease."

"You're an infatuation."

"That's better?"

The server came back and poured them each a glass of wine. When they were alone again, he leaned forward, putting his elbows on the table. He looked at her as if he was looking *into* her. She reached for her wineglass to break the eye contact. The crisp, cold white wine quenched her thirst.

"So, you're telling me that you haven't thought of me since we were together."

Had she ever. "It's only been a couple of days," she reminded him. "But you might have crossed my mind. Once or twice."

"Is that right? Care to tell me when?" He grinned, and his voice lowered. He leaned closer. "Lonely in your bed before you go to sleep?" He reached across the table and covered her right hand with his. "Did this hand find its way between your thighs? Did you close your eyes and pretend it was me touching you?" He dragged his middle and forefinger over her own to the table.

"It might have, but I'm left-handed," she told him with a smirk.

Tom poured her another glass of wine, and a water for himself, and looked at the woman who sat across from him. His short, surprise trip to Miami had been one of his best ideas, and as he sat across from Gemma, he was only disappointed that he didn't have more time there.

Gemma Rexford wasn't just a smoking-hot woman he'd slept with in Jamaica. She was funny, sharp, astute, with a biting wit and a tongue just as keen. The woman gave as well as she got. She was one of the most impressive women he'd ever met. They'd talked all night over their food, and he felt a real connection between them. It made it easy for him to forget that they were professional rivals.

When the server returned with their bill, he was

sad that the evening was coming to an end. He'd expected to come down to Miami, find Gemma and ravish her, to get her out of his system, and be back on a plane home. But the minute he laid his eyes on her, her hair up, no makeup, in her tattered coveralls—he knew it would never be that easy. He'd been hooked.

He handed his credit card to the waiter. "So, what now, Gemma? Dinner's over. Do we just say our goodbyes now, or can that wait until tomorrow?"

With her wineglass halfway to her lips, she froze and looked at him. She didn't answer for a moment, and he wondered if he'd pushed too hard, misread the evening or the fire and promise he'd felt between them. She finally finished her wine and lowered her glass. She was wearing a smile on her face. "I think we can put that off until tomorrow morning."

CHAPTER SEVEN

GEMMA'S HOUSE WAS a two-story modern-style rectangle that was mostly made of glass. Her yard was lush. Thick trees and bushes that, along with a high wall, preserved her privacy. He could see that Rexford Rum was doing well. "This is a nice place. I like the garden," he told her. His only outdoor space in New York was a small balcony off his condo. "You must have a green thumb."

"My thumbs only know rum. This is the work of a fabulous gardener. But you should check out the place in the daylight," she said over her shoulder as she keyed in the code to unlock her door.

He came up behind her. Not touching her, but close enough to feel the heat of her body. "To me, that sounds like an invitation to stay the night," he leaned over and murmured in her ear.

She didn't answer as she opened the door and walked inside. He followed closely behind. The lights came on, and he saw that the interior was just as modern as the exterior, open concept, clean and neat. "Can I get you a drink?"

"That depends," he said.

"On what?"

"On whether or not I'll have to drive back to my hotel tonight."

She paused for a moment, and she seemed to be mulling over her response in her head. After far too long of a pause, she turned and walked away from him and into her kitchen. She pulled a wine bottle from the rack on the way. "I guess I'll get you that drink."

"That's what I thought. So I will get to check out that view of your garden after all." He went to a glass wall and looked out into her yard. Security lights illuminated some of it.

She handed him a glass of wine and held her own glass and the bottle. "Forget about that for now," she said, nodding in the direction of the stairs. "My room's this way."

"Lead the way."

They climbed the stairs, and he saw that her bedroom encompassed the entire second floor. "Wow, this is quite a bedroom."

She smiled. "There used to be three rooms up here, but when I bought the place, I had the walls torn down to create one big bedroom, a giant closet, and the ensuite of my dreams. I live alone. I figured, why not?"

"It's amazing." His eyes landed on the king-size bed that held more pillows than necessary. "Looks comfortable."

Gemma put the bottle of wine on the end table

and walked into her closet. When she came out, her dress was gone, and she was standing in front of him in a pink bra and red panties. "I'm sure most of your dates normally have it together enough to wear matching underwear."

He laughed at her comment. But she was right. The women he went out with were typically well coiffed, impeccably dressed, recently manicured, eager to impress. Not that there was anything wrong with that. Hell, he'd more than enjoyed it in the past. But that was what charmed him about Gemma. She hadn't been worried about impressing him with thousand-dollar lingerie. But seeing her in front of him excited him more than any other woman ever had. "I wouldn't worry too much about that. You won't be wearing it much longer."

When Tom stalked toward her, Gemma stopped caring about her mismatched underwear. He put a hand on her shoulder and plucked the bra strap from her skin and dragged it down her arm. He dropped his lips on her shoulder and kissed her lightly. His touch tickled her, and she drew her bottom lip between her teeth when he kissed that sensitive spot on her neck. He reached back and unsnapped her bra. He pulled it away from her, and it dropped to the floor. Taking her breasts in his hands, he cupped her, squeezed, brushed his thumbs over her nipples, and she arched into his touch. She hooked her thumbs under the sides of her panties and shimmied them down her hips.

He groaned, not taking his eyes from her chest. "Get on the bed," he told her.

Gemma smiled and knelt on the mattress. Her reflection in the full-length mirror in front of the bed entranced her. She watched her reflection as he approached. He'd removed all his clothes, and he knelt behind her. He smoothed one hand over her stomach, and the other up her torso, over her breasts and to her throat. He held her head in place and put his face beside hers, looking at them in the mirror, as well. "Look at us," he said, his voice rumbling through her. "We look good, don't we?"

"Yeah," she said, her voice so breathy she could barely hear herself.

"Keep your eyes on us in the mirror," he told her. She nodded. He smoothed his hand down over her stomach to her pussy and cupped her in his large hand. She flexed her hips against him, and he returned her eagerness by dipping two fingers inside. At his touch, she closed her eyes and threw back her head. But Tom's grip on her neck tightened ever so slightly, getting her attention. "Eyes open and on the mirror," he commanded.

"Okay," she said again in a whisper, afraid that if she spoke any louder, it would break the spell he held over her.

The pads of his fingers circled her clit, and she moaned.

He removed the hand that he'd had around her throat and dragged it down her lower back. He pushed her down so that she was on all fours on the bed, her ass raised to him. In the mirror, she saw Tom behind her, his eyes on her ass, as he picked up the condom he must have pulled out earlier and opened it, and his face looked pained as he rolled it over his cock. He lifted her ass a little bit and pushed inside her. His thrusts were rough, fierce, and his grip on her hips was strong.

She cried out, and their eyes connected in the mirror.

"You're so goddamn hot, Gemma," he rasped. "I'm not going to last long."

"I won't, either."

"Touch yourself."

"What?"

"You heard me. Touch yourself."

He didn't have to ask her again. Her left hand dipped down her front. She found her clit, which was already swollen and needy from his previous touch. She circled it only a few times and looked in the mirror again, seeing that his eyes were locked on her.

She moaned again. The pleasure built within her, and she pushed back against Tom's thrusts. Her breath stuttered, and her body tensed. She cried out when her orgasm hit her at full force. Tom followed her right over the edge, proving that he was barely holding on by a thread and waiting for her to finish before he came.

Gemma and Tom both collapsed on the bed as their breathing returned to normal. "Wow," she whispered.

"Yeah," he agreed.

"I'm glad you decided to come down here."

"Me, too."

The next morning, Tom sat by Gemma's pool. It was December, but because he was acclimated to the typical New York winter, he found it downright tropical in Miami. He was wearing his button-down shirt and pants from the night before. He thought about the traffic and noise of New York, and he closed his eyes, savoring the silence of Gemma's property. Her home was an oasis. He could get used to this. Gemma joined him, handing him a mug of coffee. *Yup*. He could definitely get used to this.

She was wearing a pair of leggings and a large sweater, which somehow still managed to show off her incredible body, instead of covering her up. She was by far the sexiest woman he'd ever met. "Enjoying the weather?" she asked.

"It's unreal. I can't believe I have to go back to winter in a couple of hours. It's like a paradise down here."

She looked around and seemed to revel in it, taking it all in. "It's pretty great, right? Where do you live in New York?"

"I've got a place in Manhattan."

"Paying a fortune for a shoebox?" she asked.

"Pretty much."

"I can't imagine living in the city like that. I like my space. My privacy."

"You've got a great place here."

"Yeah, it wasn't always. There were a ton of renovations to do. It took a lot of time, and even more money. But it was worth it all." She sipped from her coffee. "What time is your flight?"

"I took the private jet," he told her. "I need to leave in about an hour." He'd come down to Miami to get Gemma out of his system, but his plan had backfired. All his night with her had done was make the cravings for her worse. It shocked him that he was reluctant to leave Gemma.

Gemma laughed. "The private jet," she repeated. "Well, look at how fancy you are. I mean, the Rexfords don't have a PJ."

"Well, you're definitely missing out," he told her. "Maybe if you're nice to me, you can borrow ours." He put down his mug and stood over her, holding out his hand. "Are you going to miss me?"

She took his hand, and he pulled her so she stood in front of him. She put her arms around his neck and drew him in for a kiss. Despite the coffee she'd had to drink, Gemma tasted just as sweet as she had the night before.

When they broke apart, she smiled and shook her head. "Nah. Just wondering when you'll be out of my hair. I've had you, and I'm tired of you now."

He skimmed his hands down her back to cup her backside and squeezed. "I know that's not true."

"You don't think so? I'm one hundred percent ready for you to leave."

"I think you'll miss me the second I'm out that door."

She pressed her body more fully against his, and he responded in kind. "You're so sure of that."

"I am. In fact, I think we'll see each other again real soon."

She smiled up at him. "I know it's a bad idea," she started. "But I think you might be right."

CHAPTER EIGHT

"So, what's all this?" Gemma asked, flipping through the report Reid handed her. She saw the Cain name printed on several pages.

"We're making an aggressive push up north," Reid explained.

"Cain Rum territory," she noted. She'd known it was coming, and even though she welcomed the challenges of a new launch, she couldn't help but think of Tom, and she was left feeling conflicted.

He nodded. "Now's the time."

Quin spent the next hour detailing a condensed version of the information in the report. It involved some new blends and a new marketing plan to target young, hip, but sophisticated adults—the Wall Street and Hamptons type, exactly Cain's customers. Quin had put together a great plan, and Reid looked more than satisfied.

When Gemma remained silent, Quin turned his attention to her. "What do you think?" he asked her.

"I like it. And I have a few different batches that should fit that profile in the barrels now."

Her brothers smiled at her, pleased with her enthusiasm, and she attempted a smile back, but she knew it didn't reach her eyes. She felt a pit of guilt in her stomach. She was lying to her brothers—hiding a huge truth from them. She'd never lied to them before, and she knew that they would never approve of the night she'd spent holed up in her house with Tom Cain, and how every part of her wanted to see him again.

She noticed that Reid was still watching her. "You okay, Gemma?"

Apparently, she wasn't putting on a very good act. "Yeah, I'm fine. I'm a little tired. I'm trying to relax and decompress after all the catch-up I had to do after Jamaica."

"I called a couple of times last night," Quin told her.

"Sorry," she said. "I wasn't around my phone." The truth was that she had seen Quin's calls, but she hadn't felt like talking. She'd needed some time for herself. Residual guilt from how much she'd enjoyed her date with Tom had kept her from answering. "Anything wrong?"

"No. I just wanted to talk. You seem a little distracted. I just wanted to make sure you were okay."

"What's that supposed to mean?" she asked. She knew they were right, but she hadn't realized she was acting any differently. Her forbidden encounters with Tom had changed her. She knew she was acting strangely, but she couldn't come clean now. They wouldn't understand. "I'm under a lot of pressure lately. Sure, we're all responsible for the success, and I'm not doing this alone, but I personally put a lot of pressure on myself to continue pushing to get better." That was the truth. Being on top meant she had to stay there. "I'm just tired."

Neither Reid nor Quin said anything for a moment. Quin spoke first. "We're sorry. We didn't realize how you felt. But how do you expect us to know what you're going through if you don't tell us?"

"I tried to not dwell on it, to push past it, but it just made it worse. I had to disconnect for the night. But I won't shut you guys out anymore, okay?"

"That's all we need," Reid assured her.

"God, what's happened to you guys? You settle down in relationships and now you're all about the feelings?"

"Yeah, it's pretty good, huh?" Quin added.

She stood from the table. "I wouldn't have you guys any other way." She picked up her copy of the report. "Now, let me get out of here and get back to work, okay?"

The mood in the boardroom was somber and serious as Tom and the rest of the men took in the recent profit and loss numbers. Once, Cain Rum had been on top of the industry, but their market share had fallen dramatically in the past year. If they didn't act quickly, they would lose everything.

"John," Tom started, addressing his father. "We need to turn this around. We need an overhaul of how we do things. We need to explore new markets, new processes, a new approach to marketing."

His father waved him off. "Tom, I've been in this business since before you were born. We've had downturns in the past, and we've come out of them. It'll be fine."

Tom tried to keep his emotions in check. "The world has changed in the last fifty years," he insisted. "I believe this is more than a downturn. This is a downright slump, but there are ways out of this. We need to adapt."

"And how much do you think all of this would cost? What, we'll just take the money out of thin air?"

Tom thought of the way the company spent money. The private jet he'd taken to Miami. "There's room in the budget. Changing is the only way we'll survive—"

"I won't hear of this kind of talk. It's negative and not helping anything."

"Sir, perhaps Tom is right—" Shane, Tom's friend and one of the corporate accountants, agreed.

John glared at him, cutting him off.

"You gentlemen might think you know what's best, but you're young in this business and have no idea how to maintain a brand over a long time. The only course of action is to ride it out. The fad distilleries, the craft places—like Rexford, especially—are trendy and will fall out of favor soon enough. And we'll still be here, doing what we've always done. An old, familiar standard."

Tom sat back in his chair, frustrated at not being heard. His fears were coming true. His father was too stubborn and set in his ways to see it, but based on Tom's own projections, Cain Rum was going to fail, and as much as he tried, there was nothing he could do about it.

CHAPTER NINE

HOLIDAY MUSIC PIPED through the speakers at the Bal Harbour Shops, and the crowd bustled around Gemma, Celia and Lila as they made their way through various stores. Gemma loved the holidays, but she hated the crowds, the noise, the chaos, and generally preferred to do her gift shopping online. But when Lila and Celia had invited her along for a girls' day, she couldn't refuse. Otherwise, she would just stay at home and fail to talk herself out of calling Tom.

As they waited for their coffee orders at the café, Lila sighed. "I have no idea what to get Reid for Christmas," she confessed. "He's a grown man with his own money. If he wants something, he'll buy it."

"Why don't you plan a vacation for you two?" Gemma suggested. "I know Reid sucks at taking time off unless he's forced to do it."

Lila mulled that over. "That's a good idea. Maybe I'll throw in never talking to him about wedding planning ever again."

"It's going that well?" Celia asked with a laugh.

"Every time he sees me on Pinterest, his eyes start to glaze over," Lila said, picking up her latte. "How about your secret mystery man, Gemma?"

"Large iced Americano for Gummo," the barista called.

"That's *Gemma*," she told the barista, but the words didn't seem to register with him. It was the holiday season, and he had more customers waiting for drinks. "You don't care what my name is, do you?"

"Peppermint tea for *Sheila*!" he said.

"That's close enough," Celia said, reaching past Gemma for her tea.

When the three were out of the café and back into the crowded, open-air mall, Celia sipped her tea. "Don't think you're getting away that easily. What's up with you and that Cain guy?"

"Oh, boy," she said. "I don't need to bore you with that."

"What makes you think we'll be bored? Do you know us?"

"Fine. He was here."

"When?"

"Earlier this week."

"What?"

"Just for one night. He took his private jet and surprised me. We had dinner…" She trailed off, hoping something would come along and distract them. But no such luck.

"And what else?"

"I brought him home."

"He flew down here for one night with you? So romantic," Lila said, putting a hand on her heart.

"What we did that night sure wasn't romantic," Gemma joked, remembering the way he'd taken her, his commanding hand on her throat.

The girls all laughed. "So, when are you going to see him again?"

Gemma thought about it. "I don't know. I probably won't." She shook her head. "It's just too complicated."

"Why is it complicated?"

"Because of his last name," she said. That was the simple answer. "What, am I supposed to invite him over for Christmas dinner and say, 'Hey, Reid and Quin, I know we've spent years fighting with this guy and his family, and your ex-wife stole from us and married his father, but we're banging now, so can't we put that all aside for the holiday?'"

"That's some real Shakespeare shit, you know?" Celia told her.

"And see how it ended for those kids?" Gemma asked. "I told you, it's complicated."

Celia stopped in front of a store. "Oh, look, Lila, here's the perfect gift for the man who has everything," she said.

Gemma looked up and saw they were standing in front of Agent Provocateur. She recalled the night she stood in front of Tom wearing mismatched underwear. It hadn't concerned him, but she'd felt like an idiot. Too bad she hadn't come here last week…

"All right," Lila said. "We're going in."

"Maybe I can find something Quin will like." Celia held up a lace teddy that had more straps than Gemma knew what to do with. "Like this."

"You know, it kind of makes me uncomfortable that I'm here with you while you pick out sex clothes for my brothers." But Gemma's eyes caught on a piece of red material. It was a sheer bodysuit. It was kind of plain, had no extra straps or buckles. It was simple but it was stunning.

"Ooh, you *need* to get that," Lila said over her shoulder. Gemma had never been one for expensive lingerie, but god, there was something about it that drew her in. "Your Mr. Cain will love it."

"Please," she said. "I don't even know if I'm going to see him again." She tried to tell Lila that she was wrong. But she knew that it was the truth. *Mr. Cain would love it.* She fingered the sheer material.

"Are you going to buy it?" Celia asked.

Gemma thought about it. It was ridiculously expensive—more than she'd ever spent on lingerie—but she nodded and plucked the hanger from the rack. "I think I will." Maybe she'd have to show it to him in person.

The Saturday game night rush was in full swing when Tom entered the sports bar where he was meeting his friends. It was only Thursday, but their favorite place was packed. He'd known Shane and Darren since college. After graduation, they'd both gotten jobs at Cain Rum's corporate office. They might be adults now, but they still found time for beer, wings and a hockey game, just like they had back in the day. He walked into the crowded restaurant and found them sitting in their usual corner booth.

"Hey, guys." He took a seat and poured himself a beer from the pitcher in the center of the table. He drank. "It feels like forever since I've done this."

Shane tapped Tom's glass with his own. "Yeah, you were in Jamaica. And you bailed on us last Monday."

He'd completely forgotten about the plans he'd made before his impromptu trip to Miami. He had no regrets, but he should have told his friends, and he knew he'd have to account for his absence. "Yeah, I had some things to take care of in Miami."

Darren drained his glass and poured another. "Man, you should have invited us along. Miami's great—we could have partied it up."

"It was a pretty unexpected trip."

Darren narrowed his eyes at him. He worked in the corporate travel division of the company. "What did you have to do down there? I didn't know about any business trips to Florida."

"Well, it might have been a personal trip," he revealed.

"So, it's a woman, then."

"Isn't that where Rexford is based?" Shane asked. "What are you doing, a little corporate espionage?"

"I wouldn't mind doing a little espionage with Gemma Rexford," Darren said with a snicker.

"Man, she is hot," Shane added as Tom balled

his hands into fists under the table. "I swear, I saw a picture of her in the trade newsletter from the conference..." He trailed off with an appreciative, wolfish whistle.

"You tell us, Tom. You were there. Did she look that good in person?"

Tom's body was tensing with the talk of Gemma. He'd had enough and didn't want to talk about her any further. "Guys, she's also one of the best distillers in the world, and we owe her the respect she's due."

His friends were shocked into silence. Tom hated to admit that he'd been just as bad as them when it came to talking about women. It wasn't right, and he wanted to change. But he knew Darren and Shane could sense the difference in his behavior.

"Sorry," Shane said, putting his hands up in surrender. "What's up with you?"

"It's nothing." He couldn't tell them that he was currently infatuated with the woman who was partly responsible for the decrease in Cain Rum's profits. "I just don't think it's appropriate to talk about a woman, especially a colleague, that way. But sorry, I'm frustrated lately."

"With your dad?"

Tom nodded. They'd been in the last meeting with him, where John had ignored Tom's warnings and desire to change. Shane and Darren had been his main confidants over the years, and he'd vented many times about his frustrations with his father. He wouldn't normally turn to anyone outside the family with his issues, but Darren and Shane were his best friends. He trusted them, and they felt the same way. "Yeah, and the company. You've seen the numbers. He's convinced it's only a temporary dip and not part of a downward trend. He's a dinosaur who doesn't understand where the market is and is too stubborn to step aside." He didn't want to see Cain Rum fail. It had been in his family for generations, and until recently it had been successful. It was important to Tom to keep the family business going. The only way they would survive would involve following current trends, adapting and changing strategies.

"Just look at what Rexford is doing," he started, his temperature rising at the thought of Gemma. "They've grown considerably in the past couple of years because of their willingness to diversify. They have a huge online presence, and they adapted to make the changing market work for them."

"But tell that to your dad," Darren said.

"Man, I've tried. We have to do something, though." He thought about it. Maybe if he spent more time with Gemma, he might get a little more insight into how Rexford worked. It couldn't hurt. He had to do something to save the business.

CHAPTER TEN

IT WAS FRIDAY and even though it was after 7:00 p.m., Tom was still in his office. He was unimpressed with the current numbers on the pages in front of him. He studied a graph that had shown profits of the past five years. Cain Rum was once the top of the pack, one of the preeminent rum brands in the country. But they'd been complacent, and they'd stagnated. And with the influx of other high-end, handcrafted brands—Rexford, especially—they'd begun their decline.

He cursed his father's decisions, his resistance to change and edict to just perform at the status quo. He didn't understand how the business and the market had changed. Would he listen? *Of fucking course not.* He was happy to do nothing until he retired. Tom looked over the numbers again, and the graph he'd made that charted Rexford's latest success. They were beating them handily, and Gemma's rum was why. She put care and attention in her craft, and one could tell from just a sip. If he had a master distiller of Gemma's caliber working for him, Cain would be unstoppable. He frowned. If he couldn't turn it

around, there would be no Cain Rum Distill... ...
for him to fix when his father retired.

He turned in his chair and looked out the large
window behind him. A light snowfall was blanketing
the city. He thought back to the Monday of the week
before, when he'd gone to Miami to see Gemma. He
wanted to be back there with her. The weather had
been hot—but it had been Gemma who had burned
herself onto his skin. They'd spoken a couple of times
during the week, shared some innuendo-laced text
messages. But a phone call was no substitute for
being with her in person. Since that night in Jamaica,
they'd formed some sort of connection—it wasn't a
relationship, but it was fun.

Tom's phone, which was on top of his desk,
buzzed and, as if she'd known he was thinking about
her, he saw it was Gemma calling for a video chat.
He couldn't fight the smile that formed on his lips
as he accepted the call. Her gorgeous face filled the
screen. She didn't normally wear much makeup, but
he saw her lips were covered in cherry-red lipstick,
paired with dark eyeliner and false eyelashes.

"You look great," he told her. "Got a hot date?"

She laughed. "Maybe." Tom tried to swallow
the lump of jealousy that had formed in his throat.
Whether Gemma had a date or not was none of his
business. They weren't exclusive, and he had no
claim on her. "What are you doing?" she asked.

"Still at work, unfortunately," he told her.

She frowned, and the red lipstick left him transfixed. "Everything okay?"

He wasn't about to confide in her that he was worried about the state of Cain Rum. He might like her, but she was one of the reasons his family business was in such trouble. He shook his head casually. "Just some things to catch up on. Someone's been distracting me lately."

She pursed her lips again. "I guess you need to start prioritizing," she told him. Tom smiled. Even though he had a pile of things to address on his desk, he already was prioritizing. Time spent with Gemma was better than any minute he spent at the office. "How much longer do you have to be there tonight?"

He scrubbed a hand over his face. "Maybe another hour or so."

"It's Friday—shouldn't you be out having fun? Happy hour with your friends, hitting on women or something like that?"

He'd thought of doing just that, minus the hitting on women, but he hadn't been interested. "I've got enough to do tonight."

"Maybe you need a little pick-me-up."

Well, now we're talking. He smiled. "What do you have in mind? Is that why you look so done up?"

"You caught me, I guess." He watched her look around. "One minute."

Tom settled back in his chair, holding his phone, and his breath, as he waited for whatever illicit thing she had in mind. There was a knock on his door. He didn't know there was anyone else in the building. Who was knocking? Goddammit, he wanted to see what Gemma was going to show him. He didn't want to deal with whoever was about to come into his office.

"Hold that thought," he told her. He pushed up from his desk and walked across his office. Whoever was on the other side of the door knocked again, impatient. "Jesus," he muttered. "I'm coming," he called out. He opened the door and was surprised to see Gemma standing on the other side.

"You're coming?" she asked, and her lips, still bright red, pursed as she looked him up and down. "It doesn't look like you are yet."

Tom was speechless and stepped out of the doorway as she walked into his office and he closed the door. He could fully appreciate her outfit as she walked away from him farther into the room. She was wearing thigh-high boots and a wool coat that came to midthigh; to the casual observer, she might appear covered. But he had a feeling that underneath that coat, she would be downright indecent. He was surprised, flabbergasted and looked at the phone in his hand he'd used to video chat with the woman he thought was in Miami, hoping at best for a racy video, and then at the woman who stood in his office.

"What are you doing here?" he asked, mimicking her reaction when he'd turned up at her distillery. "How'd you get in here?"

"What kind of welcome is that?" she asked, walking closer to his desk with slow, purposeful steps, not even looking at him.

"A shocked one." He turned the lock on the door

and followed her farther into his office. She was the last person he'd expected to see here.

She stood in front of his desk. "You weren't kidding about doing work, huh?"

"Oh, I never kid around about work." He walked around the other side of the desk, and as he straightened the papers he'd scattered on top, his eyes landed on the Rexford graph. He quickly covered it with another and pushed all of it into the top drawer.

"Sit down," she commanded.

"What?" he asked, caught off guard.

"I told you to sit down," she ordered again, her hands on her hips, assuming a dominant posture.

Tom wasn't usually one for taking orders, but he surprised himself when he obeyed, eager to see what she wanted to with him.

He watched her as she slid her fingers from her hips up her torso to the belt at the waist of the coat. Holding his breath, he watched her toy with the ends. She opened her coat and dropped it on the floor with a flourish, so that she stood before him in a sheer red lace bodysuit and those damn high boots. He'd been right. She looked downright indecent, but she was about the sexiest thing he'd ever seen.

"You make quite an entrance," he told her as every drop of blood in his body traveled south to his dick.

"I thought you'd like it."

"And I do." His eyes were fixated on her, drawn in by the dark color of her nipples through the bodysuit. He wanted to taste them.

She shook her dark, wavy hair over her shoulder.

"Thank god for that. It would have been pretty embarrassing if you had plans or something and you'd sent me away."

"I would never send you away."

"That's reassuring." She sat on his desk, and in a move more graceful than he could manage, without knocking anything off the desk she swung her legs over and swiveled so that she was now on his side, with her thighs spread to him. He almost swallowed his tongue when he saw that there was a slit of an opening over her pussy. The bodysuit was crotchless.

"Goddamn," he murmured. He started to stand again—he needed to be between those smooth, tanned thighs—but she raised her leg, the bottom of her heeled boot landing on his sternum, stopping him.

"Did I tell you to stand?" she asked.

"You did not," he said with a chuckle. "Is this your game? You're a dominatrix now?"

"Not always," she said. "But sometimes I like to call the shots."

He nodded in approval. He normally wanted to be the one in control, but— "You know this is *my* office, right? I'm the boss here." Gemma pouted, her cherry-red lips rounding in a disappointed expression. "But I can live with this. For tonight." He looked her up and down, trying his best to put on a show that he wasn't as affected by her as he was. He sat back down in the chair and held up his hands. "What do you want to do with me?"

"I'll show you."

While he was still seated, Gemma slid off his desk and straddled his thighs in his chair. Her pussy, exposed by the crotchless nature of the bodysuit, grazed against his already rock-hard dick. Whatever she wanted him to do, there was no doubt he would do it!

She kissed him with passion, no doubt smearing the red lipstick over his mouth. She shifted her hips, sliding against his dick again. Her heat transmitted through his pants, and he groaned. He grabbed her ass, gripping her, digging his fingers into her flesh. He pulled her in, tighter to him, and took her mouth in a kiss he'd been craving for almost two weeks, since he'd last seen her. Her scent, the taste of her tongue, the feel of her ass in his hands—he'd been starving for it all.

He pulled back from her to catch his breath. "God, you're incredible."

"You haven't seen anything yet." She slithered from her place in his lap and knelt on the floor. Not taking her gaze from his eyes, she unbuckled his belt, unsnapped the button on his pants, and so slowly that he thought he might pass out, she dragged down his zipper, reached into his boxers and wrapped her fingers around his shaft. He raised his hips and helped her push his pants down over his thighs.

She leaned in and swirled her tongue around the head of his dick. She took it all in her hot, wet mouth, and as she enveloped him, he pushed his fingers into her hair, wrapping the tendrils around his fingers.

When she came up for air, he saw that she'd left

her mark on him—that red lipstick covered his dick, and he almost came just looking at it. But not yet. She reached into the top of her boots and pulled out a condom. He breathed a sigh of relief. "I'm glad you were prepared."

"Always." She took her rightful place, straddling his lap. When her pussy in her crotchless bodysuit slid along his dick again, he groaned and threw back his head, thinking he might explode right then and there. "You like that?" she asked with a grin. He didn't have a chance to respond before she did it again. This time, the movement of her hips was slow, deliberate, dragging out the delicious torture. They both moaned in mutual pleasure.

He grasped her hips in desperation, stilling her. He nodded at the condom in her fingers. "You'd better hurry up with that thing," he warned her.

"You got it," she said, breathless with lust. She quickly removed the condom from the package and rolled the latex over his rigid length. Gritting his teeth, he took over, grasping himself and pulling her over him, entering her.

She cried out and arched her back, pushing her full breasts closer to his face. He tongued her nipple through the sheer material. Wanting more, he pulled the straps from her shoulders, removing the barrier between them.

He was close to exploding, but he needed to hang on for her. Luckily, he wouldn't have to wait for long. Her movements became quicker, and her breathing more strained. Already, he was so attuned to Gemma that he knew she was coming. He pulled her closer and moved with her, bringing both of them to climax together.

As their movements quieted, he held her close and inhaled against her throat. Her scent filled his lungs, and he would trade it for oxygen any day. He maneuvered a hand between them and removed the condom, throwing it in the wastebasket under his desk, and pulled her closer again. He kissed her. Her lipstick was smeared over her face, and he was proud that he'd done that. Her makeup had marked them both. He wasn't sure what had happened, when it had happened, but he had feelings for Gemma Rexford.

"Why don't we leave? I'll get you home." *Home. That'd be nice.* He thought of Gemma being in his house every day. Jesus. What was happening to him? He didn't fall for women so quickly, and here he was making wedding plans. He had to remember that Gemma was a hookup. That was it. He thought about the graph that he'd pushed into his drawer, the one about Rexford's rapid rise and success. She might be a casual hookup, but she was an inconvenient one at that.

Several hours later, they were lying naked on the rug in front of Tom's fireplace. One of the logs in the fire snapped, bringing Gemma from her pleasure-induced coma to look up at the man who'd wrapped his arms around her. He pulled the blanket that he'd used to cover them tighter, and she snuggled closer to his chest. She sighed against his skin. Despite every reason she shouldn't be with him, this was bliss.

"You okay?" he asked.

"Yeah, I'm great," she said, and he saw her smile against the soft hair on his chest. "This is incredible."

"It is. I'm glad you're here," he told her.

"I am, too. I wanted to surprise you."

"And you certainly did."

"So," she started before she could stop herself.

"What?"

"Nothing, never mind."

"You can't say *never mind* and then pretend you weren't going to say anything. What is it?"

She took a deep breath. "I was just wondering if you're seeing anyone right now. I know we didn't put a label on this, and a casual thing is fine with me, but I want to know you aren't exclusively seeing anyone."

"No," he told her. "Not seeing anyone exclusively or casually at the moment. Are you?"

She shrugged and hoped Tom wouldn't judge her too harshly. "I date," she told him. "But I'm not see-ing anyone right now. There was this guy recently. I saw him *very casually*," she emphasized, "before going to Jamaica. But I broke it off with him when I got back."

"After me."

"Yes. After you."

"Why'd you break it off?"

"You're really going to make me say it, aren't you?"

"Not if you don't want to."

She sighed. "The truth? I think a part of me knew we weren't done, you know? That I'd see you again." He hugged her tighter, and she was glad she hadn't scared him off. "Why are you still single? You're gorgeous, sexy, funny, and you have all the free rum you want. I figure you would have your pick of the guys in Miami."

"Oh, stop," she said, playfully smacking his chest.

"Seriously, though. Why weren't you seeing anybody? Why was I able to scoop you up without a fight from some other guy?"

She screwed up her nose and shook her head. "I find it hard to get really serious about a guy. I'm more of a casual woman. I don't do serious relationships, or steady boyfriends, or heavy commitments, or any of that stuff. I never wanted to be tied down. I like my freedom, you know."

"What was your last relationship?"

"A few years ago. I thought we were destined to be and all that nonsense. But it didn't work out."

"What happened?"

"I really liked him. Hell, I loved him. But at the end of the day, it felt like he liked my brothers more than me. He liked the idea of being close to the people behind Rexford Rum."

"The man's an idiot."

"And he was a really good friend of Reid's."

"Well, thank God I don't have that problem," Tom said with a laugh.

"And then there was another guy. It was a pretty serious relationship. But I was never his priority."

"How could you not be his priority?" Tom asked.

"He was a real workaholic type. That always came first." Gemma thought briefly about all of the cancelled plans, and the cold dinners she'd had waiting for him, and she already knew that Tom would never do that to her.

"The man's an idiot."

"Nah. I'm over it. The more I think about it, the less likely it was that we would ever work out. In hindsight I can see that we never had that connection, you know?"

"I do. Like the connection between us?"

She blinked and looked away, not willing to put Tom in the relationship category. "So, what about you? You're handsome, rich, successful, really good in bed—you'd think there'd be a line of beautiful women beating down your door."

"Hardly. I mean, like you, I date people, but nothing serious. I'm just so busy with work. So, I guess you're not the only woman who doesn't like being second to my job."

That made her pause. It was Friday, and Tom had been at the office after seven. Maybe he wasn't so different from those men she'd dated before. But wrapped up in his arms, she didn't want to think about that and she put the thought out of her head. "Do you normally put women behind the job?" she asked quietly.

He hesitated. "I want to tell you no, especially given what you just told me. But I guess I do."

"Wow. This is quite a serious conversation."

"Are you sorry you started it?"

"No."

"Neither am I," he assured her. "And what brought it on? Were you going to ask if I wanted to go steady?" he teased.

She laughed, thinking about how juvenile it sounded "I hadn't meant to. But now that you bring it up… I won't see anyone else, as long as you do the same."

He pulled her on top of him, and her thighs straddled his hips. "Now why would I want to see anyone else when I have everything I need right here?"

Gemma thought about that. She was what he wanted now, but would his priorities shift once the newness of their relationship wore off? Would he eventually put the job ahead of her? While the thought troubled her, she wished she'd never brought it up. She wanted to get back to the warm, fuzzy, sensual cocoon they'd created on the floor of his apartment. The doorbell rang, and Gemma was grateful for the distraction. "Is that our pizza?"

"I think so. I guess I really do have everything I need now." He stood, still naked. Gemma took the opportunity to admire the view, frowning when he pulled on his sweatpants. He walked out of the living room. She heard him open the door and speak to another person. The door closed again, and he returned holding the square pizza box.

"You know, I'm surprised," he said.

"About what?"

"When I was in Miami, you brought me to that restaurant—we had that great seafood, remember?"

"I never forget good oysters," she said.

"That wasn't the only good thing that night."

"Okay, so what? What are you surprised about?"

"New York is foodie heaven, and all you wanted to do was stay in and eat pizza."

"Sometimes I like a quieter time." She reached out and, grasping the waistband of his sweatpants, pulled lightly, dragging him back to the floor. "Sometimes I like cheese and pepperoni. And there's nothing out there that beats this."

"Are you talking about me or the pizza?"

She laughed and leaned in for a kiss before taking a large slice from the box. "Can't it be both?"

CHAPTER ELEVEN

THE WEEK HAD dragged on, but it was Friday evening once again, and Gemma was back in Tom's arms. Reid and Quin had moved on their plans to target Cain Rum, and every time they mentioned it, she'd felt the guilty pit in her stomach. But she was lying in her large soaker tub, her back to Tom's warm, muscular chest, and at that moment, life couldn't be more perfect.

Tom had arrived at her home only an hour earlier. She'd been cooking dinner, but it was left forgotten to cool on the stove top when he'd knocked on the door. They'd undressed each other in the foyer and didn't make it past the living room before he was inside her.

In the bathtub, Tom cupped some water in his large hand and spilled it over her breasts. As his thumb smoothed over her nipple, she sighed. "The week feels so long now, don't you think?"

"It's true. The five days since I saw you last felt like a month," he told her.

"I guess we have to make the most of our time together, right?"

"Yeah."

An alarm chimed from somewhere in the house. It wasn't her security or fire alarm, though. It was her cell phone. "Oh shit," she said, pushing out of the bathtub. She tried to remember where she'd left it. Her bedroom. She walked quickly, naked and dripping water and soap bubbles on the way.

"Whoa, what's the rush?" Tom called after her. "Do we have to evacuate?"

She didn't answer and ran to her room, because she knew it wasn't a regular cell phone notification. "Goddammit," she muttered, looking at her phone. It was just as she'd expected.

"What's wrong?" Tom asked coming up behind her. He had wrapped a towel around his waist and draped her robe over her shoulders.

"It's the distillery."

"Everything okay?"

"I don't know." She pushed a button to close the app, stopping the noise. "Celia, Quin's girlfriend, set me up with a digital monitoring app. It's telling me that there's a malfunction on one of the tanks and pressure is dropping. I've got to get over there. It's just for a minute. Long enough to check on it. Hopefully there isn't a huge problem. Do you mind?"

"Of course not. You've got to make sure everything is okay." He dropped the towel, and Gemma was distracted just long enough to slide her gaze up his lean body as he opened his suitcase and took out a pair of jeans. She turned back to her phone.

"You had some wine," he said. "Do you want me to drive?"

"You want to come with me?"

"Yeah. If you want me to."

She thought about him being in her distillery again. Her brothers definitely wouldn't like it, especially after hours with no one else around. But if there was a problem with one of the tanks, she would appreciate the second pair of hands. "All right, then. Thanks. You'd better get dressed."

The ride to the distillery was quiet. She was worried about the equipment, of course, but it was weird to bring Tom there. He'd been there that one time before, but that had been a quick visit. This was different. It was after hours, and she might need his help to fix the equipment. She didn't know. But she knew that Reid would throw a fit if he knew that she had brought a Cain into their business.

Tom parked in front, and he followed her to the door, which she unlocked. Gemma could hear the hiss from one of the gaskets from outside. She'd been hoping it was a false alarm, but not so. She entered first and stopped, blocking his way before he could enter. "Wait, Tom."

"What?"

She looked at him carefully. "Can I trust you?" she asked. "In my distillery?" she amended quickly, hoping she could trust him there and in her heart.

"I hope you can."

"Me too." She shifted out of the door, and he entered. "Because I have a feeling that I'm going to need your help."

He cupped her cheek, and didn't hesitate to respond. "Well, you've got it."

It took several hours, but Tom and Gemma were able to fix the mechanical problem that had threatened to ruin the entire batch. When it was under control, she went into her office to call Reid and Quin to let them know what had happened and to assure them that everything was under control.

When she came back out on the distillery floor, she saw that Tom was standing in front of her quick stills. He bowed his head and she could see his gaze following the tubes, checking out the tanks. She saw his cell phone in his hand. Was he taking a picture of it?

"What are you doing?" she asked, unable to take the accusatory tone out of her voice.

"I realized that we haven't eaten yet, so I ordered pizza. It'll be here soon." He held up his phone and she saw the food delivery app was open.

Sounded logical enough, and she felt bad for thinking the worst. "We sure do order quite a bit of pizza."

"It's okay, we can work off the calories later," he said, winking at her.

"Maybe sometime I'll actually get around to cooking you a meal."

"I'll hold you to it."

"Thanks for your help here. I wouldn't have been able to do it on my own."

"I'm glad I was here for you." He looked around. "Man, it's great to get back into the distillery."

"You distill?"

"Yeah. Well, I used to. Wiping down the tanks was my first job. But I learned to work alongside our master distiller, when we had one. I would have gladly stayed down there, too. But when we started mass-producing, we shut down the small distillery and moved to a factory. I hate being in the office. The floor is where I was happiest."

"Why don't you go back to it?"

He shrugged. "I don't have time. Also, the way we manufacture now doesn't really require many hands."

She frowned.

"You disapprove, don't you?"

"It's not for me to say. But I always think about rum as an art. It takes passion, skill, love. I was worried about quick-distilling because I was afraid there would be less of me in my product."

He watched her. "I love hearing you talk about rum. You have a passion that I once felt for it."

"You miss it, don't you?"

"I do."

"Are you any good?"

"At what?"

"Basketball," she said, deadpan. "No, rum. Distilling, dumbass. Are you any good?"

He shrugged. "I haven't blended anything in years."

"Why don't we have a little competition? We'll see who makes the best batch."

"Who makes the best between me, who hasn't mixed a batch in over a decade, and you, who was just recognized as the best distiller in the world?"

"What? Are you afraid?"

"Afraid, no. I'm just realistic. I'm not a man who wastes his time."

"It's not a waste of time if you're having fun. You said yourself, the distillery makes you happy. Okay, I have a better idea than a competition," she said.

"What's that?"

"Why don't we mix a batch together?"

"Why? You're afraid I'll beat you?"

"Shut up," she teased. "I just don't want to embarrass you too badly," she said.

A couple of hours later, they sat at the workbench in the distillery, eating their pizza with their new rum in a fermentation tank.

"Why rum?" he asked. "There aren't many women in the field at your level."

She pointed at him. "That's *exactly* why," she told him. "And it's in our family. Rexford Rum goes back generations, but there aren't many female characters in the family lore."

"Tell me about your family," Tom said.

"It goes back to Joseph Rexford, the Scottish scoundrel who ended up in the Bahamas and made a career of mixing and bootlegging rum from there. He was one of the first notorious distillers and bootleggers—a profession he passed on to his sons, who passed it on to their children and so on. In fact, our family was also responsible for sneaking large amounts of rum into the US during Prohibition in the '20s."

Tom still seemed interested, so Gemma continued on. "Rexford Rum operated on a small scale through the generations. But after Prohibition, our great-grandfather legitimized the business. By the time my mom and dad took it over, there wasn't much left, but they made it a success. Reid, Quin and I took over when our dad retired after our mother died."

"I'm sorry to hear that."

"Thanks." She missed her mother every day, but she didn't normally let herself dwell on the feelings for long. "But anyway, I was a quiet kid. I didn't have a lot of friends, so I started hanging out in this building with my grandfather and dad. They taught me literally everything I know. Since then, I've traveled all over the world. Training with the masters. And here I am," she finished. "So how about you?"

"The Cain story isn't quite as long or storied, but we go back a few generations as well. When I was little, I wanted to be just like my old man. He always seemed so powerful, unrelenting. I thought that was the life I wanted. So, everything I did, I did to get his attention or praise. It's stupid."

"No, it isn't. There's nothing wrong with wanting the approval of your hero."

"For all the good it did me," he scoffed. "No matter what I did, it wasn't enough. And the older I got, the more invested in the company I became, but I started to see that my father wasn't the good, upstanding citizen I thought he was. That culminated with the emergence of Carolina in our lives." He frowned. "I know she isn't totally to blame for it. My father left my mother for her."

"Where's your mother now?"

"St. Barts, or Saint-Tropez, or Monte Carlo," he said with a shrug. "Wherever it's trendy for a professional socialite to go in the winter."

"I'm sorry," Gemma said.

"We were never a tight family, and I'm not even that mad at Dad for marrying Carolina, but it was the recipes that came from you that were the final straw. That's what proved her character to me, and made me question my father's. They were ready to put your recipes into production and manufacture clones of your hard work. I actually paid off the guys on the floor not to. I made them hand over the recipes, and no one else saw them."

"I appreciate that."

"I'll be right back." He stood and went to his coat. When he returned, he was holding a flash drive. "Here," he said, handing it over. "I was going to do this later, but those plans got waylaid and I didn't want to wait any longer."

"What is this?"

"Your recipes. I opened it and saw they were

there, but I've never opened the files. I was guaranteed that there are no more copies."

"Thank you." She clasped her fingers around the drive. "This means a lot."

"I'm sorry about what happened."

Gemma nodded and crossed her arms. "We were both hurt by her and your father."

He went to her and put his hands on her hips. She wasn't sure how he did it, but she felt immediately disarmed. "If only your brothers were as easy to win over," he said with a low chuckle.

She shrugged and wrapped her arms around his neck, drawing him in for a kiss. "I like you," she said when they pulled apart. "You don't need their approval, but I promise they'll come around." Gemma paused, she had an idea, but she wasn't sure if it was a good one, or a terrible one. "You know, Reid and Lila have an engagement party coming up in a couple of weeks. Want to be my date?"

"Do you think that would be smart? I'm not exactly Reid's favorite person."

"Actually, it was Lila's idea. At least if Reid's busy with his other guests, he won't have any time to think about how much he hates you." She smoothed her hands down from his shoulders to his chest. His shirt was a barrier that kept her from feeling his skin under her fingers. She wanted it gone and thought about ripping it from his body.

That's how it was with Tom. The second she got near him, she just couldn't keep her hands off him.

Her body was in full control—her brain just gave out the second he was near.

Tom laughed. "I'll think about it," he told her. He wrapped a finger around one of the belt loops of her jeans and tugged her closer. "But for now, let's clean up and get out of here?"

CHAPTER TWELVE

ON MONDAY MORNING, Gemma arrived at work later than normal. Tom had delayed his flight home and she'd dropped him off at the airport on her way to the distillery. The few extra hours with him had been incredible, and she was grateful for it, but it was getting harder and harder to say goodbye after each visit. She'd never had that feeling before, never had a man who left her feeling like Tom did. There was no doubt in her mind, or her heart. She was falling for him.

Before hitting the distillery floor, she stopped into the break room for a cup of coffee. Quin and Reid had beaten her there.

"Where have you been?" Quin asked.

"I slept in a little," she said. Lying to her brothers was becoming a frequent occurrence, but it wasn't getting any easier. "Sorry I'm late."

"No big deal," Reid said. "It's just not common. Is everything looking okay with the tank that malfunctioned on Friday?"

"Yeah, thankfully, we got here just in time and took care of it."

"We?" Reid asked.

"What?"

"You said, 'We got here just in time,'" he told her.

"I don't think so," she said, knowing that she had come close to being caught. There was no way she was going to tell him about bringing Tom to the distillery. "But it's fine. I've got a technician coming in this afternoon to make sure everything is in order."

She turned to Quin, who was staring at his tablet while he drank his coffee. "How's your morning going?" she asked, desperate to change the topic.

"I have an interesting proposition for you," Quin said, handing over the tablet he had in his hands. "This email came in."

She read it over. "Interesting." It was from *Men's Lifestyle* magazine, saying they wanted to do a photo shoot and interview with her.

"What do you think?" Quin asked.

"It sounds like a lot of fun," she said.

"Are you familiar with the types of shoots they do?" Reid asked, frowning.

She laughed at his stern expression. "Yeah, I've seen a magazine or two. What, are you afraid of your little sister being half-naked in a magazine?"

"I just don't think you need a sexy photo shoot. You're at the top of the industry. I don't think it's necessary."

"I don't think it's *necessary*, either," she said. She looked down at the gray coveralls she was wearing. Dressing up for the awards banquet in Jamaica had been the first time in a long time since she'd let herself be feminine or flirty. And every day she spent with Tom, she felt sexy, desired. He brought that out in her. How would he feel about her doing a shoot like that? She realized that it didn't really matter what he thought. She was her own woman, and could do whatever she wanted, but she would still give him the benefit of a heads-up before going ahead with it.

"What do you think?" Quin asked.

"I think I'm going to do it," she said. There was nothing wrong with a woman celebrating her sexiness. "It'll be a good fit for the hip, young market you like so much," she told Quin. "Can you set it up?"

"Yeah, if that's what you want." Quin didn't sound happy about setting up a sexy photo shoot for his younger sister, but that was his problem.

"I do want it," she told him. "I think it'll be a lot of fun. Something different."

Her insistence must have won him over, because he nodded. "Sure thing."

She stood from the table. "I guess I'd better get to work. Let me know what they say about the shoot."

"Will do," Quin told her, his fingers already tapping away on the screen of his tablet.

She turned to Reid. "What are your plans for today?"

"I've got some calls with distributors in the Northeast."

"The push on Cain," she said without much enthusiasm.

"Yeah, anything wrong with that? What's with the tone?"

She realized that she was about to step in it. She had little of the enthusiasm she'd once had for the plan. "Why do we bother?" she asked. "Why are we in the business destroying others? We make a superior product. Why don't we just focus on doing our best and let the customers decide?"

That got Quin's attention. He looked up from his email. "That isn't what you said before."

"Maybe I'm tired of this rivalry," she admitted with a sigh.

"It's business, Gem," Quin told her. "Taking out our competitors. That's how this works."

She wanted the conversation off Cain Rum, because the more they talked about Tom's family, the guiltier she felt. The meeting reminded her that her illicit weekends with Tom were essentially a betrayal of her family. She needed to get out of the room and away from her brothers, so she headed back to the distillery.

Gemma crossed the floor, her heart still heavy with guilt. Her crew was working diligently on the various steps in rum production. She checked in with a couple. They were a capable group, and it felt like some days she was barely needed in the place. She went into her office to work on some new ideas for their upcoming summer campaign. But not until she finished her coffee.

She sat at her desk, and her thoughts turned to the magazine shoot. It would be fun to come out of her shell a little. She could put a little more sex appeal out there. Gemma couldn't wait to tell Tom.

Her phone vibrated in her pocket. *Speak of the devil.* It was Tom. "Hey, you," she answered.

"Hey. We just landed, and I figured I'd give you a call."

She could hear the pilot in the background. "Are you taxiing?"

"Yeah."

He'd never called from the plane before. Sure, he would text to let her know he was home, but this was new. "How was your flight?"

"Pretty smooth. I'm beat, though. I was hoping to get a little sleep on the way. But it didn't happen."

Gemma thought about how tired she was and how that was a direct consequence of the man she was speaking to. She didn't feel bad for him. "Well, I've got some news," she teased.

"Yeah?"

"I was asked to take part in a feature for *Men's Lifestyle* magazine."

"Oh, really?"

"Yeah. An interview and a sexy photo spread." He didn't say anything for a while, and she wondered what was going through his mind. Did he not want her to do it? "Hello?" she asked. "Are you still there?"

There was a knocking sound on his end of the line. "Sorry, I was getting my bag," Another pause, and she could hear him thank the flight crew. "So," he continued, and she could hear the mischievous smile on his lips. "Tell me more about this sexy photo spread."

There was an email notification on her computer. She opened it, and it was already information for the photo shoot. She had to be in Los Angeles in a few days. "Well, it's in L.A. in three days. Want to meet me there?"

"Tell me where and I'll be there."

CHAPTER THIRTEEN

GEMMA EXITED THE dressing room. She'd already done the interview, during which the friendly female writer had asked her questions about her family and how it felt to be a woman in the industry. But now came the photo shoot, and she was feeling nervous. She clutched the thick robe to her body. She'd been ready to do it, but there was a nervous flutter in her belly. She looked over at the craft services table and saw Tom. He smiled when he saw her, encouraging her. She smiled back and felt better. He had been excited about the shoot and not at all jealous or mad that it would be sexy in nature.

The photographer's assistant helped her up onto the raised platform that held a mattress and several pure white sheets, made up to look like a bed.

"How are you feeling, Gemma?" Clint, the photographer, asked her as he readied his equipment.

"I'm good."

"Fantastic. You can drop the robe whenever you're ready."

Another assistant, this time a woman, held up the

sheet that barred Gemma from view as she removed the robe and handed it off.

She kneeled on the mattress and pulled the bedsheet up to her front, covering her naked body. The luxurious, impossibly high thread-count white cloth slid over her skin like a lover's tender fingers, sending shivers throughout her body. Her eyes traveled over to Tom's—his gaze was fixed on her.

"All right, let's do it," Clint said, raising his camera. "You look great, just give me confidence. Give me sexy."

With the flash in her eyes, she shifted the sheet around her body. Showing some skin, just enough to tease that, save the nude-colored thong, she was naked underneath. Her confidence soared. Shaking her head, she tossed her hair over her shoulder, the perfectly sculpted curls falling down her back. Out of the corner of her eye, she could see Tom, watching her every moment seated in the corner of the cool room. Their eyes connected, and he smiled before she looked away from him and, pursing her lips, looked into the camera lens.

"Beautiful, Gemma," Clint encouraged as he snapped another several dozen photos of her. "Just like that. Give me sexy." She arched her back and posed for a few more. She felt fabulous, and so glamorous. This was different from anything she'd ever done for work. It was so freeing and empowering to finally shed her coveralls and do something outside of her comfort zone. Her eyes caught Tom's as he sat in the corner watching her, his attention trained on her as if she was the only one in the room.

"That's great, Gemma. Beautiful," Clint said, lowering the camera. "I think we've got everything we need."

With the camera lowered, Gemma again became aware of her state of undress. She was no longer the glamorous model under the lens of the camera, but was back to being Gemma. With the shoot over, the spell had broken, and she felt self-conscious. Wrapping herself fully in the sheet, she waited for the photographer's assistant to come back with her robe. Gemma gratefully accepted it and crawled as gracefully as she could from the mattress. She noticed that Tom hadn't moved from where he sat in the corner of the room.

As the crew worked, clearing the set, Gemma sauntered over to Tom. "What'd you think?" she asked, leaning down to kiss him.

He remained seated, but his hands smoothed over her hips. "I think if I stood up, you'd see exactly what I thought," he said with a grin, nodding down to his crotch.

She looked down, and she could see the bulge in his lap, and she braced her hands high on his thighs, dangerously close to his erection. Leaning in again, she put her lips to his ear. "Well, I'm going to go get dressed, and then we can get back to the hotel and you can tell me just how much you enjoyed it."

Back at her hotel room, Gemma had barely shut the door behind them before Tom was on her. He pushed her light jacket from her shoulders, and then his hands were on the buttons down the front of her blouse. His fingers were insistent but also nimble as he slid each delicate button out of its hole. The blouse had cost more money than she was comfortable admitting, but all she wanted was for him to rip the fine silk from her body.

When she was finally free of her shirt, she took the opportunity to push Tom's T-shirt over his head, as well. She kissed him, wrapping her arms around his neck, pulling him closer. It still wasn't close enough. She was desperate for him, wanted to breathe him in, needed every piece of him inside of her. His hands went under her skirt, pushing it up over her hips, and he pulled down her panties. Without releasing him from her kiss, she kicked them away.

Tom lifted her, and she wrapped her legs around his waist. She was still wearing her strappy stilettos, and he grunted when the heels dug into his lower back.

"Sorry," she whispered against his lips.

"Don't be," he groaned back before kissing her again.

He pushed her against the wall next to the bed, and she watched as he reached down for the box of condoms they'd left on the bedside table. Tom had one hand gripping her ass, and she was wedged between the wall and his hard chest as he unsnapped his jeans and rolled on the condom with his free hand.

Gemma dragged her lips along his sharp jawline,

the short hairs rasping her lips, as he took himself in hand and entered her. She gasped, and his groan was loud in her ear as he put his hands on her hips and pulled her so she could feel him deep inside her.

Gemma grasped Tom's shoulders and held on for dear life as he thrust into her. The angle put his shaft in contact with her needy clit, bringing her higher and higher to that peak of pleasure she was seeking.

She threw her head against the wall behind her, and his lips found the sensitive spot at the crook of her neck and shoulder. That one spot that set her ablaze every time he touched her there. Using his teeth, he nibbled, putting just enough pressure to make her cry out, enough to bring her higher as she reached in vain for the precipice, but she wasn't quite there yet.

Tom pulled her away from the wall, turned and, without leaving her, dropped her roughly on the bed. He gripped the backs of her thighs and leveraged his weight, plunging into her again and again until she came with a loud cry as he brought her over the edge, where he joined her with just a couple more quick thrusts.

He collapsed on top of her, but then rolled over so that Gemma rested on his chest. With her ear to his heaving chest as he caught his breath, she could hear his pounding heart. His arms wrapped around her waist, holding her as she kissed her way up and down his throat.

"I love this," she whispered and inhaled a lung-ful of his scent. It was the first time she'd used the *L* word when it came to her relationship with Tom. She felt herself tense, and Tom's arms tightened.

His eyes found hers. "I love this, too."

She smiled and relaxed again. His fingers tickled her low on her spine, and she shivered. He pulled the hotel duvet over them. She could stay there in bed with him all day, but it felt like they spent all their time together in New York or Miami, in bed, hiding out from their families. But in LA, they had no one to hide from. They should take advantage of that.

"Something on your mind?" he asked.

"I don't want to complain about being in bed with you, but hiding what we have is generally all we do."

"I know I don't have any problems with being in bed with you," he told her. "But you're right. Do you want to go out on a date?"

"Yeah. The only time we've actually gone out is that restaurant we went to on your first trip to Miami."

"And you kept insisting that it wasn't a date," He reminded her.

She sighed against his chest. "That feels like so long ago."

He hummed against the side of her head. "It does. It's only four p.m. It might be a little early for dinner. What should we do until then?"

She raised an eyebrow and flexed her hips against his.

Tom laughed. "You might want to give me a few minutes after that last one."

"Fine," she said, rolling off him. "I'll give you

your refractory period if you need it. Why don't we go try that pool downstairs?" In the hotel brochure, she'd seen a beautiful adults-only pool. "Did you pack your swimsuit?"

"I did, and that sounds like a great idea to me."

Gemma rolled out of bed and grabbed her swimsuit and walked into the bathroom. She looked at herself in the mirror. Her cheeks were flushed, and her hair was tousled, and she looked satisfied. Happy. There was no hiding what she and Tom had done, and that was okay with her. She pulled on her one-piece suit. She'd picked it up before flying out to Los Angeles. It was cut high in the thigh and low in the front. She turned to check out the view. The thong bottom showed off the bottom half of her ass cheeks. It was risqué, of course, but she knew Tom would love it.

When she came out of the bathroom, Tom was already dressed in a pair of swim trunks and was pulling on a white T-shirt. When he saw her, his eyes fixed on her body.

"Like my suit?" she asked, knowing full well that he did.

"Yeah, it's incredible." He took a step toward her, his intent obvious in his eyes.

She held up her hand, stopping him. "What about your much-needed refractory period?"

"Seeing you in that bathing suit changed my mind, I guess."

"Well, we've got all night, just keep that in mind. But for now, I want to check out that pool." She pulled on a flowy maxidress. "I need to unwind a little."

When they walked into the adults-only pool area, they saw that it was mostly empty. It was not so much a typical indoor, tile-covered pool, but more an oasis with fountains and waterfalls and low light that mimicked the outside at night.

"This is really nice," she said, plucking a fluffy towel from a shelf.

"It is," he agreed, doing the same.

They found a couple of lounge chairs on a far side of the pool and dropped their clothes. Tom's swim trunks were short and tight, showing off so much of his trim, toned body. He was the sexiest man she'd ever seen, and she regretted her decision to come down to the pool instead of returning to bed.

She pulled her dress over her head and saw that his eyes were fixed on her body. "Come here," he murmured, and she obeyed. He put his arms around her waist and kissed her. "Let's get you wet in that swimsuit."

"Mmm, too late for that."

"You know, maybe the fact that we've spent our entire relationship in bed has nothing to do with hiding out and everything to do with me not being able to keep my hands off of you."

Gemma considered skipping the pool and going back up to their room. "Should we leave?"

"Why don't we stay here for a while. Look around—this place is as romantic as hell. A little delayed gratification won't kill us, will it?"

"It might. I think I get enough of that when you're in New York. But you're right."

He turned his head and winced.

"You okay?" she asked.

He cupped the back of his neck and rubbed. "Yeah, I think I might have pulled something."

"You definitely exerted yourself. Let's get in the hot tub, you relax, and then I'll take you back upstairs."

They both stepped into the water. It was just shy of scorching, perfect for her, but made Tom hiss. "Too hot?" she asked, settling into of the seats.

"No, I'm a manly man. I can handle it."

She laughed, resting against the jets. "God, I know we're only here for a couple of days, but this has been an amazing little getaway," she said, letting the jet soothe the muscles in her neck and shoulders. She could use a massage, too. Even though she'd been having the best sex of her life and felt perfectly relaxed every moment she spent with Tom, her secret relationship with her family's biggest rival was taking not only an emotional, but a physical toll on her. She realized that she was more tense than she'd realized. "Thanks for coming with me."

"Thank you for inviting me."

"Between Jamaica, New York and now, I need to stop taking so many vacations," she said. "I haven't had much of a chance to focus on work."

"What are you working on now?"

"Just some new flavors for our summer line," she said, keeping her eyes closed. "You know, keeping it young, hip, sexy." After she said the words, she knew that she probably shouldn't have said anything. He did work for their competition. And with how tightly she and her brothers held their secrets, she really should have known better.

"Oh really? What sorts of flavors?"

She straightened in her seat. "Why do you ask?"

He shrugged casually. "No reason," he told her. "I'm just making conversation because I'm interested in you."

She didn't respond, but she eyed him warily. Was he just making conversation like he claimed? Or was there something else to his questions? She couldn't be sure. She thought of him in her distillery, studying her equipment, cell phone in hand. Gemma wanted nothing more than to trust him.

Tom's hand rested on her thigh. She looked over at him to see his eyes were closed as he leaned against the back of the hot tub. She loved his touch, had begun to crave his hands on her body, but she couldn't ignore the fingers of doubt that crawled up her spine.

CHAPTER FOURTEEN

WITH GEMMA BUSY in Miami with her family, Tom hadn't made plans to visit that weekend. So, when his father's assistant called—on his father's behalf, of course—to invite him to dinner on Friday night, he begrudgingly accepted. Of course, he missed Gemma, but with her father visiting Miami, they'd decided it was best for her to spend time with her family without the added potential drama of their illicit affair. Funny thing, though—his time with Gemma didn't feel illicit to him.

So he made the trip out of the city to his father's home, and he parked his car in the driveway. He wished he'd hired a car, because he might need copious amounts of alcohol to get through a dinner with his father and Carolina. He wanted nothing more than to be in Florida with Gemma, or holed up with her in his condo. She was gorgeous, sexy, intelligent, funny, sassy. He loved everything about being with her. With his hand on the door handle and with one foot out of his car, he paused. *Love?*

He loved talking to her, being with her, sleeping

with her, eating with her, thinking about her. His chest clenched as he made his way to the front door. He wasn't sure when it had happened, but somewhere along the way, Gemma had gotten under his skin. She was all he could think of. He rang the doorbell, and his father's longtime housekeeper, Louise, opened the door.

"Thomas," she said with a smile, drawing him in for a hug. Louise had worked for his family since he was a child. Hell, as his guardian, she'd been more of a parent than either his mother or father.

"Hello, Louise, how are you?"

"Very good for an old thing," she told him.

"Well, you don't look a day older than when I was a child," he said, winking.

She giggled. "You old charmer, get in here."

Tom walked into the salon—it had never been called the family room. They had never exactly been a family. He nodded in hello to his father, seated in his chair, and made a straight line for the bar in the corner. Fuck it. He'd call a car to pick him up.

He poured himself a glass of dark rum. Tasting it, he realized he'd always thought they'd made a decent rum, but this didn't taste anything like Gemma's. Since they'd started manufacturing and bottling in a plant, the product was missing something. That handmade quality. The art she'd spoken of. *Love.*

He took a seat in the chair opposite the ornate couch where his father and his wife sat. Carolina barely acknowledged his presence, not looking up from her phone as she tapped the screen with the manicured nail of her thumb, holding her wineglass in the other hand. He couldn't imagine cold, calculating Carolina being part of Gemma's family, and no matter what he thought of her brothers, he knew that they were a tight, loving family. That was something that he'd never known growing up in this home.

"How have you been, son?" John asked, with as much concern as he'd show a business acquaintance.

"I've been well."

"You've been scarce around here lately."

"I've been traveling on the weekends."

"In Miami?" he asked. "The flight records show quite a few trips down there on the corporate jet."

"Yes. I have a friend down there." Carolina raised an eyebrow at the mention of her former hometown, but she didn't look up, so he tried to goad her. "You're familiar with the area, Carolina. Any tips for my next visit?"

"The place is a swamp," she answered simply while John frowned. "I wouldn't waste my time with it."

Tom smirked into his glass. He was growing to love the time spent in Miami. Although, he was certain that had more to do with Gemma. *Love.* There he went, using that word again. "I'm surprised you lived there. You seem to be quite at home in New York, what with how cold it gets."

"That's enough, Tom," his father reprimanded him. He wasn't concerned—he knew he'd rattled Carolina.

"When will dinner be ready?" Tom asked.

"Louise says within thirty minutes."

"Great." Tom couldn't sit in the room with them any longer, so he took his glass and headed upstairs. He walked to the end of the hallway and opened the door. As he entered his childhood bedroom, he looked around. It was exactly how it had looked the day he'd left for college. After that day, he'd never spent another night in the house, and that was okay with him. He looked over his sports trophies, academic accolades, old pictures that featured him with friends and Louise. But not his parents.

Tom sat on the bed. He wondered why he wanted to hold on so tightly to the family business. He'd never felt like he was part of this family. It had always been his goal to carry on the legacy, but he wondered if it was even worth it.

His phone vibrated in his pocket. He took it out and saw it was Gemma. "Hello," he said, unable to take the smile from his face.

"Hey, how are you?" she asked. Even though their connection was crystal clear, he could hear the physical distance between them, and a pang of longing hit him square in the chest. He missed her. "What are you up to?"

He leaned back against the headboard of his bed and swung his feet up on the mattress. "I'm at my dad's place for dinner with him and Carolina."

"Ugh. Sounds like a lot of fun," she said sarcastically.

"Oh, yeah. I'd much rather be in bed with you. How are you?"

"I'm good. I just got out of the shower." Tom felt a stirring in his dick, picturing her fresh from the shower.

"Oh, really? What are you wearing?"

She chuckled and he could almost see her roll her eyes at him. "You're so clichéd. I'm wearing a towel," she told him anyway.

"So, you're all clean?" he asked her. "How would you like to get dirty again?"

"What are you proposing?"

"I've got about half an hour before dinner. Drop the towel."

"Done," she said, without hesitation, the echo in her voice told him that she'd put the phone on speaker.

He smiled. He looked at the closed door to his bedroom. "Close your eyes and cup your breasts. Pretend it's my hands on you."

She hummed with pleasure, and he could picture her lying on her bed, her hands on herself, cupping and pinching her nipples. His dick hardened in his pants. Dammit, why hadn't she video called him? "How's that feel?"

"Mmm…good. Not good enough, though."

With one hand, he unsnapped the button on his jeans and lowered his zipper. He pressed his palm against his hard dick. "Why don't you slide one of your hands down your stomach to your pussy?"

"Sounds like a good idea to me…" she said, her voice wistful. He heard her gasp, and his dick shifted.

He reached into his boxers, and found his hand

was a poor substitute for the body of this woman, in another state, now lying in the middle of her bed, touching herself because he asked her to. There was moisture at the tip of him, and he rubbed it around the head, before smoothing his hand down and gripped his shaft hard. "Tell me what you're doing," he commanded, lust and need lowering his voice.

"I'm making little circles around my clit." She moaned again. "I have a finger inside me. But it's nothing compared to you."

"Goddamn it, you're fucking sexy," he ground out, fisting his cock. "Christ!"

"Tom," she gasped. "I'm going to come. I wish you were here with me."

"Me, too, baby," he said. "Me, too." He worked his hand quickly. His stomach tightened, and his heart raced. "Gemma," he whispered, trying to keep his voice down for anyone who might be in the hallway outside the room. Gemma cried out into the phone wedged against his ear, and he came. As his breathing calmed, he threw his head against the headboard. "Fuck, Gemma," he said. "How am I going to go eat dinner with my family now? Talk me out of getting on a plane to Miami right this minute."

She laughed. "I won't tell you any such thing. I want you here right now."

He stood and carefully walked to the attached bathroom. Thankfully he found some tissues and cleaned up as he talked to her. "You've got your family tonight, love."

"Come anyway. If you get down here tomorrow

morning, we'll still have two days together. I'll figure something out with my family. Don't worry." Jumping on a plane for yet another weekend in Miami was completely unnecessary. It wouldn't kill him to stay away for one weekend, would it? "As a little extra incentive, you get down here tonight and we can have a little replay of what we just did. Except instead of your hand on your cock, it'll be my mouth."

He groaned and tossed the tissues in the wastebasket. "You're killing me."

"Good. Text later with your decision."

He didn't need to even think about it. He just had to get through dinner with his father and make a quick exit. But he wasn't sure he'd be able to rouse their pilot or get a flight at such a late hour. "I'll be there in the morning."

CHAPTER FIFTEEN

WHEN GEMMA HEARD the knock on her door the next morning, she thought it might be Tom. He hadn't been able to get a flight the night before, but he was scheduled to arrive very soon. She all but ran to the door, unable to contain her smile, but it dropped when she opened the large wooden door to see Quin. And he didn't look happy.

"Hey, what's up?" she asked, a moment of panic seizing her. "Is Dad okay?"

"Everyone is fine," he assured her. "But I saw a teaser on *Men's Lifestyle* website for your interview and photo shoot."

She could tell that he wasn't happy. He handed over his phone, and she saw the website. They'd chosen a very sexy picture. The one where she was side-on, holding a sheet over her front, but the curve of her ass was exposed. She looked sexy, powerful, in charge, and she smiled.

"You like it?" Quin asked. "It's a little risqué. I don't personally see what your ass has to do with rum."

"You wanted hip and sexy, didn't you?" she reminded him.

"I certainly didn't want to think about my sister as being sexy," he said.

"Your not being able to handle my sexiness isn't my problem," she said, pointing her forefinger at him. She frowned at her brother. "Quin, you arranged that photo shoot and feature. You knew what kinds of things they do. I think it looks great," she said, reaching for his phone. "Let me see the other pictures."

He opened the gallery and scrolled through the photos. Gemma was thrilled with how they'd turned out, and she couldn't wait to see the spread and feature in the upcoming magazine. If the public liked them half as much as Tom would… Then she remembered. Tom was going to be here any minute. She had to get Quin out of her house before he showed up. She moved around him and put a hand on his arm, subtly ushering him to the door. "Well, thanks for stopping by."

He saw through her, though. "Are you trying to kick me out?"

"Of course not," she said. "I just have a lot to do today before dinner at Reid's."

He narrowed his eyes at her and stood in place for a bit, just watching her. "All right. See you tonight, I guess."

She smiled and opened the door for him. "See you tonight."

She watched Quin get into his car and then drive

off her property, and she exhaled. Obviously, Quin knew something was up, but she couldn't focus on that now. She went back to the kitchen and finished prepping the breakfast she would share with Tom.

Only a couple of minutes passed before her doorbell rang again.

This time, she knew it was Tom, and she quickly walked back to the door. She pulled it open and barely had enough time to catch her breath before he drew her in for a kiss. When he pulled away, he was smiling. "Sorry I'm late," he said.

"Don't worry about it," she told him. "Whether you know it or not, you're actually right on time."

When Gemma pulled her Jeep into Reid's driveway next to Quin's Range Rover, she turned off the engine and just sat in the quiet for a moment. She regretted leaving Tom at her place so she could have dinner with her family. She was glad to have had the afternoon with him, and in a moment of desperation, she'd asked him to join her. But he was right. A celebratory dinner with her family at Reid's home probably wasn't the best place to reveal her relationship with her family's enemy. She'd promised she wouldn't stay long, but he'd told her not to worry about him as he settled in front of the basketball game on TV.

Tonight was all about family. Her father didn't visit Miami enough, and she missed them all being together. Her brothers and their partners and her father were waiting inside, celebrating Reid and Lila's

engagement as a family before their formal engagement party the next weekend. She exhaled. She was
excited to see her family, of course, but that was
hard, since she'd left Tom alone at her house.

He'd been right to stay, of course, but it didn't
make driving away any easier. And that was what
was starting to scare her. She'd never felt so strongly
for a man before. She had always been a single, casual, fun-loving woman who didn't need to be tied
down to a man. But she was already tied to Tom. It
had happened when she wasn't even paying attention.

She saw movement in the living room window
that faced the driveway. It was Quin, waving for her
to come in. She waved back and grabbed the bottle
of rum she'd brought for her father and headed for
the house.

When she opened the door, the music and the
noise of conversation and raucous laughter greeted
her. Her brothers were talking, and her father was
busy charming, or being charmed by the newest
members of the clan—Lila and Celia.

Reid and Quin saw her first. They hugged her in
greeting, and then she moved on to say hello to her
father. When he turned and saw her, he stood from
his stool and came over to her. He wrapped his arms
around her and lifted her off the floor. "My little
Gemstone," he said, using the name he'd called her
by since she was a child.

She hugged him back. "Hi, Dad. It's good to see
you."

He lowered her again. "How are you?"

"I'm good." She lofted the bottle. "I brough this."

He kissed her on the cheek and took the unlabeled bottle. "Gemstone, if you weren't already my favorite, this would have put you at the top."

"Hey!" Reid called as he and Quin joined them at the kitchen island. "What's that supposed to mean?"

"Reid, when you're number one, you're number one," Gemma teased.

"Don't worry, baby, you're my favorite," Lila assured him, putting her arm around his waist.

Quin handed Gemma a glass of white wine and took his place next to Celia. She couldn't believe that her brothers had both found amazing women. She was overjoyed for them. Seeing them all together, as a family, made her smile.

Her father cleared his throat. "I would like to raise a toast," he started. "To my children. I'm so proud to be here with you and my future daughters-in-law. Lila and Celia, I see how happy you've made my sons. I just know my dear Liza would be thrilled to be with us all here."

The room fell silent, and Gemma knew that just as she was, her brothers and father were all remembering her departed mother. "She's definitely missed," she whispered. They all nodded in agreement. She looked around the room. Her brothers had found love. She was happy for them, but it was something she didn't have. The closest she had was Tom, and she wanted him there with her, by her side.

"To Lila and Reid." Her father got her attention,

raising his glass. "Congratulations on your engagement. May you find happiness together like I once had." Everyone smiled. Her parents had had an incredible relationship, and it was one she could only hope to model in her own life.

"To Lila and Reid," they all toasted.

"Gemstone, look at your brothers. Did you ever think you'd see the day?"

"Honestly, no."

"And I know you'll find that kind of love someday."

Gemma drank her wine and nodded. "Yeah, you never know. Who can say, really? Stranger things have happened, right?" She tried to laugh it off. When she turned away from her father, she saw that both Lila and Celia had their eyes on her. They knew her secret, even if her brothers and father did not.

After dinner, the night carried on. The drinks flowed and the voices and laughter got louder, and Gemma took a moment to slip outside. She took a seat at the porch swing and looked out onto Reid's backyard. There was a slight winter chill in the air, and she tugged her sweater tighter around her. Of course, Tom would laugh at her for being cold. She sighed, missing him. Things between them had sure developed over such a short time. But she was still so conflicted.

She heard the back door open and looked over her shoulder and saw it was her father. He joined her on the swing, putting his arm around her. She snuggled into his side.

"What's wrong, Gemstone?" he asked her.

She thought about lying, but she couldn't do that. She sighed. "That toast you gave. I think I have fallen in love."

Her father looked down at her, surprised. He smiled. "Is that right? Well, why isn't he here? Are you embarrassed of your family?"

"Reid and Quin? Yeah, sometimes."

"Who is this man? Why didn't you bring him?"

"I didn't bring him because of who he is."

"You know, with our family, everyone is invited. Who could he be? Is he an ex-con?" he asked, nudging her, teasing. "Because if he is, depending on the crime, we could probably overlook it."

She smiled. "He isn't a convict, Dad. But he might still be one of the few people not welcome in this family. He might be something worse." She braced herself. "He's a Cain."

"Cain," he said. "As in...?"

She nodded. "One and the same. It's John's son, Tom."

She waited for his angry outburst. But instead he nodded sagely. "I see," he said, his voice soft. "I take it you haven't told your brothers."

"Not a chance," she said, shaking her head. "They would be so angry. They wouldn't understand."

"Most likely," her father agreed. "And you love him?"

She thought about that. "I think I do. He's not what you think—he's a good man."

"Then that's good enough for me. If you love him, then you should be with him. I loved your mother dearly."

"I know you did."

"If I could have one more day with her, there's no way I would spend a second away from her. Life is too short to be unhappy." He pulled her closer into his side. "Did I ever tell you that your grandfather—your mother's father—didn't want me to marry Liza?"

"No. You never did."

"You know our family history. We come from pirates and rumrunners and bootleggers. Your mother's family were above my station. They saw me as a ne'er-do-well. They didn't drink. Thought the rum was immoral. When I met your mother, I knew what I was up against. Her father literally threw me out of his house, threatened to run me out of town and forbade me from seeing his daughter. You know what I did then?"

"What?"

"I still went after her. We loved each other. And I didn't give a goddamn what anyone thought of it. We had twenty-five good years before she was taken." He trailed off. "But if you love this man, and you think you have a future, fight for it."

"But Reid—"

"Will most likely be angry. He was hurt when Carolina left him and married Cain. But you have to be honest with him and give him a chance to get used to the idea." He stopped. "If you two get married, Carolina will be your mother-in-law. Are you ready for that?"

Gemma screwed up her face and laughed. "Let's not jump the gun on that. There aren't exactly any wedding bells for me in the near future. Lila said I should invite him to the party next weekend."

"That's an excellent idea."

"A public place will stop Reid from resorting to violence," she reasoned.

"I think Lila's mellowed your brother significantly. Maybe now he has love of his own, he'll understand."

"Maybe you're right, but I don't want to count on it." She shivered a little—the night air was cold.

"You're chilly. Let's go in."

"Okay. You're really smart, you know." She stepped up on her toes and kissed her father on the cheek.

"No, I'm just old," he told her. "When you're my age, you'll be this smart, too."

She followed her father back into the house. After telling him the truth about her relationship with Tom, she felt lighter than she had in weeks. She looked at Reid and Quin, wondering if they would respond just as well.

CHAPTER SIXTEEN

FROM HER PLACE in the middle of Tom's king-size bed, Gemma watched as he got ready for work. It was Wednesday, and she'd taken a few of her vacation days to go to New York. The time in between visits was getting harder and harder to bear, and they found themselves making them shorter each week. It was ridiculous how many short-haul flights they were taking, and despite how many frequent flier miles she was earning, the carbon offsets were costing her a small fortune. But it was worth it.

Tom came out of his closet with his shirt open and draped over his broad shoulders. His thick, dark hair was still wet from his shower, and she wanted him to come back to bed. His eyes skimmed over her, at the thin, white sheet draped over her middle, and her leg extended and bent outside of the sheet. He stopped as he buttoned a cuff. "Goddamn, I wish I'd taken the day off."

"It's not too late for that," she told him.

"I've got a few meetings today. But I will be home as soon as I can."

"I'll be here, waiting."

He put his hand on her knee and smoothed it up her thigh, and it disappeared under the blanket. Gemma giggled as his fingers tickled the inside of her thigh, and he went higher. He swept his fingers over her and delved deeper. His thumb circled her clit, and she gasped.

"Don't start anything you don't have time to finish," she warned him but widened her legs for him to touch her further.

He groaned and ripped the sheet from between them, exposing her naked body. He kept his thumb on her clit as she moaned in pleasure. He stood and pulled her thighs so that she was at the edge of the mattress. He unbuckled his pants and pushed them down.

"Aren't you already going to be late?" she asked him.

"I don't give a fuck," he muttered. He bent over and kissed her. It was hard, rough, wild.

She wrapped her legs around his hips and held him in place. His cock nudged against her, and she sighed, moving her hips, so that she slid against him.

He tried to back away. "I need a condom," he told her, his breath against her lips.

She reached down and gripped his dick, lining him up with her opening. "Don't worry about it."

"What?"

"You heard me. Just do it. Just fuck me. Now!"

"Anything you say," he obliged, and with a flex of his hips, he was buried deeply inside of her.

Without the barrier of latex, Gemma felt every inch of him. With fast, furious thrusts, he filled her, pulled out and then drove into her again. She cried out and clung to him, driving her nails into his back. Only he knew how to make her feel so good. Pleasure coiled inside her and tightened with every thrust. Then without warning, the spring within her snapped, and she came with a scream. She felt herself spasm around his cock, and he stilled and collapsed over her, burying his face in her neck.

He whispered something that sounded a lot like "I love you," but she wasn't sure. She stilled. "What was that?"

He straightened. "Nothing," he said, not looking at her. He pulled up his pants and looked at the bed-side clock. "I'm officially late for work."

"You can't blame me for that," she said with a smile as he buttoned his shirt.

He paused. "Are we okay?"

"About what?" Gemma asked, standing. She picked up the T-shirt he'd worn last night and pulled it over her head.

"The condom?" he asked. "Or the lack of, I must say."

"It's fine. We've both been tested, and I'm strict with my birth control. So I figured, why not?"

He kissed her tenderly. "Thanks for a great morning. But I've really got to get to work." His look turned dark. "But when I get home, I want you right here, in this bed."

"It's a deal."

* * *

"We can all agree that we need to make some drastic changes in the way we do things," Tom said, addressing the men in the boardroom. "There are changes I want to make that I think are a long time coming."

The door opened, and his father walked into the boardroom. "What are you doing here?"

John shrugged casually. "It's been a while since I sat in on one of these marketing meetings. I'm just keeping an eye on my interests."

"That's why I'm here," Tom said. "My interests and the interests of everyone in this room are the business's interests. I'm sure you have other things you could be doing."

"Never mind that," John said, waving his hand as he took a seat at the head of the table. "But you mentioned some changes. What are they, exactly?"

"Our marketing research shows that customers are looking for a more specialized product. I want to change our focus from mass-produced to hand-crafted." He heard his father scoff, but he kept going. "There is a big push now for small batches, high-end products. Look at the things Rexford Rum in Miami is doing. They're on top of the game, and they've done that through high-quality products. Not large vats of mediocre rum."

The men in the room grumbled. "That would lead to a large scaling down in production. What about the lost jobs?" one asked.

"We would retrain them in actual distilling processes," Tom said. Every time he thought about it, he became excited.

"We're not going to change how we do things to sell this hipster, millennial rum you're so fond of. We'll devote all of our time and money to the change and what happens when the next trend comes along?"

Tom closed his eyes, tying to hold onto his patience. "This will take time and money, but I've done the research. We can do it, and we'll be successful. I know it."

"But what about the money for rebranding, retraining, retrofitting our machines?" John asked. "Tom, I see your vision, but it isn't practical. That's your problem."

"We're losing money and our brand is stagnating every day we do nothing. This isn't going to be easy, but I will set us up for future success. Customers are looking for handcrafted, artisanal rum, and we can be the ones to fill that demand."

Tom looked around the room. He could tell most of the team clearly sided with his father. They'd barely listened to him. The stubbornness of the people in the boardroom was what would bury Cain Rum, and there was nothing he could do about it.

If he was going to succeed in the rum industry, he might have to do it on his own. As the meeting continued around him, Tom was lost in his own thoughts. Maybe it was time for him to strike out on his own.

When Tom came home that evening, he was tired and frustrated. It seemed that every day at Cain Rum became slightly more burdensome than the one before. His father's stubbornness and refusal to acknowledge that times have changed would ruin the company. They needed a plan. And it needed to be enacted soon, before it was too late. Rexford Rum was thriving because they adapted to the environment and targeted new markets. Why his father wouldn't, he had no idea.

At one particularly dark moment that day, he'd considered packing up his office and just leaving. But he hadn't. Cain Rum was all he knew. He couldn't just walk away from the family business, could he? If he wasn't part of it, then what did he have?

The answer to that was standing in his kitchen when he opened his door. But he was willing to forgive Gemma, who'd broken her promise to be in his bed, when he saw her hovering over a steaming pot wearing nothing but an apron, a black thong and a pair of sky-high red stilettos.

She looked over her shoulder at him. "Honey," she said, her voice dripping sex. "You're home."

He loosened his tie and dropped his bag by the door, not hesitating to make a beeline for her. He stood behind her, his hands pushing under the apron to cup her breasts and smooth over the small curve of her stomach. He loved every part of her body and would gladly spend the rest of his life touching her. "You'd better go get ready for dinner."

With his hands still on her, he leaned over her shoulder and looked into the lightly colored sauce simmering in a small saucepan. "What are we having?"

"Steak with béarnaise sauce and asparagus spears."

"And dessert?"

She looked at him, her lips pursed, and raised her eyebrow. "Me."

He hummed his approval. "My favorite. Any way we can move that dessert course to now?"

"Only if you want this sauce to burn," she warned him. "But why don't you go freshen up? We've got the next few days together before we even head to Miami."

She was right. They did have a longer time together this week. *Five days*, he thought with remorse. It wasn't nearly long enough. What he wouldn't give to have Gemma in his home, in his kitchen, in his bed every day.

An hour later, they were seated in front of their empty plates. Gemma had unfortunately changed out of her apron, but he had no arguments against the skintight black minidress she'd put on. She'd pulled out all the stops for a romantic stay-at-home dinner, and it couldn't have come on a better day.

"Are you okay over there?" she asked. "You've been quiet."

He blew out a breath and topped up his wineglass. "I had a tough day."

"Want to talk about it?"

He shook his head and drank his wine. "It's just my father. I'm—" He stopped talking, not sure if he should discuss the distillery with Gemma.

"When we're together," she started, "I'm not just

Gemma Rexford. I'm your girlfriend. I want you to know that you can talk to me if something is bothering you. And I hope I can talk to you."

"Of course you can."

"So if you want to talk, I'm here."

"Thank you." Even though he'd told his friends of his frustrations with his father and the company, he hadn't told them the fear he felt of losing everything. So he told Gemma—his insecurities, his problems with his father, his fear that his family and the business would sink before he had a chance to right the ship.

"Some days," he said, taking a deep breath, "I think about quitting the business altogether."

Her eyes widened in surprise. "Really?"

He nodded. "Yeah, I realized today that my father is never going to give up control if he doesn't trust me. And I can't stay under his thumb forever. There are things I want to do with Cain, but as long as he's in charge, he won't let me. Sometimes I think it'd be easier if I branched out on my own."

"On your own?"

"Yeah, I finally realized that night we were in your distillery. I had so much damn fun with you, making rum, that I realized that's what I want, it's what Cain is missing—a handcrafted product. We made the biggest mistake when we automated the process. A small place is what I want. I'm like a stranger every time I walk onto my own production floor. It's all very mechanical, with computers and robots running the show. I want to be hands-on." He took a deep breath. "If my father doesn't step down soon, I'm thinking about walking away."

"That's a big move."

"Yeah. I know."

"And I assume you haven't told your father."

"You're the only person I've told."

She moved from her seat across from him and sat in his lap. "Thanks for telling me." She paused, pushing her fingers through his hair. "It's a good thing I'm your girlfriend, and not your rival, right now, because I have something I want to say to you."

"And what's that?"

"I'm really proud of you." Tom shifted uncomfortably, having never heard those words before. "And I want you to know that if you decide to open your own distillery, I'll help you in any way I can."

He smiled. God, he couldn't fight it anymore. He wasn't just falling for Gemma; he was in deep. He loved her. "Good thing you're my girlfriend, because master distiller Gemma Rexford would never offer her help to a Cain."

"That's true. Good thing we all have layers, though, right?"

Tom smiled and smoothed his hand over her ass. "As long as you think so, why don't we get some of these layers off you?"

Outside Tom's building, Tom was helping Gemma into the car that he'd called to take her to the airport. She had to return home to prepare for the engagement party that she was hosting for Reid and Lila. Tom would be joining her the next day.

He normally drove her, but that afternoon, they'd sipped a few too many glasses of wine with dinner. She'd used the wine to dull her sadness at leaving Tom again. It didn't work. Even though she knew she would be seeing him the next evening, saying goodbye to him filled her with such a sorrow. It was so painful leaving him, but she knew that just like every other time, their next meeting would be even hotter and more full of love than the last.

"I've really come to hate this," she said with a slight shiver. It had started snowing again, and as she looked around, she realized that she was caught in one of those movie-magical New York–at–Christmas moments. The city hustled and bustled around them, and a light layer of snow covered the sidewalk.

"Me, too." She shivered and Tom reached out and pulled her coat closer to her neck. "You need to get a real winter coat," he teased.

"I live in Miami. This *is* a winter coat," she said of the thin coat she wore every time. And she was cold every time.

"Call me when you land, okay?"

"I always do."

Tom wrapped his arms around her and drew her in for a kiss. She pressed against his chest, taking his warmth. When they parted, neither of them made a move to separate. The entire city hummed around them, but with the snow, the lights, it was too much to resist.

"Tom," she said, but then hesitated.

"What is it?"

She grabbed a deep breath and took a chance. "I think I'm falling in love with you."

He didn't say anything at first, and she felt embarrassed and wanted to take it back. "You know, I'm sorry I said that. I just got caught up in a moment, I think."

He took her chin in his hand. "I'm in love with you, too."

He kissed her again. And while Gemma should have been focused on the moment between them, all she could think about was where they could go from there. What was their future?

She backed away. "Come with me," she said, taking yet another huge chance. But she realized that was a mistake when he shook his head.

"What? I can't. I have work tomorrow."

"It's fine. Quit your job and move to Miami," she told him with a laugh. "Don't worry. I'm kidding."

He laughed. "Good. Because you know I can't do that."

"But I thought you wanted to leave the distillery."

"That was just frustration talking. I can't just walk away."

Gemma realized then that any future she'd thought she had with Tom was shakier than she thought. He wasn't going to walk away from his family business. He wasn't going to run off to Miami with her. "Okay," she said, the blissful feeling of their moment fading. "Well, I'd better get to the airport."

His eyes narrowed as he pulled open the back door for her and she got into the car. "Okay. Have a safe flight."

"I'll call you when I land," she promised.

"Thanks." He paused. "I love you."

"I love you, too."

When the car pulled away from the curb, Gemma turned her head to see him. Tom was still standing on the sidewalk, his eyes on the car, but the frown on his lips left her wondering. What type of future did she have with Tom? He'd talked about leaving Cain Rum and she didn't want to admit that it had given her a small beat of hope, but as he said, he couldn't just walk away.

She'd told the truth. She did love Tom, and she was glad she'd said it, but if he wasn't her future, then what was the point in keeping it going? She would see him again tomorrow, and then she was going to tell her brothers that she and Tom were together. She hoped that she was making the right decision. How would they react? Was she risking everything—her family, her business—for a man who wouldn't do the same for her?

CHAPTER SEVENTEEN

"Do you really think this is a good idea?" Tom asked Gemma as she finished putting out the rest of the food for the party. "Your brother's engagement party is tonight. I don't know if this is a great time to drop this on him."

Gemma turned to him. The minute he'd arrived, she'd forgotten about all her doubts from the day before. She was in love with Tom, and even though she wasn't sure how he felt about it, she saw her future whenever she looked at him. "I feel like there's no better place to tell them about us. If I love you, they'll learn to love you."

"You have more faith in that than I do."

"Well, I'm hosting the party, and you're my guest. If he doesn't like it, it's too bad." She saw Reid's car pull into the driveway. Reid and Lila exited, and Quin's car pulled up next. Quin, Celia and her dad, who'd come back to town for the party, got out. "There they are. Go wait in the living room until I'm ready."

"So I can jump out and yell, 'Surprise'?"

She rolled her eyes. "Come on, let's do it."

She went to the door and greeted her family. She'd asked them to come early, before the rest of the guests, so she and Tom could tell them about their relationship. She hugged and kissed each of them, inviting them in.

"Thanks for coming a little earlier, guys," she told them. "I've got something to tell you."

"What's going on?" Reid asked her. He looked concerned.

Her heart pounded. Lila, Celia and her father already knew her secret, but she was terrified of telling her brothers. She didn't want to disappoint them. "Well, I wanted to gather you all here first to tell you that I've been seeing somebody."

"Really?" Quin asked.

"Is he here? Where is he?" Reid asked, looking around.

While it might have seemed like she was talking to the group, her words were directed at Reid and Quin. Gemma's eyes slid over to Tom's as he waited against the wall, out of view of her family. He nodded, encouraging her, letting her know that he was with her. She carried on. "Yeah, and I want you to know it's going really well. I'm so in love with this guy. And it's someone you know."

Reid smiled. "Really? That's awesome, Gem. Who is it?"

She took a deep breath before waving for Tom to join her. "You remember Tom, right?"

The smiles dropped from both Reid and Quin's

faces. Reid took a step closer. "What? What the fuck is he doing here?" he asked, pointing at Tom.

Lila stepped in front of Reid. "I invited him," she told him. "I thought this would be a good time for you to find out."

He turned to Lila. "You knew about this? And you didn't tell me?"

"Don't get mad at her, Reid," Gemma interjected. "Talk to me."

"Fine. How could you do this, Gemma?"

"And with him?" Quin asked her. "How could you be so stupid?"

"Hey!" Tom said, stepping in front of her, taking on Quin. "Don't call her that."

The room erupted into loud voices, each trying to be heard over the next, and Gemma couldn't stand seeing all her favorite people fighting. "Stop!" she shouted. "Everyone shut up!"

The room fell silent. How she thought this could ever be a good idea, she didn't know. "I'm sorry," she said, realizing that she'd probably ruined what should be a happy family event.

"You know what," Tom said, stepping forward. "I'm going to leave."

"Good idea," Reid said, which earned him Gemma's glare.

As he turned toward the door, she grabbed his arm. "Tom, wait. I don't want you to go."

"Let him go, Gem," Quin called after her.

"I'll go to a hotel. Just call me later, okay?"

"No, wait. I'm coming with you."

"No, you aren't," he told her. "Stay here with your family. Enjoy the party."

"I don't really want to be here right now."

"Gemma, you don't mean that," Quin told her.

"I'm not exactly feeling very welcome in my own home right now."

She walked to the door with Tom. She closed the door so she wouldn't have to see her family, who she knew were watching them through the glass walls of the house.

"You're not coming with me," Tom told her. "This is a night for your family. I knew it wasn't a good idea for me to come tonight. I'm sorry."

"You didn't do anything wrong," she told him. "It's Reid and Quin. They just need to get to know you. Like I do."

He shook his head. "I think they already know everything they want to." He cupped her cheek and kissed her. "Call me tonight, okay? We can get together later." Gemma held back the tears as she watched Tom get in his rental car. When he was gone, she walked back into the house.

"Gem—" Reid said, his voice was soft. He'd no doubt already been scolded by either their father or Lila and Celia.

"No," she said, cutting him off. "I don't want to hear it. Not tonight. I was hoping this would work out better. I thought that my word that I loved him would be enough for you, but clearly it wasn't. Can we just forget about it now? Your guests will be here soon."

She noticed Celia elbow Quin in the ribs, prompting him. "Why don't we all have brunch tomorrow?" he asked her. "Invite Tom. We can hash this out tomorrow."

There was nothing to *hash out*. She was in love with Tom, and her brothers would have to deal with it. She didn't want to talk to either of them about it, especially if they couldn't refrain from yelling. But a public place might better to keep their emotions under control. "Yeah, sure. Let's do it."

CHAPTER EIGHTEEN

THE LAST PLACE Tom wanted to be was at a restaurant, waiting for Reid and Quin Rexford to arrive for brunch. The only reason he was there sat next to him and put her hand on his thigh.

"Thank you for doing this," she said to him.

"I'm only here for you," he said, closing his hand over hers. "I know this is important to you, and you're important to me."

She smiled. "I know they can be a lot to take. They're pretty overbearing."

"I know, and I don't mind. If I had a sister, I would probably act in a similar way. They're just trying to protect you. But when they say anything nasty to you, that's when I have a problem."

"Don't worry about me. I can handle them."

"I know you can. And if it gets too intense, we'll just order booze."

She smiled. "Good idea."

A shadow slid over the table, and she looked up and saw that Quin and Reid were taking seats across from them.

"Good morning," Gemma said.

Tom could have jumped across the table when Quin grunted back a response. "You don't have to like me, but you'll show Gemma the respect she deserves," he warned.

"Good morning, Gem," Quin said solely to Gemma.

"Well, this is off to a great start," Gemma muttered. The server came and poured them each a coffee. "Where are Dad and the girls?"

"They all decided that this is something we have to work out without them."

"So, what are we doing here, Gem?" Reid asked.

"This brunch was your idea," she said. "Both of you. I want you both to just sit down with me and Tom. Let's work out whatever problems you have with this."

"This will always be a problem with me," Reid told him.

"With me, too," Quin added. "Of all the guys out there, you pick him."

Tom rolled his eyes as they discussed him like he wasn't even at the table. And he was completely over it. "Look, guys, I understand you're pissed. And given the history between our families and what happened in the past, I don't blame you. Saying that, I do want to apologize for coming to the party. I knew it wasn't smart. I shouldn't have done it. But I won't apologize for being with Gemma." He felt Gemma's grip on his thigh tighten, but he didn't pull his eyes away from Reid's.

"I see," Reid said.

Tom continued. "And before you say anything else to berate Gemma for our relationship, I would advise you not to. And I think if you haven't already, you owe her an apology."

Gemma waved down a server and ordered a round of drinks for the table. It probably wasn't going as well as she'd wanted. But Tom felt good. He'd said his piece, and there was nothing else to say.

"I'm sorry, Gem," Quin muttered.

Reid cleared his throat. "Me, too."

"Thank you," she said.

Tom leaned back in his seat, as did Reid and Quin. It was a while before anyone spoke. The server returned with a pitcher of sangria and four glasses. "Are you ready to order?" she asked, pouring them each a glass.

"Not quite yet," Gemma told her.

"Let's get this out of the way," Reid said, leaning forward, resting his elbows on the table. "I don't like you. I don't like your family. I don't like that you're with my sister."

"Reid," Gemma whispered, her anger evident.

"I completely understand where you're coming from. Carolina screwed you over. I can't excuse what she did, but I don't feel the need to apologize for that woman. But here's the thing. You don't have to like me. I don't particularly like you, either. But I like Gemma. In fact, I love her."

Reid said nothing to him but turned his attention to Gemma. "We can't tell you what to do. Gemma, you're a grown woman, capable of making your own decisions."

"Thanks for your permission," she said with ice in her voice.

"This isn't about permission. You don't need it," Reid told her. "How long has it been going on?"

"Since Jamaica," Gemma told them.

"Since Jamaica?" Quin echoed.

"You heard me."

Tom laid his hand over hers. She didn't need him there. She was more than capable of handling her brothers.

"How could you keep something like this secret? I just wish you would have told us sooner," Reid said. "Instead of blindsiding us with this."

"In what situation would telling you have been easy? I know that any way I did it you would have freaked out." She paused. "Okay, maybe it was a little dramatic, doing it before the party. But I wanted you to meet him. The right way. Without any of the business involved."

"That's another matter altogether," Reid said, turning to Tom. "What's your game here with Gemma? I know your company is on its way down. Are you here to mess with your competitor? Maybe steal more of our recipes—"

Tom had had enough. "You wait a goddamn minute," he said, probably a little too loud for Sunday brunch, earning them looks from surrounding diners. He lowered his voice. As far as he was concerned, Reid could say what he wanted about him, but when it came to his relationship with Gemma, he wouldn't hear it. "There's no fucking game, and I'm disgusted that you think there might be. I love Gemma," he repeated. "And we're going to be together whether you like it or not."

"Fine. If you say so. I don't like it, but I guess it isn't up to me."

"No, it's not," Tom said. He could feel Gemma's hand on his thigh. He felt comfort from the small gesture. The simple fact was that the more time he spent with her, the closer they became. He had fallen in love with Gemma, and there was nothing her brothers could do to stop it.

CHAPTER NINETEEN

BY THE NEXT MORNING, Gemma wasn't feeling any better about the uneasy truce Tom had formed with her brothers. She hadn't heard from Reid or Quin since they'd parted ways after brunch the day before. That was strange, because they were normally in constant contact.

She sighed as she walked into Reid's office for their weekly Monday morning meeting. Quin and Reid were already there. The air was ripe with tension. And she knew it was because of her. "What's on the agenda today?" she asked, knowing full well what they were going to discuss.

"Are we okay?" Reid asked.

"Yeah," Gemma said.

"Where's Tom?"

"He went back to New York this morning."

Quin scoffed. "Reid, I know you aren't really interested in what Tom is doing. Neither am I. So, let's just focus on business, without any of the personal stuff getting in the way."

"Up until now, the distillery was personal,"

Gemma pointed out. "But I'd like to carry on like we always have, and just get down to work."

"Even though you're sleeping with our biggest competitor."

"I'm completely over this conversation. Can we just move on?"

"Yeah, I'd like that, but we still need to talk about our goal of moving into the Northeast, and directly competing with Cain Rum." He looked at her with a frown. "Still think you can keep the personal separate form the business?"

Gemma knew it was coming. It was a plan that they had discussed before she and Tom had become more serious than a casual weekend hookup. Although they'd been racking up the frequent flier miles to see each other, they had never actually been casual. "Absolutely."

"How well do you think you'll be able to separate yourself when it comes to taking down your boyfriend's family business?"

"I'm going to keep making rum. What you guys want to do with it is up to you."

"We used to make these decisions together," Quin reminded her.

"I want to do what's best for the distillery," she told them.

"Then can I ask you to dump Tom Cain?" Reid asked with a smirk.

She said nothing. She knew that this wasn't going to go away. For the rest of her relationship with Tom, however long that was, she would have to keep him separate from the other parts of life—her work, her family.

Quin closed his laptop. "Gemma, can I ask you a question?"

"You're probably going to ask it anyway."

"Probably. You said that you're in love with Cain?"

Gemma didn't hesitate. She wasn't eager to admit to her brothers just how deeply she was in. "I am." She shook her head. "I didn't mean for it to happen. We were just hooking up. I thought it would be like every other guy. But he wasn't. I didn't mean to catch feelings."

Quin nodded, as if he understood where she was coming from. "Happens to the best of us, and we don't even see it coming." He nodded at Reid, who was stoic.

"You've got that right," she agreed. "At first it was just about letting off a little steam. It had been such a heavy year for me, and I wanted to forget about all of the pressure for a few minutes."

"A few minutes, huh?" Reid said with a derisive chuckle, rolling his eyes. Of course, he would take the opportunity to take a dig at Tom.

Gemma whipped her pen at him. "I would have said a couple of hours, but I didn't think you wanted to hear that. Then when he showed up here one weekend, I thought I could shake him. But I couldn't. It just kept happening." She turned to Reid. "You probably think it's stupid."

He sighed. "No, Gem, it's not stupid. Lila turned

my life completely upside down. And I know I'd risk everything to be with her. And look at Quin."

"I scuttled a deal that was worth millions because of Celia."

"Your situation is different," Reid said. "But we both understand what it's like to have someone you can't live without. But I won't pretend to like that you found that with Tom Cain. I'm worried that you're literally sleeping with the enemy, and it could put us in danger."

"And I can understand that. We both know what's business. And what's personal."

"Do you think you can keep your personal life separate from the distillery?"

"Yes. It's about family and making sure this business is as successful as we can make it and setting it up for the next generation. Even though that's far in the future, right?"

She looked over at Quin and saw that he had a small smile on his face. "What's that look for?"

"What look?"

Gemma was grateful that the attention was shifted from her to her brother. Gemma quickly looked at Reid, who had also noticed their brother's change in demeanor.

"What's going on?" Reid asked.

"You can't tell anyone," he started, a smile growing on his face. "But Celia's pregnant."

"Holy crap!" Gemma exclaimed. "That's amazing."

"Congratulations, man!" Reid said.

"Thanks. We were going to wait until dinner with Dad before he goes back out west to tell everyone. But you guys pulled it out of me."

Gemma couldn't believe it. She was going to be an aunt. It dawned on her as Reid and Quin discussed the pregnancy. "Let's do it," she said, interrupting them. "I want what's best for the distillery. Let's move into the northeast."

"What about Tom?"

"It's about family now. You guys are right. We need to set ourselves up for future success." She had to talk to Tom, but she knew she couldn't discuss anything distillery-related with him. But with her business directly targeting his, how was their relationship going to work?

She put all of that out of her mind. At least for the moment, she wanted to focus on her work. "Why don't you guys come downstairs? I've got some bottles that might be good to launch for the summer line."

"Yeah, let's go down."

They left Reid's office, and even though she felt better about her relationship with her brothers—and she claimed to be able to keep those parts of her life separate—it could have grave ramifications with Tom. That niggling of apprehension still gnawed at her gut. She'd made the right decision for her family, but it wasn't sitting right with her.

"So, what do you have for us?"

"Well—" Gemma drew out the word "—it's definitely light. And it's been infused but not fully flavored with tropical fruits. Pineapple, mango, strawberry. But it isn't overpowering and would be good in a cocktail, with soda, and also on its own."

"Sounds promising. How is it?"

"I haven't tried it yet. I was waiting for you guys."

"You haven't mentioned it," Reid said.

"I was mad at you, remember?"

"I didn't know you were working with flavors like that," Quin said. "It's not our usual profile."

"That's why I made it. I wanted to try something different. I didn't know how it would work out, and I didn't want it to get out. It's something I've been developing for a while now. With the popularity of hard seltzer, this could pair well with soda water. I thought if it was good, it might be a good addition to our product line."

"What other surprises do you have down here?" Reid asked her as they entered the distillery.

She winked. "Not many. A girl has to have a few secrets, doesn't she?" Gemma was always excited when she had something new to show them, and this was no different.

They walked into her office and she bypassed the drum that contained the rum she'd made with Tom and went for the bottle on the end of the shelf in her office. She opened the bottle and poured the rum into three small tasting glasses. Even though it wasn't a fully flavored rum, but rather just infused with a light flavor, she could still smell the tropical notes. She already knew it was going to be a hit. She handed the glasses to each of them.

"To the family," Reid said, holding his glass up, toasting to their name and the distillery as they did whenever they tested a new batch. Gemma and Quin echoed his words, and they all drank at the same time.

The rum was light and crisp, with a hint of tropical fruit. She was glad that she'd followed her gut on an infused rum. They quick-distilled their mainstream offerings, and she knew that she could have enough made and bottled for their launch in the spring. She watched her brothers eagerly as they tasted the rum.

Quin spoke first. "Gemma," he said, and his voice held an awe that embarrassed her a little. "That's incredible."

"Yeah," Reid concurred. "On its own, with juice or with seltzer, it'll be incredible."

They all drank in silence, savoring the new rum. When Gemma saw Reid's eyes catch on the barrel in the corner that held her and Tom's rum, she knew what was coming. Her brothers normally left the distillery floor to her. But they both still had a keen eye on what happened. Reid pointed to the small barrel. "What is that?" he asked. "Another infusion? Something new?"

"Yeah, kind of," she said, hoping they'd drop it and focus on what she was putting in front of them. They'd just come to an understanding about Tom, and she was reluctant to bring him up again. Gemma thought about lying, but she had nothing to hide. Even if her brothers didn't like him, she was in love with Tom and was proud of their relationship. Reid and Quin would just have to get used to it. She straightened. "That's the batch that Tom and I made."

His eyes narrowed. "Wait, what do you mean? You and Tom made a batch?"

"I knew you would hate this. I didn't want to tell you," she muttered. "He was at my place a few weeks ago, and I had that emergency with the tank. I had to come in and fix it. It was a Friday night and I didn't want to call in any of the crew, so he came with me and helped save a huge batch. We ended up making some ourselves."

"You let him into the distillery?" Reid asked, angry again. "Jesus, Gemma, how could you be so stupid as to let him in here?"

Her mouth dropped in a mix of anger and surprise. "Stupid?"

"What would you call it?" he challenged. "You're sleeping with this guy. Our families have been at odds for years, and this is what you do? You invite him into our distillery? What about family loyalty?"

"Fuck you, Reid. I thought we were past this. What I do is none of your business."

"Cain Rum almost ruined us once. How could you have forgotten about that? And you invited him in here after hours?"

Here we go again. "I haven't forgotten what Carolina did—not for a second. But that has nothing to do with Tom." When Reid rolled his eyes, she slammed her fist down on her desk in frustration. She would never get through to them. Quin casually stepped between her and her oldest brother.

"He stole our recipes," Reid maintained.

"He did not!" She sighed and walked to her desk. She opened the top drawer and took out the flash drive that Tom had given her—the one that contained the recipes Carolina had stolen. She tossed it to Reid, and he caught it in one hand.

"What is this?" he asked.

"It's the recipes that Carolina stole. The same ones that Tom paid his distillery workers to hand over and forget about." That shut him up, but she was still angry. "I'm done with this conversation. What I do in my personal life is none of your business."

"It's my business when it comes to protecting the distillery and this family." His voice was softer.

"Reid, you don't need to protect me."

"He could have taken anything," Reid said. "Or seen anything, sabotaged something. We have sensitive equipment here that a lot of people want to get their hands on." He wasn't letting go of it, but he seemed tired of fighting. But not as tired of it as Gemma was.

Gemma didn't want to admit to Reid that he was right. Something like that could have happened. But not with Tom. She trusted him. *Didn't she?* She thought back to his questions that he'd had about their future plans. She thought about him studying her equipment, but she shook it away. "He wouldn't do any of that."

"How do you know that?"

"Because I know him."

"How well?"

Gemma had given Tom her heart. Her body. Her love. She trusted him with those things. But she eyed the glass of rum in her hand. Could she trust him with her family?

"Why did you choose him?" Quin asked. "Just tell us that."

"The truth? I didn't choose him. Did you choose Celia?" She pointed at Reid. "Did you choose Lila?" She stopped. "Wait. Is that what this is about? Do you think I'm choosing him over you guys?" Neither of her brothers looked at her, telling her that she might be right. She felt kind of sad for them. "Guys, I'm choosing to be happy. And Tom, whether he's a Cain or not, makes me happy. It doesn't have to be so black-and-white."

"It's not just black-and-white," Quin said. "It's what's realistic. Where is your future going? He's poised to take over Cain. Do you think he's just going to drop everything and move down here to be with you?"

Hearing it out loud made her heart pound. Reid had echoed her own concerns. "I don't know. I haven't thought about it," she lied. "We haven't talked about it yet."

"I mean, if you're not looking for a future with him, if it's casual and that's all right with you, then fine. We just don't want you to be hurt."

She wouldn't let on that their words hurt like knives driving into her heart. They were right, of

course. But she straightened, looking firm and reso-
lute for her brothers so they wouldn't know she was
crumbling inside. She needed to have a serious conversation with Tom—as soon as possible. "I won't
get hurt, Reid. I'm a grown woman. And I can look
after myself."

Reid nodded. "Okay. You know I trust you, Gem.
And I'm sorry for freaking out a little there."

"A little?"

"Okay, a lot. Lila's already mad enough at me for
butting into your life. I'm trying to ignore the part
of me that wants to protect you."

"You're allowed to want to protect me. But you
have to let me make my own decisions."

"I will. I'm sorry. I'll trust you when it comes to
this. But please be careful. If you won't listen to me
about your relationship—"

"I won't."

"I know, but please listen to me about protecting
the distillery. I know how it feels to be betrayed and
sold out by someone I loved."

She nodded and understood where Reid was
coming from. Carolina had blindsided him—all of
them—when she'd done what she did. "I'm sorry
she did that to you. But it won't happen this time."

"Okay, I trust you," he said, wrapping his arms
around her, drawing her into a strong hug. "I'm
sorry," he said again.

"I'm sorry, too. I should have been honest," she
told him, and then hugged Quin. She loved her brothers. They'd had conversations about Tom before. But

now she felt like they all understood each other and were on the same page.

Now she had to make sure she and Tom were, as well.

now she felt like she'd never get to... ...each other into
you're on the same page.
"Yeah," she said to make... ...her and "Yep," were
as well.

CHAPTER TWENTY

"WHAT THE FUCK?" Tom said when he saw the photo and copy for the ad campaign they would be launching. It was the first time that a campaign had been pushed through without him seeing it. And when he saw this one, he was livid.

It featured a nearly nude woman, on a bed, covered with a white sheet. Her dark hair was long and wavy, and she bore a striking resemblance to how Gemma had looked in the *Men's Lifestyle* spread that had debuted the week before. Gemma's feature had made a splash. She'd always been Gemma Rexford when she was hauling barrels in bulky coveralls, but in a short amount of time, she'd become a sex symbol in the rum community.

He seethed at the Cain ads he saw on his computer. The ad copy was the worst part, however: "We don't need sex to sell fine rum… But it doesn't hurt." The marketing department must have worked overtime to find a way to degrade Gemma and her accomplishments and get this out in such a short amount of time.

He picked up his phone and called Bill Edwards, the head of marketing. When the man answered, Tom didn't waste time with pleasantries. "Where did that ad come from?"

"Did you like it?"

"Does it fucking sound like I liked it?"

Bill was silent.

"I know it isn't your style," Tom said. "Who did it?"

"Your father."

"What?"

"It came from him—he suggested it."

"Pull the ads," he ordered.

"Why?"

"I appreciate that your team did them, but they aren't Cain Rum. They're a cheap shot at Gemma Rexford, and it's obvious. That's not how we promote ourselves."

"But your father—"

"It doesn't matter. Do what you have to do. Just pull it."

"Okay," Bill said.

Tom hung up without saying goodbye. He had someone else to talk to. He walked down the hall to his father's office. He knocked on the door.

"Yes?" his father called from the other side.

Tom stalked into his father's office. "What did you do?"

His father narrowed his eyes at him, but his face otherwise remained impassive. "I'm sure I don't know what you're talking about."

"The new ad campaign. Don't pretend that woman isn't based on Gemma Rexford."

"That woman you're sleeping with? Don't think I don't know about your weekly trips to Miami."

"How do you know about that?" he asked.

"I saw the magazine with her on the cover on your desk. All those trips to Miami—I connected the dots."

"You went in my office?"

He shrugged. "I went to find you, and you weren't there. I saw the magazine."

"You had no right to go into my office."

He shook his head. "You know, son, I never thought you'd betray the family and the business with a competitor. Especially a Rexford." Now his father was starting to sound like Reid and Quin.

"What I do in my personal life is none of your business," he said. "And it in no way affects what happens here."

"It's my business when you're seen with our competitor," his father told him. "You've never gone against the family like this before. I believe that woman is a bad influence on you."

"A bad influence?" Tom asked. "I'm not a goddamn teenager." He was so angry he almost forgot the reason he'd gone in there. "What are you doing running ad campaigns, anyway? You're not in marketing. You've never had any input into it at all."

"I still run this company, and that means I still make the decisions. When Carolina showed me those pictures of her online—"

Tom caught his father's slipup. "Carolina showed you? I knew she was behind this. You did this to embarrass Gemma and slander her name in the industry. Typical—we can't beat her product, so you do something shady like this."

Since his father had married that woman, Tom hadn't taken the opportunity to get to know her. He didn't trust her. All he knew about her was that she had been capable of betraying the Rexfords by stealing their recipes. There's no way he could trust someone who could do that, and he didn't understand how his father could, as well.

"That's besides the point. You're threatening the future of the company with Gemma Rexford. How do we know you aren't trading corporate secrets? A little pillow talk."

"Why would I try to ruin the company that's been in our family for generations? I'm the only one who's trying to save this business."

"Son, you have a choice to make. You want to run Cain Rum, right?"

"Yes. I always have."

"You can't run this company if you're seeing Gemma Rexford."

Tom had been expecting the words. He'd often thought them as well during those nights he'd spent with his arms wrapped around her body. He'd heard them clearly as he said them to himself. Deep down, Tom had always known he would have to make a choice, and as he stood in front of his father, his anger rising, he knew which choice he wanted to make. He wanted to storm the fuck out of there and never return. But he knew it wasn't that simple. He couldn't walk away from the business, not like that. No matter how he felt about his father, the business was his birthright, and was something he'd always striven for. It had been his goal for as long as he remembered.

Maybe he needed some space from Gemma, just a little time on his own to figure out what it was he wanted. He knew what he wanted, but what was for the best was a different matter altogether. But first, he had to make sure that the ad featuring the Gemma lookalike didn't see the light of day.

His father, always astute, was watching him carefully and must have seen the indecision on his face. "Let me know what you decide," he said. "Now, if you'll excuse me, I have work to do."

Gemma was in front of her makeup table, getting ready to go out with Celia and Lila, when her cell phone rang. She'd had plans to go out for dinner and drinks with the girls. Well, drinks with Lila, she realized, and smiled, remembering that Celia was pregnant. But either way, Gemma was looking forward to dressing up and having a good time. She paused in applying a steady black line to her upper eyelid and frowned, because she knew she would never be able to complete it so flawlessly again. She looked at the screen and, seeing it was Tom calling for a video chat, she smiled and accepted the call. "Hey babe, what's up?"

He sighed. "I'm still at the office." He looked tired, and she wished she was there with him. "Are you going out?"

"Cocktails and tapas with the girls," she told him. "It's been crazy at the distillery lately." *Especially with the plans for the aggressive summer launch that will target Cain Rum*, she thought, but left it unsaid. They had been working hard for the launch, and even though she was seeing Tom, her brothers didn't care. They were moving ahead with it. "Is everything okay?" she asked.

"Oh, you know, just the typical frustrations that come along with a family business."

"Oh, I know what that's like."

"I know you do."

"But at least it's almost the weekend," she said with a smile. "You know what that means."

His sigh caught her attention, and she frowned. "Listen, Gemma, I don't think I'll be able to come down this weekend."

"Oh, really?" she asked. Since they'd started their relationship, they'd managed to spend every weekend together. Gemma hated how desperate she sounded.

"Yeah, sorry," he said. "Something came up, and I can't get away." His lack of an actual response was startling.

"Something came up? Anything you want to talk about?"

"No, not really," he said.

For the first time, she could feel the distance between them, and it wasn't just physical. "I hope everything is okay."

"Yeah, it will be."

She frowned. "Work?" A black pit formed in her stomach. Gemma had a bad feeling about the conversation. She was worried for him, sad that he didn't confide in her, annoyed that he was being so dismissive. This was why she didn't deal with serious relationships.

He sighed. "It's nothing I want to talk about right now."

His tone made herself feel like she was being dismissed. "Okay. Well, that's too bad." She shrugged, trying to not let him know how much it did bother her.

"Are you okay?"

"I'm great," she told him. "We'll probably see each other next weekend."

"Probably?" he asked. "Are you still coming up here?"

"Yeah, sure thing," she said, noncommittal.

"Gemma, are you okay?"

"Me? I'm fine." She wasn't sure why she was being so confrontational, or why him not making the trip down this week bothered her so much. She was annoyed by herself. For even letting it affect her. "I'm going to go now so I can finish getting ready."

He frowned. "Okay. I'll talk to you later."

"Sure thing."

"I love you."

She looked away from the phone and nodded at

her own reflection. "I love you, too," she said before disconnecting the call. She'd said the words; she'd meant them. But as she thought about the conversation, and the confusion she felt at his lack of information, feeling it tore her heart out.

Picking up her liquid eyeliner, she attempted to continue the line she'd started on her eyelid. But her hand was shaky, so she threw down the wand in frustration and wiped at the mess she'd made.

She was frustrated with herself for behaving that way. She'd never let herself feel that way about a guy. So what if he couldn't make it this weekend? It wasn't the end of the world. She could get by for one weekend without him. He told her something had come up, and that should be enough for her. She had no claim on him. She trusted him, but she was left with the impression that there was something he wasn't telling her.

Tom stared at his phone screen for probably a minute after it turned black. Gemma obviously hadn't been happy by the way the conversation had turned out, but hell, neither was he. He'd had every intention of going to Miami tomorrow. But since he'd seen the new ad campaign, he knew he had to work to cover it up before it debuted. But not only that. He'd made the right decision for himself. He had some feelings he still had to sort out. And he couldn't do either of those things from her bed in Miami.

His phone rang again. He hoped it was Gemma,

but instead, it was Bill from marketing. He answered. "Any news?"

"We're not pulling the ad."

"Why not? It can't be too late."

"If we wanted to pull it, it would take a matter of minutes to write a few emails."

"Then what is it?"

"Tom." Bill sighed into the phone. "I don't know what kind of family drama you and John have going on, but I don't want to be in the middle of it."

"What is it?"

"Your father and his wife came to visit my office about an hour ago."

Tom frowned. "Yeah?"

"They told me that under no circumstances are we to stop it. No matter what *you* said."

Tom formed a fist with one hand, and he could have crushed his phone with the other. Every day he entered the building and worked with the other employees, never once bringing his father's name into his business. But now his father had gone around him and brought him up to an employee in a disagreement. No, that wasn't appropriate at all. He thought about asking Bill if there was another way, but he'd already made the man's day hard enough.

"Okay, thanks, Bill," he conceded. "I'm sorry about the awkward position we've put you in. It shouldn't have happened."

"Thank you. I appreciate that."

"Have a good night."

He'd once looked up to his father, had once respected him. His opinion of his father's actions of the past several years had lowered his opinion of him, but this time? This time he'd gone too far. The old bastard had found out about his relationship with Gemma. His goal was to embarrass them both and drive them apart.

Tom had no idea how to make it right with Gemma. He already knew that she would be pissed about it. He would have to tell her—get ahead of it—before it was plastered on billboards, magazines, posters and internet banner ads. He picked up his phone again and called her. It went straight to voice mail.

"What the hell?" He said the words aloud in his empty office, completely shocked that she hadn't taken his call. He pushed redial. Again, it rang only once and then went to her voice mail.

"Hi, this is Gemma. I'm not around, or I'm screening, so leave a message."

"Hi, Gem. Sorry I missed you." He started rolling his eyes, annoyed that she hadn't answered, knowing that she was ignoring his call. "Um, I'm not entirely happy with how our last phone call went. And I've got something important I need to talk to you about. So please call me back. I don't care when. Even if it's late. I love you."

He'd done what he could. He couldn't stop them, but he needed to warn her before the ads mocking her went public. He'd skipped his Miami trip to deal with this and try to wrap his head around what he wanted for his future—the company or Gemma. But

now going down there was his only option. He'd have
to tell her face-to-face.

The campaign would be live by morning. Hopefully she wouldn't see it until he saw her.

Two hours later Gemma was seated at a high-top
table drinking sangria with Lila, Celia opted for
water. Her mood had improved considerably, and
she had managed to forget the disappointment she'd
felt earlier—at Tom, at herself.

"Are you okay?" Celia asked her.

It was the second time she'd been asked that.
Maybe she hadn't done quite as good a job at hiding her feelings as she'd thought. "Yeah, I'm fine."

"Liar," Lila told her. "What's going on?"

She sighed. "It's stupid," she said rolling her eyes.
"Tom was supposed to visit this weekend, but he isn't
going to make it."

"Is there something else?"

"No. That's what he said. But he didn't really explain. Just said he didn't want to talk about it."

"Wait, he said that?"

"Yeah, and I think that's what's bothering me the
most. Like, we don't have to spend every weekend
together, but I feel like I deserve a little more information than *I don't want to talk about it*."

"Yeah, that's definitely weird."

"But the weirdest thing is that isn't what I'm upset
about."

"So what is it?"

"I hate that somehow I've become this woman

who cares what this guy is doing. I shouldn't care that he doesn't want to get a flight to another state. It's not even a big deal. I'm going to New York next weekend." Gemma dramatically put her head on the table. When she looked up again, she saw that Lila and Celia were watching her, both of them looked amused by her current predicament. "What?"

"That's what happens when you're in love." Lila said. "You're supposed to care. You're supposed to be irritated when he flakes."

"I don't know," Celia added. "It sounds like he was being shady—not telling you why he couldn't make it."

"Exactly," Gemma agreed. "I just don't know what's up. I feel bad if he's going through some heavy personal thing, and doesn't want to share, but we've already shared so much. He knows he can be honest with me. No matter what it is." She drained her glass of every drop of sangria. The way she felt, she could use another pitcher of the stuff. "This is ridiculous," she muttered to herself. She waved to the waiter and ordered more sangria. "I'm just going to forget him for tonight. If he doesn't want to be here, that's his loss."

CHAPTER TWENTY-ONE

THE USUAL NOISE of the distillery was no match for the pounding inside her skull. It might have been fun hanging out with Celia and Lila, but she'd stayed out too late and drank too much sangria. Gemma didn't go out often, and this was a clear reason why.

She was still upset by how her conversation with Tom had gone the night before. And she'd ignored him and the missed calls and the voice mail notification that showed on her phone with his message. She needed a little bit of space to give herself time to figure out how she felt about him. She was in love with him, but her own reaction to him not visiting her had scared her. She didn't want to be the obsessed girlfriend who couldn't go longer than a week without seeing her long-distance boyfriend.

She looked at the clock. It was barely 1:00 p.m. She envisioned going home, lounging in her bathtub, soaking off the rest of the hangover, and then she made big plans to order a pizza and lie on the couch in front of her TV. She wouldn't have thought so yesterday, but a small part of her was glad that Tom wasn't coming down this weekend. She realized that space was what she needed. She wasn't mad at him, but she was madder at herself for being bothered by it. He was allowed to take a weekend off from their relationship, and so was she.

Her office phone rang, and she squeezed her eyes shut against the trill. Not opening her eyes, she answered it. "Gemma Rexford."

"Hey, Gem," Quin said on the other end. "Reid and I are in my office." He paused, and she knew from his tone of voice that something was wrong. "We think you might want to come up here."

"Is everything okay?" she asked.

"Um, just get up here."

"Yeah, sure. Just give me a couple of minutes." She hung up and shook off her coveralls. "Jose," she called to the floor supervisor. "I'm heading upstairs for a few minutes. You've got this under control?" He shot her a thumbs-up in response.

Despite her fatigue, she jogged up the stairs. When she walked into Quin's office, he and Reid were both seated—with matching deep frowns on their faces. "What's going on?"

"You look like hell, Gemma," Reid said, frowning.

"Gee, thanks."

"Yeah, were you out late or something?" Quin asked innocently, obviously knowing what time Celia had come home last night.

"You can both ask your women about last night," she muttered, taking a seat in the chair next to Reid.

"Is that why you called me up here? To ask me about my hangover?"

"No, we wanted to see if you've seen this." Quin handed over his tablet.

"What is it?" She looked at the screen and saw that it was on Cain Rum's website. At first, she saw the images, and thought momentarily that they were the ones she'd shot for *Men's Lifestyle*. But she looked closer and saw it was another woman. She looked up at her brothers, not understanding, but then she saw the ad copy that accompanied the pictures. *We don't need sex to sell fine rum... But it doesn't hurt.*

"What is this?"

"Cain's new campaign," Reid said.

She came to a quick conclusion. "It's obviously a dig at me," she said.

"We thought so, too."

She laughed without humor, trying to act like it didn't bother her. How could Tom do this to her? "And look at the copy. It's not even good. These guys are failing at everything."

"Gemma," Reid said, reaching out and putting his hand on her shoulder. "Have you spoken to Tom?"

"No," she said. "Not today. Not since last night before I went out."

"*Last night,*" Quin repeated. "And he didn't mention any of this?"

"No."

"He had to have known about it, though, right?"

She nodded. "Yeah, I guess so." Even though she

was trembling with anger, she calmly put the tablet back on the desk. "I'd better get back to work."

"Don't you want to talk about this?" Reid asked her, standing as well.

"Why?" she asked equal parts confused, angry and weary. "So you can say 'I told you so'?"

"We wouldn't."

"No? You always hated Tom. You hated that I was with him. You knew something like this would happen."

"No, Gemma, neither of us agrees with your relationship, but we would never want you to be hurt."

"I've got to get back to work."

"Wait, Gemma," Quin said, catching her before she left.

"What?"

"Did you have a chance to read the summer launch information packet that I left on your desk?"

"Not yet. I put it in my bag."

"The team added some of our ideas for taking on Cain Rum."

"You think the best time to bring this up is now?" she asked, incredulous.

"You would have seen them anyway," he reasoned. "I was going to go over them with you today. It's not my fault that the circumstances have changed."

She had no idea what the circumstances were. She wouldn't know until she talked to Tom—to ask him what the fuck had happened, to tell him to go to hell, to hear whatever his side of the story was. She sighed. "I'm going home," she told them. "I'll let Jose know. If you need anything from the floor, tell him. I'll look over the information later."

"Sure," Reid said. "Call later, okay?"

"I will."

She was halfway down the stairs before she dug out her phone and dialed Tom's phone number. It rang once before his voice mail picked up. She huffed in frustration. And now he wasn't taking her calls? She didn't even bother to leave a message. She didn't need an explanation. He'd completely screwed her over. He had to have known about the ad.

She went back to her office. Her head was spinning. She couldn't stay there any longer. She went over to Jose, where he was watching over the bottlers. "I'm not feeling well, so I'm going to head home. You've got this under control, right?"

"Yeah, we're good. You go home and feel better. We'll be fine here."

Gemma hated to leave the distillery when they were so busy filling orders, but there was no way she would be able to focus on any of it with the way she felt. She felt humiliated, betrayed. And whether Tom had seen the ads or okayed them, he still represented Cain Rum. She went to her office and tried calling him again. Voice mail. She huffed in frustration and threw her phone into her backpack and slung it over her shoulder, and she picked up her keys and left.

On the drive home, Gemma's mind wandered. She mentally reviewed their entire relationship, looking for clues that he would betray her. And the more she thought about the blissful, fun, loving moments between them, her mind shifted to the questionable things. Like the questions he'd asked her about the distillery, his interest in her equipment. Was he just interested in her, or had he been digging for information? God, she'd been so stupid.

The closer she got to her home, the tighter she gripped the steering wheel. Her knuckles were white, and her hands cramped. She relaxed her grip as she slowly climbed the driveway. She would try to call Tom again, and if he refused to take her call, then that was the last time she would reach out to him.

She felt the tears form at the corners of her eyes. This was why she didn't do relationships. She hated that she was letting herself get so emotional over some guy. She should have seen what was happening after his first visit to Miami. He'd transformed from a secret, illicit one-night stand to someone she'd cared for. Someone she'd somehow fallen in love with, and had been willing to sacrifice everything for.

When Gemma's house came into view, she saw that there was another car in the driveway. "What the…?" There was a man sitting on her porch, and she sighed in relief and frustration, when she realized it was Tom. He was sitting with his forearms across his thighs, his head thrown back against her door. She had given him a key, but he hadn't used it. He was waiting for her to come home before letting himself in. He noticed her and stood, but averted his eyes from her gaze. She was unsure which emotion he wore on his face. Shame? Remorse? He stood and jammed his hands in his pockets, the movement slumping his broad shoulders into a curve. He looked at her briefly before looking down at the ground.

Gemma grabbed her backpack from the passenger's seat and slung it over her shoulder. She stepped out of her vehicle. "Why are you here?" she called to him.

"To explain."

An explanation was all she wanted. But she didn't know what he could say to make it better. With whatever he said, it would likely signal the end of their relationship. She walked past him, and her arm brushed his. "I'd love to hear it," she muttered sarcastically. She unlocked the door and walked in. He followed behind her.

He closed the door. "You've seen the ad, then."

Gemma tossed her open backpack to the floor and turned to face him. "Yeah, I have. The real question is though, when did you see it?"

"Yesterday."

"You saw it yesterday. Funny, you never mentioned it when we spoke on the phone."

"I thought I could stop it before it launched. But I was too late. I was just as blindsided as you are."

"I highly doubt that. Nobody's publicly embarrassed you."

"I wouldn't say that, but my family has greatly embarrassed me, too."

Gemma shook her head. No matter what Tom and his father disagreed on, he had never been publicly mocked within their industry. "Why did you target me?"

"I didn't target you."

"No, you didn't. But your company did." She went into the kitchen, and he followed her. She pulled a bottle of wine from the rack on the wall. She didn't speak as she opened it and poured out two glasses. "Here," she said, sliding one of the glasses across the table to him.

"Thanks."

They both drank wine, watching each other over their glasses. The tension radiated between them. She hated it, hated him. No, she didn't hate him. She loved him. But she hated everything else. Finally, she lowered her glass. "I'm the best rum distiller in the world," she said, simply.

"I know you are."

"And that your company embarrassed me, mocked me, in their newest ad campaign is low as fuck."

He nodded. "I know. It shouldn't have happened."

"I wouldn't be so mad if you thought you could compete in the distillery. But that's why you had to resort to shady tactics."

He put down his glass heavily, and the wine sloshed over the rim. "You know, you keep saying that *I* did these things. It was done without me even knowing. And none of that changes how I feel about you."

"Is that why you called and said you wouldn't be coming down here?"

"It was part of it. I was trying to get ahead of it. I was hoping it could be stopped before it went live." He paused. "But that wasn't it."

"What is it?"

"I had my own doubts and concerns. My father found out about us. That's why he went after you. I was willing to work past it, but I was scared, too. I didn't know how to reconcile you and my family. But the difference between you and me is that I was willing to try. I tried to call you last night, but you ignored my calls."

"I didn't answer because I didn't want to talk to you."

"Because you were mad that I wasn't coming to visit."

"I wasn't mad because you weren't visiting. I was mad that I cared so fucking much," she admitted.

"I don't understand."

"Everything with us has been so quick—a whirlwind—and the feelings have been so intense. I fell so hard for you. I fell in love with you."

"It's been like that for me, too," he said, taking a step toward her.

"But I never wanted that," she told him, stopping him in his tracks, clearly not expecting her to say that. "At some point I lost control," she continued.

"And that's bad?"

"Yes."

"You're being ridiculous."

"I'm ridiculous?"

"Yes. Losing control is what love is about. And I'm just as lost and confused as you are. That's what I realized last night. I was so unsure of how to separate you and the business. But I don't want to."

"Well, I hate it."

"Tell me what you want."

"I want my old life back."

"Your old life?"

"I want to be content like I was before."

"I'm not following you."

"You made me realize that I want more. I was happy then—single, carefree, focusing on rum, my friends, family. That was enough for me."

"Was it?"

She looked down into her wineglass. It wasn't. It hadn't been nearly enough for her, but it sure as hell felt a lot better than she did at that moment. She'd never felt a hurt so real and powerful. And Tom did that. She loved him so hard that he alone had the power to make her feel like her heart was being ripped from her chest. She sighed and finished her glass of wine. She picked up the bottle. "Want some more?" He shook his head. She poured herself another glass, needing the fortification. "Maybe my brothers were right," she realized.

Tom visibly stiffened. "What do you mean?"

"We don't have a future."

"That's not true, Gemma."

"It is. What kind of future do you expect to have? What kind of relationship is this—traveling between two states. Hell, I'm on a first-name basis with the flight crew at this point."

"So we spend a few days a week on a plane."

"But it's not just the distance," she said. "It's what's happening right now. We work for competing businesses, and I thought we were strong enough to just forget all of that."

"We are," he told her. "We can be."

She shook her head. Tom wasn't even the issue anymore. It was what he represented—every one of the feelings of mistrust she had. "It's too much. Every conversation has that little bit of secrecy because we can't talk about work. Every time you ask me a question, I feel there's an ulterior motive. And then this ad thing. Do you understand how much it hurt, how embarrassing it was to have my brothers show me an ad that mocked me and what I do?" He thankfully said nothing, and she proceeded, her emotions at an all-time high, raising her blood pressure, making her hands flail as she spoke. "And not even to mention our plans to target Cain next year. How could I agree to that if we're in a relationship—"

"What was that?"

She paused, knowing that she'd accidentally said too much.

"You're targeting us?"

"It's business."

"And you said you agreed to go along with it. Before any of this happened?"

Who was he to turn it back on her? She nodded. "Yes, I did. And you know what? Your concerns that your father is ruining your company, that you could fail and lose everything, didn't even sway me." In reality, the decision had given her pause. She had thought about what Tom would think. But with the way his eyes narrowed at her now, she realized that she'd scored a direct hit on their relationship. It was her out. Her way to push him away and make him hate her before she could let herself be hurt by him again.

Tom's laugh held no humor. He put his hands on his hips. "I see what you're doing, Gemma. You're trying to make me mad so that you feel better about me walking away. If you don't want to be together, you only have to say the words."

Gemma tried to stand tall, even though she could feel the quiver in her bottom lip. "It's over."

Tom looked away from her, and she could see the rise and fall of his shoulders as he took several deep breaths. She saw the moisture gather in his eyes, and he nodded his head. "I love you, Gemma. I'm sorry for what happened with the ad. But maybe you're right. Maybe this has been too complicated from the start."

Even though her heart might be breaking, she nodded. She wanted to take it all back. She wanted him to throw his arms around her and kiss her. But she stood her ground. This—ending it now—was for the best. "It never would have worked." She sat on the couch. While her head said she couldn't imagine a future with Tom Cain, in her heart, she couldn't imagine her life without him.

He sat next to her. Even though they weren't touching, she could feel his warmth, and she had to clench her fingers into fists to stop them from reaching out and touching him.

"I'm sorry," he said, shaking his head, but looking straight ahead, not at her. "About the ad. About everything. That none of this turned out the way we wanted."

"I'm sorry, too."

Tom pushed his fingers through his hair in an attempt to smooth back the dark waves. "I should leave," he said finally.

"Okay." When he stood, she reached out and stopped him. "Wait."

"What?"

"I have something for you."

She pushed off the couch and went to the side room where she'd put the bottle a few days before. She came back out and handed it to him.

He handled the bottle. "What is this?"

"It's our rum."

"Have you tried it?"

"Not yet. When I brought it home, I thought we could taste it together."

There was a brief but pregnant pause between them. He held the bottle aloft. "I guess I'll go now."

"All right. Have a safe trip home."

"Thanks." It surprised her when he leaned in and kissed her on the cheek. "I'll be seeing you, Rexford."

CHAPTER TWENTY-TWO

AFTER ONE OF the most miserable weekends of his life, spending sleepless nights in his bed, where all he did was toss in his sheets and think about Gemma, Tom walked into his office Monday morning still feeling terrible. As soon as he sat behind his desk, his assistant, Alison, popped her head in the door. "Tom, your father wants you to meet him in his office first thing." John Cain was one of those old-school guys who got to work at 7:00 a.m. He'd no doubt been waiting for Tom to get in since then.

He cursed under his breath. He was too exhausted and too irritable to deal with his father first thing on a Monday morning. "I haven't even had coffee yet."

"Got you covered," she said, putting a coffee cup on the desk. She'd undoubtedly come to work, heard the message from John and walked next door for it, knowing Tom would need some fortification.

"You're the best." He took the cup and drank.

He could feel Alison watching him.

"Everything okay?"

"Not really," he told her. "I've got some personal stuff going on."

She frowned. "Anything I can help with?"

He shook his head but smiled at her. Alison had been with him for as long as he'd been at Cain, and he appreciated everything she did for him every day. "Not really, but thank you. I really have to get to John's office."

He left his shoulder bag at his desk and headed up the hallway to his father's office. He knocked on the door and heard his father telling him to come in.

When he entered, he also saw Carolina sitting in one of the wing chairs opposite his massive desk. His father was bad enough. But having to see both of them was not how he'd wanted to start his day.

"Tom, sit down," his father instructed, gesturing to the chair next to Carolina.

"Good morning to you both, as well," Tom said as he took a seat, making his annoyance apparent. His emotions were already completely raw. He didn't have the patience for whatever his father wanted with him first thing on a Monday morning.

"It's about time you got in," his father admonished, eyeing the coffee cup in his hand.

Tom sipped his coffee and then glanced down at his watch. "It's not even eight forty-five. So, what's up? What's with this early morning meeting?"

"Tom, I've made a decision, and I wanted to tell you first."

That got Tom's attention. Was it finally happening? Was his father finally stepping down? Would he now have the chance to save Cain Rum? Tom sat up straighter in his seat. "What is it?"

"I'm retiring."

"Are you?"

"Yes," his father smiled indulgently. "Effective at end of day today. And Carolina will be taking my spot."

Tom's periphery turned black as his father's words sank in. There was a roaring in his ears as he looked at Carolina. The smug smile on her face told him that she was quite pleased with herself. When he swallowed his shock and found the will to speak again, he took a deep breath. He turned to his father. "You're handing the company over to her?"

"That's right."

"Why? Cain Rum is supposed to be mine."

"After your showing the past little while, and the changes you want to make, not to mention your relationship with Gemma Rexford, I don't think that letting you take over just yet is in the best interest of Cain Rum."

"My proposed changes are the only things that are going help this company survive." He turned his attention to Carolina. "What things will you do to keep this place running?"

"I have some ideas," she said vaguely in a way that let him know she had nothing. "I'm sure we'll work together to make the best decisions."

There was no way he was going to work with her on anything. This was it. He'd worked his entire adult life to take the reins at Cain Rum. But no matter what he'd done, it was never enough for the man sitting in front of him. "You have nothing," he said, standing. He looked at his father. "And you don't have me."

"Tom, what are you saying?"

"For years, I've worked my ass off for this place. And to see it in the position it is now is breaking my heart. I'm done."

"What are you going to do?"

"For once, I'm going to do what's best for me. I'm quitting."

"You can't quit."

Tom's righteous anger was matched only by the sadness of what he was about to do. He was about to throw away what he'd worked for, and potentially any relationship with his father he would hope to have. "Watch me."

Standing outside Reid and Lila's house, clutching two bottles of wine, Gemma took a deep breath. She'd applied makeup, styled her hair and put on something cute. She, Lila, and Celia were staying in to watch cheesy movies and drink wine, but she was grateful for the opportunity to wear something other than sweats and her coveralls. She'd told herself that she was ready to get back to the old life she'd so craved. It didn't make her feel any better, though. If she'd been honest with herself, she would have admitted that she was miserable.

She knocked a couple of times on the door before letting herself in. "Hey," she called, holding her bottles up. "I'm here." She walked into the kitchen and saw that in addition to Lila and Celia, Reid and Quin were there as well. "You guys are here, too."

"Well, this is my house," Reid reminded her, standing and wrapping his arms around her.

"Sorry, I didn't mean it like that," she said, apologizing and accepting his hug. "I was just expecting the girls. Not you guys."

"You've been avoiding us all week," Quin pointed out.

"You're right," she sighed. "I have been."

"Why?" he asked.

"I just didn't want to hear the *I told you so* that I had coming."

Reid shook his head. "Gemma, like I said, we wouldn't have said that. We just want you to be okay. How are you?"

"I'll be fine," she assured them. "Probably not today, but that's why I brought these," she said, holding up the wine bottles. "I briefly forgot that Celia wouldn't be drinking. But I figured two bottles would come in handy anyway."

"All right, let's get out of here, Reid," Quin said, grabbing his coat. "Our car should be here very soon."

"Where are you going?"

"Dinner at Arlo's and then some drinks and cigars."

"Have fun," she said, moving past them. While the women said goodbye to her brothers with hugs and kisses, Gemma busied herself opening one of the bottles of wine she'd brought. She thought back to all the goodbyes she'd shared with Tom. And then the final one when she'd told him it was over.

So many times that week she'd wanted to call him—she almost had. But she'd been strong. Life was easier, and she would learn to be happy without him. She sat on a stool at the kitchen island and picked at the charcuterie plate Lila had prepared. She wondered just how long it would take before her relationship—or lack thereof—became the topic of conversation.

"So tell me," Lila said. "What exactly happened between you and Tom?"

So, not long, then. "I could say it started because of that damned ad," she started.

"The one with the woman?" Celia asked. "That was some serious shade."

"You're telling me. It's embarrassing to be on top of my industry and have a competitor pull something like that."

"Did he have anything to do with it?"

"He said he didn't, and I believe him. Apparently, he had no idea until it came across his desk, and he tried to stop it."

"So why did you break up with him?"

"It was too hard. Me being a Rexford, him being a Cain. The businesses, and our families." She didn't think she could talk about it anymore. "So, that's enough about my miserable love life. Why don't we decide on movies?"

Lila scrolled through a list of candidates they could stream. Gemma, already feeling the effects of the wine in her mostly empty stomach, stopped her. "The one about the male strippers going on a road trip is what I want."

"Again?" Celia asked.

"Listen, if any other movie features muscly guys in thongs, I'm all for it. But for tonight, I want a group of sexy guys in thongs."

"I can't argue with that argument," Lila said.

"I knew you'd see it my way."

"You've been in a shitty mood all week, Tom," Shane admonished him, as Tom plucked three beer bottles from the fridge for himself and his friends. When Tom had told them he didn't feel like going out, Shane and Darren had brought over a pizza and wings from their regular restaurant.

"Yeah, what's going on with you?" Darren asked. "The stuff with your dad?"

They knew he'd left Cain Rum, and they knew his reasons and hadn't demanded an explanation. Tom hadn't told his friends that he'd been seeing Gemma, and he certainly hadn't told them that they'd ended it. But they'd been able to pick up on his mood. He shook his head, hoping he would get away from interrogation. "Not Dad. Just personal stuff."

"And you can't share your personal stuff with your best friends?"

Tom opened each of the beer bottles and handed them off. "Remember Gemma Rexford?"

"That distiller in Miami?" Shane asked. "The hot one? Yeah, of course."

"We've been seeing each other. For a few months now," he revealed.

"You've been hitting that, and you never shared with your friends?" Darren asked. "I'm hurt."

"It's the twenty-first century," Shane said. "Nobody says *hitting that* anymore."

"Yeah, sorry about that. It was a private thing," Tom said. "But now it's over."

Both of his friends frowned. "Aw, shit," Darren said. "Sorry, man. You want to talk about it?"

"Not really," he said. "Can we just drink beer and eat pizza?"

"Yeah. We can."

Tom had settled into the friendly, easy conversation when there was a knock on the door. He dropped his pizza slice on his plate and stood. "I'll be right back." He walked to the door, and when he opened it, he was surprised to see his father. In the years that he'd lived there, Tom could count on one hand the number of times that his father had visited his place. "Dad."

"Hello, son. Can I come in?" He had never seen his father look so forlorn before.

"Yeah, of course." He stepped aside, and his father entered. When he saw Shane and Darren at the table, he paused. "You have company. I'll come back another time."

"No, don't be ridiculous. We'll just go in another room." He led his father to the bedroom he'd renovated into a study. "Fellas, I'll be right back."

When they walked into the study. Tom realized he was still holding his beer. "Can I get you a drink?"

"No, thank you." He looked around. "I went by your office. I saw it was cleaned out."

"Well, I quit, so that would make sense."

"You didn't need to quit," he told him.

"I did, though. You gave Carolina my job."

"Only for a brief period. I couldn't trust you to take over right now."

"You couldn't trust me? After everything I've done…" He trailed off. "I'm your son, for Christ's sake!"

"And you're seeing Gemma Rexford."

"I wasn't seeing her. I was in love with her." He shrugged and drank from his beer. "Not that it matters. It's over now anyway."

That made his father pause. "You love her?"

"Yes."

"What happened? Why did you break up?"

"Why do you care?"

John sighed. "We got so off track, Tom. Our relationship wasn't always like this."

"No, it wasn't."

"And I know when we took that turn," he said.

"Do you?"

"It was Carolina."

"That was part of it. But we grew apart. It had been happening for a while. I thought I wanted to be just like you. You were my hero, larger than life. But it turns out you were only human."

"I am. And I know you don't like Carolina, and you don't like what I've done with the business, and I'm sorry we butt heads so much. The curse of us both being stubborn men. Maybe you're more like me than you want to admit." Tom said nothing. "I want you to come back to work."

He thought about the implications of going back to Cain Rum. "Not a chance."

"What are you going to do?"

"I don't know," he said, not mentioning the plans he'd talked to Gemma about to start his own distillery. "I'll figure it out."

His father cleared his throat. He was clearly uncomfortable in the conversation. "I would like to work on our relationship," he said. "Do you think we can?"

For all his life, Tom had wanted a better relationship with his father. Hearing him say the words gave him hope that it would be possible, especially since he no longer worked at the company. He nodded. "Let's start over. I'm not ready to forgive you, and it won't be easy, but let's work on it."

His father's smile was small. "That's all I could hope for," he said. "What are you going to do about Gemma Rexford?"

"That question is no easier to answer," Tom admitted.

"You say you love her?"

"I do."

"Then go after her."

"She was pretty adamant that I shouldn't." She wanted to be single, not tied down. She'd made that clear.

John cleared his throat. "If you love her, you have find a way to make it work."

Tom rolled his eyes. "You're not exactly the one to be giving out relationship advice."

"I know it doesn't make sense to you, but Carolina and I do love each other. That was something I never had with your mother, and you know that."

"You and mom were only together because it was convenient."

"It worked for both of us. She liked the status of being a Cain, and I like having her on my arm. I'm sorry that isn't a healthy household to grow up in. But we both loved you. No matter how we showed it."

Tom swallowed roughly. It was a hard conversation to hear, but he knew it was the truth. "I wish you could have been happier together."

"Me, too. But we're both happier now. And that's the important thing. I just don't want you to turn out like me and be an old man before you're truly happy. If you can have that now—whether it's with Gemma Rexford, or not—you should go for it."

"How?"

"You'll figure it out," his father told him. He held out his hand, and Tom shook it. It was ridiculous, shaking his father's hand instead of hugging, but that's where their relationship was right now. They could work up to it. It would just take time. Maybe some time was what Gemma needed, too.

Several hours and many glasses of wine later, Gemma walked, unsteady, into her house. She'd had one hell of a week, and she'd needed fun with her ladies. She made her way to the kitchen. Her house was so quiet. She saw the second unlabeled bottle of rum that she and Tom had made, and she felt sad.

She poured herself a glass of water, but she also took a small glass from the cupboard and poured herself a finger of rum. Bringing the glass to her nose, she inhaled. She hadn't tasted it yet, but she could tell it would be good. She picked up both and walked to the living room. She sat on the couch, looking into the short glass. The amber liquid caught the light, and she sighed.

She put the glass on the coffee table and picked up her phone. She opened her contacts. Her thumb hovered over Tom's name. She closed her eyes and put her head back, as her thumb depressed on the screen, dialing him, as she felt every ounce of willpower wither and die.

He answered just after the first ring, not even giving her a chance to chicken out and hang up. "Gemma?" His voice was low, sexy as hell, as he said her name.

She had no idea what to say, no idea why she'd called him, just that she was lonely and sad. "Hey," she said, her voice trailing up as she dragged out the one-syllable word. "What are you doing?"

"I'm in bed. What's up?"

"Uh, nothing. I was just out with the girls." She knew she was slurring a little, so she worked harder to enunciate each word. "We had some wine and watched movies."

"Sounds fun."

"Yeah, it was."

There was a silence before he spoke again. "It's late."

Her eyes squeezed shut, embarrassed. She checked the time. It was after 3:00 a.m. She felt like an idiot. Why had she called him? "Shit. I'm sorry. I shouldn't have called."

"No," he interrupted her. "It's good to hear from you. How are you?"

She sighed and thought about lying and telling him how well she was doing. But she went with the truth instead. "I miss you."

"I miss you, too."

"I've got a glass of our rum in front of me."

"Did you like it?"

"I haven't tasted it yet. Have you?"

"Not yet." She could hear movement on his end of the line. "Hold on a second. I've got you on speakerphone," he told her, and she could hear a glass hit his granite countertop. She could hear liquid being poured. "I've got some rum, too. Want to taste it together?"

She smiled. "Yeah, sure." Smiling, she reached for the glass on the coffee table.

She raised the glass to her lips and tasted it. It was delicious, and her stomach curled with his moan of appreciation in her ear. It brought back their nights together, and she wished he could have been there with her then.

They drank their rum in silence for a while. "We did good," she said.

"It is good. It's got me thinking…"

"Thinking what?"

"This rum is good. But it's nothing compared to your recipes, though. I think I brought you down."

"Aw, you're just a little rusty. How are you?" Talking with Tom was so easy. She'd missed him this past week.

"It's been a frustrating week. This is a conversation I would have liked to have with you in person," he explained. "My father is finally retiring."

Gemma blinked in surprise. But the sadness followed. Even if she and Tom hadn't had that fight, their relationship would never have survived this recent development. "That's great news," Gemma said. "That's what you wanted. Now you can do things your way."

"Yeah. If he would have even given me the chance."

"What do you mean?"

"I quit."

"What?" She wasn't sure if she'd fully comprehended what he'd said through the haze of the wine. "Why? Running Cain Rum was the most important thing to you."

"It wasn't the most important thing to me."

She felt tears pool in her eyes. "So why did you quit?"

"My father told me he was retiring, and then he named Carolina as his successor."

Her mouth hung open. "Are you kidding?"

"I wish I was. So, I left. I quit. They're content to keep doing things the same way until you and your brothers put us out of business. There's nothing I could even do to help if I wanted to."

"So, what are you going to do?"

"I'm not sure."

"What happened to starting your own distillery?" she asked. "I remember you telling me about that."

"Yeah. Between us, I would like to explore that option a little more."

"Like I said then, I would love to help you out with anything you need."

"Thank you. I appreciate that. But for now, I'm just trying to get used to being single and unemployed."

She laughed. "Well, seeing as how you don't have anywhere to be for a few days—" She paused. Her brain was telling her mouth to stop talking, but her lips wouldn't listen. "Why don't you come over?" She squeezed her eyes shut, waiting for his answer. It had been a stupid thing to say, and she wished that she could take it back.

He chuckled. "Did you just invite me over for an interstate booty call?"

"No," she insisted. "Because that would be a bad idea. Why? Would you want to?"

He didn't say anything, and she wished she could see his face. She could picture his every feature, every line of his body. In person, she could read him easily, but she could tell nothing from the full beats of silence. He could hear him take a breath. "I do still want you, Gemma. Make no mistake about that. I want to say yes. And if it was anywhere close to being a good idea, don't think I wouldn't be on my way to the airport right now. But I think it's best if I don't, and we say good-night here. Let's not let this get any more complicated than it already is."

Shot down. Swallowing the lump in her throat, unable to speak around it, she nodded. He was right; it was best if they said goodbye. "All right, Tom, if that's what you want—"

"If this was about what I wanted," he whispered, his voice low and dangerous—lust-filled, "I'd be down there with you right now, but it's about what you wanted," he reminded her.

"Yeah," she agreed. "You know, I guess I should let you go. It's pretty late."

"Okay. Good night, Gemma."

"'Night," she said, hanging up. She looked around her empty house. She'd made a mistake thinking that she could go back to her regular life. There was no *regular life* for her anymore. Not one without Tom, but he'd made his wishes clear. He was staying away. She drank the rest of the rum in her glass and blinked back the tears that formed in the corners of her eyes.

She'd really made a mess of things.

CHAPTER TWENTY-THREE

SEVERAL DAYS LATER, Tom looked out the window of the plane as the speaker crackled to life. "Welcome to Miami International Airport," the pilot said over the loudspeaker. He looked out the window and saw the palm trees lining the runway. When the plane came to a stop at the gate, Tom was the first person off the plane. Quitting Cain Rum meant losing his corporate jet privileges. But he would have ridden a bus to Miami if it was his only option.

A short time later, he was getting into a rental car and he was on the road. But instead of taking a route that would lead him to Gemma's home, he took a different one. Lila had given him the directions during their conversation the night before.

He drove up to a large white house and knocked on the door, hoping he wouldn't be thrown out on his ass. The door opened, and Reid Rexford stood before him. Lila had told him Reid would be there. But she clearly hadn't spilled the beans to her fiancé that he was going to show up. The other man's eyes narrowed.

"What the fuck are you doing here?" he asked.

Lila had told him to expect such a reaction. "I was hoping we could talk."

Reid crossed his arms. They were about the same size, but Reid had the home turf advantage. And Tom knew to respect that. "I don't think we have anything to talk about."

Tom shook his head. "That isn't true. We have quite a bit."

"Anything you have to say, it should be to Gemma."

"Before I see her again, I need to clear the air with you. Is Quin here? I wanted to see both of you."

Reid rolled his eyes. "Lila set this up, didn't she?" When Tom neither confirmed nor denied, Reid sighed and wiped his palm over his face, and moved out of the way of the door. "Goddammit. Come in."

Tom followed him into the house, and in the kitchen, he saw Quin sitting at the table, drinking a beer. When he looked up and saw Tom, he muttered, "What the hell?" He looked at Reid. "Did Lila set this up?"

"Yup."

Quin still ignored Tom. "Why?"

Reid went to the fridge and pulled out another beer. "He wants to talk to us, apparently." He opened the bottle and held it out to Tom. "Want one?"

Between Gemma pouring him a glass of wine before dumping him and Reid giving him a beer after begrudgingly inviting him into his house, the Rexfords were raised to be polite hosts.

He joined Gemma's brothers at the table.

"So, what are you doing here?" Reid asked. "Why did you come to us?"

"I told you before that I'm in love with Gemma."

Quin scoffed. "You've got a funny way of showing it. What do you think you were doing with that campaign?"

"Like I told her, I didn't know about it until it was too late. But what happens at Cain Rum is no longer my concern. I left."

"Is that right?"

"I quit."

"Why?"

Tom gave an abridged version of the steps that had led to where he sat at that moment. He noticed Reid stiffen when he mentioned that Carolina was now in charge. "They attacked the woman I love. I couldn't work there any longer." He drank from his beer. "I need to get Gemma back."

"Then why are you talking to us? We have no control over what she does."

"Oh, I know that. Nobody does."

"She's miserable without you," Quin revealed.

"I'm miserable without her."

"So again, why are you here and not at her place?"

"I need your help."

Even though a few days had passed, Gemma's conversation with Tom was still fresh in her mind, Gemma drank her coffee and stared off into the distance of her backyard, not focusing on any one point on the horizon. Her phone rang, and a part of her wished that it was Tom, calling and telling her that he was on his way. But she knew it wasn't. He'd made his wishes known. He might want her, but he wasn't going to act on it. They were over.

When she saw the number for Reid's office on the caller ID, she was surprised. It was Sunday morning. Why was he at the distillery? "Hey, Reid, everything okay?"

"I'm not sure," he told her. "I came in to catch up on some work, and I'm in my office and there's an alarm going off in the distillery. I think it's one of the tanks, and I don't know how to turn it off. You better get over here."

She thought about it—maybe there'd been a malfunction in the tank room again. "I didn't get a notification on my phone," she told him.

"I don't know what to tell you, Gem," he said. "But you know I don't know this new system. I don't want to risk screwing anything up with it."

"Yeah, sure," she said, pushing up from the table and grabbing her keys. "I'm on my way."

Disobeying the posted speed signs, Gemma arrived at the distillery in record time. She jogged to the door and unlocked it. Opening the door, she didn't hear the alarm—had Reid figured out how to turn it off? "Reid?" she called. "You in here?"

Gemma turned the corner out of the foyer and onto the distillery floor. The overhead fluorescent lights were off, but the room was bathed in soft yellow light from the strings of lights that crisscrossed the ceiling. There were bouquets of white flowers lining workbenches, and candles on the table.

"What the...?" she said to herself. "Hello? Reid?"

"No, sorry." She heard the voice behind her that turned her insides to jelly. "It's just me." She turned slowly and saw Tom standing there.

So many questions ran through her mind, but "How did you get in here?" was the first thing out of her mouth. Quickly followed by "How did you do this?" Did he break in? Did he force her brothers to let him in? Then she realized that her brothers must have been behind it. "Reid," she muttered. He'd set her up. But she wasn't angry about it.

"Reid and Quin," Tom clarified. "They let me in. Hell, they even helped put up the lights."

"Well, you must have coerced them at gunpoint, or they've been taken over by body snatchers," she said, taking a couple of steps closer to him. "Because that's one hundred percent more likely than them helping you do this."

Tom shrugged. "You know, I thought so, too. But I guess we came to an understanding."

"What kind of understanding?"

"They understand that I love you more than anything."

Her heart stuttered in her chest. "Is that so?"

"Yeah." He took a few steps closer to her. "What

I said about us not making things any more complicated—I'm a goddamn idiot."

Her heart thundered in her chest, and she nodded.
"That is true. Good of you to say."

"I'm sorry," he told her.

"I'm sorry, too," she said. "I was the one who
pushed you away. I was scared. I wasn't ready to fall
in love with you."

"I know. It is scary," he told her. "It's fucking ter-
rifying to give yourself to another person. But I'm
willing to try if you are."

"What about the distance?"

"I might have a solution. I'm leaving New York."

"Really?"

He nodded. "I had to get out of there. Work, my
condo, the city. There's nothing there for me anymore."

"Where are you going?" she asked, hoping that
his response was the one she was looking for.

"I think I might give Miami a try."

She smiled. "You got a job down here? Because
I'm not about supporting some guy who doesn't
work."

"I was hoping you might have an opening down
here on the floor."

"You want to work for me?"

"I told you about opening my own distillery. I
still want to do that. But I'm out of practice, though.
I was hoping you might have room for an appren-
tice."

She took one of his hands in two of hers. "I think

I can find room for you. As long as you promise to do what I say."

He chuckled, lacing his fingers with hers. "I think I can do that."

"But if you think you're used to the heat, you haven't seen anything yet."

* * * * *

PURE
SATISFACTION

REBECCA HUNTER

MILLS & BOON

To my daughter. You are a shimmering light of joy in my life, just because you are you. Thank you for choosing Ruby's name, but please don't read this book until you're much, much older.

CHAPTER ONE

THERE WERE PLENTY of reasons why the CEO might call her into a private meeting an hour before her official Christmas vacation began, and Ruby Bisset couldn't think of a single one that boded well for her. She scanned the uncharacteristically quiet marketing department of NY Creatives Media. Everyone else had left after the trays of Christmas cookies, blintzes and bottles of champagne had disappeared from the holiday party. Ruby would have ducked out, too, if Cristina hadn't taken her aside at the fig, goat cheese and honey appetizer tray and quietly asked her to meet. She also would have drunk a hell of a lot more champagne.

But the fizzy effect of her single glass of bubbly had long since worn off as Ruby headed through the maze of cubicles, sidestepping stray bits of holiday wrapping, two lost pens and a ripped envelope on the way. With each step closer to Cristina's corner office, Ruby's heart rate ticked up a notch. In preparation, she'd brought the social media calendar she had perfected for Cristina, even though she was pretty sure this was way too late for a chat about strategy. So what was this last-minute, off-the-calendar meeting about?

Some less-than-desirable possibilities came to mind, like the chance that those topless pictures from spring break during Mardi Gras had finally resurfaced. Even after four years, that possibility still lingered in her mind. Jimmy had promised he'd deleted them, but that was only after she'd caught her ex-fiancé sharing them with three of his friends. There were a lot of lessons embedded in that stupid mistake, one of which was never do anything you wouldn't want your whole office to know about.

As the company's social media manager, she should have learned that lesson the first time around with Jimmy. But, apparently she hadn't, which was how she'd ended up getting caught four years later in the hallway of a Hell's Kitchen bar during a company after-hours gathering making out with Raj, the cute, sweet guy from finance. And, of course, in her typical go-big-or-go-home fashion, she hadn't been subtle, which was why they'd been caught by hot-hole CFO, Adrian Wentworth. Who happened to be Raj's boss.

Raj hadn't so much as looked her way since, and Ruby had gotten the sense that this wasn't his personal choice. Adrian hadn't said a word to her either, though he seemed to be putting a little extra effort into his scowls at her since then. This secret meeting couldn't be about *that* incident, could it?

Probably not. More likely: a social media emergency had emerged, and Cristina was going to ask Ruby to work over the holidays.

It wouldn't be the first time she'd been given a hush-hush assignment like that, and the truth was she was having some doubts about her decision to spend Christmas alone. NY Creatives Media was closed for two weeks, and Ruby had made the mistake of telling most of the marketing department that she was locking herself into her apartment to get her photography portfolio in shape. Alone. Which had earned an outpouring of sympathy, despite Ruby's insistence that this was her choice.

Anyway… The point was she could handle trading a few of those days alone for top-secret emergency triage meetings with some high-profile celebrity trying to avoid a scandal. Not exactly what she got into this business for, but she'd get a much-needed lump of cash in the bargain, which was another reason not to say no.

If that was even what this meeting was about.

The executive hallway felt more deserted than Marketing, which didn't help the foreboding feeling. *Please don't let this be about the Mardi Gras photos.* It was probably bad luck to even think about them right now.

Ruby sucked in a breath as she passed the door marked Adrian Wentworth, CFO. Three years ago, despite the doubts he'd expressed very publicly, she had earned her place at NY Creatives Media by giving a stellar crash course in personal branding, the subject of her senior thesis. She'd spent good portions of her time since then helping the higher-ups build their social media platforms.

Well, almost all of them. Adrian had made it clear that even setting aside thirty minutes to brainstorm personal brand ideas was beneath him. *She* was beneath him, and not in the fun, sexy way which, unfortunately, she'd had graphic dreams about— dreams she now couldn't unthink.

Adrian was thirteen years older than she was— yes, she'd looked it up—and that, plus his conde- scending attitude, should have taken away his sex appeal. Sadly, it hadn't, at least not in the darker recesses of her mind. After that first fateful dream, she couldn't stop noticing him. It was as if he'd spent every one of those thirteen years between them sculpting himself into ridiculous hotness, just to taunt her.

The light in Adrian's office was still on, though that wasn't a surprise. He had more than earned his reputation as a hard-ass workaholic, and Raj had let it slip that he expected the same of everyone else. What the hell would he do with himself during the two weeks the office was closed? Reorganize his spreadsheets? Color code his perfectly tailored shirt collection?

Ruby hurried past his door and stopped in front of the corner office, her heart thumping harder.

Cristina Santos was her idol. She had started NY Creatives Media with her husband James, and to- gether, they had built it into the top firm in its niche in ultra-luxury brand publicity. Thanks to Ruby's group, they were getting more innovative with social media marketing, too. Cristina's marriage was enviable, and their happily-ever-after life was made for social media success, right down to their two adorable and camera-ready shih tzus.

Ruby took a deep breath and reached for the handle, but Adrian's office door clicked, putting her into alert mode. Curiosity got the better of her and she glanced his way.

He had one foot out of his office, frozen in the middle of his doorway, staring at her. His usual look of brusque condescension was missing. Instead, he was staring at her in open surprise. Then his gaze dipped down her body. Her skin prickled, and her hands went instinctively to the hem of her short, playful holiday dress. But he wasn't scowling. His gray eyes lit up with unfiltered heat. Her own body went on high alert, and she sucked in an audible breath. The moment the sound left her mouth, all signs of desire on his face disappeared.

What was *that*? It happened so fast that Ruby wondered if she'd imagined it. Before she could decide, Adrian was heading straight for her. Each step kicked up her pulse another notch until he stopped in front of her.

What did he want? To make a crack about her outfit? On Halloween, he hadn't hesitated to comment that they were a professional workplace, not a Midwestern high school. Okay, maybe that cheerleader skirt was a little on the short side, but everyone in the creative department had gotten into the teen zombie horror movie theme, and plenty of the costumes were more outrageous than hers. He hadn't made a remark like that to anyone else—she had asked around—so the critique was personal. There was probably something in there she could report to HR, but the truth was she had made her share of snarky comments to his face. So it was pretty much par for their course.

"Can I help you?" Ruby flashed what her roommate called her trademark Midwestern smile—which she knew got on his nerves.

He frowned. "You're welcome to open that door anytime. Or I can help if you need assistance."

If heat had been in his gaze, it was definitely gone now. In its place was his usual stony expression, paired with the dry sarcasm that seemed to be his default. But now she was a little suspicious. The secret meeting with Cristina involved him, too?

"I can open my own doors, thank you," she said, giving him another smile, "though I know offering to do it is tradition for a man of your age."

He scowled, and she knew that comment had hit its mark. He didn't strike her as particularly vain, but his age seemed to be a point of sensitivity with her, so of course she took every opportunity to bring it up.

"Just open the door, Ruby."

She kept her smile in place. "Sure thing, Mr. Wentworth."

His scowl deepened. No one went by last names here, but she tried to fit his in as often as she could. Ruby shrugged innocently and opened the door.

Cristina's office was sleek and modern, with her degrees and accolades neatly framed across one wall. She was organized and together and all the things Ruby hoped to be in ten years. Everything in Cristina's office was in its place, the way it always was, except for one detail: her husband James was sitting next to her on the couch.

"Ruby, Adrian, thanks for staying late," Cristina said.

She gestured to the chairs, where Ruby and Adrian were apparently supposed to sit. Ruby sank into the plush leather, next to Adrian. His gaze darted down to her thighs, where her dress had ridden up, exposing the tops of her thigh-high stockings. He swallowed, frowned, and looked away in clear disapproval. Ruby's cheeks warmed. Why the hell did she find this man attractive?

She blocked that out and focused on the tone of Cristina's voice, filled with the same hint of nervousness that Ruby had heard earlier over the lunch canapés. Cristina crossed her legs one way and then the other. James took her hand and squeezed it. Ruby searched for something that would make cool, confident Cristina fidgety and came up with... Nothing. This was definitely not about Christmas bonuses.

"Ruby, you're probably wondering why you were called in here, right before the office closes," James said. "I'll get right to the point. We have an enormous favor to ask of you and Adrian, and we're truly hoping that you'll consider it."

Ruby let out a sigh of relief. No Mardi Gras photos. This was about working over the holidays. She could handle that. But wait—with Adrian?

Cristina looked from Ruby to Adrian and back again. "Before we present this, I need you both to understand that this topic requires discretion, whether you take up our offer or not."

"You know I have no problem with discretion," Adrian said, then turned to Ruby, his eyebrows arching slightly.

"Nor do I," Ruby said, staring right back at him.

"Of course. We wouldn't have approached you two if we thought otherwise," Cristina said.

Adrian leaned back on the couch and crossed his arms. A short lock of his hair curled rebelliously over his forehead, the only part of him that he didn't seem to keep in line. He looked like a grumpy ancient Greek statue in a well-tailored suit.

"What's going on?" Ruby asked.

James rubbed the back of his neck, the universal symbol for *you might not like this*. He looked at her. "We need you to take Cristina's place at the Kalani Resort for the next week, and we need Adrian to take mine. Discreetly. We'd like no one to know about it, if possible."

Ruby blinked. Did she hear him right? They weren't going on their high-profile Christmas vacation to Hawaii? Instead, they wanted her to spend a week at an ultra-luxury resort with...

"With Adrian?"

"Yes."

And no one could know about it? "Like...decoys?"

James furrowed his brow. "Um...yes. Like decoys. Both in real life and on social media."

"I see." The social media campaign. The one Ruby had set up to showcase NY Creatives' growing social media department. It would demonstrate their strength with personal branding by featuring Cristina and James enjoying the luxuries of the Kalani Resort over the holidays...as a couple in love. One glance at Adrian told her that he wasn't happy with this.

"With *Ruby*?" Adrian's voice was laced with incredulity.

Ruby rolled her eyes.

"Yes, with Ruby," Cristina said dryly. She sighed. "What we're asking of you is rather...unconventional. But we really need your help. It would be paid time, of course."

Adrian frowned. "I don't give a fuck about the money."

That was easy for him to say. Living in New York City with college debt, Ruby couldn't afford to be so highly principled. Nor could she afford to mouth off to her boss.

James's forehead creased with more worry lines. "It's just a week of stepping in for us. You'd still have the second week of the holiday back home."

"Why aren't you going?" Ruby asked, still a little stunned. This was an elite resort and Cristina had been planning this trip—and the campaign that surrounded it—for months. "We have a lot of clients watching this campaign to see what kind of engagement we can get. And it's your personal brand that's at the center of it."

"I know this isn't ideal," Cristina said. "I'm really sorry, but we can't tell you why. Not at this point."

Adrian opened his mouth, then closed it without replying. The office was quiet, and Cristina shifted in her seat.

Ruby had never seen her look this uncomfortable. The more she thought about it, the more convinced she was that something big was at stake…but Ruby couldn't imagine what the heck it could be. She also couldn't imagine how a week playing this couple would even be possible.

"I'm not sure I understand how this would work," Ruby said slowly. "I'm pretty sure people can tell us apart."

Cristina waved away her comment. "I know we don't look the same up close. My skin's darker, not the same body type…"

Ruby nodded, then made the mistake of hazarding a glance at Adrian. For an instant, she caught that same look he'd had in the hallway, the look of raw sexual interest. Ruby was well-endowed and usually not self-conscious about it, but Adrian's gaze moving down her body conjured scenes from her sordid dreams. Scenes she really shouldn't be thinking about right now.

"Ruby, you created this campaign for me, and you know how many clients are watching to see how well it works, how much potential business is riding on it. I think you know we wouldn't back out if there wasn't a really, really good reason." Cristina cleared her throat. "I understand that close up, we're not similar, but if you get creative with the photos, I think you'll be able to pull off the social media campaign you planned. And there's a very good chance that no one you'll meet in person in Hawaii will know who we are."

"We're similar enough, too," James said, tilting his chin at Adrian.

Ruby had to agree with this assessment. Both were tall with dark hair and broad shoulders. When she first started with the company, she had thought they were very much alike...until Adrian opened his mouth.

But Adrian didn't look encouraged. He scrubbed his hands over his face. "And you're not going to tell us why we're doing this?"

Cristina shook her head, and for a moment Ruby could have sworn that there was a look of true sorrow on her face. "Maybe after the week is over, but that's not a guarantee."

Ruby still wasn't getting how they'd pull off this identity switch. "Okay...and I suppose you figured out how we'll work this with the airlines and the resort?"

James nodded. "We're taking a private jet, so you'll ride with us. We'll drop you off and go on from there, hopefully without notice. The Kalani is very discreet, so it shouldn't be impossible to lie low in the cabin we've reserved. We can just let the resort know we'll need privacy. They're used to high-profile guests, so they probably won't think twice about it."

A week in a cabin with Adrian? The one person at NY Creatives Media who answered every one of Ruby's smiles with a scowl? One glance in his direction told her that he wasn't liking this idea any better than she was.

But either James didn't notice or he was trying not to. "It's a private residence on the beach, with a swimming pool and unlimited food service to your door. We have a few excursions planned, but we can figure out how to work with that, too."

Ruby knew exactly what their vacation looked like because she and Cristina had spent time putting together three fun, romantic posts per day about it. Creating more buzz around Cristina's personal brand made a perfect case study in social media brand management. If it worked and clients took note of what they had done, Ruby was pretty sure she'd get a raise, and maybe also a promotion. But that required the campaign to actually happen.

"So…you want us to spend the week publishing all the posts Cristina and I worked on and taking photos to go with them, like we're a married couple?"

James hesitated. "Yes, that's the gist of it."

"The campaign is ready to go," Cristina added. "We just need you two on the ground to execute it."

Adrian was silent, and Ruby had no idea what to say. Her plans for a quiet Christmas had just turned into a week in a cabin with the grumpy

CFO…pretending to be a happily married couple. Right. This was getting wackier by the minute.

James leaned forward, resting his forearms on his thighs. "I know it's a big ask, but we really need to disappear for a week. The Kalani is a niche luxury resort, so I'm hoping you'll be able to enjoy it, even under these circumstances." He looked from Ruby to Adrian. "We'd be so grateful."

So grateful. Those were the words she had used when Cristina and James had hired her straight out of college, based on her internship and senior thesis. Now at the ripe old age of twenty-five, she could see how she had probably sounded unprofessional and extra-young. But for a company looking to appeal to a younger generation, she had more than earned her keep. Now, Cristina and James were asking for a favor. James almost certainly hadn't intentionally used the same phrase, but the point wasn't lost on Ruby.

The room was quiet. She took a deep breath, trying to make sense of what Cristina and James were asking. Almost everything about this offer was appealing—spending the holidays in Hawaii instead of alone in her apartment, the much-needed financial bonus, while still getting time to work on her photography portfolio—everything except the other half of her new fake relationship.

Adrian's expression looked pained, but he hadn't said a word to protest. He was a big boy, and he could deal with whatever his problem was. She could put up with him for a week…and ignore any future sex-fueled thoughts. And hopefully he could keep his mouth shut.

"Just let us know what you decide," Cristina said to her. "I hope this goes without saying, but if you can't do this, we'd understand. This isn't in any way an obligation. But you worked hard on this campaign, and I wanted to give you the opportunity to follow through with it."

Ruby nodded. "I'll get back to you soon with my answer. Send me the details of when we're leaving and anything else you'd like me to consider."

She started to stand up, slowing as she caught Adrian's gaze. His eyes narrowed, and the tension in the room tightened in the silence, ready to snap. Yes, she knew he didn't like her much, but James and Adrian had been close forever—everyone in the company knew that. Was Adrian contemplating turning down his friend's request? After all the times Adrian had implied that she was young and immature, was he going to pull that middle-school attitude right in front of her boss?

She gave the CFO a sweet smile. "Do you have any questions for me before you decide?"

"No."

She had no idea how that word slipped from his tightly drawn lips, but it came out, clipped and definitive.

"Good," she said, scooping up her belongings. "Because I'm pretty sure I'm a yes. Just send me the details."

CHAPTER TWO

ADRIAN CLOSED HIS eyes and massaged his temples as Ruby walked out and the office door clicked shut. Fuck, fuck, fuck. When James had mentioned taking his place at the Kalani, he'd initially said yes, but if that involved spending a week in a confined space with Ruby Bisset? If the request hadn't come from one of his closest friends, his immediate answer would have been *hell no*. Why had't it occurred to him that if he was taking James's place, someone would be taking Cristina's?

"Adrian?" he heard James say. "Let's talk in your office."

Adrian opened his eyes and tried to force a smile, but he could tell by Cristina's reaction that it wasn't working. Adrian really didn't want to discuss this topic, but maybe James would give him some idea of why they'd made this bizarre request in the first place.

"Fine." He nodded in Cristina's direction and then headed for his own office. James followed him in, closing the door behind him.

Adrian planted both hands on his desk, gathering his last ounce of restraint for this discussion. "This is a really bad idea."

"I understand this is a lot to ask, but two hours ago you were okay with it. You said you had no plans."

"I can't do it anymore."

"I'm getting that vibe. Strongly. I just don't understand what changed since we talked, besides the fact that Ruby will be there," his friend continued. "Honestly, I thought it was going to be Ruby that needed the hard sell. She's the one stuck in a cabin with your grouchy ass all week."

"Agreed." Adrian swallowed. "But she's so…" he massaged his forehead, searching for a way to say this "…young."

"—upbeat?" James finished the sentence at the same time as Adrian, but his eyebrows shot up when he heard Adrian's answer. "Oh."

Young. It was one word, but the strain in his voice clearly conveyed every single thing Adrian hadn't wanted to say. That despite every effort he had made to steer clear of her, he was terribly, inappropriately attracted to a woman who was too young for him. A woman who looked like she was straight out of some college surrounded by cornfields, bubbly and carefree and everything a thirty-eight-year-old man should not be attracted to.

Despite that—maybe even in the darkest recesses of his mind, *because* of that—he found himself fantasizing about things he shouldn't. Not the kinds of things a wide-eyed twenty-five-year-old wanted, like holding hands and walking down the beach. Instead, his mind usually went straight to dirty scenarios, the kind that would make the entire HR department gasp. Because he was on the executive team, which made Ruby off-limits. Completely. Period.

It was why he'd stayed far, far away from her. He didn't even *like* her. Ruby and her sunny smile, innocently walking by the finance department while half his team drooled. It irritated the hell out of him, especially since her smile wasn't so sunny when she directed it at him.

James was looking at him with new eyes. "Oh," he said again, driving home just how bad this was.

"Now do you understand why this won't work?"

James shook his head slowly. "How did I miss this? You're so...indifferent with her."

"Of course I am. I keep a professional distance."

"That's one of the reasons I asked you to do this— you'd never step over the line. The whole company knows that."

"I'm equally asshole-ish to all employees," Adrian muttered. "I'm fair that way."

His friend chuckled. "I was trying to be diplomatic."

James was right. Even if Adrian wasn't on the executive team, he wouldn't have any interest in an office flirtation, as his sister called it. She'd used that term when not minding her own business one evening, and Adrian had mocked her ever since. But Sydney had gotten in her share of digs, so she had it coming. His sister's heart was in the right place, but she should have known better. She'd seen him at his lowest, after the miscarriage, after Victoria left, and she wouldn't have forgotten it. Adrian had, in fact, "moved on from the past," as Sydney put it, but he would never, ever repeat it.

James knew his history, and his friend had done his own share of well-meaning prodding about not spending the holiday alone. Which was probably why he'd asked…though now the man was looking more conflicted about the request.

"Do you want me to explain to Cristina why you can't—"

"No." Adrian grimaced. "Don't tell Cristina. It's a nonissue as far as anyone else is concerned."

James's expression softened. "I'm sorry, A. I'd back out of this but… I can't."

"You really can't tell me why you need me to do this?"

"I promised Cristina I wouldn't." James had that mixture of pain and a little hope Adrian had seen before in his expression. The last time he'd seen it was when Cristina's miscarriage had started, when they still hoped they could stop it. James had come to him, knowing his history, and Adrian had never seen his friend so anxious. Whatever was happening this week, it was definitely serious. James took a deep breath. "You just need to trust me that I wouldn't ask if this wasn't really important."

"Got it. You really need this."

James nodded. The office was quiet, the city

buzzing below them. "You know, you're being a little hard on yourself. She's young, but not *that* young."

"She wore a goddamn cheerleader costume for Halloween. I left early that day."

James's eyes widened, and he put his hands up. "Okay," he said quickly. "I get where you're coming from. But she's in her twenties, and desire is different than actions. Just keep to your side of the bed."

"What?"

"Just kidding. But the place only has one bed, so one of you needs to take the couch. I'm sure it will be a nice one, considering the price of this place." James rubbed the back of his neck. "Sorry. We really weren't planning on this scenario."

"I'll sleep on the couch," Adrian grumbled.

"One more thing." By the look on James's face, Adrian was pretty sure he wasn't going to like this thing either. "This resort is all about granting guests' wishes. Ours was to surprise us with romantic dinners from around the world, and we planned a few romantic outings, too. The staff takes these requests very seriously."

Adrian squeezed his eyes shut. "Fantastic."

Ruby held up the top half of a red-and-white string bikini, inspecting it…or what there was of it. It was tiny and fun, and after her minimalist purge last spring, this was her only swimsuit. It was also true to the minimalist spirit, size-wise. Was wearing a barely there bikini a good idea, considering she was going to spend the week trying to ignore her very unprofessional fantasies about Adrian? Should she even ask herself this question?

Hell, no. She could keep her hands to herself... probably. And she was definitely not in charge of Adrian's. Was he debating the wisdom of wearing his swimsuit around his coworker? Probably not.

Besides, the idea of Adrian in anything but a suit was impossible to imagine. Even in the most lurid of her fantasies, he was always dressed, with just his pants unzipped. She, on the other hand, wasn't. She'd reach in and take out—

Ruby squeezed her eyes shut. She was *definitely not* thinking about that.

She grabbed the bottom half of the bikini and dropped both pieces into the suitcase next to her cover-up. This was, in fact, her most practical choice in that it took up less room than a one-piece, which was why she had opted to keep this one in the purge. Currently, the only suitcase she owned was a rolling carry-on, so everything she packed for the week needed to fit in there, including her camera and lenses.

Was calling Cristina and saying yes to this crazy plan a mistake? Her finances could definitely use the boost. Cristina had made it known that her assistant also posted on her account, so Ruby decided that one more person posting wasn't too much of an ethical stretch. And pulling off this campaign for Cristina would be great for her career—that was certain. Her mother would say she should go. This was exactly the kind of adventure her mother had spent the last twenty-five years feeling like she'd missed out on. But it was making Ruby a little nervous.

A week with Adrian Wentworth? He was the definition of a hothole: a hot asshole who didn't deserve his looks and made her question the biological wisdom of physical attraction.

How could she have sex dreams about this man? She dated easygoing guys like Jimmy. Raj was her type, or he would be if he hadn't suddenly started avoiding her. She'd never been interested in the kind of guy who told her flat out that she was wrong in that bored, irritated voice of his. She was from Ohio, where niceness was practically a religion. She'd never met anyone so blunt—and so smug about it.

There would definitely be taunting this week. Would she do something stupid?

Well, she was still allowed to make stupid mistakes up until her thirtieth birthday. That was the point of her pact with her mother: Ruby promised she'd keep her twenties for herself. She'd do what her mother had never gotten to do: take chances, pursue dreams, et cetera. Her mother's rationale: when Ruby's thirties came around, she'd be ready to make compromises without regrets—and by compromises, her mother meant marriage and family.

There were times when this route was a little lonely, especially since most of her friends who'd stayed in Ohio were already married, and a few had kids. Sometimes it was hard to even talk to them without wanting those things, too. There were also times when she felt like she was following her mother's lost dreams more than her own. But parenting a newborn Ruby instead of finishing college and starting her career had been hard on her mother. Ruby had never quite shaken the feeling that she owed this time to her mother.

Still, her mother's advice had paid off so far. She'd dumped Jimmy and applied for long-shot dream jobs in New York City, and she'd gotten one. Now she lived close to art galleries she'd give anything to be represented by, and her roommate, Dena, was the most interesting friend she'd ever had. Yes, their apartment was the size of her Ohio State dorm room and just as outdated, and yes, she regularly ate ramen to make ends meet on a salary that would have bought her a two-story house back in her hometown. But she was in *New York City*. Even after three years, it was still hard to believe. The other things she wanted? When she hit thirty, she'd worry about that part.

Ruby dug back into the bin marked Summer Clothes, which she'd dragged out of the closet. She sifted through a small stack of tank tops, shorts and sundresses, picking out a few favorites in holiday-themed colors. Low-cut red dress? Yes. Flowered halter top and matching skirt that showed off her stomach? Hell, yes. Working in an air-conditioned Manhattan office year round meant that she rarely had the chance to wear true summer outfits, so she had kept very few, only her favorites, all more adventurous than her office choices.

Ruby lifted her favorite red tank top from the bin.

As she debated, her phone rang. She glanced at the screen. *Dena.*

Her roommate had been gone less than twenty-four hours, and frankly, Ruby had expected a call sooner, though she still hadn't decided exactly how to handle the conversation about her change in plans. She really didn't want to lie, so that left her with the plan of intentional vagueness and an attempt to keep her mouth shut as much as possible. There was a ninety-five percent chance that Dena would attempt to coax out the location of her getaway and about a twenty-five percent chance that Ruby would accidentally slip and say something important. All of which meant she had to keep this conversation short.

"Hey, Dena. How's Southampton treating you?"

"Good so far. The snow is beautiful out here, and I haven't strangled my mother yet. How is life in our empty apartment?"

"Quiet."

Ruby looked around at the sparse decorations that had made the cut in her spring purge. A red tablecloth and some red and silver ornaments in a glass bowl, plus live pine trimmings she had paid way too much for at the flower shop downstairs. It was a little empty without Dena around, but less clutter, less stress…and hopefully, more focus.

"Don't forget that the Long Island Railroad makes trips out here every day," Dena said. "You can change your mind at any time."

"Um…thanks."

When Dena had found out that Ruby was not,

in fact, planning to visit her parents in Ohio for the holidays, she immediately invited Ruby to join her and her boyfriend to spend the holidays at her family's house in the Hamptons. But the fact that Ruby would be the only single person there made her turn the offer down.

The line was quiet, and then Dena let out a sigh. "You really shouldn't spend Christmas alone."

Ruby massaged her temples. "Well…as it turns out, I won't be."

"What?" Another pause. "Are you having a mystery guest?"

"Nope," she said quickly. "I'm going on a secret… uh, retreat."

"With other people?"

"Yes."

Dena was quiet again, and Ruby held her breath, hoping this topic would die.

"Are you going with a guy?"

Oh Lord, how did she answer that? She wasn't going to lie about the trip, especially not to her best friend. "Kind of?"

"What does *kind of* mean? And where?"

Ruby rolled her eyes. "I just said it was secret, girl."

"Even from me?" Dena sounded a little hurt. "Fine. But you better be posting some good photos on your account."

"Uh… I don't think so." She bit her lip, waiting for Dena to reply.

"Are you involved in something shady?"

"No," Ruby said quickly. "Really. I'll tell you more about it when I get back."

But as she ended the call, she wasn't even sure she wanted anyone to know about this setup—ever. No matter how much Cristina and James allowed her to reveal in the future, spreading the word that she'd gone on a fake romantic holiday vacation with Adrian Wentworth wasn't the best career move. The last thing she wanted was for her colleagues to ask about—or speculate on—what happened in Hawaii. In a cabin with only one bed.

Luckily, she was almost sure that, for once, Adrian would agree with her.

CHAPTER THREE

ADRIAN WALKED OUT of the airport toward the car. The warm humidity of Hawaii seeped through his dress shirt and up the legs of his pants. He unbuttoned his collar and tugged at the neck of his undershirt. After eleven hours on the plane, he was beyond uncomfortable. The sooner he could change, the better. Which meant getting into this resort as fast as possible.

He glanced back at Ruby, trailing a couple steps behind him. Her sweater was around her waist, leaving her in tight red leggings that showed the shape of her legs and a white tank top that showed plenty of sun-vulnerable skin. Which he definitely wasn't going to stare at. The red, wide-brimmed sun hat and large sunglasses hid a good portion of her face, but she seemed to be looking around at the scenery... with only a rolling carry-on bag? Did she forget the rest of her bags back on the plane?

Cristina and James were long gone, off to whatever secret hideout they were headed for this week. Adrian frowned. Irresponsibility was a personal pet

peeve. Ruby was very organized at work, but m.
in the rest of her life she was a mess...

He cleared his throat. "I think you forgot your luggage back on the plane."

She stopped, looked at the tiny rolling suitcase she was pulling, then back at him. "Right here."

He let out an exasperated sigh. "I mean the *rest* of your luggage."

"This is it," she said, gesturing with her hands like she was presenting a game show prize. He narrowed his eyes, and she smiled. "I'm spending a week on the beaches of Hawaii. Bikini, sunscreen, beach wrap, sandals...did I miss anything?"

"One carry-on for a week in Hawaii? Are you sure?" They both looked at her little rolling bag, then at the full-size suitcase and rolling carry-on he was juggling. "I thought that women—"

"Stop." She held up her hand. "I need to plug my ears before you say that stereotype aloud." And then...she really did plug her ears. "Go ahead."

She smiled at him, waiting. He just stared at her, completely at a loss, as she continued to watch him.

"Done?"

He didn't know how the hell to respond to this little show, but there was no way he was going to stand there like a gaping idiot. Quick comebacks had never been his strength, which was why he'd always leaned heavily on his repertoire of scowls and glares. But both those approaches were significantly less effective from behind his "disguise"—sunglasses that Cristina and James had suggested—leaving him scrambling to find a way to dig himself out of this.

"We're supposed to be discreet," he said. "We're disguising ourselves as Cristina and James. Walking around in a bikini and flip-flops might make that difficult."

She shrugged. "I am discreet."

"Red leggings?" He gestured to her outfit with a flick of his hand.

"If someone sees a person in a floppy hat, sunglasses and red leggings, they're thinking about her style, not the specific person who's wearing it. And this is the kind of thing that Cristina would wear. So yes, this outfit is discreet, even if it's not subtle."

She said this all with that sweet smile, one that he had long ago mistaken as naive. Wrong. She gestured to his suit, which wasn't at its best after a full day on the plane. "You, on the other hand, are wearing the kind of thing that makes people ask who the hell is wearing a suit and sunglasses on a Saturday in ninety-degree heat? Which calls attention to you."

He glared uselessly at her through his sunglasses. So much for digging himself out of this hole.

She sighed. "We should go. You're probably dying to get out of that suit."

Adrian was aware he was still staring at her, but he hadn't come up with a single retort. The temperature and the plane ride and everything else about the last twenty-four hours was getting to his head because for the first time in weeks, he had the urge to laugh. He covered his mouth, trying to hide any traitorous signs of a smile.

"But a free packing tip for next time," she continued, giving him that cheery smile. "If you leave the office wear at home, you won't need that extra suitcase."

A little chuckle escape from his mouth, and he turned away before another came.

"Ready when you are," she said, heading for the car, but he caught a hint of satisfaction in her expression.

They found their car, and the driver loaded their luggage while they settled in for the ride to the northeastern side of the Big Island. Adrian kept his gaze out the window, trying to forget that Ruby was in the seat next to him.

It was impossible. Even when he shut his eyes, that faint coconut scent found its way across the car to him. He'd spent the torturously long plane ride trying not to think about it. The scent was from her hair. He'd confirmed that in a moment of weakness when she'd dozed off and tipped her head toward him. Ruby had fallen asleep immediately after take-off and slept almost the entire plane ride in a way that seemed incredibly unfair, considering he'd only nodded off a couple times. Plus, it meant he'd had to actively ignore her thigh, resting against his a few times, and once, the way her shirt rode up, exposing a little portion of the soft-looking skin of her stomach. Which he definitely hadn't stared at.

As the car started through the barren lava landscape, Ruby took off her hat and sunglasses and turned to face him.

"We need to talk about the week," she said, giving his crumpled suit a skeptical glance. "I have some ideas."

He, on the other hand, had been trying hard not to think about spending a week in an enclosed space with her. "Go ahead."

"Most obviously, we'll keep close to the cabin as much as possible. I brought along a project to work on, and I'm sure you have lots of work to do."

He actually hadn't brought any work, a first in a long time, but he nodded anyway.

"The social media plan I created for Cristina included posts three times per day. We'll need to start right away with the photos."

He suppressed a groan. "That's your area. You make the plan and let me know what I'm supposed to do."

"Perfect."

Well, at least they agreed on something. At least this time he had resisted the biting sarcasm he used when she offered to help him develop his "personal brand" a few years ago. No one was ever going to see photos of what he ate for breakfast or what he was wearing, and absolutely no one's life was worse for it. Social media felt like an elaborate project in deception, and besides, he already had a personal brand of sorts.

Blunt was the term his family favored, though *asshole* was probably used more often at work, which was perfectly fine with him. Ruby almost probably had used it. Which he definitely didn't care about one way or another.

"Cristina and I planned to post one photo a day emphasizing the luxury, one fun or adventurous activity, and one post focusing on intimacy." Ruby listed them on her fingers in that upbeat voice she used in meetings, like the idea of intimacy was just another part of her job.

His heart thumped harder in his chest, and he swallowed, trying to ignore it. He could get through this.

"The photos should be aspirational," she added.

"They will be, considering that we're photographing a fake vacation."

"They won't be aspirational if we're arguing or glaring at each other, for example…" She gave him a pointed look. "That also applies to pulling off our roles as decoys. Acting like an unhappy couple will get people to take note of us, which we're looking to avoid. And as the person who's fixed more than one public mistake, my experience says it's always the whiff of drama that gets the word out."

He blew out a breath. Ruby was probably right. "So act like a couple in public. Got it."

When he glanced over at her, he caught the challenge in her gaze. "Can you handle that?" she asked.

"Of course I can," he grumbled.

She smirked but didn't comment.

Of course, they were going to act like a couple. What that absolutely didn't mean was provoking her by putting his hand on her thigh right now, just to see if that challenging look would turn into something else. He wasn't even going to think about that.

"So what do you think Cristina and James are up to this week?" she asked after a while.

He shrugged. "No idea."

Ruby raised an eyebrow.

"Seriously. James said nothing."

"Huh." She wrinkled her brow. "You don't think they're going to do something drastic with NY Creatives Media, do you? Like sell the company and move to Nepal?"

He crossed his arms. "Over Christmas? Without telling me, the CFO?"

"Good point." She tapped her chin. "Do you think Cristina is pregnant again?"

The question stunned him, draining all inappropriate thoughts about Ruby and reawakening memories better left buried.

The year before, the couple had miscarried well into their pregnancy, long after they'd picked names and redecorated their spare bedroom. Long after they'd announced the due date publicly. The experience had wrecked James for months and had reawakened Adrian's own memories of loss, still so sharp. Though he'd never say this aloud, the truth was he hoped that Cristina wasn't pregnant—not if it meant the possibility of all that suffering again.

This was the last thing on earth he wanted to think about right now, so to distract himself he focused on Ruby, the lesser of the two evils. She was lovely, really, and he hoped she had no idea about loss like that.

Adrian shrugged a little of the tension out of his shoulders. "Last I heard, babies took nine months, so I'm not sure where they'd need to go for a week over Christmas. And if it's just about getting pregnant, they could have done the job in the bedroom of a Hawaiian resort."

"I suppose you're right," she said, leaning back in the seat of the car.

Of course he was. The truth was that he had spent a good portion of last night trying to figure out the answer to this same question. It was surprising that James had been completely tight-lipped about where he and Cristina were going and why it was so secretive. Something significant was going on, and Adrian didn't even know where to start guessing. Something that required disappearing for a week, without anyone's knowledge?

Adrian took the quality-over-quantity perspective on friendships, and he cared deeply about the friends he had. He had to trust that James had a good reason for the secrecy and try not to take it personally.

But what could that be? As the CFO, he would have certainly heard about large potential business mergers or partnerships. James wouldn't hide something like that from him…would he? And why the secretive visit at this time of the year? Though…there were plenty of companies that didn't close down for Christmas.

Adrian scrubbed his hands over his face. He'd

had a long, boring flight to think this through, and he hadn't gotten any further in figuring out what the hell was going on. The pained look on James's face yesterday was enough to stop Adrian from asking him again. So he was letting it be for now. And concentrating on ignoring Ruby as much as possible for the next week.

Adrian held the door to the cabin open. He had that look on his face that Ruby had seen more than once since they left New York, like he was trying his best to be polite but still wasn't sure if she deserved it. To be fair, he looked at everyone like that, but not everyone was rooming with him for a week. And presumably, not everyone had sex dreams about him either. He was also particularly good at getting under her skin, so the best solution, though possibly not the most mature one, was to get under his.

He had taken off his suit jacket, leaving the button-down shirt that showed off his wide shoulders and biceps. Ruby was trying hard to ignore that, in her dreams, he looked pretty much like this, his hair a little tousled and the sleeves of his shirt rolled up, like he was ready for a different kind of work. She swallowed.

"After you." He gestured into the entryway.

"Thank you," she said, ignoring the hint of irony in his voice.

She stepped through the door, tugging her suitcase behind her. The place was gorgeous, with low furniture, white walls and exposed wooden beams that spanned the high ceiling. In the corner was a palm tree in a tall, white pot, decorated with tiny white lights and red ribbons. There were a few other festive hints of Christmas in the room: red flowers on a woven red linen on the glass coffee table and red candles on the entryway table. She could see straight through the main room to where the private pool shimmered, just beyond the shade of their lanai. Beyond that was the bright blue of the Pacific Ocean, which stretched as far as she could see.

She glanced over her shoulder at Adrian. "I guess Christmas is—"

She stopped midsentence when she caught sight of Adrian's expression. He was staring right above her head with a look that could only be described as abject horror. Quickly, she looked up, ready for some mammoth spider to fall on her head. But there was no spider. Instead, dangling from the exposed beam above was a generous bouquet of mistletoe.

Her heart jumped in her chest, and she glanced back at Adrian, but the panic she had seen on his face was gone. It *had* been there, she was sure of it. This was definitely interesting.

"You're scared of me," she said, fighting a smile.

Adrian frowned. "Don't be ridiculous."

"You totally are," she said, letting a smug smile curve her lips. "What's the matter? Are you scared of finding yourself under the mistletoe with me?"

He didn't answer, but his jaw tightened, giving her all the answers she needed. This was dangerous territory. Though he wasn't her boss, he was still part of the executive team. Did that make him off-limits according to HR rules? Maybe. Did she want to know for sure? Not really, especially considering this whole week was a secret. Which meant what happened in Hawaii stayed in Hawaii. Plus, the fact that she was getting under his skin…this was too fun to stop now.

"It's true," she said, her voice bubbling with glee. "You're scared of kissing me. Have you never kissed a woman, just for fun?"

She was one-hundred percent sure that was not true, but it was clear the comment hit the mark anyway. His jaw was clenched, and his eyes were hot with simmering frustration, but he didn't answer. This was definitely not business-appropriate, but she just couldn't help herself. After all the scowls and the disapproval she and everyone else had endured from this man, she had finally found a little chink in that impenetrable armor. And she wasn't going to ignore it. He deserved a little goading, didn't he? They were spending the week together, and this was a perfect opportunity to level out the playing field a little more.

"Don't worry. It's just a peck," she said sweetly. "I can make your first time good for you."

His expression turned stormy, but he still said nothing. Now she was far too drawn into this game to give it up. What would it be like to brush her lips against the mouth of this unfairly hot man for real? Would it be one more thing he'd approach with cool detachment, like numbers and schedules, or was there another side of him that she'd see? Time to find out…if he took her bait.

Slowly, she untied her sweater from her waist and dropped it on the floor. Next came her hat and her sunglasses. Her tank top was tight, and the neckline dropped low, revealing the tops of her breasts. His eyes darted down, and the fear was back.

"Don't be scared. Many men like…"

Her voice trailed off as Adrian dropped his bag and headed straight for her. She stared as he stopped right in front of her. His gray eyes were filled with the raw sexual hunger she had seen glimpses of, but he was making no effort to hide it this time. A rush of heat coursed through her as they both stood under the mistletoe, so close. There was no way in hell she was backing down now. Looking up into his eyes, backing down was the last thing she wanted.

"Experience isn't the problem," he gritted out.

"Oh, sorry. Is it skill level? I won't judge, I promise."

She could barely contain her laughter. All this taunting was also distracting her from just how badly she wanted to touch him, but it was a losing battle. Her body was alive with the electric spark that jumped and sizzled between them. Holy hell, this might really happen.

"It's been a long day," he whispered. "You. Are. Pushing me."

"And it's so much fun." She stepped closer, so their bodies just barely touched. Tension was pouring off him, mixed with the sultry midday temperature.

It didn't look like a peck was what he had in mind. Not even close. If he gave in, he was going to kiss her the way he did everything else—to win. Ruby wasn't sure what was at stake anymore, but she was definitely going to come out on top.

"You should walk away now," he growled. "You're getting in over your head."

Ruby laughed softly. "Are you sure we're not talking about you?"

His pulse was jumping at the base of his throat. He was so close to giving in, and she was, too. He lowered his head, so his lips were almost touching hers. "You are way, way too young for me to kiss."

Her breath hitched in the back of her throat. Those words shouldn't be a turn-on, but they were. Her defenses were crumbling fast, and she had to end this standoff.

"And you're way too old for me to have a sex dream about," she whispered, her lips almost brushing over his. "But here we are."

A deep groan rumbled in his chest, and then his mouth descended on hers, hot and hard, like he was making a point. A very sexy one. She opened her mouth to his and answered each stroke of his tongue with her own, gently biting his lip, inviting him for more. Another groan came, this one lower, and his lips softened. Then they were kissing, really kissing, and she could feel pent-up hunger simmering just below the surface. Her hand was in his hair, pulling him closer, and his body was a hard wall against hers.

You are way, way too young for me...

Oh, those words. They fueled each slow grind of her body as she moved against his growing cock. This was going to end with them naked, and she didn't even care—

Adrian pulled back without warning, first his mouth and then his body. She opened her eyes and stared at him, a little stunned at how quickly that had gotten out of hand. His expression was wild, turbulent, and he took another step back.

She drew in a steadying breath. "That was definitely not a peck."

"What that was..." He paused, shaking his head slowly. "...was a really bad idea."

CHAPTER FOUR

ADRIAN WAS TRYING to avoid Ruby, but that was nearly impossible in the confines of their resort cabin. Not that the place was small by any stretch of the imagination. It was built in a U-shape that enclosed a pool and opened to the ocean. The entrance was at the bottom of the U and led into the main room, with its high ceilings and low couches. It had an airy, modern design but was still relaxed.

On one side of the building was the bedroom. The only bedroom. It was open, with large windows that showcased the ocean and a king-size bed facing the view. The walk-in closet was big enough to be a room in any Manhattan apartment, and the en suite bathroom was enormous, with sleek gray tile. There were probably lots of other details he might have picked up on if he hadn't been in such a hurry to get the hell away from the room.

He told Ruby that she could take the bedroom and he'd take the couch. She gave him a skeptical glance and told him he could at least take the walk-in closet.

He wasn't sure if it was supposed to be a joke, but he left his suitcases in there anyway.

So that left a little over one hundred and fifty hours to get through before he was safely on the plane and out of bedroom-distance from Ruby. Soon after the kiss that he was not going to think about, she'd asked him to pose for a set of photos that involved his hand, some flowers and the handwritten welcome note from the resort's "wishmaker," who was responsible for granting a wish to the resort's elite clientele during their stay. Why anyone would be interested in pictures of these things was beyond him, but he didn't have any better ideas, so he kept that comment to himself.

After taking photos, Ruby disappeared with her computer, and he tried to sit in the living room and focus on a book. That proved impossible.

A flash of red caught his eye, and he couldn't look away as she walked out of the bedroom and onto the lanai, wearing only a tiny red-and-white-striped bikini. He watched the scene through the glass of the French doors, like a movie he'd buried deep in his mind. She dropped her towel on a chaise lounge chair and wandered over to the pool. Her long, dark hair rippled down her back as she walked, brushing against her skin, leaving the arch of her back exposed.

Fuck. Before his brain had fully registered that he was staring, his dick was hard, and he was right back where he'd been in the hallway, dying to push her up against the wall and give in to all the torturous temptation of her soft body. But he had already messed up once. He really, really shouldn't be watching her like this.

Off-limits. Period.

Now even the living room was a land mine, so that left the kitchen. Adrian paced, the tile cool against his bare feet, trying to figure out what the hell he was supposed to do with himself.

Having a fully functioning kitchen seemed like overkill in this place, considering all the full-service meal options. But there was a coffeepot, a reminder that waiting around for service wasn't really his idea of paradise. What else was the kitchen stocked with? Adrian walked over to the row of cabinets and began his inspection, opening doors, noting the selection of pots, pans and utensils. There was also a curious assortment of food in one of the cabinets, with basics like flour, salt and coffee—thank God—but also some sort of chili peppers and...banana leaves? Huh.

The white cabinets were topped with gray stone countertops, and there was a small oven and gas burners. He opened the refrigerator and found it stocked with fruits, vegetables and an assortment of other foods, including a big hunk of dough labeled *masa*, whatever that was. A list hanging neatly on the refrigerator door included all the food he had found, suggesting that these items must have been ordered by Cristina and James. In their preoccupation with whatever was happening that week, they probably hadn't thought to cancel.

Adrian frowned. It would be a shame to put all this food to waste. What had they planned to make with all this?

He stared at the cilantro and chicken breasts in the refrigerator. He had spent some time learning to cook for himself—it was that or a lifetime of take-out—but he hadn't gotten much further than the basics. Once, in his early days of culinary exploration, he'd seen some show where cooks were given a few, random ingredients, and they had to make a meal using all of it…

The beginnings of a plan began to emerge, one that would hopefully occupy him for a while. He pulled out a stool at the breakfast bar and brought the tablet on the counter to life. Time for a little research. Tomatoes, chicken, masa… He typed a handful of ingredients into the search engine and scrolled through the results.

It was a testament to how well this puzzle was occupying his thoughts that he didn't hear Ruby approaching until she was close. Really close. She passed by him, and he forced himself not to watch her. Step, step, step. Her flip-flops hit the tile, then the quiet knock of cupboard doors and the clink of glass mixed with the shush of the ocean off in the distance. The water from the faucet ran, then stopped. Adrian swallowed and kept his eyes on the screen in front of him. He was *not* going to stare.

Step, step, step. Ruby was coming closer again. He steeled himself against the onslaught of desire shooting through him. *Block it out. She'll be gone soon.*

Then her glass clinked down on the counter, really close.

"I see you brought shorts and T-shirts, too." Her voice had that low, husky tone, and he could feel her sizing him up, heating every part of him. Ignoring her wasn't going to work.

Reluctantly, he schooled his expression to neutral and looked up at her. Ruby was leaning on the counter just a few inches away, resting on her forearms, her breasts barely covered by the bikini top. He was absolutely not going to look directly at them.

"I even brought a swimsuit," he said, trying to keep his tone dry. "There are benefits to a larger suitcase."

He caught a hint of a smile on her lips. "What are you doing?"

"Looking up recipes."

Ruby's laughter filled the room, unrestrained, musical and filled with delight. He fought to hold back his own smile.

"That is not what I expected you to say," she said, catching her breath. "You know this place has meal service, right?"

He grunted in response, then sighed. "Cristina and James ordered a bunch of ingredients, so I thought I'd put them to use."

"Interesting. And perfect for taking photos." She tilted her head a little, watching him. "Well, what did you find? Maybe I can come up with something."

"Do you cook?"

"Not really."

The corners of his mouth tugged up, and he met her gaze. "Generous of you to offer your help."

Ruby rolled her eyes. "The ingredients?"

"Chicken, cilantro, tomatoes, something called *masa* and banana leaves." He crossed his arms and waited, trying not to look too smug.

Her brow wrinkled, and she was quiet. Then she smiled. "Are there peppers? Hot and regular?"

He blinked. "Yes."

"I'll be right back." Ruby disappeared from the kitchen and reappeared a moment later, phone in hand. After a few moments of scrolling, she looked up from the screen. "Cristina was going to make tamales."

"What?"

"Tamales are traditional Christmas food, not just in Mex—"

"I know what tamales are," he grumbled, cutting her off. "I mean how the hell did you figure that out?"

Ruby flashed him a smile. "Her posts on social media. They're a great example of personal branding."

Adrian groaned. Three years ago, when she'd confronted him on his refusal to go through her personal-brand tutorial, he may or may not have described it as "a useless waste of time." Apparently, she had been waiting for this moment to prove him wrong, judging from the smug satisfaction in her smile.

"I thought I remembered seeing these when I was

scheduling some posts. Cristina and her assistant documented taste-testing some of her grandmother's recipes last month." Ruby turned the phone for him to see. "She and James must have planned to make tamales for the holiday."

He looked down at her phone, and sure enough, there were many of the ingredients he had found, all chopped and presented in matching white bowls. Ruby scrolled through more of the magazine-quality photos of Cristina stewing the chicken, Cristina folding the banana leaves…

Adrian's mind started to wander, and he made the mistake of letting his gaze wander, too. Her phone was right in front of her breasts, round and barely covered by little triangles of red-and-white-striped material. Her nipples poked at the bikini top. Two perfect handfuls. Or mouthfuls. His mouth watered as his brain came to a stuttering stop.

"Um, Adrian?" The sound of his name shook a little sense into him, and his gaze snapped up to meet hers. "You want Cristina's recipe?"

She tapped the photo on her phone, the one she had been trying to get him to look at. But he had been too mesmerized by her breast to notice.

"I'll figure the food out on my own," he grumbled, ignoring her phone. Hopefully she'd take the hint and walk away. Far away.

But Ruby didn't move. Her eyes narrowed, and a mocking smile teased at her lips. "Were you… dismissing me?"

"I think we're done with the conversation." He frowned, and her smile grew wider.

"I'm not. I came in here because we need to look at our schedule to figure out what we're doing this week." She gestured to the tablet.

Adrian cleared the screen and clicked on the resort's scheduling app. Ruby leaned closer, and the scent of coconut conjured images of the beach, of sex on the beach…

"It doesn't say where we're going tomorrow, just that we've reserved a boat and two guides." She scanned through more of the days. "No outings on Christmas Eve or Christmas Day, a coastal beach tour on the twenty-sixth, and horseback riding on the day after. Then we leave the next morning."

"Those dinners from around the world are scheduled to be delivered every night except Christmas Eve."

"Which is probably where the tamales come in." She paused. "I've also been thinking that calling each other by different names is going to be difficult."

He shrugged. "I suppose it might be."

"So I propose we make up nicknames for each other, like honey or sweetheart. Something that comes naturally."

He frowned. "None of that comes naturally."

Her eyes sparkled with amusement. "What about dumpling? Or maybe pumpkin?"

He gave her his driest look. "I'll think about it."

He waited for her to leave, but she didn't. She was still close enough to touch, and it was killing him.

"I think we should talk about what happened in the hallway."

"No. We *definitely* should not." Adrian shook his head vigorously, trying to block out the memory of her warm mouth opening, her soft, lush body against his… "No. I made a mistake. I shouldn't have done that."

Ruby gave a snort of laughter. "*You* did that? I believe I taunted you."

"Still, I should have cut it off. It was completely inappropriate."

He frowned at her, but it clearly didn't put a dent in her amusement. "In the best possible way."

His jaw was clenched tight, so he grunted his dissention.

"Come on, you know it was." She waggled her eyebrows at him.

She was teasing him now. Adrian massaged his forehead. He had to get this conversation under control before she took her taunting to a new level. He swallowed. "It's inappropriate just by nature of my higher status in the company."

Ruby's eyes widened a little, and then she laughed. "Just listening to you talk like that makes me hot, you know."

Adrian scowled at her, but she ignored it.

"I know we probably shouldn't but…" Her eyes glittered with mischief. "I'll admit I thoroughly enjoyed that kind of inappropriate."

Adrian blew out a breath. It was time to just level with her, no matter how bad it made him look. "I'm glad you enjoyed it. I, on the other hand, feel like a goddamn lecher. Like the kind of guy who'd go to high school football games long after he graduated just to watch the cheerleaders."

Understanding registered in her eyes. It was a reference to the damn cheerleader Halloween costume that had him in knots for days. That he still thought about some nights. Except the gleam in her eyes suggested his comment was having the opposite effect he'd intended. A flush spread over her cheeks. "You *were* into my cheerleader costume." Delight bubbled in her voice. "Marita said she caught you looking, but I thought she was joking."

Clearly, he wasn't as good at hiding his attraction as he thought he was. Adrian gave her his stoniest glare, but she ignored it.

"Guess what?" she fake-whispered. "I wanted you to notice me that day. And when I got home, I did more than just think about it."

His cock was hardening in his shorts. "You're not helping."

She laughed. "I'm not trying to. Just getting my head around it."

He had the urge to escape. If they were anywhere else, he would have walked out by now. It was how he handled everything he didn't want to deal with: exit. But here at the Kalani Resort, mostly cabin-bound for a week, she had him cornered.

She wasn't going to let this go. He massaged his temples, trying to figure out what the hell to say.

From the first time she'd walked into the NY Creatives Media office, Ruby had made him feel ornery, even more than usual. So why the hell couldn't he stop getting hard for her? She was young and careless and got drunk at the office happy hour. Who had such exceedingly poor judgment to hook up with a coworker in the hallway of a Hell's Kitchen bar? Ruby, that's who. Yes, Raj was a good guy, and yes, some of Adrian's judgment was mixed with the jealousy that had slammed into him when he'd caught them. Why had he been jealous?

Ruby was the opposite of what he was looking for. He wanted a family. A partner to eat dinner with, to sleep next to, to laugh with. Someone who understood him, respected that it took time for him to sort out what he wanted to say. Who wouldn't use his weaknesses against him. It was that simple, or at least it should have been. So why did he have yet another hard-on for a woman who intentionally provoked him? Ruby was so foolishly, seductively carefree. Five years ago, in their first weeks of pregnancy, he'd had these same thoughts about Victoria. Maybe Ruby wasn't any of the other things that Victoria was, but that still should have been enough to make him steer clear of her.

And yet, ever since she'd waltzed into his office at the ripe age of twenty-two, going on in that cheerful voice about social media and his "personal brand" for God's sake, he couldn't get her out of his head.

Adrian ran a hand through his hair. "Look, what happened earlier was a mistake. Let's just agree not to do it again and move on. It's that simple."

Ruby raised an eyebrow. "Does it work like that?"

She was leaning over the counter, her breasts dangling in front of him like two peaches in the middle of his own personal desert. He bit back a groan as all his reasons to stay away faded. Holy hell, he wanted her, and he was absolutely not going to do anything about it.

Off. Limits.

"Of course it works that way," he grumbled, then added, "for *adults*, it does."

Ruby gave him an irritatingly sweet smile. "I'll take your word for it. You have many, many more years of experience in that area."

CHAPTER FIVE

RUBY SCROLLED THROUGH the photos she'd uploaded from her phone. She'd already scheduled all of today's posts not long after they arrived, and now she needed to plan photo scenarios and play around with the wording for tomorrow's. It wouldn't take long to fine-tune the images and captions. Ideally, she could get ahead enough to have a few days at the end without work, which shouldn't be difficult. After all, she was surrounded by paradise. The ocean was straight off the back of their place, just past the row of pineapple bushes—pineapples grew on bushes?—and in the shade, the temperature was hovering right around perfect. Getting a week's worth of beautiful pictures should be easy…if she could just get Adrian to do some more intimate poses.

She looked through the French doors, into the main room, where he was currently reading a book on the couch. Good God, he was so irritating. The only way to handle him was to beat him at his own game. In this case, it meant finding a way to make him regret that "adults" comment. Mature? No. Satisfying? Definitely.

Ruby sighed and closed her laptop, then headed through the French doors to the bedroom. She plugged it in next to her phone and stretched. It was time to put away work and figure out how to occupy herself with real-life experiences in this tropical heaven. She'd been swimming twice today, and both times had been half for her own enjoyment and half to toy with Adrian, though he may not have noticed. A couple had passed by on stand-up paddleboards, which might be fun, but it would be a lot better with someone else. Considering the way Adrian had been avoiding her since they arrived, Ruby was pretty sure he'd say no if she asked.

She wandered back outside, passing the table where she'd been working in favor of a lounge chair. She lay back on the warm cushions, propping one leg up, soaking in the sun. What time was it? Too late to get a sunburn, hopefully. Sunbathing never had been her thing, but the chair was perfectly positioned for a view into the living room.

Ruby slipped on her sunglasses and watched Adrian as he studiously read his book. Despite teasing him for wearing a business suit on arrival, she actually hadn't pictured him wearing anything else or even doing anything but sitting at a desk at work. The serious, older man. The idea itself sparked a shiver. In her fantasies, he sometimes lost the suit jacket and rolled up the sleeves of his shirt, but he'd be entirely focused on spreadsheets or whatever finance people did…until she unbuttoned her shirt or did something that found a crack in all that intense focus.

She studied him more carefully. His shorts and a T-shirt showed off broad shoulders, muscular arms and legs dusted with just the right amount of hair. He was fit, in a way that required the kind of attention Ruby was sure he gave to everything. The only remainder of his work image was his hair, still mostly neat with a few defiant curls sticking up from when he'd run his hand through it in the kitchen. She squinted, trying to get a look at what book he was reading. He must have brought it with him— apart from a few glossy travel guides on Hawaii, the cabin was entirely devoid of books. His expression wasn't relaxed, but she could tell he was giving it his best effort.

They really were opposites. Ruby was barely making enough to keep her ground floor studio in the Bowery, while he lived on the Upper East Side in a building that faced Central Park and had a doorman—yes, she'd looked it up. He'd already made tons of money off one company earlier in his career and was still uber-dedicated to his work, while she wasted entirely too much time on social media instead of getting her photography portfolio ready. On the other hand, they had one similarity that had struck Ruby as particularly interesting: they'd both been planning to spend Christmas alone before Cristina and James dropped Hawaii in their laps. Were his reasons anything like hers?

The doorbell to the cabin chimed, and Ruby sat up. Was it already time for dinner? The change in time zones had thrown off her internal clock, so it was hard to tell. She scrambled out of the lounge chair and headed toward the entrance.

Adrian was already halfway to the door as she ran into the living room. He turned as she approached and froze, midstep. His gaze dipped down to her breasts and his mouth parted.

Ruby slowed to a stop. Her breath caught in her throat. They were so close, close enough to touch. His eyes were intense, so hungry as his gaze dipped lower, raking over her exposed skin. Her breath caught in her throat. Grumpy, by-the-book CFO Adrian Wentworth was giving her the most deliciously lust-filled look, like he was one breath away from picking her up and heading for the bedroom. Oh my, she wanted this version of him.

The doorbell rang again, and the hunger in his gaze dissolved.

"You get the door," he grumbled and headed for the bedroom.

Ruby dashed for the front door, her heart pounding double time as Adrian's *very* adult stare played back in her mind.

After a deep breath, she turned the knob. A man carrying two insolated bags stood on their doorstep.

"Come in."

He gave her a once-over, his eyes widening when he got to her very small bikini. The guy immediately looked away and cleared his throat. "Where would you like your meal served?"

"On the lanai, please."

He made an effort not to look her direction again, and she suppressed a smile.

"Thank you," she said. "We'll leave the dishes outside when we're done."

"Very good, ma'am." he said, his eyes focused on a spot somewhere above her head, then he quickly turned and headed for the lanai.

Ruby headed for the bedroom, closed the door and let out a long sigh. She was pretty sure that, number one, the server hadn't suspected she was a decoy for Cristina and, number two, she had just stumbled on to a great distraction trick to avoid discovery if they needed one: the bikini. Another win for minimalism.

As effective as it had been at getting under Adrian's skin, she was pretty sure that showing up for the day's romantic dinner photo session dressed in three tiny scraps of material was pushing her outfit's useful limits, so she headed to her suitcase in search of something a little more subtle.

Adrian was in the walk-in closet, presumably changing for dinner. As much as she'd enjoy the shock on his face if he opened the door and found her half-dressed, she figured that game would be better played without the staff around. Instead, she grabbed a few things and headed into the bathroom. She took down her hair and changed into a red dress that dipped low between her breasts but hung demurely at her knees. After a bit of debate, she brushed a layer of glossy red lipstick over her lips. Just to get in the mood for the photo session, of course.

After the front door closed—presumably the server leaving after setting up dinner—Ruby headed out for the main room. Adrian was waiting there, his hands shoved stiffly in his pockets, pacing. He had put on a button-down shirt over his T-shirt, and the sleeves were rolled up, just like in her dream. He stilled when he saw her, his gaze drifting down her body. He swallowed visibly. Then he frowned.

"You're bringing your phone to a dinner table?" He eyed said phone.

"I need to take some photos for social media posts, focused on intimacy."

"Fantastic," he said in his driest, most Adrian tone. "Can't wait."

He was using that tone from the office, the one that she found both irritating and inexplicably hot. Ruby searched for something to say that would have the same effect on him, but before she came up with anything good, he was heading for the lanai.

Her steps slowed as she walked out the French doors. The table had been transformed. It was covered in soft white linen, with some sort of red tropical flowers strewn everywhere, between the plates, arranged around the glasses, and at the base of the candleholders. A bottle of wine chilled in a silver bucket, and plates with silver covers were arranged in front of each seat, presumably in the order in which they should be eaten. In the middle of the table was a card. She picked it up and read it aloud.

"Merry Christmas from South Korea." Underneath the greeting was a handwritten menu from

the chef, Alana, which included bibimbap, barbe-
cued ribs, kimchi and a few other dishes she didn't
recognize.

Ruby circled the table, inspecting the flowers.
Adrian took a seat and reached for the elegantly
folded red napkin.

"Wait—don't touch that," she said, shooing away
his hand. "Let me take a couple photos first. Then
we can eat."

Adrian sighed but said nothing, so she got to
work, focusing her phone's camera on different ob-
jects, playing with the settings, capturing the ocean
in the background. She walked around to the other
side, and got a photo of a wineglass, surrounded
by flowers, with Adrian blurred in the background.

"Uncross your arms," she said. "We're going for
relaxed."

"Like this?" He rested his forearms on the arms
of the chair and raised his eyebrows a little, like he
was both humoring her and waiting for instructions.
He sounded…well, *not* annoyed at her, and when he
wasn't frowning and taking jabs at her, it was hard
to ignore how gorgeous he was. That dark hair with
a hint of curl, dark eyes, broad shoulders, long, capable fingers…

Ruby cleared her throat and focused on the screen.
"Um, that's perfect."

"I'm not the expert here, but didn't you say the
theme of these posts was intimacy?" He gestured
to the table. "Not sure a view of our meal is very
intimate."

"I'm getting extra photos, in case I'm short on good ones on future days or if Cristina wants to do anything with them in the future." She winked at him. "Don't worry. We can eat a little, then get intimate soon."

Adrian frowned, and she suppressed a smile.

Ruby finished with the shots of the table and headed for the empty chair, and they both started on the food. Ruby hadn't realized she was so hungry until she was staring at her empty plate. She blinked up at Adrian. He was watching her with that intense look he had. The server had set their places close together, next to each other and facing the ocean, and he was so…there.

"The rest of the photos," she said as she took her last bite. She had almost forgotten them. "Let's use the wine."

It was still untouched. She poured a little into each glass. "And maybe hold hands," she added, resting hers on the table.

He hesitated, and then he laid his hand next to hers, palm up. It was a big hand, much bigger than hers, Ruby ignored the thumping of her heart and placed her palm against his. An electric zing ran through her as his long fingers closed around hers. Her breath caught in the back of her throat, and liquid fire traveled through her.

She hazarded a glance at Adrian. His expression was tight, almost pained. She may be melting into a pile of molten lust, but she was almost sure he was struggling, too.

His words came back to her, laced with condescension. *Of course it works that way...for adults.* He didn't look nearly as impenetrable anymore. This could be fun, and the opportunity to tease him about his own declaration was so tempting.

Ruby fumbled with her phone camera in one hand, trying to get a good angle on their hands. "I don't think this is going to work," she said after a few shots. She slipped her hand out of his. "We need to be closer together. Maybe if I sit on your lap..."

She stood up, and Adrian's eyes widened. "That's...that's not a good idea."

Ruby laughed. "What were your words earlier? Something about adults?"

"Fine," he grumbled, scooting back his chair.

She gave him an innocent smile and slid onto his lap. His thigh muscles tensed under her weight. She wobbled a little, and his hands settled on her waist to steady her. His warm breath blew over her neck. She swallowed, trying to steady the hard thump of her heartbeat, and leaned forward to grab their wineglasses.

"We'll do a toast for the camera," she said, handing one to him.

He took it, and she moved farther back on his lap, leaning against the hard muscles of his chest. He let out a soft groan. Her plan to make him rethink his smug comment was working a little too well...on her.

"Hold out your glass," she said, grabbing her phone with the other hand. "Farther."

"Like this?"

She was pressed against him, and his voice was a rough rasp in her ear. She swallowed, trying to focus on the camera. "Yes. Just like that."

She took a few shots, playing around with the lighting. She adjusted his hand, trying to ignore the electric zing each time she touched him. Finally, she set her wineglass down on the table.

"Let's see," she said, scrolling through the photos. "What do you think about this one?"

"Mmm," he said absently, like he wasn't listening. One of his hands was still on her waist, and his thumb moved up and down in a slow caress. Her breaths were coming faster.

"I think this one," she whispered.

"Mmm," he said again, his mouth closer.

Her whole body tingled, and she shifted to adjust herself. Her rear brushed up against something firm, and Adrian hissed in a breath. He was hard, and it turned her own libido onto high. She shifted against his cock again, this time more deliberately, and his hand tightened around her waist.

"If you keep doing that, you might regret the outcome," he said, his voice tight.

"I doubt it."

"I'll definitely regret it."

"Or you might feel really, really good."

He let out a pained laugh. "Most likely it will be both."

She spread her legs, and both his hands slid down to her hips. Slowly, he moved her against his stiff cock.

"You feel so good," he said.

She brought one of his hands to her breast, showing him how she liked to be touched. "Like that. Pinch my nipple."

He did it, and she moaned. "More."

His cock jumped against her, like it was begging for attention, and a low rumble escaped from his chest. "Fuck. Your tits drive me insane. I've wanted to do this all day long."

"But you shouldn't." She pushed her ass against his cock again. "What would people at the office think of you if they found out?"

"That I was the biggest hypocrite. That every time I warned someone away from you, it was because I was dying to touch you myself."

"But you still want to."

His chest rumbled with a pained groan. "Yes. Hell, yes. I still want to."

"No one has to find out," she whispered.

She shifted to the side and turned so she could see him. They were so close, their height difference gone now that she was on his lap. His eyes weren't guarded and distant. They were filled with enough heat to take her breath away. She was bursting into flames right now, and his stare still burned into her, making the flames shoot higher.

She smiled. "Aren't you curious?"

CHAPTER SIX

ADRIAN HAD TO bite back a groan. Was he curious? He had spent the longest twenty-four hours of his life trying not to be, and right now, he was failing miserably. That word didn't even begin to cover what he was feeling. Ravenous. Desperate. On the edge of doing something really unprofessional.

But with Ruby on his lap, pressing up against his cock and smiling a real smile for him, he couldn't resist touching her. Her cheeks were flushed, and she looked so fresh and ready for whatever came next, so upbeat, like the world wasn't full of disappointments. And damn, that red dress. It was cut low enough in front to give him a nice view of the tops of her breasts. She had shown him how much she liked his hands on them, making little moans of pleasure, begging him to squeeze her nipple again. What would she sound like if he teased her with his mouth instead? He was pretty sure he could come just thinking about it.

Her lips were so close. He swallowed, forcing himself to think of all the reasons he should cut this off. "I'm the CFO. I'm not supposed to be fooling around with you."

Her breath quickened, and her smile grew. "Say it again."

His cock gave a jolt. She was turning his last grasp at being responsible into dirty talk? Oh, he was so fucked. Her pulse at the base of her throat was jumping, and he lowered his mouth to it. "I'm the CFO," he whispered, his mouth so close. "I'm not supposed to be fooling around with you."

She gasped as his lips met her soft skin. "And you're much too old for me."

"I'm much too old for you," he echoed, his voice raw. Her skin tasted like coconut and sex, the same scents he'd caught in the kitchen.

"It's so wrong." Her hand traveled down his chest. Lower. Lower. It was so close to his cock. If she touched it, this was all over. He was going to fuck her right here in this chair.

He put his hand around her wrist, stopping her explorations. "So wrong."

Ruby pulled back a little, and he recognized her expression too well. That sweet smile of hers was laced with challenge. She tugged her hand away and stood up. His instinct was to reach for her, to pull her back on top of him, just to touch her a little longer, to ease that incessant ache for her. He shouldn't, but holy hell, he wanted to. Needed to. The last of his willpower was eroding.

He lifted his hand but stopped as he caught sight of what Ruby was doing. She was inching her dress up her thighs. His hand fell to his lap as he watched her, mesmerized. She pulled up the dress farther, revealing red panties…curvy hips…a soft stomach…a red bra that held the most beautiful breasts he had ever seen. She lifted the dress over her head and draped it over the arm of her chair, her breasts jiggling with each movement. Then she sat back on his lap, crossed her legs and raised her eyebrows, smiling. "What were you saying?"

His brain had stuttered to a stop, and his cock was heavy, heading for full alert. Adrian had no idea what he had been saying, but he was one hundred percent sure it was not nearly as interesting as what was happening right in front of him.

"You're…" His voice faded as he searched for the right way to finish that sentence.

"Almost naked?"

Somewhere, his brain was registering that she was using the tone he had mistaken for innocence. This was definitely not innocent.

"I'm ready to see what *so wrong* feels like," she whispered, her voice husky.

It took him a moment to realize she was waiting for him to speak. But the last thing he wanted to do right now was talk. Right now, the last three years of talking to her felt like one giant web of foreplay, intricately woven for this moment: when Ruby Bisset voluntarily took off her dress for him and only him.

It was like she had peeked into his secret fantasies, where he buried his face between her legs until she screamed his name, like she'd never had any-

thing like it. The fantasy played out in his mind…
After she came, she'd look up at him and ask for
more. With his cock ready to explode, she'd get on
her knees, her hair wild and her cheeks flushed, and
he'd—

No. Hell, no. If he was going to break the cardinal
rule of employee/executive relations, it was going to
be about making sure Ruby was satisfied. He pictured her legs spread for him, her eyes hazy with
satisfaction. His cock gave another jolt, begging for
attention. *Keep it together.*

He nodded to the lounge chair she had sat in earlier. "I watched you on that chair in that fucking bikini this afternoon. Want to know what I was dying
to do?"

Her smile brightened. "Show me."

Before he could respond, she stood up and headed
for the chair. Adrian watched her, memorizing this
view, from her long hair that hung down to her waist,
to the panties that left most of her ass exposed, down
her long legs. He had tried so hard not to look when
she walked around in her bikini, but now, now he finally could stare. He rested his hand on his cock as
he followed the curve of her waist, her hips, imagining what they would feel like under his hands right
now.

She stopped at the same chair that she had chosen earlier, sat down and lounged back, with one
leg bent, exactly the way she had sat that afternoon.
Ruby didn't pay any attention to him. Instead, she
closed her eyes, like they were back to earlier that

afternoon, before they had discussed limits and parameters. Like she was inviting him to just come and take.

Adrian took his time. He adjusted his cock, squeezing it as he anticipated the scent and the taste of her. Imagined kissing her. Licking her.

He stood up. His erection was in his hand as he walked across the lanai, onto the uncovered portion of their private deck. Her gaze was on the pool, glittering with the echoes of the setting sun, but when he came closer, she feigned surprise. She looked down to his cock, her eyes wide. It pulsed in his hand, jutting out against the material of his shorts.

He said nothing. Instead, he lifted one of her legs and placed it gently on the ground. He took the other and set it on the other side of the lounge chair, so she was spread for him, exposed, with just the scrap of her red panties covering the place he wanted to be more than anywhere else on earth right now. He knelt down on the wood of the deck, in front of the lounge chair, positioned between her legs. The distance was just about right if he bent forward, so he did. With his hand, he traced a slow line up one thigh then the other, feeling the softness of her skin under his fingertips. Then he used his mouth, tracing that same line up one leg, tasting her skin. This was heaven.

"Closer, sweetheart, closer," he whispered, slipping his hands under her ass and urging her forward. "Let me show you."

He kissed a trail up her other thigh, listening to her sighs, noting each time she quivered. She liked when he used his tongue, so he did it again, teasing, moving higher. She gasped, and his cock throbbed in his pants. Slowly, he lifted his hand and traced the lines of her panties, one side, then the other. He slipped his fingers under the fabric, brushing over her soft folds, and moved the material aside. Finally, right in front of him was the place he had been dreaming about for far too long.

He took a moment to simply look. Then he leaned forward and kissed, soft and reverent. That was just for him. But her gasp told him to do it again, so he did. He worked his way up to her clitoris, kissed it first just with his lips, then with his tongue. How did he resist so long? All that time, he could have been tasting her, listening to her moans.

She was trembling, and then she was begging, *please, please*, and it took all his willpower not to give in, unzip his pants and give her his cock, too. The sounds, the soft breeze from the ocean, her voice, it was all too much. Her trembles turned to shakes, and her moans turned to cries until she came. He eased her through it, milking each shudder of pleasure until her cries turned to breathless sighs.

He had given this to her.

His cock was painfully hard, and seeing her like this was too much to resist. *Mine.* Years of pent-up want for this woman pulsed through him. Before he could think through what he was doing, Adrian rose and set one knee on the lounge chair and one foot on the ground. His fingers grasped for the zipper of his shorts, but a reminder rang out from the back of his mind.

Her pleasure. The transgression wasn't as bad if it was about her pleasure. If he followed the cardinal rule of keeping his pants zipped.

He forced his hands away from his zipper. The darkening sky and the want throbbing through him blocked out everything except the woman in front of him.

Slowly, Ruby rose, propping herself up on one elbow, then the other. She looked so sexy with her cheeks flushed and her hair messed, and it took everything in him to resist. She blinked up at him. "We're stopping here?"

"I'm dying to fuck you." He swallowed, summoning the last of his reason. "But I can't."

"What?" She gestured to the erection straining against his shorts. "But... I know you want to."

"This isn't the first hard-on I've had for you, Ruby," he said. Then he couldn't resist adding, "I'm an adult. I can handle it."

Her eyes widened, and for one heart-stopping moment, Adrian was sure she was mad. But then she tipped her head back and laughed.

"I'll remember that," she said, shaking her head.

He'd probably regret those words later, but seeing her laugh was worth it.

Ruby pushed herself up to sitting. Her breasts moved, taunting him, reminding him of how much he still wanted her. The lacy red panties were his own private bullfighter's cape, taunting him. But he wasn't an animal. He could resist.

She leaned closer, tracing the edge of his shirt collar with her fingers. "It makes me hot all over again to see that you're still dressed."

With a little smile playing at her lips, she stood up and headed for the pool. She slid her panties down her legs, bending over, giving him a breathtaking view. His cock gave another jolt, this one of regret.

Adrian forced himself to squeeze his eyes shut and keep them that way until the splash of the water told him he was safe.

CHAPTER SEVEN

WHEN HER ALARM went off the next morning, Ruby was already awake. Was Adrian awake, too? No sounds from the living room yet. She lay under the soft, warm covers, last night playing through her head. The teasing, the waiting, the touching, the pleasure…and Adrian's restraint.

She wasn't sure if she was frustrated at him for holding back or if she felt sorry for him. Afterward, he had sat on the lounge chair, watching her swim, like he was her grumpy lifeguard, until she climbed out. Then he walked off to take a shower, presumably to take care of business, so she didn't feel that bad.

But oh, Lord, was last night hot…and totally against the rules. Far, far sexier than anything she'd done with Jimmy, who had been too concerned with his own image as a college football star to pay too much attention to her experience, in bed or out.

After the Mardi Gras photos debacle, Ruby had been tempted to take up the larger how-not-to-treat-women discussion, but it was easier just to break up…much to her mother's delight. Her mother had warned her that settling down at a young age was exactly the kind of trap that led to twenty-five years of resentment. And her mother would know. Still, before Mardi Gras, Ruby had been tempted.

Those photos still haunted her, and it wasn't just because of the threat that they'd resurface one day. Jimmy had betrayed her trust when he'd shared those photos with his friends. This was the person she'd lived with her senior year, instead of her friends? What kind of judgement did that show on her part? The kind that suggested she had a lot more growing up to do before she made any serious decisions about her life. Was fooling around with Adrian another impulsive mistake she'd ultimately regret?

Yet she wasn't supposed to be spending her twenties second-guessing herself. Plus, the pictures had their upside. They had been the push Ruby needed to try out her mother's advice and do the most exciting, most intimidating thing she could imagine—pack up her belongings and move to New York.

Ruby decided she wasn't going to worry about last night with Adrian. If it was a mistake, there was nothing she could do about it at this point. Besides, there were more immediate things to consider, like the fact that they were going to spend the day pretending to be Cristina and James, happily in love... or at least not conspicuously avoiding each other. Even if avoiding each other was a completely believable portrait of many marriages...like her parents', for example.

Ruby frowned. What made couples happy together? The ones she'd met seemed to have a mix of lucky circumstances, great sex and a little magic.

She stretched and rolled out of bed, heading for the bathroom as she contemplated the idea. Her only experience in a real relationship was with Jimmy, which was fun and comfortable but nothing close to magic. Still, they'd discussed marriage at the end of college, when the future stretched out like a hazy abyss in front of her and everyone around her was pairing off. Of course, he'd said he'd support her photography, but that support wavered as soon as it involved her "unrealistic" idea of moving to New York City. Yes, her mother's advice had definitely been spot-on.

Ruby splashed some water on her face and brushed her hair, studying her reflection in the bathroom mirror. Her loose white tank top made for a passable nightshirt, though it was more than a little see-through and barely long enough to cover her ass.

Maybe she should go out and make some coffee in the kitchen, dressed just like this, just to tease Adrian a little. How would he react the morning after if she was only half dressed? If Adrian's power lay in his silences, hers was in her ability to throw him off, to shake that control he wielded over everything. And here in Hawaii, it was so much fun to let that take a sexual turn.

Ruby yawned. Yes, half-naked coffee was definitely in order.

She searched her toiletries kit for a hair tie. Then, twisting her hair high over her head, she wound it around into a bun. As she secured it, she caught a flash of movement in the mirror. Adrian stood in the doorway, frozen midstep. His mouth was parted, and he licked his lips as his gaze traveled over her rear, barely covered in skimpy underwear, and down her legs. A fresh streak of heat shot through her.

Ruby looked over her shoulder and smiled at him. "Good morning."

He stiffened, and the open lust disappeared from his face. "Shower," he muttered and walked away.

Oh. They were back to caveman grunt mode.

She walked out of the bathroom, and Adrian disappeared into it without a glance in her direction.

Ruby changed into her bikini and a gauzy, white cover-up with long sleeves that would hopefully keep the sun off her while they were on the boat today. She headed into the kitchen and found the coffeepot full, with an empty cup next to it. A pang of guilt ran through her as she surveyed the tray of fresh croissants and fruit on the counter, decorated with flowers and with more than enough food for the two of them. Her mind was on teasing Adrian because he'd resisted the night before, while he had thought to order breakfast for the two of them. Maybe she should ease up on him a little?

To be decided. Ruby poured herself some coffee and filled a small plate with an almond croissant and a few slices of some kind of orange fruit. She sat down on one of the bar stools at the counter, checking her phone for messages. There were missed calls from earlier that morning.

Her mother had left a message saying the house was very quiet and that she'd call back on Christmas, if Ruby had the time to talk—quick and guilt-laden, as usual. Dena's message was longer, filled with guesses about where Ruby was. A silent meditation retreat? A nudist colony? Dena's message ended with a plea to call her and give her more hints, which Ruby took as a reminder not to talk to her friend— she'd definitely start spilling more details.

It was probably better to just block out all the things she missed and focus on what this Christmas had going for it: an ultra-luxury resort and hot, frustrating but amusing Adrian Wentworth.

Adrian appeared in the doorway not long afterward, looking freshly showered and sexy in shorts and a T-shirt. He was making it hard to focus on the practical details.

"So…we're spending the day in public," she said, brushing the crumbs from her hands. "Are we ready to act like a married couple?"

He lifted his eyebrows in that same way he always did, like he was assessing whether or not he should respond. "You mean calling each other sweetheart and looking lovingly into each other's eyes?" he asked, deadpan. "Always ready."

She snorted. In a million years she couldn't imagine Adrian doing either of those things. "Today I'm hoping to take a lot of photos I can use for the scheduled posts over the next few days. Ideally we can get all of the photos done soon."

His eyes widened. "And then you're just…done? Days before we leave?"

She shrugged. "Great photo opportunities don't come on schedule, three times per day. But I'll spend some time responding to comments, so I won't be done."

"You'll respond from Cristina's account? You're ruining the last of my illusions about social media."

Ruby grinned. "Yeah, right. I'm sure you're devastated by the news that people's posts are collaborations…and rarely spontaneous."

Adrian's mouth twitched up into a smile.

"Seriously, I'd like to get some great photos today on all the themes." She winked at him. "Including intimacy."

Adrian's eyes went dark, like they had when she caught him looking at her in the mirror earlier. He was definitely thinking about intimacy right now… in detail.

And now she was, too. She flashed to the kiss under the mistletoe yesterday. His big, hard body against hers. The groans of pleasure he made when he came back for more, more.

Adrian swiped a hand over his face, and the look was gone. "You ready? Let's get this over with."

Ruby took the last swig of her coffee and stood up. "You are in a tropical paradise, you know. Not many people just want to get a day on the ocean 'over with.'"

This got the first real smile from him all morning. "I am not many people, Ruby."

She gave him her best skeptical look as she passed by him on her way out of the kitchen. In the bedroom, she gathered a few essentials in a bag, brushed her teeth, let down her hair and plopped the enormous, red sun hat onto her head. Adrian was waiting for her by the front door, sunglasses in hand. She adjusted her hat in the mirror.

"Do I look like a passable version of Cristina?" she asked over her shoulder.

"You look lovely, Ruby."

For once, he sounded completely sincere.

Slowly, she turned around. Her breath stuttered when she met his gaze, full of want. Memories from the night before came back—the way his fingers flexed against her skin, the way his tongue moved between her legs, and the look of dark lust when she came. What had happened between them last night wasn't even close to over.

She glanced up at the mistletoe, hanging halfway between them, then back at Adrian. How could one little twig hold so much temptation? He swallowed visibly.

"Should we practice kissing like married couples do?" she tried.

He shook his head, but he was walking toward her. He stopped right in front of her, almost touching. "You know exactly where that will lead."

Adrian turned around and walked out the door before he did anything stupid. Like kiss her, just one more time. But after last night, he was pretty sure

they'd wind up on the floor, with his mouth between
her legs all over again. Or worse. He'd managed to
keep his pants zipped last night, but he wasn't sure
he had the will power to do it again.

He headed up the path from their cabin and
stopped to wait for Ruby at the main trail. She didn't
appear. He sighed. Tapped his foot. Checked his
watch. They had ten minutes to get to the docks before they were running late. Which drove him crazy,
even on a vacation.

Finally, she appeared, moments later. Her cover-
up was more see-through than he had noticed earlier, and for the first time, it occurred to him that
they were spending the day with other people...who
would also be free to look at her in a bikini.

Nope. Not thinking about that.

"We need to walk fast to get there on time," he
said and started toward the docks.

They walked through the resort, passing a series of tiered pools connected by waterfalls and an
open-air restaurant across the resort's small pen-
insula. They passed another couple, well-dressed,
both a little older than Adrian. The man's gaze slid
from Ruby to Adrian and back to Ruby in a way that
had him itching to step up to the guy and tell him to
keep his eyes off her. The man was probably twenty
years older than her, and he was looking at her like
he wanted her.

Mine. The word rang through him, and his whole
body came alive with echoes of last night by the

pool. Her soft skin, her moans of pleasure, the scent of her everywhere.

Adrian gritted his teeth. He'd do anything to make this lust for her go away. Last night had left him restless, on edge. Even though he'd gotten himself off in the shower, both last night and this morning, the ache for her hadn't eased. Both times, he'd tried to keep his fantasies in line, forcing himself to imagine making love to an age-appropriate wife as they tried to get pregnant. *That* was what he wanted, not a young, carefree coworker who was supposed to be off-limits. Unfortunately, the off-limits part still had the opposite effect it was supposed to. Still, he persisted, focusing on what he really wanted. Contentment.

The fantasy worked for the first few strokes, but the images of Ruby crept in. Of her spread out on the lounge chair. Of unzipping, giving himself a few hard strokes, and then sinking into her.

Both times, as soon as his mind went there, his whole body seized up, and he came with a force that left him slumped against the shower wall, shaking. But as soon as his breaths slowed, the ache for her came back, nagging incessantly at him.

It didn't even make sense. This was the opposite of the kind of ease and contentment he wanted. Sex was a red herring in relationships, irrelevant, and a distraction from all the things that mattered to him, like companionship and a readiness to start a family. This was why he'd made a dating rule about no sex until after six dates: to make sure he was thinking clearly about his compatibility with a woman, not just whether he wanted to have sex with her again. Unfortunately, he never made it to six dates these days, and the lack of sex certainly hadn't left him thinking very clearly, considering last night's events.

"What are you frowning about now?"

He shook his head.

"Come on," she said, slipping her arm through his. "I'm your wife, remember?"

He suppressed a groan. The word *wife* together with the bolt of electric want that raced through him when Ruby touched him was jarring. Adrian swallowed, trying to focus.

"None of your business, wife," he grumbled.

She gave him her sunniest of smiles. "Of course it is."

Adrian sighed. She wasn't going to drop this. "That guy we passed was leering at you."

"I didn't notice."

"Doesn't it bother you? He was probably in his fifties."

Ruby chuckled. "Maybe I like older men."

He scowled, but that only made her laugh harder.

"Seriously, you think I should care about some married dude who can't keep his eyes to himself? That's not my problem." She shrugged.

Fantastic. She didn't care. It was bad enough in the office, when he'd barked at Raj to keep his eyes to himself. Now it wasn't even his business.

She tipped her head to the side, like she was considering it further. "I guess it's a little depressing to think about, generally. It doesn't speak highly of marriage."

"You're not a fan of marriage?"

"Not true. I'd like to get married after my thirtieth birthday."

He blinked down at her. "What?"

"That's my plan. It's not very interesting."

"Humor me."

She sighed. "When I moved to New York, I made a pact with my mother that I'd be selfish until I turned thirty. You know, do all the things I want, follow my dreams, et cetera. Then, after I turn thirty, I'd do things that take a lot of compromise, like relationships and family."

Why would anyone make a pact like this? And what the hell kind of plan was that? Did she think getting married was something you just decided to do, like joining a gym or choosing a restaurant? It was ridiculous. If it worked that way, he'd be married, with a couple of kids and living in the suburbs.

But his irritation was mixed with a twinge of disappointment that settled in his stomach, which only irritated him more. Ruby Bisset was the opposite of what he was looking for. Her view on relationships had absolutely nothing to do with him. Why it bothered him… Well, he didn't want to even think about it.

"Interesting," he muttered.

"That was very diplomatic of you, Adrian. I can see that frown of yours."

He suppressed a smile. He wasn't the only one

paying close attention. "And what are you doing with all this follow-your-dreams time?"

She shrugged. "Have fun. Travel. Live for the moment. All those clichés."

He rolled his eyes.

"Seriously, I've been exploring photography. Techniques, but also why we take photographs. I mean, these days, we can find incredible professional photographs on the internet of just about everything. So why do people still come to New York and take photos of the Empire State Building or the Statue of Liberty? Not to get a better photo. I want to explore that."

He thought about her question. Actually, it was a good one, an interesting one.

"And then you have people on social media taking amazing, professional-quality photos of everyday things, like books or coffee, making that kind of everyday, mundane reality extra special. I want to explore the why behind that, too."

"I see." He thought about those ideas. "That's interesting. Really interesting."

"Even though it's about social media?" she teased.

He gave her a look that was probably lost behind his sunglasses.

The path split, and they took the turn toward the water. Ruby slowed as they passed a couple lounging in an outdoor canopy bed, the long white curtains half drawn. A Kalani staff member was serving them drinks on a tray decorated with the same red flowers on Ruby and Adrian's dinner table the night before.

Adrian checked his watch. Two minutes.

"You ever been somewhere like this?" she asked.

He looked at his watch again, but she didn't take the hint. He sighed. "I've been to Hawaii but never to a resort like this."

"This is the kind of place I dreamed of when I was younger."

"Hawaii?"

"Anywhere with palm trees. Not many of those in Ohio." She smiled up at him, and some of his tension about being late faded. "I'd look at photos of places like this, wondering what it would be like to be there."

He blinked down at her as she watched the couple talk and laugh with the server, little snippets of their conversation floating toward them in the breeze. She wanted this. He, on the other hand, had the money to come to places like this, but he found no joy in traveling alone.

"Someday I'll come back, for real," she said quietly.

There was so much longing in her voice that he had the strange urge to promise her it would happen. He squashed that thought and tipped his chin in the direction of the docks just down the hill. "Ready?"

Ruby nodded, and they continued along the path toward the water. A private boat was waiting for them, tied to the longest dock. It was a large speedboat, with white seats and a sun canopy over a portion of it. As they approached, a man wearing a captain's hat stuck out his hand.

"Mr. and Mrs. Santos? I'm Kiran, your guide."

Mr. and Mrs. The words sent a zing through him. Santos wasn't his name, and Ruby was so very far from his wife, but still there was a rush of satisfaction in that moment.

Adrian blinked, reality coming back into focus. Damn. Maybe Ruby was right—some sort of nickname was a good idea. It was definitely better than hearing Mr. and Mrs. all day. He glanced over at Ruby, who was giving her sunny smile to their guides. Adrian suppressed a frown. He had to work so hard to get real smiles from her, and they mostly came when she was laughing at him. Why did the rest of the world get them so easily?

"This is Dan, my assistant," Kiran said, gesturing to the man who was lifting bags and boxes from the dock and loading them into the boat. Dan smiled and took their bags. Kiran handed them each a map.

"We're going to drive down the west coast of the island and stop in a few areas that are particularly good for viewing marine life," he said, tracing the route on Ruby's map. "It'll take us over an hour to get to our first spot, and then we'll work our way home."

Ah, viewing marine life. That was what they were doing here.

Dan handed them life jackets and helped them into the boat. He pointed to a white, L-shaped bench. "If you want to stay out of the wind and sun, this is a good spot."

"Thanks," Ruby said, settling onto the bench.

Adrian's steps slowed, and his body went on high

alert. For the next hour, he was going to sit next to Ruby, who was wearing an almost nonexistent bikini and see-through cover-up. While pretending to be her husband. Somehow, he hadn't seen this coming. How the hell was he going to keep his distance?

She brushed her long, dark hair over her shoulder, seemingly oblivious to his struggle.

Three years of shutting her off at work told him that he was capable of doing just about anything if he forced himself to. He swallowed, thinking about yesterday. She'd pushed him a little and most of his self-control faded. What would it take to shred the last of it? He swallowed. Hopefully he wouldn't find out.

Adrian headed for the bench where Ruby was seated and sat down, leaving room for a whole separate person to fit between them. He leaned back, trying to look more easygoing, which was a stretch even on his best days.

Ruby slid over on the bench until she was right next to him. She gave him a cheery smile. "Hello, *husband.*"

He shifted, trying to put a little distance between them.

"You're not supposed to be scared of your wife," she said, just over the buzz of the motor. "You're supposed to be charmed by me."

"I'm completely charmed. Can't you tell, *darling*?"

She laughed, which put him a little more at ease. The boat sped up, and she lay her hand high on his thigh to steady herself. His cock jumped to life, and a groan slipped out, covered by the hum of the motor. It was beautiful torture, and if she didn't move her hand soon, he was going to have a full hard-on right here for the boat crew to see.

"Sorry," she said, not sounding very sorry as she moved her hand away.

They raced along the coast, the wind blowing around the side of the canopy, with Hawaii on one side and the volcano of Maui rising up in the mist on the other side.

Ruby pulled her phone out from her handbag and captured a few shots of the water and the mainland. She switched over to selfie mode, getting photos of her hair or her shoulder with the scenery in the background. He stayed close as she switched seats, making sure she didn't fall as the boat bounced over the waves.

"What does this function do?" he asked, pointing to an icon she hadn't used.

"It's filters for selfies. I'll show you." She held up the camera so he was in the frame, too, and just as he opened his mouth to protest, she said, "Smile," and took a picture.

"Not cool," he said, shaking his head.

"Should I have let you fix your hair first?"

His grumbling response was completely lost in the noise of the motor.

The image of the two of them came up on her phone again. Ruby looked so happy with her carefree smile. His mouth was parted a little but...was that a smile, too?

"Perfect." She elbowed him in the ribs. "That wasn't so painful, right?"

Before he could think of an answer, she turned away to slip her phone into her bag. Then she pulled out her own camera and started taking photos of things he wouldn't have expected, like the spray of the water coming off the boat and the pattern of the clouds. He watched her work, trying to keep up with what she was doing as she adjusted aperture and speed settings. After a few quiet minutes, she seemed to notice his interest.

"Just watching," he said, nodding to the screen of her camera. "I wouldn't have thought to take any of those pictures, but they really capture the feel of being here, on the boat. Impressive."

She met his gaze from over her sunglasses. "I could have given you some photography tips…if you'd agreed to my social media training."

Of course, she had to bring that up.

He swiped a hand over his mouth, trying not to smile, but it was impossible to hold back. "Fine. You were right. I shouldn't have turned it down without knowing anything about it."

"I forgive you. But I reserve the right to gloat, too."

She put her camera back into her bag and tucked her legs under her, watching the landscape. He had the urge to pull her onto his lap and tease her back, giving her a little of the sweet torment that had dogged him all morning. Maybe put his hands high on her thighs, just to see how she'd react. She was so close…and this was so not a good idea. He had to remember that last part.

The drier landscape of the north shifted to the greener hills of the south as they rode past beaches and inlets. The boat slowed as they turned in toward a cove, just beyond one of the tall coastal hills. As they puttered along, Dan took a seat on the other stretch of the L-shaped bench. He smiled at both of them, but Adrian could have sworn that the guy's gaze lingered a little longer on Ruby than necessary.

Adrian put his arm along the back rest, behind Ruby, hoping his point was clear.

"Is this your first time out on the Pacific?" Dan asked.

Ruby glanced at Adrian, looking for help. When was the last time James had been to Hawaii?

"It's, uh, been a while," Adrian hedged.

"Are you from the island?" Ruby asked.

Dan shook his head. "Southern California. But I've been here for almost five years now."

Ruby took over the conversation, deflecting anything that was remotely personal and steering it back to Dan. The guy was young, probably about Ruby's age, with a deep suntan, an overgrown haircut, and the kind of laid-back attitude that would be trampled all over in New York. But here in Hawaii, he looked completely at ease, like there was nothing else on his mind besides the day ahead of them.

In other words, Adrian's polar opposite. The only thing he had in common with this guy was their mutual attention on Ruby. And now that Adrian had noticed, he couldn't unsee it. He watched Dan closely, looking for hints that behind his sunglasses, Dan's gaze wasn't staying on her face.

If Ruby was here on her own chosen vacation instead of being locked up with Adrian, was this the kind of man she would have flirted with? Adrian watched as their conversation flowed easily back and forth. It was a skill Adrian had long given up on mastering. Then again, it didn't matter. Even if she would have chosen someone younger and more fun, Adrian was the one playing her husband. And he was the one who had made her come last night. Even if he shouldn't have.

"This little bay has everything," Dan said, pointing out toward the shore. "It's a beautiful spot for just about any water activities."

Ruby turned to look, and Adrian caught the guy's head dip down, in the direction of her bare thighs. Adrian gritted his teeth, battling the strong urge to show this young frat dude that this was *his* wife. Well, she was his fake wife, but right now, it didn't matter.

Adrian lifted his arm from behind the seat and rested his hand high on Ruby's thigh. She turned to look at him. Her sunglasses made it impossible to read her expression, but a smile teased at her lips, so he bent down and brushed his mouth against hers. Goddamn, he'd been aching to kiss her all day, and it felt too good to stop. Soft lips, the electric spark jumping between them, and the scent of coconut everywhere. Oh, how he wanted this woman. Adrian could feel his resolve to keep his pants zipped waver, but he could worry about that later. Right now, he didn't care.

She paused, pulled back, and her smile grew. Then she came in for another kiss, this one so far from soft. She opened her mouth and sucked on his bottom lip, and the sensation went straight to his cock. His fingers tightened around her thigh, and her breath hitched.

Oh, yes. Why the hell had he thought he could sit next to this woman for an entire day without touching her? Not after last night, and definitely not when some dude sized her up.

Ruby licked her lips and backed away, her breath uneven. Adrian glanced over at Dan, who clearly hadn't missed a thing. Adrian bit back a smile. Message received.

CHAPTER EIGHT

AFTER THE KISS, Adrian was the perfect fake husband. The Adrian version of perfect, at least, which she had to admit she liked a lot. It had taken her a bit to put together what had caused the sudden shift, especially considering the way he'd barely spoken to her this morning. But when she caught Adrian looking at Dan with smug satisfaction, she'd almost laughed aloud. For a man so insistent on appropriate behavior, that kiss was beautifully hungry and unrestrained.

She wasn't even convinced that Dan had been flirting with her—though she'd been known to misjudge men's intentions in the past—but clearly, that was Adrian's interpretation. Now Adrian was actually playing a convincingly hot, possessive, fake husband. She had to admit it was fun.

Kiran steered the boat into a cove and moored just outside the reef. The rest of the cove was lined with black lava. One side of it looked like a park, with white sand, a smattering of palm trees and buildings with thatched roofs. Most of the rest of the land around the cove was a lush tangle of tropical plants and trees, but the road was visible, with cars parked along it. People were scattered along the black rocks and on the beach with fold-up lounge chairs and coolers. It was a far cry from the luxury setting of the Kalani, and she couldn't wait to explore it.

"That area, just beyond the black rocks, where everyone is sitting," Dan said. "That's one of the best snorkeling spots on the island." Bright snorkels poked out of the water in clumps where he was pointing.

"Sea turtles live just inside that part of the cove," he said, gesturing to one side, "and there's a pod of dolphins that drops in right beyond the reef. If we're lucky, they'll make an appearance."

Kiran finished tying off the anchor, then sat on the side of the speedboat. "We brought the small inflatable boat you requested, as well as the snorkeling masks and fins. Which would you like to start with?"

"The boat," she said quickly.

"Snorkeling," Adrian said at the same time.

She looked over at him, and he sighed. "I guess it's the boat."

Ruby smiled at him. Their fake marriage was coming along very well.

She pulled off her cover-up while Kiran and Dan took out a small self-inflating boat from under the deck and brought it to full size. They lifted it into the water and tied it to the side of the speedboat.

"Kiran will stay here," Dan said as he fitted the oars into their sockets. "But we have another inflatable raft if you'd like a guide with you."

Before she could answer, Adrian jumped in. "We'll be fine on our own."

Kiran nodded. "The turtles live in that area and swim through the channel. Just make sure to avoid the coral. Dan can come out and meet you for any reason."

Dan held the boat while they climbed in, first Adrian and then her. It was…intimate, and no matter how they adjusted, their legs were touching. Dan untied the boat and gave them a push toward mainland. "Just wave if you need anything."

"Yeah, right," grumbled Adrian.

He looked grumpy and uncomfortable in his life jacket, his legs shoved up against hers in the little dinghy. It was obviously well made, but Adrian was much too big for it, even by himself.

"How the hell is this James and Cristina's idea of a luxury vacation?" he added, grabbing the oars.

"I think it's romantic," she said, smiling. "I'd like to find those sea turtles, *sweetheart*."

"Of course, *darling*," he deadpanned. But she swore she caught a hint of a smile as he said it.

Adrian had taken the rowing position, and he seemed to know what he was doing as he maneuvered the boat toward shore.

"You really should be wearing a hat, *darling*," she said. "You're going to get sunburned."

"Didn't bring one."

"All that room in your suitcase and no hat?" She tsked. Then she pointed off to the side. "I see the channel that way, where the boats are coming out."

"I've got this under control."

"Oh, that's right. My *husband* doesn't like when other people give him directions."

"Your *husband* is doing just fine without direction, as you might have noticed." It was true. They were entering the channel, and he navigated the little boat through the maze of coral that led to shore.

"He's also sounding grouchy," she said. She put a finger to her chin, like she was thinking. "Hmm. What could I do to put him in a better mood?"

"Agree to go snorkeling instead of sitting in an inflatable dinghy in the hot sun?"

She shook her head. "I don't mind the fish, but I'm not sure I want to be swimming around with things that are bigger than I am."

"So if I want to snorkel, I'm doing it alone?"

"I'm afraid so," she said. "But I don't mind. I can stay back on the boat while you swim."

"With Dan? Fantastic."

Ruby bit back a smile. "Is my husband jealous?"

He muttered something she couldn't hear. Oh, there were so many fun ways she could play this, especially since they were stuck in this tiny boat together. But she was making him row in the heat, so she went for the sexiest one.

"I can make you feel better," she said, resting a hand on his thigh.

He jumped under her touch, rocking the dinghy. Ruby grabbed onto the sides, and she was pretty sure Adrian was glaring at her underneath his sunglasses.

"That's not how married couples act," he said, like he was the authority on this subject.

He looked so scandalized that she couldn't resist teasing him. "Do I need to explain how babies are made?"

"I mean out here, in public," he grumbled.

She shrugged. "I'm pretty sure married couples have a little fun."

At least in the beginning they probably did, though it was hard to imagine her parents even smiling at each other. Maybe Cristina and James didn't seem like the kind of couple that locked themselves in their office for a lunchtime quickie, but still…there were a lot of married couples out there in the world. Some of them had to be more sexually adventurous. She blamed her own skepticism about what marriage meant on her parents, but what was Adrian's excuse?

"What's your family like?" she asked.

His brow creased. "They're great. Why?"

She waved off his question and focused on the answer. She wasn't sensing a lot of tension on the general topic of family. Hmm. Was he divorced? That wasn't part of the office gossip, but maybe it was old news? Thirty-eight was old enough for him to have been both married and divorced long before she joined NY Creatives Media. "Have you ever been married before?"

"No." The answer came out sharply, and he scowled. "What are you getting at?"

"I'm just trying to figure out where you picked up on your aversion to marriage."

It was hard to read his expression behind the sunglasses, but she was pretty sure it was surprise. "I'm not against marriage. Not at all. Pretty much the opposite, in fact."

Then why the hell aren't you married? She almost asked the question aloud but, thank God, thought better of it. Honestly, though, she couldn't imagine why Adrian wouldn't be married if that's what he really wanted. He was wealthy, fit and good-looking, so that alone should attract a good deal of candidates.

The other reason this surprised her was that he showed absolutely no interest in women at work. To be fair, he treated all employees with equal bluntness, regardless of gender, though his critiques were usually fair. *Usually.* Still, Ruby couldn't make sense of him. What was stopping Adrian Wentworth from getting married? Well, besides the fact that he could be an asshole sometimes.

Everything she knew about him suggested that he didn't lie or even skirt around the truth, so she could just ask him why he wasn't married. But she was pretty sure that when questions got too personal, he'd just clam up. Ruby searched for a way to carefully continue probing.

"If your vision of marriage is not your wife pleasuring you in a dinghy out at sea, what is it?"

He froze, pausing in his rowing again, as if the idea startled him.

A rush of desire shot through her as the scene took shape in her mind: unzipping his pants, listening to his torn groans as she licked his cock. A real-life version would probably involve tipping the little boat over and end with a call to the police to report public indecency. In her imagined version, his carefully controlled exterior would crumble, and all that would be left was that raw hunger from the night before. Damn, that was hot.

He shook his head like he knew what she was thinking. The boat had drifted off course, and he maneuvered the oars to point them in the right direction again, then kept rowing toward the channel.

"Come on, Adrian," she said, flashing him a smile. "Tell me what marriage should look like."

He rowed in silence for long enough that she suspected he'd stonewall her all the way to shore. But then he sighed. "I can't believe you want to have this conversation."

"I'm not going to let it go, and you're stuck in a boat with me."

"Fine," he said, pausing midstroke. "Marriage is about building a family, not blowjobs in public. It means a partner you can depend on."

Ruby rolled her eyes. "You and my parents would get along well."

He frowned. "I'm probably closer to their age than yours, so I wouldn't be surprised."

His words were clipped, but she could hear that same hunger leaking into them. A shiver ran over her skin. An older man. Someone far beyond Jimmy's frat-boy years. Someone serious. Focused. Just thinking about those ideas made her hot.

"It's true. My parents were young when they had me." She made air quotes. "An accident."

But that was the wrong thing to say, because he frowned—and not the good kind of frown. "That's an awful way to say it."

She blinked at him. When her mother had first used that phrase, it had hurt. Badly. But she'd used it so many times since then, the edges had dulled until it no longer cut. Just bruised a little. But Adrian wouldn't understand that...would he? "So marriage isn't about finding a soul mate?"

Adrian gave his driest laugh and started rowing again. Definitely not a believer in magic connections.

"And it's not about great sex?"

"The average couple has sex just over one time per week. Maybe it lasts thirty minutes? An hour?"

"That's generous. I'd say ten minutes tops."

"Maybe if you're twenty-five," he said, giving her a skeptical look over his sunglasses. "The point is that there's one hundred and sixty-eight hours per week. I sleep an average of seven hours per day, so that leaves one hundred and nineteen hours to consciously be aware of a relationship. Sex is less than one percent of married life. And it should be treated that way."

She stared at him. "You made this into a math problem?"

"Of course I did."

"What about the spark?"

"Overrated."

"So how do you keep sex out of the equation?"

"None of your business," he grumbled.

She gave him a sweet smile. "Everything's my business, *husband*."

After a few silent strokes of the oars, he paused. "If you really want to know, I wait until date number six to have sex. Just to make sure it's a good match in other areas."

"Really?"

He huffed out a breath and continued rowing. "Really."

It was just so…clinical. She could see him on one of these stuffy dates, stiff in his chair, assessing the candidate from across the table. Did he have checklist of wifely qualities? It was the opposite of romantic or anything else she'd want in a marriage.

Ruby frowned. "Have you ever been in love?"

Adrian gave her a sigh of exaggerated patience. "Not that it's any of your business, but yes."

"And the sex was good?"

He hesitated. "Yes."

"But it ended."

"Yes."

She blinked. He had spoken just one word, but there was vulnerability in it. Maybe a few days ago she wouldn't have picked up on it, but she heard it now, loud and clear. Why had it never occurred to her that his heart could have been broken? Even when she'd asked if he'd been divorced, she'd assumed he'd left someone, not the other way around.

Ruby was insanely curious. Who was this woman? How long ago did it happen? But the question she most wanted to ask was impossible to answer: What did Adrian in love look like?

Before she could ask him any of those questions, he spoke again.

"She was fun and sexy, and there was always something going on when I was with her. We fought a lot, and I didn't know what to do with that." Adrian was rowing harder now. "She probably would have left if the company I worked for hadn't taken off. I can see that now, though at the time I didn't. Or I didn't want to. And then…"

His voice trailed off, and his movements slowed, like he was lost in thought. Ruby waited, frozen in place, for him to say what happened next. Whatever it was was heavy, weighing him down. What had happened? Then he frowned and shook his head. "It was a long time ago, and I was young and stupid. But it did help me see what I'm looking for," he said, all traces of vulnerability gone from his voice. "And it's not lusting after a woman thirteen years younger than me, who wears a cheerleader costume to work."

The words took her breath away. They were the truth, but why did he have to say it like being herself was somehow lacking? Still, it shouldn't hurt for him to state the obvious. Marriage was so far in the distance for her, too. So why did it feel like he'd just slapped her?

Adrian was watching her now, his frown deeper. He dropped the oars and swiped a hand over his mouth. "Shit. I'm sorry."

"You really can be kind of an asshole," she said flatly.

He flinched, like her comment had hit its mark, and a little guilt seeped in for lashing out. She swallowed and turned toward shore. There were couples everywhere, sitting on beach chairs, fitting on masks and snorkels, like being together was so natural, so easy. The two of them couldn't even be a decent fake couple together.

Adrian muttered a few more curse words under his breath, and she could feel his gaze, heavy on her.

"You're incredible, Ruby," he said softly. "You're smart, you work hard, and you're upbeat and nice to everyone. Even me, when I don't deserve it at all."

He took his sunglasses off when she turned back to him, so he was looking at her. Her heart thumped in her chest. Goddamn her heart, traitorously swayed by his words. His praise was so rare and hard-won, never insincere, and her entire body glowed from it.

He took a deep breath and added, "Whoever you're with is an incredibly lucky man. You're exactly what any man your age would want."

"Like Raj?"

Adrian winced. "That was another asshole move on my part. I let my own... Never mind. I apologize."

She blinked, and a reluctant smiled tugged at the corners of her lips. So he *had* deliberately sabotaged things between her and Raj. A tiny part of her had suspected as much, but she'd never have guessed in a million years that he'd come right out and say it. Yes, it was an asshole move, and she figured Adrian deserved more tormenting, so she pushed him a little further.

"What feelings are you talking about?" she asked, giving him her most innocent smile.

He frowned, rowing silently, so she prodded him a little.

"You're not afraid to mock my age and Halloween costume, but you can't discuss feelings? Hmm…"

"Fine." He huffed. "I find you incredibly hot, and it's taken all my willpower to ignore that. Seeing you with Raj pushed me over the edge. I know you have a right to choose whoever you want, but that night I just couldn't handle it. There. I said it. Satisfied?"

She smiled. "Very."

And very turned on. She'd gotten Adrian to admit he'd been jealous, and her imagination was going wild. If he had been the one in that dark hallway, what would have happened? More than kissing, that was for sure. Her breath caught in her throat as she pictured it. Her back to the wall, Adrian's big, hard body against hers, his cock pressing between her legs…

Did she still want him, despite the fact that he'd just hurt her? That felt more than a little messed up. She looked up at him again, wondering where this was going.

"But now that we're staying in a cabin alone," she went on, "your current plan is to avoid me as much as possible, with an occasional insult thrown in?"

He gave her his signature Adrian stare, like she didn't know what the hell she was talking about. Except she did.

They were in shallow water now, and he climbed out, soaking half his shorts. He walked through the water, pulling the dinghy behind him with her in it like she was royalty, though the life jacket took away from some of the dignity of it. Ruby stretched out her legs and propped them up on the sides of the raft as he pulled it out of the water and onto the sandy beach.

He reached out his hand to help her up. The sides of the little inflatable boat were round, and he had to practically lift her. Her hat fell off into the sand, and she grabbed it, brushing it off. Before she could put it back on her head, Adrian was there, standing close.

He lifted his hands, and she held her breath, waiting for what he was going to do. Tangle his hand in her hair? Kiss her? But he didn't do either of those things. Instead, he unsnapped the buckles of her life jacket.

"I'm so, so sorry I hurt you," he said softly.

She opened her mouth to lie, to tell him it didn't matter, but he shook his head.

"Hear me out, please."

His breath was warm and sweet, and she closed her eyes, just enjoying the feeling of being taken care of.

"I'm so fucking hot for you, and it's driving me insane," he said, his hands slipping inside the life jacket onto her barely there cover-up. Her skin prickled as his palms traveled lower, brushing over her nipples. She shivered with pleasure. "I keep telling myself all the reasons I should leave you alone. That's what you heard, Ruby. What I've been telling myself to keep this attraction under control. It has nothing to do with you and everything to do with the fact that I'm trying not to be the asshole executive who sleeps with the woman he absolutely shouldn't."

He sounded so repentant, like it was tearing him up inside. She reached her hand up to his face, caressing his cheek.

"You're forgiven," she whispered, and she meant it.

The tone between them had shifted, like that part of him he'd been trying so hard to shut off was now on, full blast. He slid the life jacket off her shoulders, and even this had a sexual feel to it. God, she wanted this man. There was no way they could spend the rest of the week ignoring each other.

His Adam's apple bobbed up and down, and his jaw clenched. She unsnapped his life jacket and pushed it over his big shoulders, tracing the muscles of his arms with her hands.

"Is this really so wrong? What's the worst that can happen?" she whispered as his life jacket dropped to the sand. "That this thing between us gets hotter? That we can't keep our clothes on around each other?" She moved her hands back up his arms and shoulders to his neck. "That no matter how many times you come, you're never, ever satisfied?"

A groan rumbled in his chest, deep and raw.

Ruby smiled up at him. "God, I hope that's what it's like for both of us."

She took off her sunglasses, folded them and hung

them on the neckline of her cover-up. She squinted, the sky bright and blue behind him. Slowly, he took off his own sunglasses and shoved them in his pocket. The wind blew gently, carrying voices from farther down the shore. But it felt like they were alone, the warm sun shining down on them, just Adrian and her.

His dark lashes fell, and he licked his lips. His hand wove into her hair, and, slowly, so slowly, his mouth dropped to hers. His lips lingered against hers, barely touching. She took his bottom lip between her teeth, and his whole body shuddered. Then they were kissing. All the tension of the morning exploded, bursting again and again with each delicious slide of his tongue against hers. His mouth was hungry, almost desperate. She held onto him, pressing her body against his, the warm water dripping from him, his hard muscles tensing, moving, and his erection growing against her belly. She was desperate for him, and they were so far from their cabin.

She cupped his face and pulled away. He was breathing rapidly, and she swallowed, trying to get her own breathing under control.

"You're pushing me again, Ruby," he whispered. "And I deserve it."

She smiled.

"You just want a kiss? Or are you looking for more?"

His touch was gentle, almost reverent. Each word, each stroke of his hand in her hair echoed through her, setting off new sparks of pleasure.

"Why do you want this?" he asked. "Too many ten-minute fucks with college boys who have no self-control? Is that why you're looking for someone older? If we do this—if—it will be the hour-long version, and it'll be dirty."

Oh, yes. She knew this had been simmering somewhere inside him. This was the Adrian she craved, his protective layers down, his lust raw and urgent. Just like her own.

"That's exactly what I want," she whispered.

He stilled under her hands, and for one heartbreaking second, Ruby was sure he was going to call it all off. But then his mouth was on hers again, hard and demanding.

Before she fully registered what was happening, Adrian was backing away again. He took a long breath and let her go, taking a step back. She looked up into his eyes, stormy and intense.

"Goddamn," he muttered, slowly shaking his head. "Ruby Bisset, you are going to be the death of me."

Then he swiped a hand over his face and pulled his sunglasses back out of his pocket, slipping them on. "Now where the hell are those sea turtles?"

CHAPTER NINE

ADRIAN HAD REACHED his breaking point. This craving for Ruby Bisset was wrong. James had asked him to play decoy this week because he was sure Adrian would never touch Ruby. Yet he'd done it last night, telling himself it was just for her pleasure, telling himself he'd stop there. Now he couldn't stop thinking about giving in. All the way. It was still just as wrong as before, but it was better than what happened on that dinghy: he'd hurt her. Enough that she'd called him an asshole and meant it. He'd treated Ruby Bisset like an asshole, and he was finding that it bothered him, really bothered him.

As the boat raced along the shore, back toward the resort, he felt the last threads of his self-control slip. They were under the boat's canopy, just out of the afternoon sun, and her shoulder brushed against his with each bounce of the boat. Adrian looked down at his hand, resting high on Ruby's thigh again, but this time it wasn't a message for Dan. It was just for her. Her skin was soft and salty from the ocean, and his mouth watered as he imagined licking it.

Adrian took a deep breath and tried to focus on something else. Ruby was looking through the photos she'd taken on her phone, enlarging them on the screen, deleting some, and turning the phone in his direction when she found one she liked. Images from their day scrolled across her screen, and each one she chose was uploaded to a site. She copied and pasted texts full of hashtags, adding sentences with details from the beach, then scheduled the post.

It was strange to think of the pictures as a fake day in James and Cristina's life since each one held a memory of Adrian's. His feet buried in the sand with Ruby's, the sea turtle climbing onto the beach, the lunch spread in the shade of the boat's canopy. The more he watched what she was doing through her eyes, the more impressed he was. It was no wonder that James and Cristina had hired her right out of college. She was good, really good, and even though he still considered social media a waste of his personal time, he respected her work. Ruby approached it as an art, even if social media didn't deserve her skills.

The boat pulled up to the dock, and Dan tied them off. Ruby climbed off, her hair blowing in the breeze around her shoulders in mesmerizing ripples. Adrian stood off to the side, arms crossed, trying not to stare. He let her handle the rest of the talking.

"I'm glad we found that pod of dolphins, Mrs. Santos," Kiran said. "If you'd like to go back out to do some snorkeling, just let us know."

"Thank you. We will."

Adrian shook hands with both guides, and they

headed up the hill back toward the cabin…where he and Ruby would finally be alone. The afternoon sun warmed his back, and Ruby was uncharacteristically quiet as they made their way along the path through the resort.

They passed a couple holding hands, both men fit and tanned, maybe in their early forties. They looked so…at ease, so comfortable together. *That* was what he wanted.

Instead, he'd spent the night awake on a couch, fighting yet another hard-on for his much-too-young coworker, and then he'd spent the day playing her fake husband. Pretty much the opposite of comfortable. How could he get out from under this incessant craving for Ruby? It wasn't helping that she seemed more than ready to indulge.

They passed the restaurant and the pools and then finally, finally, they were back at the cabin. As they turned down their private walkway, Ruby's steps slowed. She took off her sunglasses, and he did, too. Next came her hat. Adrian hung back, watching as she shook out her long hair, powerless against the anticipation that was building inside him. He really shouldn't. Fuck. He was probably going to do it anyway.

Ruby waved the key card in front of the lock, and they walked into the quiet cabin. The Christmas lights shone in the living room, twinkling in the daylight. Ruby was so close, looking up at him, a smile playing at her lips.

Adrian dropped his bag on the floor. He set his

sunglasses on the table, then took Ruby's out of her hand and put them next to his. Ruby watched him.

"What comes next?" she asked.

Fragments of erotic dreams flashed through his mind. Sitting at his office desk, with Ruby in front of him in that cheerleader skirt. Adrian swallowed.

Ruby waited for his answer, looking up at him. Her long lashes fluttered, and her cheeks were flushed pink. She looked so young and trusting, making this feel even more wrong. And even more tempting. What would happen if he gave in? Maybe this fascination with her would fade…or maybe in a few days, when they returned, he'd be back in his empty apartment, his mind echoing with every detail of her and that aching loneliness even worse than before. It had started this way with Victoria, and she had learned to use it against him, to manipulate him by withholding, rewarding, fighting, and making up. But Ruby wasn't calculating the way Victoria had been. It was his own hunger that made him wary.

He stared into her eyes, mesmerized by the way she watched him, not hiding her own want. It was almost irresistible. But even if he was willing to risk repeating all his old mistakes with Victoria, holding onto something that couldn't work, he still couldn't get around the fact that he was an executive and Ruby was an employee, no matter how far they were from New York.

"This is wrong," he whispered.

She nodded, her eyes sparkling with mischief. "Deliciously wrong."

His cock gave a hard jolt. "I already have a reputation as the biggest asshole in the company," he said gruffly.

Her soft laugh. "I'm aware of that."

"I'm not interested in living up to it, not in this way." Adrian made an effort to soften his expression. "We work together. I sit much higher in the organization than you do. And no amount of pleasure is worth risking your livelihood."

It was painful to think about in such stark terms—that he could put her at risk.

But Ruby just shrugged. "The only people who know we're here are Cristina and James. They had to be sure you wouldn't take advantage of your position if they sent us here." She tucked a strand of hair behind her ear and looked out at the ocean, like she was thinking this through. "I suppose this puts you at risk, too. I could claim sexual harassment. So fooling around could make both of us vulnerable. In the end, this takes some trust that neither of us are going to take advantage of our positions. That we'll both respect each other here in Hawaii and then let it go when we leave."

He blinked. She had summed their situation up so neatly, and he was a little embarrassed that he was so impressed. Then he shook his head. "I don't 'fool around,' Ruby."

"Of course not," she said, mimicking his tone with a little smirk.

He blew out a breath. After years of their back-and-forth in the office, of course she was going to tease and torment him. Her pulse was ticking fast at the base of her neck, like she was anticipating this as much as he was. "These are things I should never say to someone I work with."

"I can't wait."

Then she licked her lips. He had been trying to ignore the jolt of his cock each time it ran through him, but this time, he couldn't.

"I've thought about it," she continued. "What would it be like if all the times we argued ended a different way?"

What kind of endings had she wanted? Before he thought to ask, Ruby turned, heading for the bedroom.

"I'm going to take a shower," she said over her shoulder. "By the way, I'm on birth control. And clean."

The sentences connected in his mind, setting him on fire as he watched her disappear into the bedroom. Ruby had just invited him in for sex. Without a condom. It was reckless for her not to wait for his answer, not to demand it. She was putting way too much trust in him to do the right thing.

He hadn't been with anyone in a long time—his dating rules had left him celibate…and horny as hell. Damn, how long had it been? Definitely long before his last doctor's appointment, so his most recent tests were still valid and he was clean. And soon, Ruby would be naked and wet. If he went in to tell her how irresponsible trusting him was, she'd probably just laugh and invite him in. He wasn't going to be able to resist this.

He lingered in the living room, then wandered into the bedroom, trying to calm the fuck down. But the room was filled with reminders of Ruby everywhere, so he headed for the bathroom, resting his hand on the door handle. Inside was his biggest fantasy. One that could lead him down a path he couldn't come back from. Still, he opened the door and walked in.

The bathroom was covered in gray tile, and the shower was large and enclosed in glass. Inside, there was a bench on one side and two showerheads, but right now, it was all just a backdrop for Ruby.

She stood in the middle of the shower, her eyes closed, water running down her gloriously naked body. She didn't seem to hear him. She ran her hands over her water-slicked hair, squeezing the ends, like she was rinsing out the shampoo.

Adrian watched, mesmerized, taking in each movement, his gaze lingering on her breasts. He could've stood there, just looking at her, for hours. He probably would have, too, just stared at her with his hand over his cock, if she hadn't opened her eyes and smiled at him.

"You're still dressed," she said, then turned around and grabbed a small bottle from the bench, giving him a perfect view of her ass. She unscrewed the top and poured the liquid into her hand. Then she set down the bottle and massaged the liquid into her hair. The smell of coconut wafted through the steamy room. Oh, hell, *this* was the scent. He had caught it enough times that it had become her scent in his mind. Which meant he'd tried to avoid it.

Finally, he could let go. Adrian let three years' worth of pleasure course through him. Her hands were over her head, her breasts bouncing, and then she stepped under the water, rinsing her long hair again. It was almost too much to resist.

Adrian crossed his arms. "You're not going to ask if I'm clean?"

"I trust you to do the right thing." Her voice echoed off the tile and glass, the sound of her surrounding him.

"You shouldn't," he said, his voice rough. "My cock is hard from watching you naked in the shower. And I'm an executive where you work. I don't do the right thing."

She turned to look at him. "I trust you."

A rush of some unfamiliar emotion flowed through him, and he didn't bother to examine it. He pulled off his shirt in one quick motion over his head. Unlacing his swim shorts, he eased them over his straining erection. He folded his clothes and set them on the countertop. In three quick strides, he was at the glass door. He stepped in, and finally, Ruby was within reach.

She shut off the shower. The bathroom was quiet, just the dripping of water and the sound of her body moving. She glanced at the counter and smiled. "You fold your clothes even when you're about to have sex?"

"That's what you want to discuss right now?" The

words came out dry and impatient, and he froze. For one, quick breath, he thought he'd messed it all up. But Ruby let out the sexiest laugh, low and full of desire, and his heart took off, pounding in his chest.

Adrian inhaled deeply, focusing on her. Her eyes raked down his body in one long stroke. He took another step toward her, and she took a step back, still looking over him like she was trying to get a better view. But he followed her. Step, step, slowly they moved until her back was against the wall. He didn't stop until he was right in front of her, almost touching. He inhaled the scent of coconut, and his whole body shuddered with pleasure.

"I've never seen you naked," she whispered. "Let me look."

He shook his head. "Not the best use of our time right now."

Adrian rested his forearm on the tile and leaned over her. His eyelids were heavy, and his breathing was rapid.

Ruby was about to combust. Never had she been so turned on just by the way a man looked at her. But there was no *just* with Adrian. He put every ounce of his attention into each thing he did. Right now, that attention was on her, and oh, my, it felt amazing.

He leaned down and brushed his lips over hers. "Do you know how hard I've been for you? How long I've thought about this?" His voice was rough, strained. "The very first day you walked in, I couldn't stop staring at you."

A smile tugged the corners of her mouth. "More like you couldn't stop scowling at me."

"Because I was mad as hell that I had the biggest hard-on of my life for someone who looked like jailbait."

His cock jumped between them, pressing against her belly. His words were like a drug, pumping through her, and she never wanted them to stop. "But you also liked it."

Adrian groaned. "It was torture." His mouth moved to her neck, hungry. "I tried to fight it. Fuck, I tried. But it never went away."

Ruby lifted a hand to his stomach, tracing the ripple of his abs, down, then up again. He let out another groan, this one louder, so she continued her exploration. He had the body of an older man, defined and toned, all hints of softness gone. The patch of dark hair sweeping his chest brushed against her, and with her hand, she followed the trail of coarse hair down his stomach. Her fingers brushed against his erection, and a hiss escaped from his mouth.

His biceps flexed, so close, supporting him as he leaned in closer. "You want to see what this feels like for real?"

Oh, yes, she did. Ruby wrapped her hand around his cock, feeling its weight, the strain of it against her fingers.

His jaw clenched, his lips in a tight line, and his eyes were stormy. "You want to know how good I can make you feel?"

His voice was raw, and her body was alive with anticipation. "I want to make you feel good, too."

His cock jolted in her hand. *"Fuck me,"* he muttered under his breath. "Everything about this feels good. Everything about *you* is perfect."

This was the side of him she wanted to explore. She had seen his grumpy Greek statue side, the aloof hothole CFO of NY Creatives Media. This was different. Not a statue at all but a man with wants and needs, focused completely on her. Every compliment out of his mouth rang like a bell inside her.

His other hand was resting on her hip and he brought it lower, over her ass, moving his big hand in slow explorations. He took a harsh breath, and his hand moved over her hip again, then down her leg. He teased one thigh, moving his hand higher, playing but never reaching the place she needed the most.

"Touch me," she moaned.

Her legs wobbled as his hand stroked closer, closer, until finally, his fingers brushed over her clit. Pleasure shot through her, leaving her a trembling mess. Ruby let go of his cock and grabbed onto his shoulders for support.

"You're so young," he rasped, "and I bet you're so tight."

He circled his fingers over her clit again, his strokes firm this time, and bursts of heat rushed through her.

"I've been thinking about how tight you must be for three years now, Ruby." Adrian's mouth moved down her neck, sucking on her skin. "I'm ready to find out."

His finger slipped over her clit one more time and moved lower, further, until he finally found the place that ached for him the most. He took an audible breath and slipped his fingers inside. His groan rumbled in her ear as she cried out. Oh, this was the most delicious paradox of relief and tension, and Adrian was the one who was giving it to her.

"You like that, Ruby?" His voice was taut, ready to snap at any moment. "Because my cock is a lot bigger than my finger."

"Show me."

His hand was gone, and before she could miss it, he was kissing her. His mouth made demands, and she answered *yes, yes*, over and over again. She had gotten a taste of his hunger, but this was something more. He was claiming her with his mouth, searing her with his need, and she responded, bringing her hands to his cheeks, touching him as she stroked his tongue with hers. Nothing else existed, just this kiss, all-consuming. It tapped into a deep, dark, well of want, buried inside her.

His hand moved around her ass, and he pulled her tight against his rock-hard erection. His other hand moved over her wet hair, stroking her almost reverently.

Take care of me.

The thought cut into Ruby's haze of lust, and she pulled back. What the hell was she thinking?

Adrian's touch gentled, and he shifted back so their eyes met. "Is this okay?"

God, yes. It was so much more than okay. And the last thing she wanted was to stop.

"So much better, Adrian," she said, standing on her toes to press her lips against his.

He was still, his gaze locked on hers, his eyes bright flames. She could dissolve in those flames, burn down to ashes and not even care. He seemed to be waiting for her to make the next move. It was too much to look in his eyes, to see the way he was looking down at her. Slowly, she turned around in his arms, adjusting herself so her ass was up against his cock. She looked over her shoulder at him and whispered, "I'm ready."

"Jesus," he muttered, his hands low on her hips. He stepped back, tugging her hips so that she bent over at an angle. She rested her hands against the wall, and closed her eyes, losing herself in his voice, in his touch.

"You want my cock inside this tight, wet pussy?" he rasped. "Do you need to be fucked by me, Ruby?"

"Yes. Please, yes." She barely recognized her own voice, begging for him. She barely recognized herself.

And then, it didn't matter. Nothing mattered except the feeling of him entering her. His head pushed into her slick opening, filling her, taking her breath away. He pushed farther, farther. The glass shower filled with groans of pleasure. He pushed until she was full, so incredibly full, and then he stopped. His lips brushed against her shoulder.

Then he whispered words so softly she almost missed them. "Oh, Ruby."

Two words, whispered reverently. His voice traveled through her with that same, heady rush she had resisted earlier. But before she had the chance to fully process it, he started to move. He pulled out and then pushed back in, gently at first and then harder. His strokes were thorough and methodical, as if designed to hit her at her most vulnerable places.

But she didn't want to stop. Her breaths were pants, and her cries were desperate with need. She was at that place, that beautiful plateau, fully immersed in the connection with Adrian. Was he there, too?

His hands moved around her hip and between her legs. His fingers lingered close, and she squirmed to find the pressure she needed. Finally, he circled over her swollen, aching clit. Her insides exploded with ecstasy, and his cock swelled even more. He growled and came deep inside her, holding onto her, his voice low and tortured.

Ruby collapsed against the wall, her mind in a fog of pleasure, with Adrian's body slumped against hers. He slipped his still-hard cock out of her and coaxed her over to the bench in the shower stall, where he sat down. He guided her onto his lap, and she sat with his arms around her, leaning against his big body. Resting on his chest, his heart pounded in her ear.

She wasn't sure how long they sat there, skin against skin. But when she finally thought to speak again, the steam had cleared from the shower stall.

"I think that's the most I've ever heard you talk."

He laughed, his chest shaking under her. "And I'm sure that's the least I've ever heard you talk."

Adrian stood in the bedroom, slowly buttoning his shirt. He stopped to watch as Ruby rushed in to grab her hat and sunglasses, then ran back out to answer the door. Dinner had arrived, apparently, but he let Ruby deal with it. Selfish, yes, but he'd make it up to her.

He couldn't remember the last time he'd felt so relaxed. It had been a long time since he'd had sex, so that was undoubtedly part of the relief he felt, but it was more than that. Something inside had loosened, some part that had been clenched for years. Five years, actually. Since Victoria left.

He hadn't thought about her in a long time, so why had his mind wandered to her more than once in the last few days? He had worked hard to move on from that part of his life, to make sure he'd never make the same mistake again. But the similarities were there. He'd been trying like hell not to think about this, but if he let himself think it, maybe he could figure out what the hell he was doing.

Victoria had been his opposite, impulsive where he was controlled, talkative where he was silent and moody. She got under his skin, made him laugh and turned him on, even when he didn't want to be. Especially when he didn't want to be. Was that what this preoccupation with Ruby was—she reminded him of Victoria?

It wasn't the first time this idea had crossed his mind. Adrian hadn't realized that Ruby's comment about being selfish until thirty had struck a nerve until he'd found himself thinking about it yet again. It was too much like the way Victoria had wanted things her own way, from where they lived to where they ate dinner. He'd told himself it was because he didn't care that much about any of these choices. He was happy anywhere as long as it was with her. But the unexpected pregnancy had shone a light where he'd tried so hard not to look. Even a baby wouldn't come first. Victoria's own wants and needs would always be her priority. She wouldn't change just because a baby was coming. Not even for a family.

He'd probably never fully get over the miscarriage, but he could clearly see that if he'd had a kid with Victoria, all three of their lives would've been a mess. Still, there were a few months before Victoria miscarried where he'd seen a future in front of him, one that he wanted badly. One that he still wanted, though not with Victoria. With someone who wanted it just as much as he did.

Maybe it wasn't the similarities between Victoria and Ruby that were triggering his memories. Maybe it was that Ruby reminded him of his own past self, when he couldn't see anything clearly.

God, he hoped that was what his fascination with her was about. Then it would fade as soon as he found a good match to date, who wanted a family and a quiet life and all the things he wanted. Which meant he should line up a series of dates right after they got back to New York.

The idea felt wrong. Like the last thing he wanted to do, ranking below tasks like getting a dental filling or spending another work happy hour in that bar. Then another idea followed, even less appealing: What if Ruby did the same thing—planned dates with other men right now, when her hair was still wet from the shower, where he'd fucked her?

Hell, no. The thought was as jarring as it was disturbing. It was the kind of thing that Victoria would have done to him, and he would never, ever treat Ruby that way, even if they were just "fooling around." He could deal with untangling himself from her after he left the island. He shouldn't be thinking about the future right now.

Footsteps came from the main room, along with the sound of Ruby's voice mixed with someone else's. Then the front door closed, and finally, they were alone again. Adrian left the bedroom and found Ruby sitting at the table on the lanai. She had put on another red dress, this one shorter and tighter than the last one. Her hair was still damp from the shower, and her cheeks glowed a rosy pink. He still couldn't get used to the fact that he was allowed to look, especially since once he started, it was hard to stop.

"Sweden is tonight's theme." Ruby gestured to the table overflowing with dishes.

It was a small buffet with breads, cheeses, vege-

tables and a lot of other foods, some more recogniz-
able than others, including...pickled beets. Huh. He
scanned the dishes, arranged in a neat circle around a
Swedish flag. The meatballs were a definite yes, but
the little squares of what seemed to be fish, floating
in a yellow sauce with little green bits? No, thanks.

Ruby inspected what looked like a creamy potato
dish. "The server gave me a menu, but I thought it
might be more fun to taste it all first."

"Interesting idea," Adrian hedged.

He sat down next to Ruby and followed her lead,
filling his plate with everything except that fish in
the yellow sauce.

"To an unexpected week," she said, raising her
glass.

He chuckled. "In more than one way."

"Tomorrow is Christmas Eve, which is tamale-
making day," she said, buttering a piece of freshly
baked bread. "Then Christmas Day is mostly on
our own, aside from the meal. Considering the fact
that we're pretty much confined to this cabin, what
should we do to occupy ourselves?"

Immediately, the memory appeared in his mind of
Ruby naked up against the shower wall, him holding
onto her hips with his cock buried deep inside her.
The direction of his thoughts must've been obvious,
because Ruby laughed.

"Besides that, I mean," she added. "I planned to
put together my photography portfolio, but it seems
a little depressing to work on Christmas."

He leaned back in his chair, forcing his mind off

sex. "I brought a stack of books. You're welcome to take a look at them."

Her eyes widened. "You brought books?"

He raised an eyebrow. "Believe it or not, I do read."

Ruby's face opened with laughter. "I mean in your suitcase. Is that why you brought so much luggage?"

"One of the reasons, yes." Adrian tried to keep a straight face, but it was hopeless. He swiped a hand over his mouth so she wouldn't see his smile. "Though maybe I shouldn't offer them to you."

"Okay, I admit that maybe there are legitimate reasons for bringing more luggage." Ruby's laugh was musical. "Now will you let me borrow one?"

"I suppose," he said.

"What did you bring? Maybe a suitcase full of sexy romance we could read aloud?"

He chuckled. "I wish."

"Hmm…what kind of books would Adrian Went-worth read?" She took a sip of her wine and leaned back in her chair. "My guess is mystery, where the world works the way it should. Mysteries get solved, bad guys get punished…that kind of thing."

"Interesting theory."

"Am I right?"

Adrian flashed her a smug smile. "Nope. Try again."

She furrowed her brow. "Then literary fiction is my next guess. Something deep and boring."

He shook his head.

"Ooh, now I really want to know."

He waggled his eyebrows, just to drag out the suspense a little, and she cracked up. After years of false smiles and gloats and irritation, she was smiling, really smiling just for him. And it felt good.

"Most of the books are science fiction, but there are a couple of fantasies in there, too."

She fake gasped. "How completely impractical of you. I'm impressed."

He just lifted his eyebrows a little, trying not to smile.

"Is there sex in these books?"

"Sometimes."

"Do you skip over those parts?"

He crossed his arms. "You want to see what I do when I get to those parts, Ruby?"

"Definitely. But not at the dinner table." Ruby flashed him a sassy smile, then took a bite of the potato dish. "Are there anchovies in the potatoes?"

Adrian shrugged and popped a meatball in his mouth, their day replaying in his head. The more time he spent with her, the more he was curious about…well, just about everything. But most things weren't any of his business, so he started with the question he'd been mulling over since the meeting in Cristina's office.

"Can I ask you a serious question?"

She nodded.

"Why were you planning to spend Christmas alone?"

Her playful smile faded. She opened her mouth to answer, but then closed it. Finally, she sighed. "It just seemed like the best option I had."

"What about your friends? Wasn't there anyone you wanted to spend a few hours with?"

"My roommate's family has a house in the Hamptons," Ruby said. "That's where I went last year, but it was pretty depressing to be the only single person with a bunch of couples."

Enough said. That one Adrian definitely understood. "And your own family?"

As soon as the words left his mouth, he regretted them. Her whole body tensed, like she was steeling herself.

"Sorry," he said, trying not to frown. "None of my business."

Ruby shook her head. "It's fine. Christmas was never a lot of fun growing up. My mom is a flight attendant, so she spent a lot of time away. It was mostly just my dad and me. But they thought it was important for my sake to have Christmas together. I always looked forward to it, hoping they'd put aside their own problems for a day. It never happened. They never figured out how to compromise." She sighed. "That's another reason I made that pact with my mother. To avoid all that resentment my parents built up. I need to make sure I'm over my hang-ups about relationships from growing up with all that resentment. I'm hoping that age will bring me some wisdom. Though I've heard it doesn't always."

She raised an eyebrow at him, and he heard the crack she was taking at his age. But it was deflection. He could hear the hurt in her words, too, the sadness of her hope evaporating each year. How could she still look forward to holidays? But, of course, she did. Of course, sunny, upbeat Ruby would still hope.

It was quiet for a while, then Ruby gave him a little smile and added, "I know. That story is always a buzzkill. But I'm fine."

Adrian frowned. That's what she thought was going through his mind? He had to think of something decent to say to her right now, and, as always, he was coming up with nothing. So he pushed his chair back from the table.

"Come sit with me," he said. "Please, just for a few minutes."

She blinked, and for a moment he thought she was going to turn him down. Really, none of this was his business, and he was prepared for her to remind him of that in some way. But then she pushed back her own chair, stood up and settled into his lap. He wrapped his arms around her, telling her the only way he knew how that she deserved so much more.

They sat that way in the warmth of the evening. He looked out beyond the privacy of their cabin, past the pool and the screen of flowering bushes to the ocean. The urge to solve this, to do something to make her feel better was getting stronger. Even if it was none of his business. But what could he do?

He could give her pleasure. The longer she sat on his lap, the more the other night came back. Ruby's legs spread, her ass moving up and down against his cock…

No, sex was about forgetting, gone when the afterglow faded. Pleasure wasn't enough. He was looking for something more, something that would last longer. Maybe he could figure out how to make this year's Christmas a really good one. He needed to come up with something…and quickly. As in, within the next twenty-four hours. Something so she'd understand how highly he thought of her, something to make that careless comment in the dinghy earlier today disappear.

Ruby shifted in his lap and kissed him. "Thank you, Adrian. That felt good." She gave him another kiss, this one lingering, and then she sat back down in her own chair.

She wasn't in his arms anymore, and the moment was already fading. Adrian searched for a way to hold onto it.

"I think we should celebrate Christmas. Just the two of us," he said quickly. "In my family, we get up early, open presents and then have brunch."

"Presents?" She raised an eyebrow. "That's not really my thing. Minimalism, remember?"

He blinked. How could presents not be *her thing*? He had plenty of money, enough to give her something useful and meaningful…and she didn't want it?

"Please? We'll make it fun," he said softly.

Her brow furrowed, and she was quiet. Finally, she sighed. "As long as we have a twenty-dollar price max."

Adrian frowned. That was not at all what he had in mind. On the other hand, this was about *her* holiday. He ate the last meatball off his plate, promis-

ing himself he'd find a way to make twenty dollars
meaningful. Somehow.

"Fine. Nothing expensive," he conceded. "I'd just
like to do something to celebrate."

"Great. And I have a condition of my own."

He chuckled. "And that is..."

"No more sleeping on the couch for you. The bed
is king-size. Even if you're not the snuggle-up type,
there's more than enough room for both of us. We
can build a pillow wall if you want us to stay on our
own sides."

Adrian chuckled. "As long as you're okay with
sleeping in the same bed as me, I'm more than happy
to be there. No pillow wall necessary."

She smiled that smile of hers, all traces of hurt
gone. Her whole face lit up, and his chest tightened.
That smile was for *him*. He was the one making her
happy, and damn, he wanted to do it again and again.

Except that wasn't how this worked. Would she
still smile at him like that when they got back to New
York, or would they go back to how they'd always
been? The idea that everything that happened here
in Hawaii would be gone hit him hard—that he'd
go back to watching other people make her smile
while she frowned at him. It made him never want
to go back.

CHAPTER TEN

ADRIAN PACED BACK and forth in front of the kitchen counter. Where the hell was Ruby? She'd been gone for over an hour now after announcing that she needed to "take care of something." It was the first time they had actually been apart since they'd gotten on the plane in New York, and Adrian really didn't like the uneasy feeling of not knowing what was happening with her.

He frowned. How would it feel when they got back to New York, after things between them ended? She could be hit by a taxi, and he wouldn't even know it, let alone be around to help her.

Over the years, he'd found that the best thing to do when these kinds of uneasy thoughts surfaced was to force his mind on something else. Something specific and fact-based. Like Ruby's Christmas gift.

He had stayed up late the night before, searching the internet for the perfect gift under twenty dollars that could be delivered by tonight. Unsurprisingly, his options weren't very satisfactory. Admittedly, he didn't know her very well, but he was pretty sure he was on the right track with photography. In the end, he ordered a book of erotic photographs as a sort of gag gift but had gone to bed unsatisfied. He needed to think of something else…that cost two dollars and fifteen cents. Right.

What did she want? All the camera components he'd looked up were far over the spending limit, and he didn't know what accessories she already owned. The minimalist thing was yet another pain in the ass when considering presents. She'd mentioned getting her portfolio together this week, and he'd secretly checked out her photography website, which showed a contest she'd won. How the hell could all this translate into something she really wanted?

Then, the perfect idea came to him. He could give this other "gift" to her along with the book since, technically, it cost nothing. Arranging it would take some last-minute finagling, but he was almost sure he could pull it off. All he needed to do was get ahold of his sister.

Adrian stopped his pacing and found his phone, typing out a quick message. If Sydney could help him figure this out, it would definitely make this Christmas memorable.

He took a deep breath and let it out as the relief ran through him. Then he surveyed the neat line of bowls in the middle of the counter. Inside each bowl was an ingredient for tamales that he'd chopped or minced or rinsed in whatever way the recipe had specified. The large bag of *masa* was sitting at one end, along with a package of banana leaves. Had he missed anything? The chicken had to be—

"Honey, I'm home." Ruby's voice, bright with a hint of laughter, came from the front hallway of the cabin. "That's fun to say."

Adrian rested both his hands against the counter and hung his head in relief. He wasn't going to look too closely at what his worries about her whereabouts meant. *Just move on.* He straightened up and headed for her.

"Wait," she called as he entered the main room. "Turn around."

He did. Her footsteps moved through the living room and into the bedroom. Then he heard her come out again.

"Okay. You can turn around now."

He furrowed his brow in confusion, which she dismissed with a little wave.

"You'll see later." She walked across the living room and stopped in front of him. Then she put her hands on her hips and batted her eyelashes at him theatrically. "Did you make yourself useful while I was gone?"

"Maybe." He gestured toward the kitchen. "You can decide yourself."

Ruby's steps slowed as she caught sight of all the bowls filled with ingredients. She turned to him, her eyes shining. "I should have known. Anything you do, you fully commit, don't you?"

"How kind of you to notice."

Her face lit up with laughter. "Aw, Adrian. Have I not been nice enough to you?"

He raised an eyebrow, but the effect was probably ruined by the real smile he couldn't stop. In the past, her comments almost always had little barbs, critiques of his tendency to obsess over the details, to get things exactly right. He searched for traces of that now, but she seemed genuine. His heart raced as he took in the admiration in her voice. Was this new, or had she appreciated this side of him all along, too? Had he simply failed to notice?

Before he could fully process an answer, Ruby was in the kitchen, looking businesslike.

"So where do we start?" she asked over her shoulder as she washed her hands.

"I found a recipe from Cristina's posts with the ingredients we have, so you should focus on cooking that. I can start assembling the tamales without chicken, since I already watched a video online that showed how to fold the banana leaves."

He glanced up, and her expression was full of humor. "If that's acceptable to you, of course," he added dryly.

She widened her eyes innocently. "Of course it is. You know best, Adrian."

So much for all that admiration he'd heard in her voice just moments ago. She was mocking him. Yes, maybe his ideas sounded a lot like commands, but he had spent the last hour prepping the food and coming up with an efficient plan.

"Of course I know best," he said, because he just couldn't resist.

Adrian headed around the counter and took a step closer, then another. With each step he took, she backed up. The electric pull between them buzzed and sparked, charging him up. There was definitely hunger in her gaze, but there was also defiance. She took another step backward, then another until her back was flat against the wall. He rested one hand on the wall next to her as the smell of coconut flooded his senses, making him lose his train of thought.

"Just because I admitted I'm hot for you doesn't mean you can order me around," she whispered.

He struggled to keep his expression stern, but it was hard to when she was so close.

Her eyes narrowed a little. "You think you're right about everything, don't you?"

"I don't *think* I'm right. I *am* right."

The statement was arrogant as hell, but it felt so satisfying to say exactly what he meant. She huffed out a little breath, but her cheeks were flushed and her nipples were hard, poking through her dress. If this didn't end with sex, he was going to need some serious time in the shower. And knowing Ruby, there was a good chance she'd hold out just to get on his nerves.

He, on the other hand, was long past any game that required him to hold back. He was all in. His head hung heavy over her as he took long drags of her scent. Resting his weight against one hand on the wall, he brought the other hand to her cheek. Her breath hitched, and her pulse pounded at the base of her throat. Still, her eyes were rebellious. His gaze wandered down farther, over her flushed cheek, to her lips, pouting at him.

"Does it turn you on to argue with me like this?" he whispered.

She narrowed her eyes. "Only if I win."

Adrian's laugh was rich and deep, wreaking havoc on her already keyed-up body.

Ruby was lying, of course. There was an ache between her legs that she was trying hard to ignore. Arguing with him did turn her on. The truth was that everything that happened between them turned her on. He was so close, almost touching her, and her body burned for his.

Ruby lifted a hand to his thigh. He stilled at her touch, his breath a sharp hiss. Slowly, she moved her hand higher, higher, until she reached his cock. It was straining against the material of his shorts. She gave it a stroke. He swallowed, and that look of smug satisfaction slipped a little. Good. He was playing dirty, using her attraction against her, so there was no reason she shouldn't play dirty, too.

"Is this what you're going to do in the office the next time you want to make your point? Close your office door and press your hard, aching cock up against me?"

His dick jumped against her hand, and his body stiffened. Ruby smiled up at him. She'd hit a nerve, the forbidden line they'd stepped over. And oh, it was so satisfying to get under his skin. So she went for it again. "But what happens if you catch me in a dark hallway with Raj again? You gonna make your point the same way?"

She had absolutely no intention of making out with Raj anymore, but she couldn't resist bringing it up.

One look at the dark glint in his eyes told her that sentence had turned their taunting into all-out sexual warfare, and it made her giddy, light-headed.

He lowered his mouth to her ear. "You're not making out with him at happy hour again."

The rough hum of his voice was turning her inside out. She tilted her head, looking up at him. His mouth was so temptingly close, but she gave him her most skeptical look. "Is that so?"

"Yes. It is." He moved her hand from his cock and pressed the long, hard length in just the right place, against her clit. She moaned, her whole body thrumming with need, and Adrian was watching her with his relentless stare.

So she stared right back. "Because you say so?"

"Because you won't be aching for Raj. You'll want my mouth, my cock." He slipped his hand under her dress, sliding it up her leg until he came close, so close. And then he stopped. She glared at him, and he gave her his smug smile. "Right now I'm gonna fuck you against this wall so you'll remember it. So you'll be thinking about me whenever your back is against the wall."

His voice was a low rasp, and his body was tense, like he, too, was holding on to his last ounce of self-control. And how she was dying to give in right now if it meant a relief to this aching need.

"Do it," she whispered. "Make me think about you every single time."

He let out a groan, and his mouth descended on hers. The kiss was wild, all hungry need. She slid her fingers into his hair, pulling him close, and he let out a deep rumble. He tilted his head, and their mouths fit together, like the missing piece of a three-year-long puzzle. Everything clicked into place. Frantic hunger turned into the long, sensual glide of his lips over hers. She met each stroke of his tongue with her own.

When he moved to her neck, Ruby tipped her head back against the wall, exposing every vulnerable part, and he let out a hiss of satisfaction.

"You taste so good," he said, lips against her skin. "So sweet."

He sucked at the base of her neck. The sensation shot through her body, hitting her core. She gasped. "Again."

Adrian's laugh was low and satisfied, and he went back for more. The friction of his mouth, the heat of his big hard body against hers, it was so good. Ruby closed her eyes and pulled him closer, grinding against his erection.

He flexed his hips, dragging his hard length along her clit. White-hot sparks exploded inside her.

"What's the matter, Ruby," he whispered. "Do you need something from me?"

He was pushing her to beg. She knew it, and she was almost past caring. Almost.

"Is this what you want?" he coaxed, rocking his hips again. Another round of white-hot pleasure ran through her. "Do you need my cock? Tell me how badly."

Her breaths were coming so fast, one after another. Damn him. He really was going to make her beg.

"You're an ass," she hissed.

Adrian laughed. "We both already know that. But I have a nice hard cock to fuck you with. So I guess you'll have to overlook that part."

"I should go back in the bedroom and take care of this myself," she said, giving him her best glare.

He must have taken her at her word because he stilled against her. When he pulled back a little, his smug smile had slipped. Did he think he'd pushed her too far? Not even close. He took a deep breath.

"I am an asshole, Ruby. But the only thing I want right now is to please you." He was so serious, and the truth of it, the vulnerability in his voice, hit her hard.

She slid her hands to his cheeks and gently tilted his face so they were looking eye to eye. "I know."

His expression was unreadable, and she held his gaze, watching him closely. Finally, after a few moments, he nodded.

She stroked his cheek, and his cock throbbed against her. "Now fuck me," she whispered.

His mouth crashed down on hers again, and a deep groan rose from his chest. She couldn't get enough of his mouth, his body, everything. She lowered her hands to his waist, finding the button of his shorts, fumbling with the zipper. Finally, it came loose, and she shoved his shorts and boxers off. He kicked them aside, still kissing her. He broke off and tugged his T-shirt over his head in one swift move. Ruby pulled her dress off, dropping it onto the pile.

Then his hands were on her again, big, warm hands moving over her skin, sending trails of delicious fire over her stomach, her sides, her breasts. She moved to unhook her bra, but he shook his head.

"Just like this," he rasped. "Please."

Both of his hands came around her ass, and he lifted her. She wrapped her legs around his waist so his cock settled between them, lighting sparks and making her dizzy. He pressed his cock against her, just the silky scrap of her panties between them.

"What do you want?" The question was out of her mouth before she could think better of it.

"You, Ruby. I want you."

Then, before she could fully register his words, he moved her panties out of the way and sank deep inside her. His cock stretched her, sliding into her with the most beautifully satisfying friction. In those last inches, her body surrendered completely.

"Fuck," he muttered. "So wet. So good."

He was trembling, or maybe she was. Maybe they both were. It didn't matter anymore because they were both winning now. Or maybe they were both losing.

Then he started to move, his thrusts long, hard and relentless. Over and over, he slid in and out. The pleasure was building inside, growing, blooming, taking her breath away. She tilted her hips and dug her heels in so his cock dragged along the perfect spot.

"Oh, my sweet Ruby," he rasped, his head buried in her shoulder. "So sweet. I can't take it."

His biceps, his chest, his abs, everything flexed with each thrust. He was covered in a sheen of sweat, but he showed no signs of slowing. Just those thrusts, long and hard, until she was so close.

"Harder," she whispered.

He bit down on her neck on the next hard thrust, and everything exploded. Ecstasy pulsed through her in wave after wave. She gasped for breath, and his name was falling from her mouth, over and over. "Adrian. Oh, Adrian."

His cock grew inside her, and then he was coming, too, filling the room with growls. His arms tightened around her, and for one moment, everything else was gone. Just the two of them. He brought them to the floor, a tangled mess of arms and legs. She clung to him, his hard muscles under her hands, as her breathing slowed.

They were in Hawaii. Playing a fake couple. Except this didn't feel very fake right now.

Adrian pulled back a little, his eyes serious, like he was trying to read her. Like he was making sure she was okay. It was intense, and it felt so good. Then he raised an eyebrow. "Did I give you something to think about?"

A bubble of laughter rose up inside her. "You're being an asshole again."

The corners of his mouth twitched up. "I know."

"I can't believe how much fun I'm having this week with such an asshole," she mused.

A smile spread across his face, and this time he didn't try to hide it. "You are definitely going to be the death of me," he said, shaking his head. "But right now, I'm okay with that."

CHAPTER ELEVEN

RUBY WOKE UP Christmas morning to the low hum of Adrian's voice. It was a sexy sound, so she lay there, just listening to it. Slowly, she opened her eyes, and he came into view through the bedroom's French doors.

He was stretched out on one of the lounge chairs on the lanai, facing the ocean, so she couldn't fully see him. He seemed to be wearing only pajama bottoms, and he was talking to someone on the phone. Clearly that someone was under the age of five, judging from his questions about stuffed animals and finger paints.

She closed her eyes again, the details of yesterday's kitchen adventure coming back. His voice in her ear. His hard biceps flexing under her fingers as he thrust so deliciously deep inside her. Holy hell.

How could this be the same Adrian Wentworth, CFO of NY Creatives Media, a man of few words and fewer smiles?

Ruby stretched lazily, then slid out from under the soft sheets. She took her time pulling on a tank

top and shorts, then she wandered toward the French
doors for another view of him.

Adrian ran a hand through his hair, his toned
muscles in relief in the morning sun. The man was
beautiful. After a moment of gaping, she registered
a change in Adrian's tone.

"Merry Christmas to you," he said, his voice gentle. "And I'm not all alone, Mother."

Ruby froze as the silence stretched out. Listening
in when he was talking to a child hadn't felt like an
invasion of his privacy, but a conversation with his
mother was different. Ruby shifted on her feet. She
should really leave, but she was so curious. It wasn't
much of a conversation, actually, more just a series
of yeses, noes and other one-word answers. This was
more like the Adrian she knew…except she could've
sworn there was longing in his voice.

She didn't know anything about his family. Had
he mentioned a sister at some point? Why was he
here in Hawaii instead?

"No one important," he said with a hint of irritation. "It's work related."

No one important. The words should not have
stung, but they did. Even though he was probably
just trying to cut off his mother's questions.

Still, after the dinners and the sex, it hurt to hear
the words come out of his mouth. Just like it'd stung
a little when he'd stayed up long past her and was
out of bed before she woke up, like he had silently
drawn an intimacy line. It was ridiculous. This was
just a few days of fun. And she never got sensitive

about men. Why was she starting now, after a couple days of really good sex?

Slowly, she backed away from the doors. The sinking feeling was settling in the pit of her stomach as she turned around.

Pull yourself together, girl. If she wanted to dwell on this, she could do it some other time. Today was Christmas, the day she'd hoped to make her own kind of special this year. Ruby was absolutely not going to let Adrian's words ruin it—words that might not be true and definitely weren't even meant for her ears.

She blew out a breath, straightened up and focused on the first step to a good morning: coffee. She headed for the kitchen, but as she walked out through the doorway into the main room of the cabin, she came to a stop.

The room was covered with red and white flowers. They were strewn across the glass coffee table and hung from soft white lights that lined the windows. Flowers sat on the branches of the decorated palm tree in the corner, and they were spread along the floor, making a trail that lined the wall. Beneath the tree lay a single present, square and flat, wrapped in red paper with a white card on top.

Ruby stood in the doorway, frozen in place, her gaze darting from surface to surface as she took in all the flowers. She had never seen anything like it before. It was as if the whole room had bloomed overnight. The ache in the pit of her stomach from moments ago faded. It didn't compare with what was right in front of her, breathtakingly gorgeous. She could spend Christmas Day just sitting in this room.

She ducked back into the bedroom and grabbed Adrian's present out of her beach bag. She tiptoed over to the tree and set his present next to the red package.

Adrian had left the French doors open, and a soft breeze blew off the ocean, rustling the petals of the flowers on the table. He was still on the lounge chair, and she could hear the low rumble of his voice through the wind, though she couldn't make out the words.

A little of that sinking feeling came back, so she turned and headed to the kitchen for a coffee. But the kitchen was full of surprises, too. Gone were the dishes from their tamale-making project. Instead, in addition to the fresh pot of coffee, she found a bowl of cut fruit, a small pitcher of juice, hard-boiled eggs and a flat basket of pastries, doughnuts and rolls. The napkins were candy-cane patterned and the plates were red. Ruby stared at the spread.

Adrian must have ordered breakfast. Had he also arranged for the flowers? Or was that part of the resort's romantic Christmas setup?

Before she could decide, Adrian's footsteps came through the main room and into the kitchen. Her heart sped up as he came closer. *Forget about what he said. It doesn't mean anything.* Ruby took a calming breath and turned around.

Oh, Lord, he looked so good shirtless, his muscles defined and on display. For once his hair was a mess, and he didn't seem to care. Her heart stuttered in her chest as he crossed the kitchen in long strides, coming straight for her. He stopped right in front of her.

"Merry Christmas," he said, shoving his hands in the pockets of his pajama pants. "No touching the food until we've opened presents."

"Merry Christmas." Her voice was breathless. *Easy, girl.* "Coffee isn't food, is it?"

"Hmm. I suppose we could work something out."

She reached for the mug on the counter next to the coffee maker. By the time she had poured herself a cup, Adrian was next to her, holding the carton of milk.

"Thanks." She took it out of his hand, poured in a bit, and handed it back to him. "The place looks amazing. Do they decorate everyone's cabin like this on Christmas?"

He gave her a very Adrian stare. "Not everyone at the resort celebrates Christmas, Ruby."

"Well, it's the loveliest idea for a Christmas morning surprise that I've ever seen," she said, keeping her gaze on him. "Whoever is responsible for it."

Adrian's eyes were fixed on hers. He opened his mouth, hesitated, then spoke. "I want this to be the best Christmas you've ever had."

Ruby blinked up at him, her heart pounding in her chest. He looked so determined, like he was going to make sure it happened. This was the same Adrian who had given her his snidest comments and most judgmental stares? It seemed impossible that the Adrian she knew from the office was also the same person who'd spent yesterday morning prepping their tamale meal, then dedicated himself so thoroughly to really good sex. Now he'd arranged the most beautiful flower display, just to make her Christmas special. Why didn't he show this side of himself more often?

"Thank you. Truly." Ruby stood on her toes and met his lips with hers. "Let's open presents."

He blinked at her, like the kiss was the last thing he'd expected from her.

She grabbed his hand and led him into the main room. She plopped down on the couch, next to the tree, and Adrian sat next to her, stretching his long legs. Without his shirt, he looked much more relaxed...and ridiculously sexy. She was about to make a comment about what kind of package she wanted, but he spoke first.

"Open your gift," he said lifting his chin in the direction of the red present.

She knelt under the decorated palm tree and brought the gift back to the couch, setting the card aside on the coffee table. She tore off the paper and found a book, just like she'd guessed. But it definitely wasn't one she'd guess he would buy for her. On the cover was a close-up of two people, visible from their mouths down, entangled in a kiss. The woman wore red lipstick, and hints of the man's tongue could be seen. Ruby knew about this book because a handful of bookstores had refused to carry it, claiming the photos were too explicit.

"Thank you. I love Stef Yang's work," she said,

smiling up at him. "We should definitely look through it together."

His eyes widened. "Do you already have this one?"

She shook her head. "I've just heard about it. It's perfect, really."

Had he peeked inside yet? Ruby opened the book to the middle. One of the pages was white, blank except for the word *Richer*. On the other page was a photo of a woman's bare breasts. Hanging in between them was a pendant with a diamond wrapped in a silver nest. She glanced over at Adrian, but he wasn't looking at the book. His gaze was fixed on the coffee table, and he looked a lot less relaxed now, which was a little odd.

"You should open the card, too."

Ruby cringed. "Sorry. I'm one of those rude people who goes straight for the presents."

He didn't say anything, though she had left herself perfectly open for one of his little jabs. Something was off. Adrian reached forward and set the card in her hand.

She tore off the flap and opened the envelope. The card had a palm tree with Christmas lights on the front, and as she opened it up, a piece of paper fell out. She set the paper aside and read the card. Printed in Adrian's careful writing were just five words:

You deserve the very best.

So simple, but her heart thumped like mad. What the hell was she supposed to make of this?

Ruby bit her lip and unfolded the paper. It was a printout of…an email? It was to Adrian from a Sydney Wentworth. Same last name, so a relative? She read on.

Hey, look! A note from my brother, who ditched us for Christmas this year. Just kidding. :) Hope you're actually enjoying yourself for once.

I checked out the photos from the contest she won and the work she's done for NY Creatives Media. You're right. She's good. I sent a note to three galleries I've worked with that might be a good fit. She'll probably get an email from them after the new year, and she can take it from there.

But I still have questions about her, and you know exactly what I mean. When you get home, I'll expect answers. It's either that or I tell the rest of the family. Mom being who she is, I'm pretty sure I'm your best bet. The rest of the family says hi.
Merry Christmas. Take care yourself.

Ruby stared at the letter, her head spinning. Adrian had a sister, and they sounded close. What was his mother like? And most important, three galleries? There was too much to process.

"It's not a guarantee," Adrian said softly. "Just a connection, something to get your foot in the door. Like Sydney said, you can do what you want with it."

"How…how did you know I won that contest?"

"The internet knows everything, Ruby," he said gently. There was something new in his voice, something she hadn't heard before. Then after a pause, he added, "I looked on your social media."

She gave him a look of mock horror. "No, you didn't."

A smile teased at his lips. She blinked at the man in front of her, still stunned by the note from his sister. Still stunned by what he'd done for her. His gift to her was so…unexpected. So thoughtful. The usual stern, implacable stare, the condescension—all of it had faded. His expression was softer. Maybe even a little vulnerable. Before she could get over her surprise, he bent down for a kiss, just a brush of his lips, his body so close, making her body light up.

"You did this for me?" Her voice was barely there. "I'm not sure what to say…except thank you."

"I stayed under twenty dollars, too," he said with a hint of smugness.

Slowly, she shook her head. "Of course, you figured out how to give me something that's worth so much more than its price tag."

Adrian gave a little grunt of acknowledgment. A week ago she might have read it as dismissive, but now she could see hints of the pleasure he was taking in her response.

Her mother used to lavish her with expensive gifts from wherever she'd traveled recently, but those always felt more like an apology for barely showing up than a gesture of generosity. Adrian's gift was real, both cleverly within the boundaries and outrageously generous. If she didn't distract herself soon, she was going to get too emotional.

She dropped the card and the paper in her lap and reached for the white box still under the tree. She had found the perfect gift in a boutique not far from the Kalani…or what she'd thought was the perfect gift, before Adrian had raised the bar moments ago.

He took the box and lifted off the top, peering in. Then he chuckled.

"A hat?" He pulled out the black, newsboy-style hat and fit it on his head. Then he leaned back on the couch, his mouth twitching up into a smile. Oh, my. This new side of Adrian, lounging shirtless on the couch, was beautiful. Why didn't he smile, really smile, more often?

In the middle of her shameless gaping, Adrian sat up and grabbed the hat off his head. "There's no way this was under twenty dollars," he said, inspecting it. "It's much too nice."

"You mean *thank you*?"

"I love it, Ruby," he said quickly, his gaze meeting hers. Then he looked back down at the hat, and she knew he couldn't let the money piece drop. Ruby let him suffer a little in silence until he couldn't take it anymore. "But this was over the twenty-dollar limit, right?"

Ruby tried to bite back her smile. "Just a little bit." More than a little, actually, but once she caught sight of it in the store, she'd known it was perfect. It was stylish, a little old-fashioned, and a lot sexy. He had mentioned on the dinghy that he hadn't brought a hat to Hawaii, and from the hint of redness across his cheeks and over his nose, he definitely needed one.

Adrian looked thoroughly scandalized. "But those were *your* rules."

"Oh, Adrian," she said, shaking her head. "Don't you know that there are times when the rules don't matter?"

He met her eyes, and in that moment, it felt like they were both thinking about much more than just the hat. Was he thinking of rules about executives not sleeping with staff? Rules about marriage? Rules about avoiding commitment? At this moment, it was feeling less and less like any those rules mattered.

He didn't answer her. Instead, he put his hat back on his head and then scooped her up. In her next breath, she was lying on the couch, and he was on top of her, looking down at her with those serious gray eyes. His skin was warm under her hands, and his erection was growing against her.

"Merry Christmas, Ruby," he said, kissing her. "I hope it's a memorable one."

She looked up at him, smiling. "Very."

The full weight of his gaze fell on her, and bolts of giddy anticipation rushed through her. His eyes were dark with hunger. How could she have ever thought him unaffected? This resort really did grant wishes because this unveiling of the real Adrian had become hers.

"Want to know a secret?" she asked.

He nodded.

"I used to think of you as a grumpy ancient Greek statue," she said, her voice breathless. "So beautifully built."

She lifted a hand to his face, running her fingers down over his cheekbones, along his jaw. He shuddered as her fingers reached his neck. She moved her hand lower, over the flat planes of his chest, down his sides. A groan came from deep inside his chest, so she moved her hand lower, to the space between them, until she reached his cock. It was hard but still tucked away. She cupped her hand around it and adjusted it, and he let out a breath of relief, but like a good statue, he didn't move.

A hint of amusement glittered in Adrian's eyes, but he said nothing. She ran her palm down his hard length. Another groan escaped him, deeper, and his whole body tightened. Taunting him was so deliciously fun, and she could see how close he was to his breaking point. His jaw was clenched, and his pulse was ticking hard at the base of his throat.

Ruby lifted her other hand to her chest. Her nipples poked through her flimsy tank top, the two darker circles showing through.

"Is that what you want to be, Adrian? A beautiful statue, hard, impenetrable?" She teased her nipple, moving her fingers over it, and she moaned as sharp pleasure burst through her. "Or do you want to give in? Do you want to let yourself go and indulge in the things you crave?"

His eyes were fiery, and he stared down at her with single-minded intensity, like a starving animal ready to devour her.

"You're not a statue," she whispered. "Not even close."

She pinched her nipple, giving it a little tug, and another burst of pleasure shot through her. She shut her eyes, and Adrian's hand closed around her wrist.

He guided her hand down and squeezed his cock with it, hard. Ruby's pulse exploded as euphoria raced through her. This was what *she* craved, this moment when she knew it was finally happening.

"I want to give in, too. Take care of me." The words were dangerous, the ones she wasn't supposed to think.

Adrian dropped his lips to her cheek as he thrust into her hand. "I'll take care of you, sweetheart. You know I will."

Oh, the satisfaction those words brought her. Everything about this was driving her crazy. Every inch of that beautiful body covered her, and he wedged his cock right between her legs so it pressed on her clit. He rested on his forearms, taking long, deep breaths, his expression stormy and intense. Then he lowered his mouth to hers for a kiss. It was a devastating kiss, slow and calculated to make her fall apart.

Her hands tangled in his hair as their tongues slid together, and his hips ground against hers, sending more sparks of pleasure through her. One of his hands traveled down, and he tugged at the waistband of her shorts. She shimmied them off, turning the kiss sloppy, but she didn't want to stop. God, she had never been as hungry for anything in her life as she was for Adrian right now. His hand moved over her mound, and he slid two fingers inside her.

"So perfect." His voice was tight and barely there.

The words filled her with a new wave of warmth, hitting her deep inside. Then his fingers were gone, and he guided his cock through her folds, pushing the tip inside. Then more. More. Slowly, so slowly.

He gritted his teeth as he sank into her. He had dirty-talked his way right through sex before, but this time he was silent. The implacable look on his face was gone. His whole expression lit up with a kind of wonder as he stilled, deep inside her. Then he started to move. In and out, in and out, adjusting the angle so he hit her clit each time. He held himself over her, looking down as the heat built inside. His thrusts were relentless, and his eyes were on fire.

Over and over she met his hips until she came, crying out her pleasure. Adrian buried his head in her neck and shuddered, groaning against her.

His breaths slowed, and he pulled back a little. The morning sun shone through the window, lighting up his face as he gazed down at her. "Merry Christmas, Ruby."

CHAPTER TWELVE

THE WARM AFTERNOON breeze blew across the lanai, nudging Adrian back to reality. He was staring out at the ocean, his mind wandering to places it shouldn't go, instead of concentrating on his book. He'd read the same paragraph three times, and it still hadn't sunk in.

Ruby lay with her head in his lap and her long, bare legs stretched out across the outdoor couch. She was wearing tiny shorts and a tank top with no bra. He'd already had her once, on the couch, and now, just a few hours later, he wanted her again. The intensity of his want wasn't fading.

Ruby, on the other hand, looked the opposite of intense. She looked thoroughly engrossed in a sci-fi mystery she'd decided on. Her hair fell over his legs, and her mouth was parted a little. She also didn't seem to notice just how distracted he was by her, which was probably a good thing.

Not that she'd mind. She'd probably encourage it, in fact. But it felt wrong, mostly because he couldn't stop himself from thinking about the future.

What would happened when they sat in the same

room together back in New York? It had already been difficult to block her out before Hawaii, and now he couldn't even read a book with her next to him. He'd have to get this under control.

Because how the hell was he supposed to find a wife who wanted a family and a quiet, settled life as badly as he did if he couldn't stop thinking about Ruby, who wanted nothing to do with relationships? How would this emptiness of being alone ever stop?

Except…it had faded a little today, spending Christmas with Ruby.

The thought made him a little uneasy, so he tried to block her out and picture his goal: wife, kids, a house, a dog or two. But that image didn't come, just the guilt of trying to erase the woman next to him.

Ruby sighed and bent one leg, tucking her foot under her leg. Damn, she looked so young right now, reading on the couch. She seemed so relaxed. And he was afraid to think too much about the tenderness he felt as he looked at her, so content. It was dangerously close to the feelings he'd been searching for… But it was with Ruby, the staff member he shouldn't be touching, who had explicitly stated she was staying away from anything that required compromise. The warmth that ran through him now felt even more risky than just lusting after her. Because no matter what happened here in Hawaii, it wouldn't last.

Pushing that aside, he set his book on the table in front of the couch, next to his new hat, then leaned back and rested his hand in Ruby's hair. He stroked it off her face, and it tumbled over his legs. She smiled a little but kept reading.

"I can't believe you're missing out on a perfect intimacy photo here," he murmured.

"Nah. No social media photos today. I'm way ahead on my posts, and I took a walk through the resort with my own camera this morning."

His hand stilled as her words registered. Today they weren't playing Cristina and James. Today was private.

A burst of happiness flooded his body. What was he supposed to do with all these...feelings? Maybe he could figure out some middle ground. Maybe this didn't have to end right when they got back to New York. Maybe they could let whatever this was run its course. Without anyone finding out. All the realities of their differences would certainly make this obsession fade, wouldn't it? She'd almost certainly be okay with that since she wasn't looking for anything serious.

He closed his eyes as he stroked her hair, memorizing the way the silky strands felt under his hand.

"What's on your mind?"

He opened his eyes to find Ruby staring up at him.

"I know it's something good," she said with a laugh. "Are you going to fill me in on it?"

Adrian weighed his options. Telling her the truth about wanting to continue this when they got home could end with their clothes off, but there was a chance it could go the opposite way. Was it better to dodge the question and explore this quiet moment together? What would she want?

Just then Ruby's phone played the Ohio State fight song. She froze, her gaze locked on his. "My parents," she whispered.

The call she had been waiting for all day. Lazy, relaxed Ruby was gone, and so was her easy smile. His gut twisted as the unease in her gaze took over, and he didn't know what to do with that feeling.

The phone rang again.

She sat up.

"I do want to talk to them," she muttered, as she reached for the phone on the coffee table. "Really. I do."

He couldn't think of anything to say to that, so he reached for her hand instead, but she was already too far away.

"Merry Christmas, Mom." Ruby's voice was bright and cheery. Adrian wondered if her mother heard the hint of tension in it, too.

He watched her walk away, into the living room. She must have stopped there and sat on the couch because he could still hear her clearly.

"Yes, it's been…very nice so far… No, I'm not alone. But I'd be fine if I was."

With each response, he could hear her voice getting tighter. He really shouldn't be listening in on her private conversation, but…

"Yes, he's a man."

More silence.

"No, this isn't a distraction. My career and my photography are still my priorities." Her voice was tight.

"I know, Mom." Her voice had gone from tight to apologetic. "Can we talk about this some other time? How was your visit to Grandma's?"

Adrian hung his head. He was listening in on her private conversation, and now he was starting to read into it. None of his business. He grabbed his hat off the coffee table, then stood up and headed toward the beach, far from listening distance. He pulled the hat low on his head as he walked off the lanai and across the pool deck, Ruby's voice following him.

But as he started down the wooden steps that led to the beach, a thought occurred to him that made him stop in his tracks.

Had Ruby heard him this morning when he spoke to his family earlier? He'd shut the door to the lanai, but judging how well sound carried in their little cabin, it was possible. What had he said during his call? His mother had definitely asked who he was spending Christmas with. How had he answered?

Shit. He couldn't remember, but he definitely hadn't waxed poetic about spending time with Ruby—his mother would've never let it go if he had.

Had he said something that could've hurt her? Just the thought alone made him ache... If he focused on making the next few days perfect for her, maybe that would outweigh all his asshole moves.

Adrian walked down the last two steps and started across the beach. The afternoon sun sparkled over the water, and the sand was hot under his feet. He walked to the water's edge. *Just focus on the next three days.*

He wasn't sure how long he'd been standing there making plans before Ruby's hand brushed over his shoulder. He turned around. She still hadn't put on a bra, just a tank top, short shorts and sunglasses. Her hair was piled on the top of her head in a messy bun, and she looked sexy as hell.

"Your parents have a good Christmas?"

She chuckled, surprising him. "As good as it gets for them, I think." She was quiet for a while, and then she added, "You know, I think not going home for Christmas these last couple years has been good for them. I mean, I'm pretty sure my parents stuck together for my sake more than for theirs." She gave him a tight smile. "My mom missed out on a lot because she got pregnant earlier than she'd planned. She told me that more than once. But now that I'm not there, they can't use me as an excuse anymore."

She stared out at the ocean. "Back in November, I told them I wasn't coming. It was long enough ago that both of them could've made other plans. My dad's been talking about taking a Christmas cruise in the Caribbean forever, and my mom's always wanted to visit her sister in California for the holidays. This is the second year in a row I gave them the perfect opportunity to do the things they finally wanted to do, and neither of them took it." She shook her head slowly. "I have no idea what the hell that means."

Adrian ran his fingers down the soft skin of her arm. "That their relationship is more complicated than it looks?"

Ruby laughed. "Yeah, I got that part."

"Is that why you're spending Christmas alone?"

She shrugged. "Partly."

"The other part?"

She was quiet.

He waited a couple moments, but she still didn't answer, so he tipped his chin down the shore. "Want to walk?"

"Okay."

She stepped into the shallow water and started down the beach. It splashed around her ankles, getting her legs wet. "Adrian?"

"Mmm?"

"Why didn't you spend Christmas with your family?"

He sighed. "For the same reason you didn't go to your friend's place, I think. Because it's hard to be single during the holidays when you're surrounded by happy couples. I just needed a break from it."

She nodded, like she understood.

"I told you that I was a mistake," she said after a while.

He frowned, waiting to see where this was going.

"It's not that my mom didn't want kids. She did, just not when she was twenty. It meant she had to drop out of college, and she never ended up going back. She always wanted to travel, see places, explore more of the world, so when I was five, she got a job as a flight attendant." Ruby sounded so different than she usually did. So serious. "She was gone a lot. It was a compromise, both for her and for my dad and me. None of us were happy, really."

The wind blew wisps of her hair across her face, and she tucked them behind her ear. He had so many questions, but he waited, giving her time to tell the story the way she wanted.

"I don't think my mom regrets having me, not exactly, but she really, really doesn't want me to make the same mistake."

Adrian stiffened. Those words weren't sitting well with him. She didn't think her mother regretted her...but she wasn't sure? Every protective instinct in him was going off, but he gritted his teeth and just listened.

"That's why we made that pact I told you about. She was giving me permission to make choices based on what I want, not compromising for anyone. Men do it all the time, but women...less often." She raised her eyebrow at him, waiting for him to argue, but he didn't. "I broke up with my college boyfriend when I had to choose between him and moving to New York."

"Definitely a good decision," he muttered.

Ruby smiled. "It was. My mom pushed me to leave him behind, and she was 100 percent right on that one."

"And I'm guessing your mom also advises not to get married or have kids?"

"Not until thirty. In her mind, those are the ultimate compromises."

"What about in your mind?"

Ruby hesitated, then nodded. "She's probably right."

"But you're not twenty years old still working on your college degree."

Ruby laughed. "Are you weighing in on this topic?"

"Of course. I'm older and wiser," he said with an arch of his eyebrows.

She gave him a little shove, and he feigned a stumble in the sand.

"I've been following my mother's advice for a while now, trying to decide based on what I want. It's harder than one would think."

"Not for me."

Ruby laughed. "I know. That's something I really like about you."

He smiled at the compliment. "And this is related to not going home for Christmas?"

She sighed. "I didn't want to go. Like I said, Christmas has never been a lot of fun in our family. But I wondered, what happens if I'm selfish about my decision and stay away? Will my mom stand by her theory, or will she make an exception and ask me to come home?"

"And?"

"She stood strong." Ruby kicked a little water and looked out at the ocean.

"Is that what you wanted?" he asked gently.

A tiny set of waves broke on the beach, spraying on his feet, getting him wet.

"I don't know," she said after a while. "Part of me was glad that she held herself to her own standard, even when it was personal. Especially after all those years of hammering her advice into me."

She bent down and picked up a shell out of the water, studying it for a moment. She pulled her phone out of her pocket and snapped a couple photos of it, then threw it back in the ocean.

"But part of me wanted to be the exception," she said softly. "To be important enough to make her break her own rules."

Adrian swallowed, feeling the pain in those words. He wanted to say something comforting, but of course, nothing came. The only thing he could think to do was touch her, hold her. He had crossed so many forbidden boundaries, but somehow, comforting her this time felt even more intimate. He was slipping further into dangerous territory, but right now, he couldn't bring himself to care.

He waded into the ankle-deep water next to her and put his arm around her shoulders. She looked a little surprised, but then she smiled and wrapped her arm around his waist. They walked that way through the water, their hips bumping, her soft body against his. It felt good, so good.

"Are you having a merry Christmas?" he asked.

She smiled. "Yes. Definitely yes."

Adrian nodded, ignoring the clench in his chest. He'd pleased her during the day and stayed on his side of the bed at night. It was a delicate balance, but as long as he remembered the limits, this wouldn't get out of hand. Hopefully.

CHAPTER THIRTEEN

Merry Christmas. Tried to get ahold of you. Our flight is leaving soon, and we're coming tomorrow morning to pick you up. Sorry about the last minute change, pls let Ruby know. I'll explain when we get there.

ADRIAN HAD NO idea how long he'd been sitting on this lounge chair, staring at the message from James. Long enough to get hungry again, even after the lunch picnic. All he knew was that the sinking feeling wasn't going away.

James and Cristina were coming back early. He and Ruby didn't have a few more days in Hawaii. They had one more night, and then it was over. All of it. It wasn't a big change. So why did it feel like his legs had just been cut out from under him? Why did a few more days really matter when the end would be the same?

Somehow, it did.

An idea floated through his mind for the second time: What if they didn't stop? What if they met up back in New York? Working together would be complicated, and getting caught would probably hurt her career. Adrian frowned. Sneaking around wouldn't work, but maybe they could see each other a few more days, before the office opened again. They could even set an end date: January 1. Just until the end of the year.

The more he thought about it, the more he wanted it. He just had to figure out a way to bring it up.

He stood up and headed toward the beach, where Ruby had disappeared to get a few more photos. She was sitting in the sand, not far from the water, looking at her phone. She was barefooted, her long legs crossed, and she was wearing short shorts again. His blood was rushing south, and it was far from the first time today. He was beginning to appreciate her love of minimalism.

He sat down next to her in the sand. She turned and smiled at him. "Hey."

She smiled each time when she saw him now, like she was truly happy to see him. Adrian's heart beat faster, and he swallowed. It was better to just get this over with. "There's something I need to show you."

His voice sounded raw to his own ears, and her brow wrinkled. He pulled out his phone and showed her the message. They sat like that for a long time, just looking at the words. The screen went black after a bit, and he shoved the phone back in his pocket.

"So…" she said, letting the words linger. "No horseback riding tomorrow."

He shook his head slowly.

"Damn. I'm a good rider."

He raised an eyebrow.

"Really, I am. I learned at summer camp."

"When was that? Last year?"

Ruby poked him in the side. Her smile was so warm, so beautiful, and Adrian couldn't help but grin in response.

She was quiet again for a while. Then she sighed. "It's our last chance to bet on the real reason why James and Cristina needed us here."

Adrian shrugged. "I'm going with family emergency. Not James's family or he would've probably told me. I still can't figure out why they'd want to keep it secret, but that's all I've got."

"Interesting."

"Is that skepticism I hear?" He tickled her stomach, and she laughed.

"It's just not very specific. Kind of a cop-out answer."

He tickled her again, and she squirmed against him, which made him think about getting naked. Again.

"What about you? You have a better guess about where James and Cristina went this week?" he asked, trying to steer his mind off other subjects.

"I definitely think it's something personal, maybe family."

Adrian poked her in the side. "I already took that one."

"No way. Your guess was much too broad to claim it," she said, laughing. "I'm going with a private family matter in El Salvador, where a lot of Cristina's family lives."

"Not specific enough."

"Fine, I'll go with my first guess, even if you're going to laugh," she said. "I still think it's something about being pregnant."

He didn't laugh.

Ruby turned to him, and her smile slipped. "You don't like that guess," she said softly. "Because of what happened last time?"

He nodded. James and Cristina's miscarriage wasn't a secret. They had announced their pregnancy right when they found out, made a whole campaign on social media about it. In the days after the loss, the scheduled posts were still going up, and the congratulatory comments were still coming in. Dealing with the public as the private devastation hit them had been too much. It had almost broken James.

"Experiences like that don't go away," Adrian said.

He could hear the rawness in his own voice, and by the look on Ruby's face, she could, too.

"And you would know?" she asked, her voice gentle.

"Yes, I would."

Adrian looked out at the ocean, trying to bury the memories that were rising up inside him. The hope that could be so easily snatched out from under him. The woman who'd so easily moved on, both from the miscarriage and from him.

"Was it with the woman you mentioned before? The one you fell in love with?"

He nodded. "Victoria."

She tilted her head a little. "And you really wanted the baby."

"More than anything I'd ever wanted."

The words were so hard to speak, so painful, but it was the truth. When it happened, he couldn't shake the sadness, the loss, which had increasingly irked Victoria. *It's not your only chance to have a baby*, she'd snapped not long before she left. That she hadn't understood why he couldn't move on a few weeks later, even looked down on him for it... He never wanted to be in that position again. After all these years, it still hurt to even think about it.

He braced himself for more questions, but they didn't come. Instead, Ruby rested her hand on his leg and gave it a gentle squeeze. Maybe someday he'd be ready to say more...except there wasn't a *someday* for them. She wasn't ready for a relationship, let alone a baby. This would end tomorrow. Unless he convinced her to continue just a few more days in New York.

Adrian looked at her, really looked at her. He could see hints of Ruby's eyes through her sunglasses, but he couldn't read her expression. But it didn't matter. It didn't change anything, so he simply looked, taking in her lips, the shape of her face, the soft skin of her neck, where he'd kissed her a dozen times today, and the long silky hair blowing against her shoulders.

After a while, she gave his thigh one more squeeze. "Is it time for our grand finale sex marathon? If you're not too old for one of those..."

Adrian let out a laugh as he tackled her, wrapping his arms around her. Something inside him broke free, and the heaviness of the past faded as he looked at Ruby. Her sunglasses sat askew on her forehead as she lay in the warm sand, with him half on top of her.

"You're getting sand in my hair," she said, smiling up at him. "How do I always end up on the bottom?"

"Because it makes me hot," he whispered in her ear.

Her eyes were shining. "Me, too."

Ruby lay in the sand with Adrian on top of her, staring down at her in that way he had, his mouth stern and his eyes bright. His growing erection was pressing against her hip, and she welcomed it. Craved it. Because tomorrow this would be over, too soon, just when she was starting to understand him. Just moments ago, she'd seen a glimpse of real hurt, buried somewhere inside, and everything in her wanted to ease it.

What would her mother say about that? Probably that it was a trap. That the urge to nurture someone else's wounds was a slippery slope of compromises, the kind that could trigger an avalanche of priority shifts that grew until it buried her in other people's wants and dreams, snuffing out her own.

Okay, maybe that was a little melodramatic, but nothing about this man was casual. He was intense, and her chest swelled with the pleasure of all that intensity focused on her.

Adrian slipped a hand up her shirt, finding her

bare breast, closing his hand around it. That knot loosened a little. She needed more to ease the tension deep inside her. She wasn't ready for the end, but it was happening. And really, sex was what they had.

"What do you want from me, Ruby?" His breath was a rasp in her ear. "You want me to wear you out tonight? You wondering if I'll keep getting hard for you, over and over, all night long? Because I already know the answer."

His teeth grazed her neck, and she let out a quiet moan. His words flipped a switch in her, and all the tension in her exploded into hot streaks of lust. She was so ready for sex right there on the beach.

Ruby craned her neck to see if they were alone. They weren't. Farther away, a couple wandered next to the water, holding hands, heading away from them. The woman stopped to pick something out of the sand, and the man stooped down to look at it, his head bent to hers.

Adrian's hand came to her chin, gently coaxing her gaze back on him. "You really want to think right now? Or do you want something else?" He brushed his fingers over her nipple, then squeezed it, sending sparks of pleasure through her. "If James and Cristina's names weren't on the line, we'd do it right here, in the sand. Could you keep quiet while I fuck you, or would the other guests hear us?"

Oh, Lord, the filthy things he whispered were turning her inside out. His cool facade was melting with every word he spoke, and in its place was hunger. For her.

"You wouldn't dare," she said, her voice full of challenge. "Not here, in front of everyone."

His cock pulsed against her and he laughed. "You're pushing me again, and you can feel how it gets me going." He flexed his hips against her, his erection rubbing against her clit, shooting a burst of pleasure through her. "I think I know what to do with you."

Then he was off her, lifting her like a bride.

"What are you doing?"

He didn't answer, just marched her across the beach and up the steps with a smug smile on his face. He walked them across the deck of the pool, heading straight for the deep end.

"Hey, wait—" Her words were cut off as Adrian dropped her in, fully dressed.

She remembered to close her mouth just as she hit the water. It was cool and refreshing, and she swam to the surface, her clothes weighing her down. She took in a gasp of air and clung to the side with one hand, rubbing the water out of her eyes with the other. She looked up at Adrian, who was now shirtless and working to unbutton his shorts.

"You just threw me in the water with my clothes on?" she said, breathless.

"That's not a real question, Ruby." He had that condescending tone from the office, and his smile oozed triumph.

"Asshole," she muttered. She was caught up in that mix of emotions that was so familiar: frustrated, reluctantly amused, and a lot turned on.

Adrian seem to interpret her silence as hesitation because he added, "I can buy you new clothes if those are ruined."

She shook her head. "I would never let you off that easily."

He tipped back his head and laughed. It was deep and unrestrained, a laugh she had never heard, and she found herself smiling. He shook his head. "No, you wouldn't." He eased his shorts and boxers down, revealing his growing erection. "I love that about you."

Ruby froze, her heart jumping, her breath stopped. The words had slipped from his lips so naturally, and now they colored everything between them. *Love.* Was that word a careless mistake? From a man who was never, ever careless?

Slowly, reluctantly, she met his gaze. His smile had faded a little, and she couldn't read the expression that was in its place. Was it the same, uneasy combination of surprise, agitation, and whatever else was brewing in her? What they had together wasn't love, but the word echoed inside, insistent, defiant.

Before Ruby could make sense of the moment, Adrian scrubbed his hands over his face, took a deep breath, and then leaped into the water, cannonball style. She was too surprised to duck as the water splashed over her, drenching her face again. When she wiped the water from her eyes, Adrian was next to her, his face glowing with laughter.

"Damn, that felt good." He shook his head and

water sprayed from his hair, across her face. He reached up to wipe the drips off her cheeks.

"It had the potential to be painful," she said, glancing down between his legs.

"I was careful."

She rolled her eyes. "You always are."

He swam closer, grabbing onto the wall next to her with one hand, his face just out of reach. The word *love* still rang inside her like a bell, and she didn't know how to make it stop. He found her thigh with his other hand and closed in for a nip at her bottom lip. "Let's figure out how to get you out of these clothes."

He caught the bottom of her shirt, bunching it as he lifted it. She grabbed more of it with her free hand, and together they brought the material over her head. It hit the deck with a splat.

Adrian's hand glided around her, down her back, and he eased off her shorts and panties, lifting her legs to pull them off. He held them out of the water for a moment, staring at them with a hint of a smile, then set them next to the shirt. He swam behind her, his erection nudging against her rear. Treading water, he unhooked her bra. He came in closer, the warmth of his body at her back, as he eased the bra strap over her shoulder and down her arm.

Was this the last time he'd ever undress her? Uneasiness ran through her, and she bit her lip. No, she couldn't start thinking that way.

"Are we having pool sex?" she asked, dropping her bra onto the pool deck.

He kissed her neck. "I really hope so. And I think the ledge that's built into the other side of the pool would be the perfect place for it."

With a deep breath, he disappeared underwater and started for the shallow end. Ruby pushed off from the side, taking long slow strokes, then flipped over onto her back, stretching her body out, enjoying the water and the sun, and the knowledge that Adrian would be at the other end, waiting for her. When she reached the other side, he was sitting on the ledge. The water came up to his chest.

Ruby swam up to him, straddling him, wrapping her legs around his toned waist. She reached between them, stroking his cock, feeling the difference now that they were in the water.

"Does sex even work in the pool?" she asked. "Everything is much slower."

He shrugged. "I guess we'll find out." His hands settled on her hips. "You ready to try?"

"Mmm. Very ready."

His teeth grazed her neck, then sank into it, sending a sharp ripple of pleasure through her as he entered her, slowly filling her, pausing when she gasped, giving her time to adjust. It was a different sensation, dreamy and languid. Then, when she was fully seated on him, he leaned forward and kissed her. The kiss was thorough and deep, and her hands tangled in his hair as she pulled him closer, the sensual slide of their tongues stoking her hunger for him. The erotic scrape of his teeth against her lip was a shot of ecstasy, chased with an aching tenderness as he caressed her. Her body was melting in the flames of their kiss, and still she wanted more.

"You feel so good," he whispered, his lips brushing against her. "I can't get over how good this is."

Before she could gather the words to reply, he lifted her and then brought her back down, letting his cock fill her again. It was a slow exploration, so new and different. Adrian's low grunts each time he entered her added another layer of pleasure. Time faded and she was suspended in this dream, her hands on Adrian's biceps as they flexed, moved. She closed her eyes, giving herself over to the sensations.

"Take care of me." The words came out of her mouth again, and before she could take them back, he answered.

"I will, Ruby," he said, his voice tight. "I will."

His words tipped her over the edge, and she let go as her orgasm rippled through her, long and deep, shaking her to the core. Adrian came with a deep groan, his arms closing around her and pulling her tight. She fell against his chest and hung her head on his shoulder. Her eyes fluttered closed as she listened to the thump of his heart.

I will.

CHAPTER FOURTEEN

THE NIGHT WAS WARM, and the light of the moon bounced off the water, casting a bright glow on the deck. Adrian sat on what was now his favorite lounge chair next to the pool, and Ruby lay with her back against his chest, settling between his legs. The waves broke on the beach, so close.

For one last night, they were spending the night in this cabin, in their own world where they made the rules. He'd brought the word *love* into this world, even though it didn't belong here. Her eyes had widened when he said it, and truthfully, it had surprised him too. He wasn't in love, but he could feel the seductive pull of it. He could fall in love with Ruby Bisset. It wouldn't take much. That should've been a reason to stand up and move far away right now, but instead, Adrian slipped his hand under Ruby's tank top. Just a little more time to make up for what they were missing with their early departure—that was all he wanted. Then he'd move on. His fingers moved over her stomach, and he focused on that feeling.

"I don't think I've had Filipino food before," she said, her voice soft and dreamy.

"It was delicious." He focused on how her inhales and exhales felt under his hand.

"I wonder what other dinner they had planned for us tomorrow."

This was the opening he'd been waiting for all evening. He'd planned his words carefully as he watched her dress. It should be an easy sell because it was what she wanted all along: casual, no-strings fun in the bedroom. He was the one who had resisted in the beginning, not her. So why was his heart beating so fast right now?

Because it felt different.

But it wasn't, not really. They still had polar opposite aims. She had her no-attachments-before-thirty thing, and if anything, this connection with Ruby made him want the real thing even more. But he could deal with that in the new year.

"I've been thinking," he said, keeping his voice light. "We've been cheated out of at least a day of sex. Maybe we should finish that up when we get to New York."

She stilled against him. His heart was doing crazy things in his chest as he waited. Then, finally, she exhaled slowly.

"No, thanks."

"What?" No, thanks? What the hell kind of answer was that?

"I said no, thanks," she said, and her voice had an edge to it.

"Why the hell not?" The question came out harsher than he meant it, and she sat up, pulling away. "You were the one that pushed me in the beginning, and now you're turning me down?"

He pinched the bridge of his nose, but that didn't stop the agitation that was building inside him. This conversation was going completely wrong. He took a deep breath and tried again.

"We would be really careful. No going out, no chance of getting caught. We could have an end date—New Year's. It wouldn't be any different."

Ruby huffed out of breath. "No. Thanks."

The frustration was building inside him. She wasn't touching him, wasn't even looking at him now. "Can you say something besides that?"

"Like what?"

"Like at least tell me why?"

Slowly, Ruby turned her head toward him. She looked…uncertain. She almost never looked uncertain, and it occurred to him that *he* was the one who'd put that look on her face. A bad feeling had been growing in his stomach, and it was getting worse.

"Did I do something wrong?" he asked softly.

She sighed and shook her head. "No."

"Then why not?" There was a hint of desperation in his voice, and he realize that was what this bad feeling was: desperation. Since he'd gotten James's text, he'd been comforting himself with the idea that they'd have a few more days. That this didn't have to be over…except she'd just turned him down.

Ruby bit her lip. "Adrian, I don't think I can be

casual about you anymore. That's why I think it's better to break it off here."

It took a moment for him to realize he was gaping at her. What the hell was going on? "What about your no-attachments-until-thirty thing?"

She rolled her eyes. "I'm not a machine, Adrian. No attachments doesn't mean I have no feelings until I'm thirty. It means that when I start to have feelings, I need to walk the other way."

That took a while to sink in. This scenario hadn't occurred to him. He'd formed a list of counterarguments in his mind, but they were all about making sure no one would find out and that her job would never be threatened. Not…this.

"What about…what about when we get back to the office?" he asked.

She shrugged. "We'll avoid each other, I suppose. I'll go out, get drunk and forget? And you go back to your sex-free marriage dates."

Everything in that statement needled him. First of all, he had no interest in sorting through marriage candidates right now. But the idea of her and Raj against the wall…that wasn't sitting well with him at all. Would he have to endure that again?

"So…" Adrian was having trouble getting words out at all. He swallowed. "We just end like this? That's it?"

"I'm a little tired for another round of sex, if that's what you're asking."

That wasn't what he was asking. Actually, he had no idea what he was asking. All he knew was that the idea of ending whatever this was between them early was emphatically not what he wanted.

"Tell me what you need. What would it have to look like for you to say yes?" The desperation was leaking into his voice again.

"It doesn't work like that," she said, shaking her head.

"There must be something."

She shook her head again.

It hurt. It actually hurt. He took a deep breath, the scent of coconut everywhere.

Take care of me.

She had said those words. It had been in the middle of sex, but she had said them. His plan had been all about making sure she had nothing to lose in this. She hadn't acknowledged that there was anything that would make her change her mind, but what if he offered her something different…something more? No. That couldn't be what she wanted. And he didn' want compromises, either.

Adrian scrubbed his face with his hands. This was a mess. It was late and all he wanted was to lie in bed with her right now. No more talking. It was the last boundary he'd kept in place, and tonight, he was going to break it. Keeping to his side of the bed didn't matter as much anymore. Sex would feel good, but he found that even sex didn't matter as much. Just touching, like they had been minutes ago.

Except now touching looked like the last thing Ruby wanted to do.

Her hair was tousled, her bare legs soft and perfect. He had a sudden desperate thought, that maybe he could suggest they go somewhere else, take a real vacation together and see what happened. His heart sped up. He could just ask.

But that wasn't what he wanted, not really. Was it? No. He'd stopped having sex on dates so he'd look at relationships logically. And right now, he definitely wasn't thinking logically.

They sat in silence, not really looking at each other. Finally, Ruby stood up. She opened her mouth, hesitated, then shook her head.

"Good night, Adrian," she whispered, but it sounded more like goodbye.

Ruby was still awake when Adrian came into the room. She'd half expected him to sleep on the couch, but here he was, slipping under the covers next to her. She was on her side, facing away from him, and she pretended to be asleep. It was easier that way. Even though she was so far from asleep.

Every inch of her was awake as he came closer, closer, until finally, he crossed the unspoken line he'd drawn the last few days when they were lying in bed together. He was touching her. His hard body settled against her back. He had no shirt on, and her pulse kicked up as his warm chest pressed against her skin. His cock was half hard, and she was dying to press back against it, feel the friction between her legs as it grew.

If he wanted sex now, she wouldn't have the

strength to say no. Even if she'd probably regret it in the morning.

His arm came around her, pulling her closer, and he rested his hand on her stomach. She was trying to keep her breaths steady, but, oh God, she wanted him. His cock was growing. If he just moved his hand a little lower, it would feel so good. Ruby waited. And waited. And waited.

Nothing more happened. Just his body against hers and the pressure of his hand, pulling her against him. They lay just like that. The distant sound of waves came in through the windows, and the sound of his deep, steady breaths was so close to her ear. It was the one and only time they'd ever lie like this, and she fought hard to stay awake, memorizing each detail, each sensation.

Finally, after a long, long time, Ruby gave up and drifted off to sleep.

Ruby slid on her sunglasses. They hid her eyes in moments of weakness, like when she found herself staring at Adrian's biceps as he lifted his suitcase or when she caught sight of his expression as he held the car door open for her. His trademark frown was back, the one that she'd seen less and less of over the last few days, and tension radiated from him, threatening to spark every time she accidentally brushed against him.

She settled in the seat of the car, the air-conditioning cutting through the last traces of the tropical humidity. As they pulled away, she got her last glimpses of the Kalani Resort, noting each bit of the luxury that she'd probably never get to enjoy again. She'd never be able to afford this place on her own, and she was trying to be thankful for the little taste of luxury she'd gotten, but it was hard not to think about the things she'd missed since it wasn't really her vacation. The pool with the waterfall they'd passed on the way to the docks, the restaurant over the water she'd only seen a picture of, the horseback ride they'd canceled...

Ruby hazarded a glance at Adrian across the long, empty stretch of the back seat. He was looking straight ahead, his jaw tense, working. Back to grumpy ancient Greek statue mode, still, impenetrable.

Actually, now that she was getting a good look, he seemed...tired. They still hadn't spoken much since she'd walked away last night, leaving him alone on the lounge chair they had so thoroughly made use of that first night. She told herself she'd tried to resist him when he'd come to bed, but the truth was she hadn't. It had felt too good to lie next to him. By the time she woke up in the morning, he was gone.

They pulled into the airport, and the driver headed for the private jet area and parked. Ruby climbed out of the car and walked around to the trunk, where the driver was removing the last of their luggage. She grabbed her carry-on and started for the jet. Out of the corner of her eye, she could see Adrian next to her, facing straight ahead, with his perfect posture and his inscrutable expression.

"You have everything?" His voice was gentler than she'd expected.

"I should be asking you that question," she said, nodding to his two suitcases.

She was pretty sure he smiled a little. They probably looked just like they had when they'd left the plane days before, but nothing felt the same.

The runway was quiet, and she absorbed the last of the Hawaiian sun. Tomorrow she'd wake up in the New York winter. Maybe she'd come back here someday, though it was almost definitely not going to be on a private jet.

The door to the private plane was open and the steps were down. A woman waiting at the bottom took Ruby's luggage before she climbed the stairs.

Ruby entered the cabin and stopped, staring at the scene. Cristina and James were sitting in the seats facing the door, with smiles full of joy. In James's arms was a tiny baby, just a little bigger and rounder than a newborn.

A baby. James and Cristina had a *baby*.

She tried to piece this together. Cristina definitely hadn't been pregnant when they left, so they must be either fostering this little one…or they'd adopted.

Adrian came up behind her, his hand gently settling on her back. "Keep moving, Ruby," he whispered.

She could feel the moment he saw the baby, too. He stilled, his hand tense on her back.

"A baby," she whispered stupidly, but she couldn't help it. That was what was behind their mystery trip. Not a company buyout but a baby.

"Meet Hector," Cristina said. "I'm sorry we couldn't tell you sooner. We got the call last week from my grandmother, and we didn't know what to do. It's not a guarantee when you get a call. These kinds of things can fall through easily. We didn't want to tell anyone until we were sure."

"But it didn't fall through," Adrian said from behind her. "You have a baby."

"Our baby," Cristina echoed, her eyes filling. She circled her arms around James and little Hector, and a tear trickled down her cheek. "Finally."

"So you sent us to Hawaii for a little privacy," Ruby whispered.

James nodded. "So sorry I didn't tell you, A. I would have eventually. Cristina's grandmother has been helping us work with an agency in El Salvador, and this isn't the first time we've been alerted. We've even flown down there once, thinking it would happen, but the mother decided to keep the baby."

"Last summer…" Adrian added.

James nodded.

"I've scheduled posts for the next two days, Cristina," Ruby said. "You want me to keep going? It would give you a little space. As long as you want."

Another tear trickled down Cristina's cheek. "Thank you, Ruby. I'd love that."

Ruby turned to Adrian, who still hadn't said a word. A week ago, she would've thought he was stoically observing this domestic scene, but now Ruby could read the longing in his eyes, and in that moment she ached for him. This was what he wanted, exactly what he saw in front of him: a family. Oh, she wanted to comfort him. She wanted to hold him and kiss him and tell him…tell him what?

She didn't want to give him a family herself, did she? A baby would be nice someday…in the future. Not now. Her mother would have a heart attack just knowing she'd thought about such a big compromise.

She'd been right to say no to him last night, and not just for her own sanity. He shouldn't be playing around with a woman just trying to get her own life started when he so clearly ached for this kind of happiness. But picturing Adrian with another woman, holding their baby…she really didn't want to think about that. Seeing him gaze down at James in Cristina, she could finally admit one more little piece of last night that had stung. He had invited her for a few more days of sex, nothing more. Had he even considered looking for this kind of happiness with her?

Adrian looked down at her. He said nothing, but he wasn't looking very stoic anymore.

Ruby bit her lip. She knew her hurt wasn't fair— she had been the one to draw the line. If they were alone, maybe they'd talk about this, but it wouldn't change anything. So she gave him a little smile, then headed to her seat.

CHAPTER FIFTEEN

"Who is she?"

"Just someone I work with."

"Try again." Adrian's sister raised an eyebrow, and she had the nerve to look amused.

He, on the other hand, was nowhere near amused. Frustrated was an understatement, and his current state of sleeplessness wasn't helping. In the days since they left Hawaii, he'd tried everything to put Ruby back into that *hot temptation he'd never give into* category in his mind. The one he'd kept her in for the past three years. It wasn't working.

Adrian scrubbed his hands over his face. He knew his sister would press him for details—he'd resigned himself to it when he'd written her that Christmas email. But he still hadn't come up with a good way to explain it.

"Come on, Adrian," Sydney coaxed, not bothering to hide her smile. She was thoroughly enjoying his discomfort. "I'll invite you over for New Year's if you give me the details."

"Too late. Amy already invited me," he grumbled.

"Consider her invitation suspended." His sister's eyes sparkled with interest. "I can see you are stewing over this big-time, so let it out."

He really, really didn't want to talk about Ruby, but maybe it was better to just get the discussion over with. Sydney knew him better than anyone in the world. She'd at least understand where he was coming from.

"Bonus for giving in right away instead of making me spend all night dragging the answer out of you. Amy is still putting Evan to bed." She gestured to the hallway of their apartment, where his sister-in-law had disappeared with his nephew just minutes before. "If you tell me now, you won't have to say it in front of my wife."

It wasn't much of a threat, considering how much a part of his life Amy was, too. But the thought of spending the evening with Sydney prying at him was enough to make him relent.

"Fine. You win." He took a deep breath and blew it out. "Ruby is a colleague at work who I spent Christmas with because of…circumstances."

"I definitely got that from the email," she said, waving him off. "What I want to know is why you look like you haven't slept in days."

"Because I haven't," he said darkly.

Sydney's eyes lit up. "Because you're in love?"

"Don't be ridiculous," he snapped, but Sydney's smile grew wider.

"You totally *are* in love," she said, giving him

that dismissive wave again. "Now let's hear your list of buts."

Only Sydney would smile at him and so bluntly tell him he was wrong. Well, only Sydney and Ruby. But he wasn't wrong. She was.

"I can't fall in love with this woman. She's twenty-five going on eighteen, and we work together. She likes to party and she's irreverent. Not at all serious." He ticked off each reason on his hand.

His sister let out a snort of laughter. "Sounds perfect. Hopefully she can get you to take yourself a little less seriously."

The comment stung, and Sydney seemed to realize this right away. "Sorry, Adrian. That came out wrong." She patted him on the knee. "But you hold yourself to such rigid standards, and there doesn't seem to be much room in them for enjoyment. Or happiness."

Adrian frowned. That might be true. "The other major problem is that she's got a thing about no relationships until thirty."

Sydney raised her eyebrows. "Really? I like her already."

"I'm looking for help here, Syd."

"So no relationships until thirty…but you think she's into you?"

He nodded. "Pretty sure."

"Why doesn't she want a relationship?"

He blew out a breath. "It's something about honoring her mother's dreams and following her own dreams while she's young."

"So she doesn't want to compromise her personal goals for a relationship?"

"Something like that."

Sydney was quiet for a few moments. "Can you give her that?"

"And have a family, too? A baby takes a hell of a lot of compromises." He gave her a pointed look. "You should know that."

It wasn't a good idea to think about babies, but he couldn't help himself. He let the idea bloom in his mind. Ruby pregnant with his child. Living with him, working on her photography in one of his spare rooms. It could be her office.

There was so much joy in that image it was hard to contain. He would take care of her. She had said those words, *take care of me*. Would she ever want that for real?

"And you absolutely need the baby to feel like you're starting a family?"

He definitely wanted a baby. Enough to give up Ruby? "I don't know," he finally said.

"I can't believe I have such a traditional brother. Haven't you been listening all those years when Amy and I talked to Mom and Dad about getting married?"

Adrian blinked, searching for the connection she was making. He was coming up with nothing. "Um, yes. I listened."

"But you thought I was just talking about wanting to marry a woman," she said, rolling her eyes. "I wasn't. It's something everyone needs to think

about, including you. Families come in many different forms. And the more we let ourselves explore
what we really want, the more we all can find happiness."

Adrian was silent. Maybe he could be a little more
flexible. He'd thought a lot about what he wanted...
but that was a long time ago. Before he moved to
New York. Before he cashed out on his start-up and
upgraded to a penthouse facing Central Park. Before
he bought his sister and Amy a place downstairs so
they could live closer. Before Ruby had started at
NY Creatives Media.

He did still want a family—that much he was sure
of—but as for what it looked like...

The more he thought about it, the more he wanted
to be with Ruby. Except his meticulously planning
brain was short-circuiting at the idea, spitting out all
sorts of worst-case scenarios.

"What if it happens again?" Just saying the words
hurt, but he forced himself to continue. "You know I
can't do anything halfway. What if I put everything
into this, and I fall in love and wait until she's ready,
and then I lose another baby? Or something else happens? I don't think I can—" His voice broke, so he
stopped there. It was too much to even speak it aloud.

"If she's a real partner, you won't go through these
things alone this time," she bit out, the old anger at
Victoria rekindling. Sydney blew out a breath. "I just
want you to be happy, Adrian." His sister's voice was
softer now. "This is big. I can feel it."

"Me, too, Syd," he whispered. "Me, too."

After a few days apart, the satisfaction of just seeing Ruby would be...well, he didn't know what to call this feeling inside. But even if he called and asked to see her, he'd still have to figure out how the hell to convince Ruby to give a relationship a try. She might not want to see him. Adrian wasn't sure how long he sat there, lost in thought, but the silence was broken when Amy walked into the room.

"Asleep," she whisper-yelled, pumping her fists in the air. She plopped down next to Sydney on the sofa. "You two are quiet."

"Just discussing my future," Adrian grumbled.

"Interesting," Amy said. "Does it include going to the Central Park Zoo with Evan tomorrow? He asked right before he fell asleep."

He imagined walking around the zoo with Evan, listening to him talk nonstop about the animals. "I'd love to."

Ruby sat on the edge of her bed, tugging on the zipper of her black knee-high boots. They were her winter favorites, the perfect combination of warm, waterproof and sexy. Exactly what she needed for the New Year's Eve party, which would probably involve a post-midnight, half-drunk walk from her friend's apartment to a nearby bar.

She tugged the zipper down instead of up, but it still wouldn't budge. She stared down at the boot. The problem with minimalism was that she didn't have a lot in the way of backup, so it was these or black pumps. Or running shoes. Ruby sighed and juggled the zipper again, and thank goodness, it came loose.

She zipped up the boot and stood. In the full-length mirror on her closet door, she smoothed her favorite black dress: fitted, just above the knee, with a low scoop neckline that showed just the right amount of cleavage. Work-appropriate with a blazer or a sweater, or evening wear with a scarf or alone, with a necklace that drew attention to said cleavage, just for fun.

Tonight called for the latter because she was going to have a fun New Year's Eve, dammit. Flirt a little, drink an extra glass of champagne and magically wake up in the new year, ready to start on her resolution: forget about Adrian.

Her phone rang, and she glanced at the screen. Her mother. Ruby stared at her phone as it rang again. She hadn't answered the last time her mother called. She'd been too unsettled about Adrian. He'd made her consider compromising everything, just to be more like the kind of woman he was looking for.

The phone rang for a third time. Maybe a talk with her mother was exactly what she needed. Ruby took a deep breath and answered it. "Hi, Mom."

"Ruby, sweetheart. I tried to call yesterday."

"Sorry. I was busy putting together a portfolio to submit to a couple galleries."

It was true. Despite everything, she'd made some good progress on putting together a coherent narrative in her photographs, based on the photo that had won the contest. She'd named it *Layers* after she realized that so many of her series were about layers in the city—physical layers of buildings, class layers, everything. When she understood her theme, the rest was much easier.

"Fantastic. That's my girl. Following your dreams," her mother said, pride bursting in her voice.

"Yep. Following my dreams." Ruby bit her lip.

Yes, she was thrilled about the chance to submit her work to galleries, but overall, she wasn't feeling very fantastic. She couldn't stop thinking about Adrian.

In a short time, the NY Creatives Media office would open again, and she would see him every single day. She still had no idea how she was going to get through that. Any time she tried to figure out a plan, the word *MISTAKE* flashed through her mind in neon lights, all caps. How many times did she need her guiding principle of *why not have fun with this?* to turn into *oh shit* for her to learn?

Don't do anything you don't want the whole office to know about. Except this time, she wasn't so worried about other people knowing. James and Cristina definitely wouldn't judge her, and her friends in the marketing department were more likely to respond with a round of high fives. No, the problem wasn't what other people thought. The problem was this ache for Adrian that wasn't going away. She didn't know what the hell to do with it.

"Are you going to tell me about your mystery Christmas vacation?" her mother asked.

"It was for work. A private assignment, so I can't

tell you about it." That was the explanation Ruby had decided on. She'd rehearsed it enough so it sounded natural. Casual.

The line was quiet. Ruby turned to get a view of her rear in the mirror, making sure her panty line wasn't showing, then grabbed her mascara.

"Ru?"

"Yeah?"

"Do you…do you think you'd consider coming home next year?"

Ruby froze, her mascara wand halfway to her eyes.

"It would mean a lot to your father." Her mother hesitated, then added, "And to me. I'd love to see you at Christmas."

Ruby could hear how hard it was for her mother to say this, to ask Ruby to do something for her, despite their pact, despite how many times she'd told Ruby do things for herself. No guilt, no regrets. But suddenly, she missed home. She missed her parents. It was a surprise, considering she'd spent a lot of time crafting excuses not to go home to Ohio and see them, but the truth was she ached for her family. It was more than a little imperfect, infinitely frustrating, but the only one she had.

She put down her mascara and made her way around her bed to the window. It was snowing outside, the kind of big, wet flakes they had in Ohio around this time.

"Yes, I can come home for Christmas next year," she said softly. "Thanks for asking."

Her mother sniffed, then cleared her throat. "I better let you go. You probably have plans for tonight. New Year's Eve in New York City."

Her mother's voice was wistful, the way it always was when they talked about New York.

"Mom?"

"Yes?"

"What would you say if I met someone now? If I was having second thoughts about waiting?"

The line was quiet again. Ruby traced the path of the snowflakes falling down to the street below, waiting for an answer.

"I pressed you to break up with Jimmy just because he was wrong for you," her mother said quietly.

"You were right about that one."

"What about this guy? Is he right for you?"

Ruby gave a little snort of laughter. "Debatable."

"Will he hold you back?"

Would he? She thought back to that moment on the plane when she'd had the urge to give Adrian what he wanted. "I'm more scared about what I'd be willing to compromise."

Her mother sighed. "That's the hardest part, Ru. Just promise me you'll be honest about what you want from the start. I think that was my biggest regret. Not saying all the things I wanted from the beginning."

"I don't even know if he wants anything with me."

"Oh, sweetheart, I'm sure he does. You're incredible. If he doesn't, he's an idiot and doesn't deserve your attention anyway."

Ruby caught her own reflection in the window and found she was smiling. She was twenty-five, and her mother's approval still made her glow inside.

"Thanks, Mom," she said. "Miss you."

"Miss you, too."

Ruby hung up the phone and stared out the window into the night. What would Adrian say if she just laid out what she wanted? Would he be willing to try dating, just to see where it led?

Chances were good he'd say no. Because in the end, he wanted a baby, and she wasn't ready for that. But if she didn't try for what she wanted, she'd never get it.

Ruby walked back to her mirror and applied her mascara. She took the cap off her cherry-red lipstick and carefully traced her lips with it. The earrings Dena had bought her for Christmas were perfect for New Year's Eve, a glittery cascade of gold that dangled just above her shoulders, and she added the chain with a simple gold pendant that her parents had sent her.

As she fastened her favorite gold bracelet onto her wrist, there was a knock on her bedroom door. Dena peeked in a moment later. "You ready, Ruby?"

"Almost."

"Benjamin thinks it'll be impossible to get a cab if we wait too long."

"I'll hurry."

Normally Ruby loved hanging around Dena and Benjamin, but tonight, she wasn't in the mood to watch them look into each other's eyes. Selfish, yes, so Ruby had kept her mouth shut.

She sighed and sifted through her closet for her black wool coat and the soft red scarf that would double as a shawl. Then she grabbed her wallet and phone from her dresser, ready to stuff them into her little black purse. But when she glanced down at her phone, she froze. There was a message from Adrian.

Her heart took off. Not once had he contacted her since they'd walked off the plane. Was it fate that he was contacting her now?

Easy, girl.

It was probably something disappointingly practical. Or maybe he'd ask her for one last night before the new year came, and his search for his age-appropriate future wife began. Time to rein in her expectations.

She took a deep breath and opened the message.

CHAPTER SIXTEEN

I miss you. Badly.

RUBY SANK BACK onto her bed, staring at the screen. Her heart pounded in her chest, and her stomach fluttered. A longing for him was filling her, from the deepest parts of her. Her body was alive with the memory of him.

"Ruby? You ready yet?" Dena's voice came through the door again.

"Hang on," she called.

Ruby typed in her reply.

R u drunk?

Nope. I'm not in my twenties, remember?

She chuckled. Adrian Wentworth probably never drunk-texted women, even in his twenties. Maybe she should invite him to her place for sex, and then bring up the dating thing? She'd meant to give this a little more thought, make a plan or something, but oh, how she wanted to see him.

Ruby stared at the phone. After a long, fortifying breath, she typed an answer.

Miss you too.

Can we talk?

After days of radio silence, he wanted to talk now, on New Year's Eve? Dena and her boyfriend were waiting in the living room for her, but this wouldn't take long. Just a few minutes. Her hands shook as she typed out her answer.

OK

She sent the message and stared down at her phone, waiting for him to call. Just one more time, listening to his voice, and if Adrian didn't want to try for something more, then she'd put him behind her.

A new message appeared.

I'm outside your building. Can I come in?

Her heart took another leap as she stared down at the message. He knew her address? And…talking in person? Right now? Beautiful, grumpy, ancient-Greek-statue Adrian Wentworth wanted to come to her apartment? The warning lights were flashing in her mind, *mistake, mistake*. This definitely could be a mistake. Or it could be the best decision of her life.

Her heart was pounding in her chest, sending a message, loud and clear. Except she didn't know what the message was. After one more breath, she ignored the warning lights and typed her answer.

Apt 214

Ruby dropped her phone and headed out of her room, straight for the front door. She passed Dena and Benjamin, sitting on the couch dressed in full winter gear. They craned their necks, tracking her as she crossed the room.

"Is everything okay?" Dena asked.

"Go on to the party without me," she said quickly. "I need to take care of something."

Dena didn't get up. She and Benjamin looked at each other, then back at her. Ruby reached the door just as the buzzer rang.

"You didn't order pizza, did you?" Dena asked. "I told you there will be tons of food at Yasmin's."

"It's not pizza. It's, um, a person." The weight of Dena's stare on her was heavy, so Ruby turned to face the door. "Seriously, you don't have to wait for me."

"I'll see who this is first, thanks," Dena said, smiling.

Ruby was too nervous to argue. She stood by the door, staring at it, as footsteps sounded in the hallway. Adrian's knock came, and her heart jumped in her chest as she turned the knob.

The door swung open, and her breath caught in her throat. Adrian stood in her doorway. Snowflakes decorated his coat and the scarf that was bundled around his neck. A few more snowflakes were stuck to the brim of his newsboy cap. Short curls stuck out from underneath his hat, and his cheeks were pink from the cold.

Ruby took a deep breath and met his gaze. Everything else around them melted away. Gone was the stern CFO of NY Creatives Media, and in front of her was the Adrian she'd known in Hawaii. He was looking at her the way he had that last time in the pool, when he was deep inside her. When she'd begged him to take care of her. When he'd said he would.

Words were gone, and her body was alive with desire and warmth and joy. The force of this swirl of emotions took her breath away.

She had replayed that moment in the pool so many times, enough to question her own memory of it. Maybe she'd imagined the intensity of it? Maybe she'd read too far into his words? But now she knew she hadn't. Everything she'd seen that last time together was here in his expression as he stood in her doorway: desire, vulnerability, hope, and something she wasn't ready to name.

Adrian took a step toward her. Another one. He was standing so close now. His gaze wandered over her face like he was taking it in, her eyes, her cheeks, her lips… He was going to kiss her. She could feel it, and there was nothing in the world she wanted more than to kiss him. Ruby tipped her head, bringing her lips closer to his, and slowly he lowered his mouth—

"Are you going to invite your friend in?"

Dena's voice snapped her back to reality, and Ruby pulled away. Adrian blinked at Dena, like he was just as thrown off as Ruby was.

"Come in," she whispered.

She took a deep breath and stepped back, and Adrian walked into her apartment. Ruby shut the door behind him, using the moment to gather herself together. Hazarding a glance across the room, she found both Dena and Benjamin staring, wide-eyed, at Adrian.

"Dena, Benjamin, this is Adrian Wentworth." She gestured to him. "He's a, um, work colleague."

Dena's eyes widened. "Hothole Adrian?"

Adrian cleared his throat, and Ruby grimaced. He'd come up in conversations about work before, and not in a good way. This was just one more reason Ruby hadn't wanted to discuss Hawaii when she came home. Dena had prodded her for more information about her mystery Christmas trip, but Ruby had skirted around the details. She'd mumbled something about work, and Dena had definitely picked up on her somber mood since she'd returned. Apparently, that was just enough information for Dena to read this situation.

Ruby glanced at Adrian. He swiped a hand over his mouth, but she was almost sure he was fighting a smile.

"You two really should catch that cab to Yasmin's." She gave Dena a meaningful look.

"You sure?" Her friend's voice was more serious.

Ruby nodded. "I'll catch up with you."

Dena let out a sigh and stood up. She and Benjamin pulled on their gloves and hats and started for the door. Benjamin kissed Ruby on the cheek and tipped his chin at Adrian.

Dena gave him a skeptical look. "Be on your best behavior, Adrian Wentworth. I like your hat."

He smiled a little. "Thanks. A pleasure to meet you."

Then she turned to hug Ruby. "Text me. Seriously."

Dena and Benjamin walked out the door, and Ruby was alone with Adrian. Truthfully, she was ready to get right to that kiss, but the interruption had brought a little more of her good sense back.

"Come in," she said again, nodding toward the couch. "Can I get you something to drink?"

He shook his head. He was looking at her the way he had when she'd opened the door. She already knew she wasn't going to turn down sex with him. Maybe it was better to just skip the conversation and get it over with right now. Then she'd have more time at Yasmin's to stave off the emptiness when he was gone again.

Adrian sat down on the couch and took off his hat. He leaned forward, his legs spread, his forearms resting on his thighs. He closed his eyes, and his shoulders rose and fell. God, it was unfair how beautiful he was. Her apartment was suddenly much too warm. She tugged at the scarf around her neck.

"If you're here for sex, I want you to know that I'm fine with that," she said, keeping her voice even. "More than fine. But I want to talk, too."

Adrian shook his head slowly. "I'm not here for sex, Ruby."

Her cheeks flushed. The longer she stood here with him, the more she realized she'd been lying to herself all along. Cutting things off wouldn't help. She was already falling for him, against all better judgment.

Adrian scrubbed his face with his hands, and when he looked back up at her, she could see dark circles under his eyes. The flush from the cold had hidden them, but they were there. He opened his mouth as if to speak, then closed it. He stood up and walked toward her, then stopped in front of her and raised a hand to her cheek. It was warm, and his touch was heartbreakingly gentle. "You look beautiful, Ruby."

She swallowed. There was so much tenderness in his voice. "I hope you didn't come all this way to say that."

He shook his head. "I came over to tell you that I'm falling in love with you."

Ruby's breath caught in the back of her throat. She stared at him. He was falling in love with her?

"What happened to not lusting after a woman thirteen years younger than you who wears a cheerleader costume to work?" She tried to make her voice sound light, but she could hear it didn't. She sounded nervous.

"You're my exception. You're important enough to make me break my own rules," he said, caressing her cheek. "Will you make an exception for me? Just the relationship part. No other compromises."

Oh, how she wanted that. But her mother's words were still fresh in her mind. She needed to be honest, right from the start.

"I saw how badly you wanted a baby when we walked onto the plane," she whispered. "I'm really not ready for that…"

"I do want a family," he said quietly. "But I can wait. And if I have to choose between having a baby and having you, I choose you."

Her breaths were shaky. She wanted so badly for this to be real. *Please, please, let it be.*

He continued, "As my sister so wisely pointed out, families come in many forms. It's love that makes a family, not kids."

That was probably the wisest statement she had heard in a long time. "Sounds like I'd definitely like her."

"She's much smarter than I am. Clearly."

Ruby smiled. "I do want kids, though. Just not right now."

He nodded. "One step at a time. Our week together was the best thing that's ever happened to me," he said with a hint of a smile. "That's what I want. Everything else is a bonus."

A smile twitched at the corners of her mouth, too. "You want me to say yes to this, right now?"

"That would be the best outcome in my mind," he said, amusement glimmering in his eyes. "But I'm prepared for the long game."

She lifted her hand to his hair and pulled him closer. His lips brushed hers, warm and familiar. Pleasure shot through her, with a hot, aching need building inside. He opened his lips, and she slid her tongue against his. He groaned and matched each stroke with his own until they were both panting.

"Yes," she whispered. "Yes."

He cupped her face with his hands. "You have no idea how much I want you right now. But I'm not going to want to leave here if we start. And I came to invite you to my apartment for New Year's Eve. Central Park looks amazing right now, and we can watch the fireworks from my living room."

Her eyebrows shot up. "You have a view of Central Park?"

"I do. Just for you." The corners of Adrian's eyes crinkled. He looked happy, really happy.

Ruby was here, in his apartment. Snow was falling, lighting up Central Park below, and she sat cross-legged on his couch, looking out the window, dressed in a short black dress and thigh-high stockings. The thought that she had planned to go to a party, drink champagne and spend the evening without him was heart-stopping. He had come so close to missing his chance to spend New Year's Eve with her, all because he was a stupid fucking idiot who couldn't let go of his own rules long enough to see what was right in front of him. Luckily, Sydney had talked some sense into him.

And now that she had, Adrian was starting to see all the ways he'd been lying to himself. Their week at the Kalani Resort was an answer to the wish he hadn't been willing to make. All his dating rules and limits weren't about finding the right match. They were to minimize risks. To avoid getting hurt again. It wasn't a baby that had been the source of all this longing. He could see that now. The kind of connection he felt with Ruby was what he'd been searching for this whole time.

"I never would have guessed you're a closet minimalist," Ruby said over her shoulder.

"Not me. It's my sister," he said from the kitchen. "She does interior design for high-end residences. I really do think you'd like her."

He'd left his apartment mostly bare for months after he bought it until Sydney had insisted on fixing it up.

"No wonder you lured me back to your lair," she said. "I'm never leaving this place."

"Fine by me," he said. "Judging by how long it took to get a cab here, I don't think you could get home anytime soon, even if you want to."

He glanced at the clock. Midnight was coming soon, and he wanted everything to be perfect when the fireworks went off. He set two plates onto a tray next to the cheese, crackers, olives and strawberries

that he and Ruby had bought at the corner store. It
had taken hours to get from her apartment to his,
but he didn't mind, and she didn't seem to, either.
They had spent it talking about the future. He carried the food over to the coffee table in front of the
couch. He returned to the kitchen for the bottle of
champagne and two glasses, then placed those on
the coffee table as well.

Finally, he sat down next to her.

"Thank you for coming to my place to invite me
here," she said softly. "Seriously. This is amazing."

"My pleasure," he said. It was impossible to de-
scribe how right it felt to see her here. The connection between them was different now that they were
back in New York, more intense, and she was looking
at him with a hint of wonder in her eyes. He studied
her for signs of hesitation but didn't find any.

"Ready to celebrate?" she asked.

"Me?" He raised an eyebrow. "Always."

She laughed and picked up the bottle of champagne, twisting off the cork. Fizz spilled from the
top, and she picked up a glass, poured and gave it to
him, then did the same for herself.

"To us," he said, and they clinked glasses.

She leaned over and kissed his neck, then wrinkled her brow. "What will we say at work?"

Adrian sighed. "I still haven't figured that out.
Maybe just say that I'm the asshole who couldn't
stay away from you?"

Ruby laughed. "And I'm your victim in that scenario? Um…no way."

He squeezed her, and a little more of the years of built-up tension left him.

"You're not an asshole, you know," she whispered. "Not in the ways that really count. I would never fall in love with an asshole."

Love. His heart expanded in his chest. "It feels like that for you, too?"

"Yes, it does." As she took the first sip of champagne, a spray of lights flashed in front of them, followed by a heavy boom.

"It's midnight," she whispered, setting her glass on the table. She slid over and rested her thighs across his. The tops of her stockings peeked out from under her dress, and he slipped his hand under the hem, onto smooth bare skin. More fireworks went off, the flashes and thunderous booms filling his living room.

He pulled her onto his lap, and she laughed as her mouth met his. She kissed him, her lips soft and hungry. He'd ached for these lips every day since they'd left Hawaii. Now he closed his eyes and kissed her, touched her, telling her in every way just how much he'd missed her.

"Happy New Year, Ruby," he whispered in her ear. "Let me give you everything you want this year."

"This is already perfect," she said. "Everything about this is perfect."

* * * * *

COMING SOON!

LET'S TALK
Romance

For exclusive extracts, competitions
and special offers, find us online:

📘 facebook.com/millsandboon

🐦 @MillsandBoon

📷 @MillsandBoonUK

Get in touch on 01413 063232

For all the latest titles coming soon, visit
millsandboon.co.uk/nextmonth

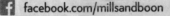

MILLS & BOON

THE HEART OF ROMANCE

A ROMANCE FOR EVERY KIND OF READER

MODERN

Prepare to be swept off your feet by sophisticated, sexy and seductive heroes, in some of the world's most glamourous and romantic locations, where power and passion collide.
8 stories per month.

HISTORICAL

Escape with historical heroes from time gone by. Whether your passion is for wicked Regency Rakes, muscled Vikings or rugged Highlanders, awaken the romance of the past.
6 stories per month.

MEDICAL

Set your pulse racing with dedicated, delectable doctors in the high-pressure world of medicine, where emotions run high and passion, comfort and love are the best medicine.
6 stories per month.

True Love

Celebrate true love with tender stories of heartfelt romance, from the rush of falling in love to the joy a new baby can bring, and a focus on the emotional heart of a relationship.
8 stories per month.

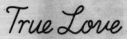

Indulge in secrets and scandal, intense drama and plenty of sizzlin hot action with powerful and passionate heroes who have it all: wealth, status, good looks…everything but the right woman.
6 stories per month.

HEROES

Experience all the excitement of a gripping thriller, with an intens romance at its heart. Resourceful, true-to-life women and strong, fearless men face danger and desire - a killer combination!
8 stories per month.

DARE

Sensual love stories featuring smart, sassy heroines you'd want as a best friend, and compelling intense heroes who are worthy of them
4 stories per month.

To see which titles are coming soon, please visit

millsandboon.co.uk/nextmonth